# Atlantic Afterlives in Contemporary Fiction

## The Oceanic Imaginary in Literature since the Information Age

*Sofia Ahlberg*

palgrave
macmillan

ATLANTIC AFTERLIVES IN CONTEMPORARY FICTION



First published 2016 by
PALGRAVE MACMILLAN



Palgrave Macmillan in the UK is an imprint of Macmillan Publishers Limited, registered in England, company number 785998, of Houndmills, Basingstoke, Hampshire, RG21 6XS.

Palgrave Macmillan in the US is a division of Nature America, Inc., One New York Plaza, Suite 4500, New York, NY 10004-1562.

Palgrave Macmillan is the global academic imprint of the above companies and has companies and representatives throughout the world.

Hardback ISBN: 978–1–137–47921–1
E-PUB ISBN: 978–1–137–47923–5
E-PDF ISBN: 978–1–137–47922–8
DOI: 10.1057/9781137479228

Distribution in the UK, Europe and the rest of the world is by Palgrave Macmillan®, a division of Macmillan Publishers Limited, registered in England, company number 785998, of Houndmills, Basingstoke, Hampshire RG21 6XS.

Library of Congress Cataloging-in-Publication Data

Names: Ahlberg, Sofia, 1973–
Title: Atlantic afterlives in contemporary fiction : the oceanic imaginary in literature since the information age / by Sofia Ahlberg.
Description: New York : Palgrave Macmillan, [2016] |
Series: The new urban Atlantic | Includes bibliographical references and index.
Identifiers: LCCN 2015033236 | ISBN 9781137479211 (hardback : alk. paper)
Subjects: LCSH: Fiction—20th century—History and criticism. | Sea in literature. | Literature and technology.
Classification: LCC PN3503 .A345 2016 | DDC 809.3/04—dc23 LC record available at http://lccn.loc.gov/2015033236

A catalogue record for the book is available from the British Library.

The New Urban Atlantic
Edited by Elizabeth A. Fay

The New Urban Atlantic is a new series of monographs, texts, and essay collections focusing on urban, Atlantic, and hemispheric studies. Distinct from the nation state mentality, the Atlantic world has been from colonial times a fluid international entity, including multiple Atlantic systems such as the triangle trade and cacao trade that extended globally. The series is distinct in three prime ways: First, it offers a multi-disciplinary, multi-cultural, broadly historical and urban focus. Second, it extends the geographical boundaries from an Old World/New World binary to the entire Atlantic rim, the arctics, and to exchanges between continents other than Europe and North America. Third, it emphasizes the Atlantic World as distinct from the nation-states that participate in it. Ultimately, The New Urban Atlantic series challenges the conventional boundaries of the field by presenting the Atlantic World as an evolving reality.

*Creole Testimonies: Slave Narratives from the British West Indies, 1709–1838*
Nicole N. Aljoe

*Stumbling Towards the Constitution: The Economic Consequences of Freedom in the Atlantic World*
Jonathan M. Chu

*Urban Identity and the Atlantic World*
Edited by Elizabeth A. Fay and Leonard von Morzé

*The Transatlantic Eco-Romanticism of Gary Snyder*
Paige Tovey

*Hospitality and the Transatlantic Imagination, 1815–1835*
Cynthia Schoolar Williams

*Trans-Atlantic Passages: Philip Hale on the Boston Symphony Orchestra, 1889–1933*
Jon Ceander Mitchell

*Atlantic Afterlives in Contemporary Fiction: The Oceanic Imaginary in Literature since the Information Age*
Sofia Ahlberg

# Atlantic Afterlives in Contemporary Fiction

*To Inga and Hans Ahlberg*

# Contents

# Preface

In September 2011, my mother fell into a coma from which she never awoke. I flew home to Sweden from Australia and kept vigil with the family gathered at her bedside. Despite the coma, we spoke with her. It was disconcerting to begin with, speaking at a normal volume and hearing only the sound of one's own voice. Soon we felt freer with the hospital staff, other patients, and their loved ones and found that we could speak without inhibition to my mother about the big and small things we had shared. It did not matter that none of the doctors we spoke with at this time could tell us how much, if anything, was received and understood by my mother. In fact, doctors cautioned us that there was no evidence that anything at all was picked up. Any visible sign of cognition—a flicker of the eye, a wrinkled eyebrow, a clenching of the jaw—was to be interpreted as purely incidental. Despite doctors' assessment of her scant cognitive abilities at the time, our communication with my mother during this time was far from one-sided. I like to think of those final words spoken by us not just as the corollary of impending loss. What we said to her was in response to what she had expressed to us loud and clear in words and deeds throughout her life, long before she lost consciousness and the ability to speak. The full history of my communication with my mother (as a continuation of her influence on me as an adult woman) supplied us with a sufficient rejoinder under the contingencies of our communication in the hospice. What passed between us then was not a monologue, but a dialogue that made it across enormous spatial and temporal boundaries. As such, it surpassed even the reach of that most extensive network of communication, the World Wide Web.

One purpose of the words we spoke to Mum was to delay the doctors' decision to switch off her life support and, ultimately, to rouse her from her coma or let her slip away. More than that, I felt our talk was in aid of a more urgent life or death matter. In our talking to Mum in that way, even though she could not answer, we were building from the past a secure shelter that might protect and safeguard for the years to come everything she had come to mean to us. I was compelled by our unique circumstance to ask questions. What is a conversation? How much space can it cover? When does it end? Where does it end? These thoughts inspired me to begin to think and write about knowledge as an environment. Importantly, this was not just to give conversation a place in the world, but also to affirm that place itself is formed by the to and fro of communication. We were ensuring that all that Mum had ever tried to impart to us would have a future. If I was right, it meant that she was intensely present in the conversation of those days, present as the one whose talk to us throughout our lives created in us the need to answer her now.

My goal in this book is to harbor the adventure of encounter across short and vast distances. My wish is to give it a lasting home by giving the oceanic imaginary the freedom Emily Dickinson in "Wild Nights—Wild Nights!" (114) finds in a wild, stormy ocean:

> Ah, the Sea!
> Might I but moor—Tonight—
> In Thee!

This book proposes to find ways in which literature and literary studies shelter encounters in a digital age. *Atlantic Afterlives* attempts to situate our discipline within a digitally enriched oceanic imaginary in the same way that Dickinson challenges her reader to imagine with her a place of tumultuous encounter in which to find anchorage.

This book has evolved in stages. An earlier version of chapter 1 appeared in *Detecting Detection: International Perspectives on the Uses of a Plot* (eds. Peter Baker and Deborah Shaller, Continuum, 2012). I wish to thank my institution, La Trobe University, Australia, for generously allowing me time to begin this manuscript in early 2012. I also wish to thank my students for enthusiastically bringing the oceanic imaginary into the syllabi at beautifully unexpected moments. Colleagues and friends, in and out of the University, as well as family, have lent the project and me an enormous amount of support, and for that I am very grateful. My thanks also go out to my children, Ayva and Albin, whose imagination is naturally oceanic and adventurous. It is in the interest of their future and the future of all our children who will be navigating the often tricky waters of an increasingly digitalized world that this book has been written. Finally, I wish to thank my husband, Nick Sergeant. His outspokenness and understanding brought a perspective to the work that helped me discover more and more of what I was really trying to say.

# Series Introduction: "The New Urban Atlantic"

Since its inception, the study of the Atlantic World has been premised on the important advances in sixteenth-century technology that made transatlantic voyages possible. Colonization of the North American coast, the establishment of plantations in the Caribbean, European adoption of African slave trade practices, and the subsequent triangle trade network have formed the mainstay of this field. *The New Urban Atlantic* adds to this set of interests by focusing on the cities (both persistent and failed) that have functioned as important nodal points for Atlantic financial, trade, diplomatic, and cultural networks. Attention to Atlantic cities, the frameworks that identify their similarities and connections both synchronically and diachronically, and their divergences from such norms expands research opportunities by allowing new questions to be asked and new problems to be posed.

Methodologically the books in *The New Urban Atlantic* will engage the interdisciplinary fields of literature and cultural history, with the historical framed by the *longue durée* of geophysical realities, the environment, and changes in that environment that have impacted human experience, and the cultural construed as the representational forms and systems that arose out of Atlantic rim interaction. Within this historio-cultural framework, the urban is meant to encompass both coastal and riverine settlements wherever large tributaries provided access to Atlantic commerce in all its senses. Another methodological feature of the series is the attention, wherever possible, to indigenous and Western immigrant cultures in dynamic and multidirectional relations with each other, as well as with preexisting histories of coastal and riverine trade, political, and social networks on all four continents and Caribbean islands, to produce a new cultural arena—the Atlantic World. In consequence of both of these attributes, the historio-cultural framework and attention to multicultural interaction, individual volumes in the series will contribute to its broad purpose of bringing pre-contact and colonial cultural history in conversation with work on the modern era, and with today's contemporary mediations of socio-cultural, environmental, economic, and technological challenges to the Atlantic World.

In addition to an extended historical perimeter of inquiry, *The New Urban Atlantic* is also framed by hemispheric interactivity in cultural networks, trade networks, and global commerce in goods, ideas, and peoples. Of utmost importance to this conception of Atlanticism, as the series' second methodological feature underscores, are interactions and exchanges among indigenous and immigrant peoples in both hemispheres, and the mutual histories these engagements produced. Although contributions of British and Dutch colonizing projects continue to inform understandings of Atlantic systems, these must be seen in relation to Spanish and Portuguese imperial projects, as well as other culturally conditioned contacts and engagements. Moreover, if the Atlantic World is an ongoing yet changeable locus of systems, networks, and identities across and between two hemispheres and four continents, it is furthermore constituted as a system within the larger framework of world systems and is thus always in dialogue with global networks, especially in terms of trade and technological circuits.

Books in *The New Urban Atlantic* will treat the Atlantic World as a still-ongoing reality that distinguishes the Atlantic rim by its shared concerns and maritime-oriented identity. Cities such as Halifax, Montreal, Albany, Boston, New Bedford, New York, Cahokia, Charleston, Mexico City, Santo Domingo, Rio de Janeiro, Dakar, Lisbon, Amsterdam, Liverpool, and Copenhagen may be defined according to many local, regional, and national factors, but are also conditioned by their geographic location on the edge of a great ocean or with riverine access to it. Whatever other economic, social, or cultural patterns of exchange in which they are hubs, such cities are also characterized by particular relationships that are best understood as part of Atlantic systems. In this sense, through a focus on cities, *The New Urban Atlantic* can also foreground urban effects on the environment for both land and ocean ecologies. The transplantation of botanical specimens, importation of livestock, changes in agricultural techniques on city perimeters, and fouling of waterways are just some of the ways in which the Old World–New World interactions have had profound and continuing effects on the Atlantic World. These continued effects influence global environmental activity just as the Atlantic World has been and continues to be conditioned by that activity.

Series Editor: ELIZABETH FAY,
University of Massachusetts Boston

# Introduction

This book is about the complexities of securing some knowledge in a world of information. I say *some* knowledge because I believe that, unlike information, knowledge is necessarily partial, incomplete. And I say *securing* even though knowledge involves us in insecure states of uncertainty, precisely because of its partial quality. Only information offers a guarantee to be, or aim to be, fit for everyone everywhere, but nowhere in particular. Knowledge does not come with such a guarantee, and it is more rare and precious for that. In the course of writing these pages, I have wanted to discover just what can be known about the world and the others with whom I correspond, often across vast distances. This book aims to chart the pleasures and costs of exchanges and encounters across the Atlantic Ocean and beyond since the Information Age. Before the technological revolution, transatlantic knowledge was tethered to a comparatively small area, and colonial America developed in the context of profound isolation from its European roots. Until the building of the first transatlantic telegraphic cable, there was no reliable postal system. When any news from Europe would take months to reach North America, the enormous distance turned the Atlantic into a creative hiatus, a fluctuating field of projection and desire.

Melville's *Moby-Dick; or The Whale* stages the Atlantic as a character in its own right, sometimes glimpsed in the manic visions of Captain Ahab, sometimes in the silky radiance of the elusive and menacing whale. The novel shows the extent to which the hunted helps define the hunter as well as their shared habitat. The vastness of the ocean in Melville's novel becomes a revealing place of reflection that threatens to drown the human subject in the process. The enormous feat of the opening line, "Call me Ishmael," cannot be overlooked. In the face of so much distance and depth, it is a powerful invitation to the reader to return the narrator's address across whatever physical or imaginary distance stands in the way. Once the telegraphic cable was built in 1858, oceanic dialogue gained metaphorical strength as an enabler of transatlantic connectivity, seen in the poetry of Walt Whitman. Only a couple of years before the outbreak of the Civil War in 1861, as his way of healing the nation and its people, Whitman celebrates communication in the verse in *Leaves of Grass* that would later be named "Song of Myself":

> I CELEBRATE myself, and sing myself
> And what I assume you shall assume,
> For every atom belonging to me as good belongs to you. (39)

In keeping with this fantasy of profound connectivity, Whitman in the poem that begins "YEARS of the modern! years of the unperform'd!" refers to the radically new by interrogating how well people now come together for the common good:

> Are all nations communing? is there going to be but one heart to the globe?
> Is humanity forming, en-masse?— (446)

The euphoria with which the first Atlantic cable was received mirrors Whitman's communitarian optimism. The New York *Evening Post* predicted that the Atlantic cable would "make the great heart of humanity beat with a single pulse" (qtd. in Gordon, 75). Also from the other side of the Atlantic, commentators referred to the cable as "that strong cord of love" (qtd. in Gordon, 76). London's *The Times* announced the end of an ocean: "The Atlantic is dried up, and we become in reality as well as in wish one country... The Atlantic telegraph has half undone the declaration of 1776, and has gone far to make us once again, in spite of ourselves, one people" (qtd. in Gordon, 134). Despite such unanimously hopeful beginnings, the image of electronic communication as the basis of a global mind has not come true. In my book I claim that, since Whitman, the Atlantic has become a symbol of loss and elegy. Even the title of Norwegian writer Knut Hamsun's 1897 short story, "Secret Suffering," says a lot about European feeling about America. There he tells of the poor treatment received by a European visitor to America, victim of chicanery in one of the nation's casinos in New York. The lesson of Hamsun's story is that the European visitor must expect to encounter unscrupulous fraudsters in America, which corresponds with a generalized fear of life in the colony experienced by Europeans at the beginning of the twentieth century.

Paradoxically, America was also conceived as a surrogate home by some of the more experimental modern writers. This coincides with a trend identified by Murray as an internationalization of the literary scene and a parallel decline of more established literary traditions and canons (219). Through the examples of Kafka and Céline, Murray depicts a tendency among European Modernists to produce a culture that he calls "a-national," in addition to international, whereby writers take a more critical point of view, "and write within a cultural framework that encompasses the entire world" (219). Thus, the image of America as an extension of self rather than a threatening other gained traction in European fiction. As the sole nation to emerge unscathed from the Great War, America became for many a sort of parent-figure of strength and resolution for Europe while still remaining a focus of cultural pessimism. It was thought that Europe had created a monster, that America was destined to destroy its maker. At the same time America was a place of refuge for many immigrants just as it was a metaphorical asylum for those European writers and intellectuals alienated by their surroundings. These tensions put pressure on transatlantic dialogue and communication. The Atlantic itself became a symbol of whatever sutured Europe to America while keeping them apart, both a safe haven of hope and a source of suspicion.

Despite improved communication technology, the early Modernists showed caution in their less euphoric attitude to these technologies. Indeed, some of the best works from this time—Djuna Barnes's *Nightwood*, Franz Kafka's *The Metamorphosis*, Faulkner's *Absalom! Absalom!* to name a few—express at their core a deep suspicion regarding the success of any smoothly meaningful communication between people. For these authors, if words reach their mark even approximately, they also do so hopefully, and faithfully, through the perseverance of correspondents in ensuring the crossing from one to the other. Much of the humor of *Krazy Kat*, the early twentieth-century American newspaper comic strip by cartoonist George Herriman, is a result of illustrating the graphic difficulty of communication and the awful messiness that comes from that failure. The strip focuses on the triangulated relationship between Krazy Kat, Ignatz Mouse, and Offissa Pupp. Nursing an unrequited infatuation for Ignatz, Krazy misinterprets the bricks thrown at his own head by the iniquitous mouse as a sign of love. Those bricks in the *Krazy Kat* strips are perhaps the result of postwar rubble not yet cleared away, but here, in a process of remediation, their use is now amorous (a ballistic signification that might give new meaning to the phrase "hitting on"!). Offissa Pupp interferes with Ignatz's brick-tossing plans and locks the mouse in the county jail, not only because he is the administrator of law and order but also because he in turn nurses a secret love for Krazy Kat.

As telephone communication is introduced in America, meaning is humorously depicted in *Krazy Kat* as being even further occluded, not less so. Krazy's encounter with a telephone in a strip that came out in 1923 magnifies the sheer difficulty of mediated conversation. In this strip, Krazy mistakes the telephone for a subject with whom one speaks, rather than an object through which two subjects speak. Set in the desert of New Mexico, famously mixing New York Yiddish and other ethnic dialects and adding its own anachronistic syntax and literalized metaphors, the *Krazy Kat* strip is already heavily invested in the idiosyncrasies of language: "Why is lenguage, Ignatz?" Krazy asks in a 1918 daily. "Language is that we may understand one another," replies Ignatz. At this, the dissatisfied Krazy asks further, whether "a Finn, or a Leplender, or a Oshkosher" can "unda-stend" Ignatz and vice versa, to which Ignatz can only respond in the negative. "Then, I would say," Krazy concludes, "lenguage is, that we may mis-unda-stend each udda." An example from Second World War European literature more somberly shows language deprivation as a form of torture. At the heart of Stefan Zweig's 1942 novella *The Royal Game* is a prisoner of war who, being denied all access to text, descends into madness. The story contains the following attempt to explain to a sympathetic listener, in the words of the prisoner, what it was like to live without text, without the expansive possibilities opened up by the symbolic: "I lived like a diver in his bell in the black ocean of that silence; and, at that, a diver who suspects his cable to the outside world has snapped and he will never be hauled back out of the soundless deep" (24).

*Atlantic Afterlives in Contemporary Fiction: The Oceanic Imaginary since the Information Age* explores the means by which we correspond with each other and with place itself. In Guy de Maupassant's story, "Sur l'eau," a fisherman recalls a moment when he is enjoying the tranquility and beauty of the river when, for no apparent reason, his enjoyment turns to fear. Fear turns to terror when he is unable to pull up the anchor from the bottom of the sea and return to land. It is later revealed that the anchor has been caught in the corpse of a woman who had committed suicide. Maupassant's story suggests that place itself communicates the horrors it bears witness to long before human action intercepts and logically reveals the causes of our disquiet. What would happen, the narrator seems to ask, if, like the fisherman, we heed what place communicates and then rearrange our boundaries accordingly? What would we discover about place and the past, if we paid more attention to it? For this conceptual leap, I am indebted to Marshall McLuhan who in 1951 with his *The Mechanical*

*Bride: Folklore of Industrial Man* challenges the reader to be as physically alert and sensitive to a source of knowledge and information dissemination (such as the newspaper) as one would be of stepping into a bath (184).

An important contention I make in this book is that if the transportation of ideas across the Atlantic can be seen essentially as oceanic prior to the Information Age, it has since become "atmospheric." Once, relations between Europe and America were given a geographic place by the terrestrial Atlantic and by what could be transmitted across it via the telegraphic cable. Much of what constitutes information in the twenty-first century, by comparison, is stored in virtual clouds, and place has consequently diminished in significance. Despite this, or perhaps because of this, I want to suggest that the pursuit and dissemination of knowledge as distinct from information is an ecological practice that protects place, and whose Ur-text I locate in literary and poetic form. Poetic form brings place into focus in the way it engages the reader here and now. Unlike information, knowledge is limited in scope, being relevant and valuable for someone somewhere. *Atlantic Afterlives* is an attempt to distinguish between information and relevant as well as reliable knowledge. This has become a matter of urgency since the Information Age, but it is not to say that considerations have not been given to it in the past. In the posthumously published essay "On Truth and Lying in a Non-moral Sense," Nietzsche challenges his readers to question overall our ability to recognize truth. The "art of dissimulation reaches its peak in humankind," he scoffs (142). As if reasoning with a child, Nietzsche talks us through the ABCs of the act of discovery: "If someone hides something behind a bush, looks for it in the same place and then finds it there, his seeking and finding is nothing much to boast about; but this is exactly how things are as far as the seeking and finding of 'truth' within the territory of reason is concerned" (147). Whereas Nietzsche here refers to truth pejoratively as it is formed out of habit and prejudice, I wish to recuperate the idea in terms of discovery beyond preconceptions in order to ask when or under what conditions do we discover anything new.

Many of the most enduring theories of how we experience the world and connect with one another have produced theoretical readings of multiple imaginary worlds. Benedict Anderson's idea of imagined communities suggests that even nationalism is little more than a shared dream. While this idea is conceptually powerful, when applied to the geopolitical, "on the ground" as war correspondents say, it is no help in upholding an ethical point of view. I think of Gaza, Syria, Iraq, or Congo, for instance, as places whose national histories are better described as, at times, nightmarishly real rather than dream. Edward Said's notion of imagined geographies is similarly a significant tool for critical thinking in a globalized world, but since the Information Age, the distinction between the real and the imaginary has become blurred and so the imagined has lost its transformative potential. The intellectual sophistication of these theories makes them vulnerable to Nietzsche's criticism because the assumptions they begin with are often disguised in their conclusions. Nietzsche warned his readers against all-sweeping, generalized ways of understanding of the world, what Jean-Francois Lyotard would later call "grand narratives." Nietzsche argued that we are no closer to understanding the world because we subsume our experiences of it under various headings or fabricated broad concepts like these. What Nietzsche dismisses as a one-size-fits-all approach—"that which is to count as 'truth' from this point onwards now becomes fixed, i.e. a way of designating things is invented which has the same validity and force everywhere" (143)—is reminiscent of the way information is delivered to us today via the Internet. Rather than being a contentious claim made with difficulty by an individual or group and offered up to be assessed as such, information is often little more than a survey of widespread agreement.

*Atlantic Afterlives* is divided into three sections that each explores the Atlantic as a trade route for knowledge as precious cargo. The first section, "Leaking Oceans," focuses on the author's ability to respond swiftly to events in the public sphere, specifically to intelligence and environmental threats, pointing toward the emergence of information itself as literature's Other (chapters 1 and 2). The second section, "Unsound Waves," investigates a range of narrative processes that help produce the very terms in which we understand ourselves as producers and consumers of information and knowledge today, with particular emphasis on the movement of people and the digitization of communication (chapters 3 and 4). The final section, "The Coastless Sea," outlines the kind of reading practices that deliver relevant, actual knowledge as opposed to information. This section investigates the bridges that bind us to place and the past while addressing the political and ethical questions that would support such foundations (chapters 5 and 6).

I began this book with a personal anecdote (Preface) to underline the interrelatedness of my two basic points about the shift from oceanic, place-based knowledge to an atmospheric, placeless circulation of information. I want to stress that far from being a neutral setting for our actions, place is best thought of as practice in the way we experience it as well as communicate and narrate it, and that knowledge is also a practice for the same reason. The awareness we bring to either the environment that we owe our biological existence to or the information we gather from it "can vary from little more than simple recognition to relatively full realization," as Walsh suggests in her discussion about literature and knowledge (87). In order to deliver transformative knowledge that can be shared, Walsh suggests, we need what she calls "virtual experience . . . structured and articulated, lifted out of the temporal flux of ongoing happening" (139). This suggests a reading practice that translates experience into narrative. Drawing on Walsh's view of literature as providing virtual experience that can be shared, I want to consider Arendt's view on what Walsh's "structured and articulated" experience could look like. In *The Human Condition*, Arendt draws attention to what she saw in 1958 as the "withering of the public realm" (60). She laments the expansion of the private sphere, its territorializing and denaturing of all areas of what she calls the *vita activa*. This is where action that is publicly visible demands courage and conviction, and the power to forgive errors, because of its long-term yet unforeseeable consequences (233). She suggests that a publicly shared arena is absolutely necessary for the adventure of the visible appearance and meaningful representation of unique instances of humanity. For Arendt, the individual human subject demands a public realm in which to risk visibility as unique and unprecedented. Lacking this we are reduced to being little more than objects of exchange, valued for what we do and what we make, never for who we are. The public realm is thus, for Arendt, the locus of original and dangerous human endeavor, always fraught with unpredictability and long-term consequences. Arendt refers to action as "the human ability to act—to start new unprecedented processes whose outcome remains uncertain and unpredictable whether they are let loose in the human or the natural realm" (231–2). Humanity, Arendt argues, has its fullest life in these actions that are unique, marked by frailty (because they are unprecedented) and inseparable from the struggle to also bring about remembrance, a secular immortality. Action in a public sphere, as Arendt defines it, is the only chance humanity has for actions that outlive the time of their doing and so partake of immortality.

In *Atlantic Afterlives* I maintain that narrative is itself a form of action that submits its representations to such immortality as readers and other writers may confer, though this can never be taken for granted. The afterlife of the Atlantic is simultaneously the passing of the traditionally troped transatlantic relationship, as well as the surviving actions, the precious cargo, in the literature from this particular area. Recalling McLuhan, I will test these ideas by assessing the literary currents of the Atlantic Ocean itself (rather than the temperature of the bathwater). In doing so I am aware that my approach goes against classic transatlantic literary studies in which the Atlantic Ocean tends to hold metaphorical weight that always exoticizes whatever lies on the other side. Part of the rationale of this book is thus to counter the fashion of producing readings of fictional texts that offer the thrills of displacing or disorienting readers' perceptions without, I contend, having discovered something actually new about place and area in the process. I concur with Spivak's affirmation of "the possibility of the *radically* heterogeneous," which, she explains, is foreclosed by too much explanation: "on the general level, the possibility of explanation carries the presupposition of an explainable (even if not fully) universe and an explaining (even if imperfectly) subject. These presuppositions assure our being" ("Explanation and Culture," 380). What would we discover about passages across the Atlantic Ocean in contemporary literature if our focus shifted from the need merely to "assure our being" toward a confirmation of the reader as discoverer of something radically new about place and knowledge? *Atlantic Afterlives* addresses concerns that Saussy details in his brief introduction to literature's role in the age of the Internet:

> The idea that a wider context will take care of hermeneutic problems, which is the assumption at the base of Google-mancy, takes for granted that text and context are co-present, "really," in some precritical fashion, a move that allows for a positivistic style of reading. But can one ask the right questions in such a positivistic setting? Is one condemned to wander a Google of endless quantitative correlations of a Yahoo! of preestablished categories narrowing down into preestablished subcategories? (33)

My book makes claims for reading practices that critically unpack assumptions of what constitutes knowledge as distinct from, but not necessarily opposed to, information. It takes up the challenge raised by media analyst Ethan Zuckerman, director of the Center for Civic Media at MIT and author of *Rewire: Digital Cosmopolitans in the Age of Connection*: "Looking for secrets—the missing information in systems we understand—we can easily glide past mysteries, events that make sense only when we understand how systems have changed" (Zuckerman, 5). Once anthologies of world literature emerged and were subsequently theorized by scholars such as David Damrosch and Franco Moretti, the literary system was perceived to be transparent to readers. Literatures of the world became available to us in an accessible way, and the assumption was that the world's cultures are somehow readable to a select number of scholars who have mastered the tricks of the trade—whether through close reading (Damrosch) or distant reading (Moretti). As such, to use Saussy's term, text and context were always thought to be "co-present." The question I want to raise is, in the words of Emily Apter, might this drive to anthologize the world's cultures itself constitute a "reflexive endorsement of cultural equivalence and substitutability" (2)? Via the Internet, comprehension of some sort or other is always on the menu, yours for the taking. However, with software-mediated access to place and people at our fingertips, our challenge, as Zuckerman writes, "is not access to information; it is the challenge of paying attention" (19). Critical to this challenge is the need to resist an ever-growing field of supposed connectivity-based methodological assumptions and models that try to program how comparative literary studies should operate.

Because of its geographically contained area of focus, the study of transatlantic literature presents an ideal opportunity to review the kind of cultural work the literatures from a specific area and time undertake. Conventionally, texts that engage with a transatlantic other are read according to a methodology that privileges exchange and circulation. Specifically, this methodology for reading is premised on what in 2007 Manning and Taylor refer to in their introduction to the inaugural reader *Transatlantic Literary Studies* as "a borderless world [wherein] homogeneity and singularity increasingly give way to transnational spaces of relation and hybridity" (3). But what of that which cannot be circulated, which resists being bought and sold? What do we do with that which does not share the same currency of either the "borderless world" or the "transnational spaces"? The heady notion of a world without borders has taken readers and authors by storm since the end of the Cold War, even if the evidence points toward an increase of man-made, physical, and legal borders. Walls today, as Brown says, are hyperbolic tokens of sovereignty, but "like all hyperbole, they reveal a tremulousness, vulnerability, dubiousness, or instability at the core of what they aim to express" (24). Brown's analysis gives a much more complex description of a world of official statelessness where, increasingly, boundaries are predicated on inequality and the failure to achieve sovereignty. There is a strange paradox at work here: on the one hand, there is a transgressive fantasy of borderlessness and, on the other, other walls are rising that have become inseparable from the contemporary global landscape. In fact, these walls are now so much a part of the economy that they are no longer seen as walls as if the form itself no longer carries meaning. I wonder if some of the vaunted push for global equivalence and connectivity can be explained by what might at its core be a deep anxiety about *disconnection*?

I wonder, for instance, if our desire to see connection everywhere is a distraction from current crises of cultural domination and exploitation in the global political economy? Books such as *Virtual Americas: Transnational Fictions and the Transatlantic Imaginary* by Paul Giles aim to "raise the specter of a transatlantic imaginary" (16), but to what end? Published just a year after the September 11, 2001, terrorist attacks on the World Trade Center in the United States, it seems a little odd to be adding comparative literature's muscle to the task of consolidating transatlantic solidarity when the significance of that particular divide is less troubling than mounting disunities elsewhere, between rich and poor, not to mention the rift between the West and Muslim communities. But the new boundless methodologies I am referring to are not equipped to discern an "elsewhere" in relation to their widening fields of interest. One might say that it is not for literature to resolve international conflict, were it not the case that comparative literature generally and transatlantic literary studies specifically intersect with the discipline of postcolonial studies and the geopolitical relationship between center and periphery. Nevertheless, in 2013 Giles's *Antipodean America* delivers more vertiginous maps of ghostly influence, this time across the Pacific Ocean. Similarly, in 2006 comparativist Wai Chee Dimock announced an alternative trajectory for reading American literature outside national boundaries in *Through Other Continents: American Literature across Deep Time*. Here, Dimock introduces "a set of longitudinal frames, at once projective and recessional, with input going both ways, and binding continents and millennia into many loops of relations, a densely interactive fabric" (3–4).

Giles and Dimock's reading of a global heart that beats inside the American and British canon, while understandable in Whitman's age, seems to me indefensible in today's world of statelessness, environmental destitution, fortress mentality, staggering inequality, and annihilation of local cultures and languages. In short, an interpretative approach that normalizes all and any points of comparison in fact sees sameness (its own preconceptions) rather than actual difference. It attempts to rival the imaginative sway of the internet without offering any resistance to the Net's own built-in normalizing force. In *The Virtual Republic*, Australian media theorist McKenzie Wark in 1997 argues rather simplistically that culture is the way a society moves information from place to place (24). By mapping out traces of cross-hemispheric influence, Giles and Dimock risk falling into a similar view of what constitutes culture. It is a view propagated in the age of the Internet and resembles a watered-down version of Deleuze's rhizome that follows multiple avenues of connection in so far as any point of a rhizome can be connected to any other. However, in a world whose sense of itself is increasingly founded on web-mediated virtuality, it seems rather pointless to argue for the existence of such rhizomatic structures and experiences since they are ubiquitous. Therefore, to look for this in our reading practices seems blissfully to ignore the essentially ecological aspect of real situations. Given that even intellectual resources are finite, what, realistically, could possibly sustain the rhizome or our study of it if we are to assume that its expansion is endless?

Instead, *Atlantic Afterlives* suggests that a comparativist today needs to consider the stumbling blocks on the surface of the ocean that arrest our endlessly proliferating interpretative progress, much like the islands of garbage in the Atlantic and Pacific. What are these but reminders that oceans are now trade routes for man-made marine debris as much as for ideas and peoples? Rather than gliding past these patches of garbage in the erroneous belief that the flow is uninterrupted, my claim is that we need to pause at these eddies to understand the new methodologies now required for reading the world. An insight into what is required can be gleaned from Deleuze in his essay "Desert Islands." Here, he describes an island that remains deserted despite its abundance of flora and fauna, despite even the presence of a castaway as well as a ship that comes to rescue him. What could change this island from being deserted? According to Deleuze, "we would have to overhaul the general distribution of the continents, the state of the seas, and the lines of navigation" (12). Nothing short of a major shift in point of view and perspective would change what we are able to see on that island. My aim in *Atlantic Afterlives* is slightly more modest. Where Wark, Giles, and Dimock see everything deliriously showing up everywhere, I see unique instances of reading and narrativizing that allow something precious to come into existence somewhere, not everywhere. In a world in which information is already hyperlinked and connected, the most important task at hand is to follow the principles of narrative and its processes of selection and privileging. As Saussy points out, "With its poor bit-stream and its requirement that we slow down to its speed, quibble over every word, literature frustrates the economy of information in which more data and faster access is always better" (33). To privilege hesitancy, deliberation and slowness over speed is an essential aspect of any reading practice that aims to share its findings with others.

To represent the world through literature, to produce narrative, is to involve human agency in a collaborative intervention in textuality in which readers and authors mutually reshape their view of the world and of the role of narrative in it. The dramatic information leaks of recent times have demonstrated that information becomes fully discernible only when liberated and represented through an authoring agency such as Edward Snowden recently and shaped into a narrative for the public to read. Like a glimpse at a flow of covert data, uninterrupted by narrative's intervening force, information is undecidable (which may still be a mark of honor for hard-line poststructuralists) and undebated, without attaining the status of knowledge. So long as we insist on believing in a borderless world in which information travels effortlessly, the islands of meanings that we hope to uncover in foreign or far-fetched literatures will remain unpopulated. What might we discover if we were to toss out that blueprint and change the lines of navigation as Deleuze suggests? For too long now, we have been taught to read America as the New World child liberated from its Old World (British) parent. What if Graham Greene's *The Quiet American*, the subject of my first chapter, "Narrative without Borders: Reading Graham Greene in the Information Age," tells another story altogether, a story wherein the transatlantic other is not the New or the Old World but the Information Age itself? Greene's transatlantic novels, *The Quiet American* and *Our Man in Havana*, reveal him as a whistleblower in today's parlance. As with Julian Assange and Edward Snowden, Greene's triumph is narrative's victory over information. He produces a narrated world that delivers the sort of enduring wisdom and counsel worthy of Walter Benjamin's ideal for the storyteller.

The second chapter, "Apocalypse Then and Now: *The Road*, *Lord of the Flies*, and the Ends of Knowledge," takes the reader into a version of Stephan Zweig's "soundless deep" (24) via a troping of the Atlantic Ocean as a terrifying sea of sameness reminiscent of our worst fears of the vacuous programmatic extension of cyberspace. This chapter offers a broad view of the range covered by the imaginary of the Atlantic as both that which divides as well as joins Europe and the United States. Here I argue that William Golding's 1954 classic *Lord of the Flies* ultimately questions any confidence placed in the salvific role of the ocean as a source of rescue post-Second World War, while McCarthy's *The Road* from 2006 presents the ocean as failing to offer anything more than a palliative function to a world whose capacity to confront otherness has become debilitated. This chapter and *Atlantic Afterlives* as a whole demonstrate that the other engaged with in the literature since the Information Age has become, like information itself, free-floating, atmospheric. In this chapter, I suggest that the liminality of an end-of-the-world perspective is essential to the way civilization sees itself. My further claim is that these vital thresholds are themselves threatened with ending, since they can only be constructed out of narrative that has become a scarce and precious resource in the Information Age. In this chapter, I put McCarthy's novel in dialogue with Golding's to show how the ocean is no longer constituted by boundaries that can be crossed, transgressed, or violated one way or another. Today, my argument goes, there is no transatlantic or even circum-Atlantic. In what I call throughout this book a "post-Atlantic" world, narratives of encounter, exploitation, or oppression can be cited by anyone, owned by anyone, and, importantly, can touch and move anyone. The good news, however, is that the ocean informs these two novels with an imaginary for thinking through the limits and possibilities of productive exchange of knowledge in post-Atlantic times when virtual encounters have become the norm. I use concepts such as terror and the apocalypse to provide the internal coherence of an alternative set of tensions in helping to locate what undermines and also what encourages the possibility of encounter between self and other in the reimagined oceanic of the twentieth and twenty-first centuries.

By charting the precarious effects of globalization, chapter 3, "Through a Border Darkly: North Atlantic Narratives of Exploitation in Peter Hoeg's *Miss Smilla's Feeling for Snow* and Annie Proulx's *The Shipping News*," shows how certain current models of communication and collaboration are consistent with colonial ideologies of Western imperialism. What emerges in my analysis of both novels is a highly localized aftermath of uneven geographical development. Hoeg and Proulx show the enormous price suffered by the most vulnerable members of society, including children and the disenfranchised, for keeping up with a neoliberal form of capitalism and progress. The aim of this chapter is to examine representations of power in the North Atlantic as they follow in the footsteps of the greed and corruption of last century's imperialism and its continuity with today's globalist expansion. These unsound waves resurface in post-Atlantic times, a stage of human development more deeply networked than ever, but at the core of which is a profound ambiguity as to the rationale of this acceleration. In Hoeg and Proulx, I read acts of resistance to what Gilles Deleuze and Felix Guattari in *A Thousand Plateaus* call capitalism's "axiomatic" in which local productivity is "decoded" and disenfranchised (143–4, passim). This chapter investigates how narrative enlists traditional and indigenous values to articulate—or "recode"—the past, present, and possible future value of the local without denying the existence and importance of the global. This chapter uncovers an ecology of knowledge in narrative that represents powerful alternatives to the unencumbered flows and often rather giddy ideals that circulate in the Information Age via the technological revolution.

Chapter 4, "A Post-Atlantic Divorce: Reading and Writing Ted Hughes and Sylvia Plath in the Digital Age," demonstrates how the Hughes and Plath saga reinstates the transatlantic divide thereby recalling the significance the ocean played just prior to the onset of the Digital Age. Afloat in a sea of discourse, the public Plath and Hughes dispute has resurrected the ocean and situated it within the "atmospheric" age of technology-mediated communication. This chapter sees that controversy as a myth of origin for the overlapping voices and competing territories now proliferating as a result of communication technology. The clamor for textual authority that emerged in the aftermath of Plath's death, even before the shouting became multimodal, is, I argue, an early indicator of the kind of writing and reading that now leaves multiple and fragmented traces on the Internet via social media. Increased traffic of information and opinion has fuelled the rush to corner the market in cultural capital from the Hughes/Plath legacy, by fans and critics who wish to claim it as their own suzerain. In this chapter, I adapt Arendt's term "pariah" to accommodate the notion of the literary outsider and the overlapping themes of secrecy and visibility that jostle with one another in my reading of Plath and Hughes's afterlife. My claim is that the strange brew of creativity and anonymous self-effacement now common in expressions of subjectivity in digital media finds a perfect setting in the Plath and Hughes story that was from the outset an early analogue of the virtual room of today. Finally, I find in my reading of Hughes's Crow poems as well as Plath's desire to divorce from the confines of her physically and socially circumscribed self an expression of the ideals of the outsider. I argue that a certain degree of disconnect from the conformist expectations of one's fellows, which we find in Arendt's pariah figure, is required in order then to reconstruct a community, although regrettably this may come at a great personal cost.

Chapter 5, "Bridging Bereavement: Narratives of Loss and Loss of Narrative in Anne Michaels," explores the role of storytelling as supporting a political narrative of loss. It asks, via Canadian author Anne Michaels' *The Winter Vault*, what reading and writing positions are available to us whereby narrative can shelter the exiled and the dispossessed even after death? *The Winter Vault* is a meditation on the limits of reconstruction in human geographies of mourning with special emphasis on the symbolism of inundation and transoceanic separation. Michaels's novel often presents loss rather than represents it, and in this chapter, I use Derrida's work on the mechanism of psychoanalytical encryption to uncover the full effect of her achievement. Reading *The Winter Vault* together with Roland Barthes's *Mourning Diary*, this chapter finds contemporary literature responding to the subjective strain of separation and division with a new conception of narrative as a bridging operation. It is striking here to find Barthes, famously responsible for "Death of the Author," offering readers this restitution of a central speaking and reading position for himself following the death of his mother.

The aim of chapter 6, "Future Perfect: The Problem of the Human in Michel Houellebecq's *Atomised* and Philip Roth's *The Human Stain*," is to carry the book's line of enquiry well into the twenty-first century by organizing its insights into technologies of connectivity around the idea of enhancements in representational and reproductive power. Houellebecq and Roth show how these factors influence us as sexual, economic, and social beings post-Information Age. Here we see an increase in the abstraction of knowledge, subjectivity, and place. This chapter extends the notion of terror produced from an insufficiency of knowing explored via espionage in chapter 1 and in the treatment of apocalyptic themes in chapter 2. Here my discussion focuses on the rivalry between the efficiencies and certainties of information and the tentative, exploratory nature of knowledge. Through a close reading of two fin-de-siècle novels, Houellebecq's *Atomised* from 1998 and Philip Roth's *The Human Stain* issued in 2000, this chapter serves as a companion to the "apocalyptic" chapter in the way it stages the Atlantic as a topos of the end of knowledge and the end of especially masculine resourcefulness. Houellebecq's novel is more extreme in its representation of technology's emasculating effect. It suggests that the scientific breakthrough of cloning will be the end of knowledge altogether since it rules out serendipity and surprise as a legitimate and important pathways to discovery.

*Atlantic Afterlives* demonstrates that rather than being remaindered in an age of electronic culture, literature functions as an enthralling stage for knowledge and a critique of forces antagonistic to its pursuit. As the ongoing invention of our social bond, the literature that is the afterlife of the Atlantic Ocean lives in our need for narrative, storytelling, and poetics.

# Part I

# Leaking Oceans

1

# Narrative without Borders

## Reading Graham Greene in the Information Age

My mother grew up in the district of Härjedalen in northern Sweden. Her small but picturesque village, Överhogdal, was given a modest mention in history books when, at the beginning of last century, a tapestry was found there dating back to 1040–1170. It had remained hidden away in a church storage room (apparently a piece of it had been used as a doll's blanket by a village girl) for more than a thousand years. Detailed and richly decorated, the Överhogdal tapestry depicts life in the Viking Age. In its woven design it is possible to read fragments of the past and predominantly they show herds of animals, as well as people on the move. There are people on foot, on horseback, as well as longboats. The extent to which the Vikings explored the breadth of the Atlantic is disputable, although there is said to be evidence of early Norse settlement at the beginning of the eleventh century on the far northern tip in Newfoundland (Winchester, 82). How much of the Atlantic the Norse men explored we do not know for sure, but this tapestry with its longboats reminds us of the role the ocean played in their imagination, despite the fact that many, like those in Härjedalen, lived inland. Even those who lived near an Atlantic shore would most likely have been unaware of its extraordinary expanse and instead they would have relied on stories about sea monsters and other dangers associated with this massive body of water. It was only after the death of Christopher Columbus in 1506 that cartographers formally named a continent now known as America and a self-contained ocean was christened "Atlantic" (Winchester, 92). Halfway through the twentieth century, these adventurous transatlantic explorers gave way to the passenger who crossed the ocean first by ship and shortly thereafter by airplane. I draw attention to the find in

Överhogdal to remind the reader first that the most recent and dramatic advances in the speed of travel and movement have themselves been accelerating so that they occupy a microscopic amount of time in contrast to the foregoing centuries. Additionally, and constituting a new scale and significance for mobility, I want to highlight the relative limitations of all technologically enhanced physical mobility in comparison to the instantaneous command of virtual spaces offered by the digital revolution. Despite their advanced performance, all vehicles today are, as Paul Virilio says, "always surpassed by the 'video performance' of the transmission of images, and by the instantaneous representation of facts" (32).

This book begins at that juncture of history, identified by Virilio, when the speed of information transfer begins to overtake any motorized or jet-propelled movements of people or populations. Now, in our own time, it seems that there are very few places that cannot be vicariously experienced via screen-mediated technology. The chapter begins with the dawn of the Information Age that has eventually led to a time when, as Isin observes, "citizens without frontiers" can traverse boundaries so as to create series of resonances, solidarities, enmities, alliances, and intensities across space and time that resist domestication under any universalizing narrative of an earthbound nation-state or territory (6). The difficulty of regulating the flows of information has become a controversial topic in the last few years especially since WikiLeaks and other whistle-blowing incidents. As technology continues to develop quicker and more efficient ways for data about us and our associations to be recorded and distributed, the gap between verifiable knowledge and detached information flow has grown exponentially. As a result, communication technology is a prime facilitator of subjective decentering with a concomitant struggle to achieve agency, political or otherwise. Isin reminds us that the contemporary subject is now imagined in terms of connectivity, the network, and the multitude (72). In this chapter I read Graham Greene's *The Quiet American* and *Our Man in Havana: An Entertainment* in the context of the role played by new communication technologies in networking individuals and society, both increasingly detached from place. This is to read Greene's prescient deposition on the state and trajectory of 1950s postwar espionage against the background of a shift from an oceanic movement of goods and information to what I call an "atmospheric" transmission of representations. This, I argue, has come to constitute the multiplatform underpinning of the Atlantic's various afterlives. As a historically contested area of exploration, communication, and representation, this is how the Atlantic still registers what communicating across geographical and cultural borders actually means. I want to read Greene in the context of the future he seems clearly to have described in these novels—our present age in which a digitally mediated oceanic imaginary of global proportions still manages to couple agency with the decentering effects of a prodigiously far-reaching connectivity. Without ruling out individual agency, this chapter is also a tentative literary critical response to Isin's proposal for the multitude to become a political subject in its own right, one that is collective and formed through various places and durations. Isin sees this subject as resisting "Empire" (74), a term he borrows from Hardt and Negri's famous text. I am sympathetic to Isin's overall claim and see one effect of a digitally mediated oceanic imaginary as furnishing the area of action for such a disparate resistance to what I see as a world order dominated by information.

Greene's *The Quiet American* is typically read as an example of transatlantic literature, but in my reading of this novel, I see a shift from the geopolitically situated transatlantic dyad to an increasing awareness of the consequences of highly mobile patterns of information. These patterns should certainly recall what Foucault wants us to know of power, being "the multiplicity of force relations immanent in the sphere in which they operate" (*History of Sexuality*, 92) with, however, two important qualifications. The first is that communication technology has made that "sphere" truly global. The second is that I do not admit Foucault's founding assumption regarding the topological impossibility of any agential position outside the network of power relations, no place from which to offer resistance to its flows. In my account, knowledge stands in opposition to information by way of an economic arrangement in which knowledge is achieved as a result of work intentionally against the flow, whereas information is consumed with far less effort. Information is a feature of the ease by which communication is automated; its very ease of assimilation, and its endless propensity to distract and digress, constitutes a seduction into a form of slavery to information masquerading as knowledge. This anticipates my discussion in chapter 3 of the Atlantic slave trade as a setting for present widespread enslavement to commodity culture. We need not conclude from this that information is an intrinsic evil, simply that it is often misrecognized for being something it is not. Information bereft of narrativity serves to disperse rather than secure agency; it is where a diverting sort of powerlessness circulates. The power of Google to exploit data about us is revisited in chapter 2 within the context of the apocalyptic themes discussed there. Opposed to this is the dogged and necessarily political production of knowledge that owes much to narrative values of structure and local relevance as distinct from the burgeoning ubiquity of automated communication. As a necessary step for creating an autonomous political subjectivity, there needs to be a concerted questioning of the pervasive effect of information, one of the cornerstones of contemporary Empire. Such an interrogation is also a productive reading of our times and texts toward knowledge as resistance to the mere consumption of information. In my reading of Greene's spy fiction, I see information being foreshadowed as that to which the multitude would increasingly be enslaved insofar as information engages them in consumption of whatever arises rather than the resistant production of knowledge as a response to whatever is happening.

The work of knowledge production draws from the multitude a particular form of agency consonant with Deleuze and Guattari's assemblage. This work drawn from the labor force of the multitude is, in each case, the singular production of an assemblage, "a constellation of singularities and traits," which is, intriguingly, "*deducted* from the flow" (*Thousand*, 448; emphasis added). The word "assemblage" (*agencement*) suggests a dynamic process as well as a spatial formation along the lines of an arrangement or alignment. The French *agencement* invokes agency, and following from this, Ian Buchanan emphasizes that an assemblage is always of several agencies and always *for* someone or something.[1] Greene's fiction might even be read via the Deleuzian axis of territorialization and deterritorialization for this would help to specify how old boundaries are erased and new ones inscribed. Nevertheless, the notion of the assemblage, especially in Buchanan's terms, constitutes a more precise account of a particularly effective and politically situated production of resistance. The boundaries of "old" and "new," "parent" and "child" within which the transatlantic relationship is commonly framed are effaced in the later half of the twentieth century as shown in Greene's *The Quiet American*. In its place, the Information Age has brought a proliferation of speaking positions to our attention, many of which exist independently of spatial and temporal demarcations. Assemblage theory makes it possible to begin to specify which among these might constitute a resistant alternative somehow "deducted" from the seductions of information.

Greene foreshadows future political turmoil in these novels as well as the increasing scale of international communication and security intelligence. Not unlike the documents released by the whistleblowers of today, *The Quiet American* anticipates the Vietnam War and *Our Man in Havana* presages many of the political pressures that later would lead to the Cuban Missile Crisis. Greene goes further than contemporary whistle-blowers because, doubtless due to his journalistic acumen, the world was readable to him as information. What is now leaked from obscurity into the public arena was already visible to his trained eye. He could translate information into compellingly plausible fiction which in itself provided a second-level "reading" of his own times. This chapter traces the changing conditions of transatlantic informationalism since the mid-twentieth century. While secret, sensitive, even scandalous information today is usually derived from accidentally open, hacked, or leaked sources, narrative is nevertheless still required to "inform" this information with enduring, relevant meaning. According to former Cold War British intelligence officer Michael Herman, meaningful intelligence in a post-Cold War setting must still be thought of as more than the collection of information but also as its selection, evaluation, and arrangement in order to be made useful as a representation whose relevance will last into the future (32). My contention is that Greene shows how narrative imbues information with intelligence, which then constitutes a grasp of present events that can also constitute a discerning perspective on what lies over the horizon. Since digital communication brought access to a virtual experience of distance, the high-speed multimodal delivery of experience has diminished the impact of any terrestrial locus of encounter, the transatlantic included. We have witnessed the passing of the Atlantic as we once knew it for the Atlantic no longer denotes a place of distance and difference, neither as the basis for anxiety nor in the form of a promise of adventure. (I revisit the extreme consequence of this in my discussion of Cormac McCarthy's *The Road* in chapter 2.) However, what the espionage novels of Greene can teach us is that, in place of the Atlantic, the network itself forms the basis of an oceanic imaginary that, coupled with narrative principles, is the setting for singular and enduring, though perhaps spatially diffuse, assemblages that continue to structure our experience of the world online and on the ground.

A methodology for a resistant reading of the Information Age can be found in Greene's *The Quiet American* and *Our Man in Havana*. Set in Cuba during the Fulgencio Batista regime, *Our Man in Havana* illustrates the extent to which information and intelligence are subject to narrative design. A British Secret Service agent offers James Wormold, a vacuum cleaner retailer, the job of establishing a network of informants in Havana for the purpose of gathering intelligence on the Batista administration. At a loss as to what is expected of him, Wormold fabricates his reports by using a fictitious group of agents that bears witness not only to a singularly creative mind but also to the absurdity of the secret service itself. Hawthorne, Wormold's minder, is suspicious of the reports that come in, including sketches of magnified details of a vacuum cleaner meant to suggest unidentified weapons, missiles perhaps, or silos. However, he is naturally reluctant to inform on his own recruit and thereby reveal his own poor lack of judgment. Both Wormold and Secret Agent Hawthorne carefully separate the real world from the world of make-believe. I shall pursue these distinctions between fact and fiction, and truth, in the following pages and argue that only after the application of narrative design to information does it ever yield its intelligence. Greene might have had the American author Nathaniel Hawthorne in mind when he named his Secret Agent. Hawthorne famously claimed not to write novels as such, but romances removed from "the possible or probable course of ordinary experience" (Porte, 95). Hawthorne's idea of romance endures in America, adapted to contemporary tastes in a narrator presented as vulnerable, even terminally ill, which I will examine in chapter 6 in a discussion of Philip Roth's novel *The Human Stain.*

In Greene's spy novels, secrets can be kept under lock and key so that only the most able of spies can uncover them. However, as I have suggested above, aspects of the novels in question also anticipate our own times in which secrets are less likely to be locked in physical safes, the virtual sites where they are housed being consequently more vulnerable to cyber attack. Today's world is intensely interconnected, and rapid flows of capital, people, goods, images, ideas, and ideologies have compressed the world into networks of practices and linkages. Due to the vulnerability of personal and state secrets, the word "security" in relation to information routinely means the opposite, arousing a sense of insecurity and a resulting stepping up of measures meant to shore up virtual bulwarks against leaks and break-ins. Apart from this specific kind of unease, the very sense of what is true and reliable about the contemporary world is shaky since the world is now very much subject to a proliferation of competing representations that owe a lot to narrative aesthetics. To a large extent this is recognizable in the present-day avatars of the gossip column, the personal interest story, as well as the so-called infotainment industry, to name only a few. In my discussion of the press in Annie Proulx's *The Shipping News* in chapter 3, it emerges that narrative principles apply to the news as much as to fiction, where the selection and arrangement—and omission—of facts makes it unclear whether the news serves anything more than a prodigious appetite for narrative. Information leaks authorized by WikiLeaks editor-in-chief Julian Assange and, more recently, Edward Snowden hit the public awareness only after a narrative scheme had been superimposed on the bare facts, which includes conflict, climax, and, sooner or later, a dénouement. What is remarkable is that although the leaked documents themselves seem to tell countless real-life stories of suffering and betrayal in war, of strategically sanctioned "collateral damage" entailing literally a cast of thousands, what hits the headlines is always the story of the leak itself. This enables the media to focus on the central character of this story, the whistle-blower, packaged as either hero or villain depending on the leanings of the news outlet.[2] Faced with a fantasy of reportage and espionage that resonates with reality, and a present-day reality that appears all the more fantastic in its peculiar and sometimes theatrical disclosure of facts, it can be concluded that truth arises, if it does, from the way it is shared and not strictly from its content. This calls us back to consider the often fraught relationship between authors, texts, and readers. *The Quiet American*, especially, anticipates a world in which the borderline between fiction and reality has become smeared, a world in which anything, provided readers are willing to imagine it, can be said to exist. Such a world is potentially dangerous, a world of terror and chaos. While narrative cannot prevent this, Greene's readers have a chance to recognize the role of the imagination and the intentions in the realm of the political, the social, and the ethical in times of war.

Between March 1952 and June 1955, Graham Greene wrote *The Quiet American*, a novel set during the French war in Vietnam in which the intricate links between politics and propaganda, as well as the status of the personal, the social, and the ethical in wartime, are unveiled. More poignantly, it is also a novel about personal ideals and professional cynicism focused on the fated encounter between British journalist Thomas Fowler and the young idealist American Alden Pyle, the quiet American of the title. The novel was written before the United States became fully involved in Vietnam, yet Greene manages to capture the dangerous paradoxes that made it such a political and military disaster. Greene's novel is not only a masterful window into American foreign policy of the 1950s and 1960s, but his blurring of the distinction between his fictional narrative and the world outside the text also resonates with twenty-first-century readers. As a journalist narrator, Fowler is in Vietnam to report on the war. Disillusioned by life, unable to end his failed marriage, and exhausted by the war, Fowler has no opinions, writes no columns, takes up no position, sporadically and dispassionately cabling observations to his editor in London. The narrative is told in flashbacks framed by the interrogation of Fowler by the French inspector Vigot as part of an inquiry into Pyle's murder. Vigot suspects that Fowler might have been involved in Pyle's death. Fowler scoffs at the investigation, suggesting that Vigot recover Pyle's dog and "analyse the earth on its paws" for clues (28), ridiculing the use of such meticulous forensic scrutiny in wartime when Pyle's death is simply one of many.

The imaginary in Greene's novels teeters on the brink of absurdity in the minds of his world-weary characters with whom his equally world-weary readers identify. It is by granting equal narrative attention to the imagination and reality, romance and atrocity, innocence and corruption, that Greene's literary world of the 1950s and 1960s intersects the world of today. Indeed, the recent development of so-called "sockpuppets" as a means of managing opinion on United States' armed operations in the Middle East and Central Asia (Fielding, 9) in the "war against terror" resonates with the war against communism as played out in Greene's novel *Our Man in Havana*. Today's sockpuppets are false online identities used to help manage official and public perceptions of politically or economically sensitive events. In Greene's novel, Wormold is part amateur, part vigilante, single-handedly constructing fake agents as well as their reports in an approximation of what he thinks is expected of a secret agent. He becomes a kind of double agent, working for himself (only to afford a pony for his daughter), but his resourcefulness foreshadows the ability of a single US serviceman to control a string of online personas in politically sensitive sites or chatrooms anywhere in the world. The satirical tone found in *The Quiet American* is matched if not word for word then certainly skepticism for skepticism in *Our Man in Havana*. As Hawthorne works to break down Wormold's resistance to becoming "our man in Havana," he points out that Wormold's vacuum cleaner business is the perfect cover. "With your cleaners you've got the entrée everywhere," Hawthorne tells Wormold (29). Wormold, who has not yet hit on the use he will later make of his cleaners, instead demands:

> Do you expect me to analyse the fluff?
>
> It may seem a joke to you, old man, but the main source of the French intelligence at the time of Dreyfus was a charwoman who collected the scraps out of the waste-paper baskets at the German Embassy. (29)

Later, when Wormold's absurdly magnified drawings of vacuum cleaner parts miraculously convince experts that he has seen a nuclear missile site, this is really no more or less darkly absurd than what today passes in the public or expert imagination for a nuclear capability or, recalling a notorious recent example, "weapons of mass destruction." Although the means by which information or misinformation circulates may evolve (postal, telegraphic, digital, etc.), the function of the imagination and the challenge it faces in extracting knowledge is far less subject to time.

Even so, the accelerating speed of telecommunications can often provoke a sense of dizzyingly rapid change in which nothing enduring can get a foothold before being swept away by further incoming signals. However, if we view Wormold's activities and their reception in terms of assemblage theory, we can see how the oceanic imaginary supports enduring constellations of agency. Although Wormold is the "author" of his fictional network of spies, both he and his "readers" (Hawthorne, his Chief, nuclear technology experts, and so on) must actively use their imagination (that is to say, intentionally) to make a shared and practical use of his reports. The result concurs with Buchanan's account of the Deleuzian assemblage in that it is *for* someone or something despite being formed out of many perspectives and intentions, some of which oppose others. In this case, this complex of differing perspectives and shades of credence does, in the end, constitute grounds for a singular and carefully evolving stance taken by Britain vis-à-vis Cuba. Even if Wormold and one or two others know the reports are bogus, the stance as assemblage exists; it might even be said to be living. The assemblage that constitutes the reports, as well as the foreign policy based on them, resists the winds of change despite any veridical shortcomings. Signals were not arriving as fast in Greene's day as they are in ours, but nevertheless the urgency of the need to know something about Cuba, as Britain peered toward the Americas, is also part of the assemblage that in Greene's novel hovers over the Atlantic. Now that the oceanic has become the World Wide Web, the Atlantic lives on in the form of its imaginary afterlives, but these too can take the form of the singular and sustainable generation of assemblages, every bit as resistant to erosion by the flows of information as the Atlantic coasts have been.

Today, any stateless terror network is almost exclusively screen-mediated, far from the wastepaper baskets of embassies. As I write this in early 2015, the US, Australian, and British forces are once again entering conflict in the Middle East, this time striking Islamic State (IS) targets in Iraq and Syria. The IS has been waging its brutal war for Islamic fundamentalist supremacy by broadcasting harrowing clips of beheadings and other horrific acts of violence to a Western audience that is partially anaesthetized to, and partially enthralled by, representations of violence that have become so much a part of contemporary culture. Similarly, the information leaks that reach the public do not discriminate between levels of importance or urgency, inviting comparatively little actual interpretative engagement from the public. Indeed, in the age of electronic dissemination and communication, little demand is made on readers to familiarize themselves with the context or to engage themselves with the facts beyond the sensational. When hackers and whistle-blowers themselves become the heroes or villains of these stories, they are standing in for a superabundance of information that rarely reaches the level of knowledge. The information that circulates is a very coarse form of signification that does not of itself feed into a properly meaningful context. As such it is unrefined and undernarrated.

Officially launched in 2006, WikiLeaks came to public attention in 2010 through its disclosure of the Afghan War Diary, the Iraq War logs, and over 150,000 US diplomatic cables, many classified as confidential or secret four years later (Pilkington). By operating as an activist for WikiLeaks, US intelligence analyst Chelsea Manning (born Bradley Manning) stepped out of his professional role and committed either treason or heroism, depending on one's point of view. An unresolved question is whether or not WikiLeaks has made the world less safe by revealing data that should have remained secret in the interest of state security. Undeniably, WikiLeaks offers the potential to translate data into something more enduring that has a significant impact on the future of organizations, governments, institutions, and private individuals, but it does not itself offer that translation. Although the *New York Times* said the leaks give "a picture of the war in Afghanistan that is in many respect more grim than the official portrayal," that picture will rarely attract more than a moment of public attention. Nevertheless, not only is WikiLeaks able to broadcast an extraordinary amount of information beyond the control of media and government, its declared agenda, "the defence of freedom of speech and media publishing, the improvement of our common historical record," gives users some guidance on where they might go next, even as far as an enraptured exercise of "the rights of all people to create new history" (Wikileaks). It is as though the providers of the information also suggest some broad narrative avenues their users might follow, which can act as a conduit for turning such acts of disclosure into a possible and imaginable "repertoire" or "infrastructure" of resistance, as Isin calls it (16). Follow-up action might include organized protests, greater freedom of expression, and a greater accountability of those in power.

Written long before such massive information leaks, Greene signals a degree of anxiety over the retreat of narrative from public life while at the same time celebrating the art of narrative such as his own as a vital ingredient for making an intervention in political affairs. By so doing, Greene recalls Walter Benjamin's despair over the reduced role of the storyteller. Benjamin equates the demise of storytelling with the end of "the communicability of experience." What he saw dying out was the "wisdom" of "[c]ounsel woven into the fabric of real life" as well as "the epic side of truth" (87). Might there be a way to recuperate the notion of literature as Benjaminian wisdom and counsel, perhaps via more recent narrative theory? James Phelan's work is located at the intersection of authorial intention and reader response theory with a specific emphasis on the reader's participatory use of judgment in achieving a political engagement responsive to an author's work. Phelan suggests a renewed engagement with the jaded contemporary reader based on a more exploratory path to knowledge and, although he does not emphasize anything like Benjamin's "epic side of truth," his approach suggests that readers can yet receive counsel from an author's work. At the same time, military or political intelligence, Herman reminds us, must persuade its readers through "a demonstrated trail of evidence, assumptions and conclusions" (10), which again must enlist the active participation of the reader in the construction of an engaged and probing response to the information. Writing that delegates interpretative and evaluative responsibilities to readers in this way is offering a version of Benjamin's counsel in much the way Greene's novels do. In my discussion of Ted Hughes and Sylvia Plath in chapter 4 and of Anne Michaels in chapter 5, I shall revisit Benjamin's gloomy prediction of the ruin of storytelling as a vehicle for wisdom and counsel. Although I aim to offer some qualified hope for narrative's power to offer guidance and understanding, it will be seen in chapter 6 on Michel Houellebecq and Philip Roth that this hope is sometimes difficult to uphold.

Today in the age of whistle-blowing, we think of truth in terms of the information distribution mechanisms by which, through leaked information, we become aware of its concealment, not necessarily by what truth is in any sense intrinsically. Rather than disclosing any one particular truth, individuals such as Julian Assange and Edward Snowden expose the practices of custodians of classified information to the general public. Even though such information is made accessible through open sources such as WikiLeaks, the public will arguably not respond to the information unless it comes with a context that delivers some form of counsel. Spy novels underscore the reading process as a most unreliable activity subject to misreadings. Greene's *Our Man in Havana*, in which Wormold constructs a make-believe world of secret agents and weapons of unprecedented scale, stages a fiction within a fiction in order to lead his readers (Greene's, not Wormold's) to the revelation of something like Benjamin's wisdom. Wormold's own deliberate fiction has no aspiration grander than his avoiding being revealed as incompetent though it ends up forming the kernel of an imaginary of Cuba, loosely based in London that has a life of its own. Instances such as these remind the reader that what he or she reads could be located neither inside the book nor inside the author, but somewhere between or somewhere outside altogether.

Greene's presentation of intelligence practices in his spy novels (of which he had first-hand experience from his work in MI6 as well as journalism) encourages the reader to compare and contrast the careful gathering and staged disclosure of information with narrative practice. The British Secret Service Bureau was formed in 1909 and used for espionage and counterespionage. It saw a great structural development during the First World War and then its peacetime importance was consolidated during the Cold War at which point it was to be forever linked with ideology and subversion (Herman, 31). Greene's spy novels collapse the boundaries between narrativized plot and the real events that inform the author's literary landscape (such as the war in Vietnam and the Batista dictatorship in Cuba). Walter Benjamin's concern that counsel can no longer be found in literature suggests that for him the narrator had been demoted from the role of supplying readers with an exalted kind of knowledge. To say that the narrator is no longer an oracle, however, is not to dismiss the power of narrative or its role in and out of fiction. Phelan reminds us that narrativity encourages two main activities: observing and judging (323). It is the act of judging, especially, that has the potential to make the reader more complicit or engaged, having to assess how his or her own values measure up to those on the page and thus encourage political awareness as a basis for action. Similarly, Herman notes that knowledge is derived from intelligence in two stages. First, secret information has to be collected via code-breaking, intercepted communications, and other covert intelligence-gathering, and second, that information must be evaluated against noncovert sources such as press releases, broadcasts, diplomatic reporting, etc. (32). In *The Quiet American*, Fowler is an investigative journalist who reminds us of the interpretive dimensions of his work when he reflects on his role as being "to expose and record" (88). Also Phelan condenses the narrator's function to that of "reporting, interpreting, and evaluating" (326). These activities certainly help to demystify narrative techniques while encouraging the reader to participate in "the ethical principles upon which narrative is built" (Phelan, 325). By engaging with text as something that, by means of that very engagement, structures what can be known about the world, the reader allows for the possibility that the experience of reading might change his or her worldview.

This is not to deny, however, Walter Benjamin's claim that the dissemination of information has undermined the art of storytelling. Indeed, one might only turn to present-day "infotainment" to see precisely how enmeshed the two have become, arguably to the detriment of each. It is strange, as Wasko notes, that one does not speak of a new entertainment age despite the fact that entertainment is as characteristic of this age as information (16). Entertainment and information now go hand in hand, each feeding off the other. The leaks made by Snowden came replete with elements of narrative, including his own character whose motivations and destiny were eagerly explored by readers around the world, showing how a figure as intriguing as he is can challenge the Empire of Information in the way that fiction can. Greene's spy novels go a long way to supplying readers with Benjamin's beloved counsel, by offering narrative strategies that demand gathering and evaluating information while at the same time showing how this might be done. As such, the novels offer a methodology for an actively engaged way of reading today's world of increased coverage of security subjects. For a start, Greene makes it clear that all knowledge arrives at its destination battered by narratology. In *The Quiet American*, the Englishman Fowler, his Vietnamese lover Phuong and her family, the Frenchman Vigot, and the quiet American himself, Pyle, are engaged in a paranoid and self-seeking battle for epistemological control that foreshadows today's competing claims for public attention and credence given to various accounts of world events that constitute a part of the current information overload.

On the surface, *The Quiet American* follows a standard plot line of detective fiction, featuring a cast of people assembled in an isolated place and the discovery that one among them has been murdered. Pyle and Fowler are the two English speakers in the novel, competing for the companionship of the beautiful but distant Vietnamese woman Phuong. The novel opens with the confirmation that Pyle has been murdered, and it emerges that this is according to Fowler's plan to limit what he sees as an escalation in American interference in the communist involvement in Vietnam. There is also more than a hint that Fowler also wanted to eliminate Pyle as a rival for Phuong who deserted Fowler for the younger man. Though placed in a war-torn Vietnam, violence and chaos in the novel are presented by Fowler—the narrator—in a rather calm and controlled manner, even when disclosing his involvement in Pyle's murder. Here war and chaos are normalized through narrative, and the same could be said of Greene's novel about Cuba, subtitled "An Entertainment." In both novels, narrative might be perceived as playing down war or trivializing the terror of Batista's rule at the time. Indeed, all narrative that aims, among other things, to entertain readers risks a similar charge when depicting real atrocities. In the case of Greene's novels, however, both *Our Man in Havana* and *The Quiet American* forestall any sense of their author's trifling with serious matters by incisively, and even poignantly, criticizing the arrogant belief held by authorities such as the British Secret Service and other custodians of classified information that they are beyond ridicule and exposure.

Fowler's reconstruction of the events leading up to Pyle's murder digresses into other areas, erotic and philosophical, and forms part of a narrative strategy to gain the trust of the reader and satisfy his or her desire for regularity, while still representing disorder. Fowler broadens the reader's understanding of the quiet American through a series of revealing, intimate exchanges in life-threatening moments. Meanwhile, Fowler's detection of the man expands beyond him in an exponential growth of knowledge that threatens to expose Fowler instead.[3] Greene's novels capture an age when information first became a properly valuable currency. As revealed in these Cold War espionage novels, intelligence constitutes both the gathering of information as well as the exploitation of that knowledge, demonstrating its enormous potential to statesmen. If Greene's vision of world affairs was uncannily prescient, he also presents what will certainly appear quaint to the contemporary reader, his novels revealing the prevalence of a sometimes naïve sense of propriety regarding knowledge transferral. After Wormold's deceit has been discovered in *Our Man in Havana*, he is castigated by the British ambassador: "The whole subject is distasteful to me, Wormold. I can't tell you how distasteful it is. The correct sources for information abroad are the embassies. We have our attachés for that purpose" (207).

Importantly, Greene's novels emphasize the feckless unpredictability of information, subject as it is to the often irrational infirmities of the human condition. The stakes for readers of this genre are increased in this way since the challenge in establishing sure interpretative ground is more difficult when partly unconscious emotions powerfully sway motives. This is certainly the case in *Our Man in Havana* in which Wormold is enslaved to his daughter's extravagant tastes and thus receptive to the Secret Service's attempt to recruit him. It is also true in *The Quiet American* where the exotic culture of occupied Vietnam, as well as the steamy climate presumably, seduces Fowler into a lifestyle in which mind is subordinate to body. Since the mind cannot be trusted, already subject to corruption in times of war and occupation, Fowler surrenders to the physical enjoyment of nights spent with Phuong and, of course, his daily opium pipe that she dutifully prepares for him with loving care. Whereas Fowler prefers a languid eroticism to the cut and thrust of politics, Pyle idealistically believes bodily gratifications to be inferior to the achievements of intellect. After his murder, Fowler rummages through Pyle's bookcase where reading for pleasure is very scant apart from a book entitled *The Physiology of Marriage*. It leads Fowler to ponder whether Pyle "was studying sex, as he had studied the East, on paper" (29). Wedded to an alternative vision of society, Pyle is an idealist to whom sexual love comes second to the struggle to save Vietnam from communist China. The conflict between hedonism and asceticism is dramatized through the doomed friendship of Fowler and Pyle. Though the matter is never resolved for these two, for readers of espionage fiction the often impossible quest for epistemological certainty is part of its attraction. Greene's *The Quiet American* is set in what was to become a major political and military watershed for America in the twentieth century. In writing the detective novel manqué that is *The Quiet American*, Greene foreshadows a world in which the trading of information becomes a way of grappling with questions of commitment, judgment, and belief. Faith in God cedes to trust in evidence and facts for the detective Vigot, a priest who has traded in his collar for a magnifying glass (139). For Vigot, and arguably Greene's first readers, the appeal of detection lies in its perceived ability retrospectively to restore order to a world of chaos and confusion. The embrace of facticity in place of faith that Greene saw in the 1950s is now at a point where information competes with religion as the main provider of succor in the form of the security of answers. Could it be that soon, if not already, the Information Age will offer the ultimate substitute for spiritual solace, an end to speculation and self-doubt, even a place of confession? Greene's Fowler still did it the old-fashioned way. While Fowler's attempt to thwart American influence in Vietnam fails, his confessional narrative testifies to his attempt to intervene in a world increasingly premised on information and power. Fowler's powers of perception and reconstruction literally demonstrate narrative's strength. Interestingly, Fowler does not attempt to persuade the reader. Indeed, his narrative voice is remarkably neutral, dispassionate, leaving much to the imagination and judgment of the reader. Fowler's detachment, however, does not preclude the reader's involvement.

On the contrary, as Phelan's narrative theory demonstrates, such "restricted narration" (326) has the potential to engage the reader more than a narrative that purports to go under the skin of its characters, since it sketches a point of view and then invites the reader in to flesh it out with his or her own experience. It is the way the reader is invited to participate in the process of what Phelan identifies as "reporting, interpreting, and evaluating" (326) that sets *The Quiet American* apart from other novels of its time. As much as Greene's novel reflects the power of intelligence and information-gathering, it also acknowledges that not all can be revealed and, by doing so, preserves some of the mystery of storytelling.

*Our Man in Havana* shows this paradox to comic effect when Wormold's drawings of new "weapons" of fearful proportions created by Engineer Cifuentes (one of Wormold's fictional secret agents) cannot be verified by the headquarters in London. The problem is that the bizarre nature of the findings would mean the intelligence is rejected by the fastidiousness of "the atomic research people." "You know what those fellows are like," the Chief tells Hawthorne. "They'll criticize points of detail, say the whole thing is unreliable, that the tube is out of proportion or points the wrong way" (78). Even so, the desire to believe in the implausible is sometimes stronger than the faith in science and empirical facts and, as we have seen, this desire wins out. Consequently the Chief as well as the Air Ministry take Wormold's intelligence very seriously. Wormold's friend Dr Hasselbacher, whose initial suggestion it was to invent the secret agents, intuits this compulsive desire for the romantic and the extraordinary:

> Medicine is my experience, Mr Wormold. Have you never read the advertisement for secret remedies? A hair tonic confided by the dying Chief of a Red Indian tribe. With a secret remedy you don't have to print the formula. And there is something about a secret which makes people believe . . . perhaps a relic of magic. (58)

Dr Hasselbacher is right on the money when he alludes to the magic of secrecy and, by extension, the way in which covert information works as a conduit for this magic. As Herman argues, "If intelligence has any single, defining characteristic in the eyes of governments and publics it is this secrecy and the mystique it attracts" (6). Hasselbacher's comment also reminds the reader that Benjamin's lament over the end of storytelling can be backdated a century or so to when science replaced primitive magic in the Western world.

Walter Benjamin's concern for storytelling dovetails with narrative and the sort of intelligence relevant to the realm of belief and faith, influencing how we comport ourselves in chaotic circumstances. As such the two senses of the word intelligence can be seen to converge. Apart from his focus on espionage, Graham Greene is, of course, well known for his personal struggle with religious faith, which is evidenced in numerous novels, including *The End of the Affair* in which the power of narrative anchors the integrity of the narrator's belief. (Recall in that novel the obverse of a Faustian contract, this time made with God, in which a woman promises to renounce happiness in exchange for her soul.) In *The Quiet American*, by contrast, faith is far more fragile, as Fowler admits he is not as "convincible" as his wife by the empty "play-acting" of religious practice (88). He finds himself in a meditative space halfway through the novel, which is for him a veritable omphalos of confusion and doubt. Fowler's interview with the Pope's deputy in the Caodaist cathedral reveals religion to him as the height of hypocrisy in its claim to the existence of absolutes and God's love of truth (85). Seeking shelter from the fierce sunlight, Fowler escapes into the cathedral in Tanyin, home of the Caodaists who at the time are at war with the Hoa-Haos. In the nave of the cathedral, Fowler ruminates bitterly on what it means to be living with faith in a world of doubt and injustice, finding in the end yet more reasons for not believing:

> But I had never desired faith. The job of a reporter is to expose and record. I had never in my career discovered the inexplicable. The Pope worked his prophecies with a pencil in a movable lid and the people believed. In any vision somewhere you could find the planchette. I had no visions or miracles in my repertoire of memory. (88)

To admit to never having encountered the inexplicable is a symptom of either profound apathy or a studied blindness to the extraordinary and the romantic along the lines of another Greene hero, the indifferent Querry from *A Burnt-out Case*. All the same, *The Quiet American* resolves the anxieties of this malaise through its internal endorsement of a secular belief in discourse and intelligence. Fowler's confessional narrative encourages the reader to gather evidence through close reading that suggests that narrative itself may fulfill the role of religion during highly skeptical or pessimistic times. This recalls a dialogue from *The Heart of the Matter* in which police officer Scobie tells Father Rank that he should have been a policeman (68). Both detectives and priests extract confessions from those who have erred through a process of detection that reveals the unreliability of text, on one hand, and the power of the word, on the other. Reading is both a source of instability as well as a powerful agent of change. Verifying information, in and out of fiction, is the process by which the reader, who may be engrossed in the narrative, also helps produce more varied and critical spaces in which to assess the matters in question. Even so, it would be far too simplistic to assume that the spy novel relies on the work of an informant in lieu of a miracle worker. Instead Greene's novels aim to question hypocrisy and the blind acceptance of any fact along with absolute tenets of belief immune to intellectual scrutiny. In her discussion of freedom, Svetlana Boym argues that intelligence in the sense I am presently using the term is "a torturous but honest road between imagination and lived experience, between contemplation and action" (6). Both senses of the word intelligence come to bear on narrative in which information that bridges the invisible with the visible must be gathered and assessed, in order also to confront the hypothetical with the actual, the familiar with the unthinkable.

Greene's novels often deal with anxieties over sexual infidelity. *The End of the Affair* and *The Heart of the Matter* are in this category, and *The Quiet American* is no exception. With inside knowledge of the plot to kill Pyle, Fowler's conscience troubles him especially since he himself will benefit from the removal of Pyle. Fowler, of course, also has cause to suspect Phuong of infidelity and interrogates her as would a detective. For Greene, however, infidelity goes beyond the sexual. In a discussion in 1948 with Elizabeth Bowen and V. S. Pritchett on the role of the writer (fragments of which later informed Greene's lecture "The Virtue of Disloyalty" from 1969), Greene considers his role as writing "from the point of view of the black square as well as of the white," adding that "doubt and even denial must be given their chance of self-expression" (*A Life in Letters*, 152). "Literature," writes Greene, "has nothing to do with edification" (151), declaring in a letter to Pritchett, "man . . . will write, as he will commit adultery" (158). Whether due to insubordination, an overheated imagination, or the war, people are not what they appear to be in *The Quiet American*. Genocide is committed for high moral reasons, murder becomes a viable option for the politically motivated as well as the disengaged like Fowler, and actual detectives are camouflaged priests. For all that, however, or perhaps rather *because* of that, the reader becomes attached to these wayward characters. Far from alienating the reader, the elements of espionage and secrecy more compellingly invite the reader to identify with a varied cast of characters, doubtless because of the way Greene is prepared to challenge conventional expectations of propriety or even of what is humanly possible. If one accepts the author's freedom to write as she or he sees fit, even if this means being equivocal, contradictory, or elusive, one must also accept that such writing enlists our own proclivities toward a dalliance with "the black square," a form of infidelity that may with some justification seek expression outside of the fiction that provoked it.

A particularly recalcitrant rejection of conventional standards of conduct is the subject of one of the longest and most ambitious of four stories in Greene's collection *A Sense of Reality*. In "Under the Garden" from 1963 a man diagnosed with cancer returns to his childhood home and recalls there an odd and complex dream. The central figure of the dream is an obscene monarch of an underground world in a cave formed by the enormous roots of an ancient tree. Slightly reminiscent of Lewis Carroll's imperious Queen of Hearts, "deeper here than any grave was ever dug to bury secrets in" (34), the foul-mouthed monarch instructs the protagonist:

> Be disloyal. It's your duty to the human race. The human race needs to survive and it's the loyal man who dies first from anxiety or a bullet or overwork. If you have to earn a living, boy, and the price they make you pay is loyalty, be a double agent—and never let either of the two sides know your real name. (48)

In a letter to V. S. Pritchett dated 1948, Greene explains "the importance of the virtue of disloyalty" (*A Life in Letters*, 154). "Loyalty," he writes, "confines us to accepted opinions: loyalty forbids us to comprehend sympathetically our dissident fellows; but disloyalty encourages us to roam experimentally through any human mind: it gives to the novelist the extra dimension of sympathy" (155). Greene may seem to be treading a fine line here though in this case he is doubtless taking the novelist's impartiality in relation to his characters' failings (or triumphs) to its logical conclusion. One cannot be loyally partisan to anyone's cherished values (even one's own) while engaging in a process of "observing and judging" (Phelan, 323), and so inevitably an author risks being charged with disloyalty to one or more sets of social constraints. According to Greene, the political virtue of a novelist's disloyalty, and by implication also a citizen's, is paramount, which he explicitly states in his letter to Pritchett:

> If we can awaken sympathetic comprehension in our readers, not only for our most evil characters (that is easy: there is a cord there fastened to all hearts that we can twitch at will), but of our smug, complacent,

> successful characters, we have surely succeeded in making the work of the State a degree more difficult—and that is a genuine duty we owe society, to be a piece of grit in the State machinery. (155)

Wormold in *Our Man in Havana* becomes that "piece of grit in the State machinery" by inventing a network of spies. Though unmasked at the end of the novel, he interestingly escapes punishment because, after all, Wormold had only invented secrets, not given them away, and so "they could hardly charge him under the Official Secrets Act" (213). Wormold finds himself in the odd situation of escaping punishment not by truth-telling but its opposite; he must embellish his lies about the existence of a network of agents. This is not dissimilar to the principle of information overload used by WikiLeaks, according to one of Assange's former collaborators, Daniel Domscheit-Berg, to obscure the uncertain basis of their actions:

> To create the impression of unassailability to the outside world, you only had to make the context as complicated and confusing as possible. To that end, I would make my explanation of technical issues to journalists as complex as I could. It was the same principle used by terrorists and bureaucrats. (45)

In the attempt to avoid discovery, subjects produce a fiction that ironically works as social critique in a way more powerful, certainly, than the sanctioned reporting of actual events in overt sources. Greene placed enormous faith in the power of fictional narrative to disclose knowledge even of an intellectually challenging kind, at the same time blurring, if not obliterating, the boundary between fact and fiction. By so doing, he places a lot of faith in the reader's involvement by which, he would hope, he or she might even become that "piece of grit in the State machinery."

As an author of fiction, Greene knows that the imagination lends the reader the freedom to seek truths that are likely to defy received wisdom. Where Benjamin laments the end of storytelling because wisdom is threatened, Greene celebrates the act of fearlessly and objectively probing the darker recesses of the human condition. He may not always resurrect "the epic side of truth," and he is prepared to risk appearing disloyal to specific personal or public principles (other than those that safeguard his art). In the passage above in which Greene describes how worldly knowledge expressed in fiction can disrupt allegiances to the state's perspective, he is more interested in the imagination's role in evoking knowledge in those who already possess it, rather than in those who do not. Insofar as Assange and other whistle-blowers wish to convert unbelievers by indiscriminately gathering and spreading information, they represent the vacuum cleaner approach to knowledge acquisition. Wormold in *Our Man in Havana* abandons his vacuum cleaner business in favor of a more considered, even discerning, assembly of fabricated information. The fact that it happens to be fictitious is not important. What is important is that his form of acquiring and giving information is orderly, selective, and purposive. And at the receiving end it is the same. The process of detecting information, unlike vacuuming it up, is reliant on the imagination to include details as well as to filter them out. In other words, it requires interpretation. The vacuum cleaner approach to knowledge does not discriminate between the insignificant fluff and the clues that might provide evidence or support a particular hypothesis the way a narrator (or a good intelligence officer) does. Still, is it possible to say, with Greene, that literature can make an intervention?

I referred earlier to the relative ease by which information reaches us. In many respects, information comes to us via a path of least resistance—and it can tend to lead us by a similar route if we are not careful. Narrative, conversely, demands of both author and reader the careful observation together with judicious assessment and selection that Phelan insists on (323). As such, narrative such as that like Fowler's is consonant with a resistant act of holding fast to a position, or a set of behaviors, for the purpose of achieving long-term goals. Such behaviors illustrate important aspects of Scott Lash's idea of practice as distinct from action (actually opposed by it) in his critique of "the global semiotic order" (32). In Lash's account, *action* is associated with individuality, consciousness, unambiguous criteria, and clear and distinct outcomes. Given second place in the Information Age, Lash informs us, *practice* is associated with community, it also "foregrounds the unconscious and preconscious," and, summing up a lengthy series of distinctions, "practice is inseparable from the very real concerns of the good life." We must be clear here that Lash is not referring to "lifestyle" or any other form of consumerist ideal. Despite demanding its own work ethic, action can be seen as eschewing the arduous daily practice of working toward the sort of long-term "good" that may well be hard to specify outside of practice and be frustratingly inconclusive. Lacking any easy or programmatic point of closure, practice for Fowler (and for Greene) is the interminable negotiation of personal agency within a setting of radical social complexity and moral ambiguity. Fowler's narrative testifies to an engagement with practice in these terms as well as demanding it of its readers.

Despite his use of a confessional form, he is not seeking any absolution, nor is he after any easy or formulaic answers. On the contrary, his story subtly puts his own values and motives to the test.

In his reading of Martin Buber and Emmanuel Levinas, Sanders notes that community arises out of social discourse and that literacy, therefore, shapes the address (68). As such, he suggests, the self, "even a vastly expansive self," is "tempered in the presence of a vibrantly alive Other" (69). At the point of Fowler's address to his reader, a community forms that is consonant with this idea, and it also allies his values with practice in Lash's sense. Writing at the cusp of the Information Age, Graham Greene's fiction is mobilized by transatlantic tensions. In its depiction of an ageing Englishman and a youthful American competing for the attention of the beautiful Phuong, *The Quiet American* transcends the personal in the way it sets up complex encounters with the other and entangles the social and the political through the body of a woman. Phuong's predicament reflects the Vietnamese situation more generally. She is represented as being subordinate to whichever power happens to be the stronger. As though it matters little to the Vietnamese people whether they are French or American forces that conquer them, Phuong does not appear to care which of the two men she resides with. Either way she submits to her older sister who acts as her marriage broker and to the power of the white male. The enigma of Phuong is the enigma of the Vietnamese people in the eyes of their conquerors. When she makes her choice, Fowler becomes vehemently anti-American. His conversation turns to the poverty of all things American—its culture, literature, politics—to the point that he even bores his French friends, who ordinarily are decidedly open to denouncing the Yanks (140).

The wider concerns of the novel do not suggest that easy solutions can be found or are being sought. There is no suggestion in *The Quiet American* that with the elimination of Pyle the Americans will change strategy in Vietnam, how can there be? On the contrary, Pyle, it becomes obvious, is merely the forerunner of many young, enthusiastic, and engaged Americans who will fervently hope to save the world from communism. The novel offers no safe and secure answers. The only certainty to arise out of *The Quiet American* is that the war will go on, the occupation will continue. Greene's novel prompts comparisons between the war in Vietnam and the interminable difficulties surrounding Western involvement in Afghanistan and the Middle East. The Vietnamese were never supported by the Chinese, as the Americans feared after China became communist in 1949, which voids a major defense for prolonging that war. Similarly, there is almost consensus now that there were never any weapons of mass destruction secreted in Iraq and thus the American invasion was justified by spurious misinformation. Yet the war on terror will continue to seek new targets affecting innocent civilians, and increasingly cruel and invasive forms of interrogation are being legalized for use in what might otherwise be routine questioning of foreign nationals, immigrants, or anyone "strange." A disturbing element of such interrogation techniques is that the intelligence they obtain is of routinely poor quality. Could it be that information obtained from someone merely trying to avoid suffering is, in quality, not very dissimilar to information sought for pleasure? In contradistinction to this, at the heart of *The Quiet American*, Fowler's self-interrogation reveals the foundations for an intervention in regard to that which passes for the truth. Truth emerges as that which cannot be revealed or unlocked and set out in any simple formula, shrouded as it is in representations that are themselves always approximations. In lieu of a sudden delightful epiphany, the reader of Greene's spy fiction must make do with what Josh Toth calls "a state of 'indecision,' a state in which the decision process . . . is animated by *both* the impossibility of the certainly right decision, or representation, *and* the promise of pure indecision" (121). Narrative maintains this state of a settlement endlessly deferred, like a gratification postponed, and arguably makes the moment of indecision a pleasurable difficulty while involving the reader in a sustained hope.

Of central importance is the way the truth becomes known or information passed on. Exposure is different from disclosure, the former being undifferentiated, unmediated, and indiscriminate, once again, rather like a vacuum cleaner. The lesson to be learned from *The Quiet American*, specifically, is that disclosure always occurs from a particular person's perspective. Fowler the narrator relies on detection and intelligence as much as the foreign correspondent and the spy. Both bear witness to what they report, or decipher, or deduce. As argued by Timothy Garton Ash in an article in *The Guardian* on the declining status of the foreign correspondent, the amateur eyewitness reports sometimes appearing in blogs or taken up by mainstream media rely on digital cameras and audio clips that bring foreign news closer to home in often evocative ways. Regarding deciphering and interpreting, local sources have been found to be more reliable, especially as they speak local languages and are familiar with local customs (22). The knowledge derived from Fowler's interrogation of self is that he is far from uninvolved and neutral, reporting on himself no less than unfolding events in Vietnam. In his use of detection and profound self-enquiry as a narrative technique, Greene addresses both the death of storytelling as diagnosed by Benjamin, while pointing out the limits of so-called objective reporting in a complex world of conflicting motives, even at war within a single heart. Fowler's narrative, of course, bears the burden of such realizations that lead him to despair and regret: "Everything had gone right with me since he had died, but how I wished there existed someone to whom I could say that I was sorry" (189). As an atheist, Fowler is unable to ask for and receive forgiveness from a higher being. As a reporter, he has broken the rules of objectivity and "become as *engagé* as Pyle" (183) even if against his will. As a narrator addressing his reader, however, Fowler discloses his ability even to report on his own vulnerable humanity, which is no small achievement.

While Fowler is never convicted of involvement in murder and punished, although Vigot highly suspects him, his narrative subtly stages the public disclosure of an unswerving inner pursuit of truth. The reader is left to prosecute as he or she sees fit. Greene is, of course, correct when he suggests that the only prosecution that matters is the internal one. Whether there is a God or not, there is always an Other, a reader in this case, or a struggle to attain a critical view of oneself. Although not convicted for his part in the murder, Fowler's freedom is severely limited by his own sense of justice refined in the process of self-detection. Vigot's suspicion that Fowler might be involved in Pyle's murder is confirmed when, following Fowler's disparaging suggestion made at the beginning of the novel, Vigot analyzes the paws of Pyle's dog. Vigot does find incriminating cement dust in the dog's paws, strong evidence that Pyle visited Fowler on the night he was murdered since builders are at work on the groundfloor of Fowler's apartment (170). It is as though the whole sorry affair was laid out complete at the outset, which in a way it was, being related via flashbacks. The structure serves to fold into one the first and the final encounter between Fowler and Pyle, Fowler's offhand epithet for Pyle—"quiet"—and finally the silencing of Pyle through death by which he became, in Vigot's words, "[a] very quite American" (17), as well as the telltale dust Vigot finds in the paws of Pyle's dog.

The novel registers a crucial weakening of the transatlantic dyad. When Pyle and Fowler are caught in the crossfire hiding in a watchtower that they share with two fearful Vietnamese guards on the rice fields at night, they are besieged by a force more powerful than them and indifferent to their existence. On that night, when Pyle ends up saving the life of the wounded Fowler, they discuss love, sex, and religion. However, the parental relationship between an ageing Europe and a young America disintegrates under the force of what is later in the novel referred to as the "Third Force" (162). Transatlantic perceptions offer little to no resistance against the Third Force. It is here we see the World Order in the form of an Information Age increasingly unmoved and unassailable by human intervention. The Third Force, as Information, cannot facilitate an intervention into its own pervasiveness though this does not make it any less destructive. The bomb that explodes toward the end of the novel kills many innocent people, and when faced with the destruction he has helped bring about, Pyle can resort to nothing but plead ignorance to Fowler:

> I forced him, with my hand on his shoulder, to look around. I said, "This is the hour when the place is always full of women and children—it's the shopping hour. Why choose that of all hours?"
>
> He said weakly, "There was to have been a parade."
>
> "And you hoped to catch a few colonels. But the parade was cancelled yesterday, Pyle."
>
> "I didn't know."
>
> "Didn't know!" I pushed him into a patch of blood where a stretcher had lain. "You ought to be better informed." (162)

Information does not of itself bestow intelligence or knowledge. Between "I didn't know" and "You ought to be better informed" lies the bewildering terror posed by the Information Age. This is a world in which there is no culpability, no one to blame, and no critical perspective from which a judgment can be made. Narrative, as Greene shows, is able to reinstate borders, but only if there is someone to whom an address can be made. The following chapter will look closer at these leaking oceans of the Information Age in which the Other has been effaced altogether by the imposition of a pervasive and fatal sameness of global proportions.

# 2

# Apocalypse Then and Now

## *The Road*, *Lord of the Flies*, and the Ends of Knowledge

In this chapter I want to examine the beginnings of an oceanic imaginary that I see overlapping and intersecting with the development of the Information Age. I propose to consider how the transfer of information and knowledge formerly via the ocean is increasingly achieved via technological means in the Digital Age. Thinking of the oceanic imaginary in digital terms suggests fresh possibilities as well as new limits for transatlantic encounters and their resulting subjectivities. Through William Golding's 1954 *Lord of the Flies* and Cormac McCarthy's 2006 *The Road*, this chapter revisits the pivotal role that the ocean, and now the oceanic, played and continues to play in conceiving the shape and design of cultural and literary interactions across virtual or real distances. Joseph Roach offers the notion of a circum-Atlantic that retains "the memory of a movement...redolent of violence and fatality, but also of agency and decision" (33). For Roach, this is where the consequences of genocidal histories endure and evolve by virtue of a memory-based diaspora of lived impressions. In this chapter I want to take further Roach's idea. My claim is that oceanic encounters in literature from the 1950s and the early twenty-first century show how, even though all history tells the history of its area, the Digital Age has changed the nature of area itself. Peoples who once encountered each other via the ocean are, since the Information Age, discovering a coastless area of interaction, because the ocean is no longer constituted by boundaries that can be crossed, transgressed, or violated one way or another. Today, my argument goes, there is no transatlantic or even circum-Atlantic. In what I call throughout this book a "post-Atlantic" world, all narratives of encounter, exploitation, or oppression can be cited by anyone, owned by anyone, and, importantly, can touch and move anyone.

Since computers have become a fundamental part of the very fabric of our existence, we are part of what Robert Hassan calls an "information ecology" comprised of networks, systems, and processes (4). For me this entails a shift from an oceanic to an "atmospheric" or cloud-based world of exchange that has rendered the notion of terrestrial place too limited, or even meaningless, for our age. And yet Roach's concept can still be applied, for what has been retained in the process just mentioned is an oceanic imaginary that also holds the memory of a movement and more. Indeed it is a movement that both looks backward and forward to those flows that we associate with global networking that offer, as Roach puts it, "a way of imagining what comes next as well as what has already happened" (33). The oceanic imaginary still convokes far-reaching flows of ideas and widespread currents of activity encompassing America and Europe, members of the Anglophone world, the North and South, and so on. Today's oceanic imaginary rides on spatially vast currents of information on the World Wide Web no less than the Atlantic ocean itself, which is itself larger than many could imagine. Counting its many rivers and tributaries, the Atlantic includes the vast network of the Congo River, the Amazon, the Great Lakes, the Seine, the Loire, and so on (Winchester, 146).[1] The value of what passes along these routes and currents has always grown or shrunk depending on what encounters are made possible by the oceanic imaginary. Now, in a post-Atlantic world, the encounters made possible by information technology demand that we rethink where agency is situated in relation to its narratives. And as we shall see, we need to appreciate when information overload diminishes agency and brings about an end of knowledge. Graham Greene's satirical *Our Man in Havana* illustrates the purposelessness of information that lacks narrative structure, intentionality, or agency. As we shall see, in McCarthy's *The Road* in which all life is on the brink of extinction, a fresh encounter with news or hope via the Atlantic ocean has become impossible, a state of affairs infinitely more wretched than Greene's world of espionage. My challenge in this chapter, and in this book, is not only to locate and identify encounters in literatures in which the ocean carries metaphorical weight but also to shed light on how the oceanic imaginary lends meaning to these encounters even in a post-Atlantic, "atmospheric," or digitally networked world. Despite the apocalyptic reflections ahead in this chapter, the Atlantic's afterlives still provide a coherent locus for imagining encounter with otherness, and that space depends no less than ever on the narratives of its authors and poets.

This chapter stages its own encounter between a world on the brink of disaster—presaged in Golding's novel and actualized in McCarthy's—and discourses of reading and writing in the Information Age that aim to territorialize the global imaginary of the future. The limitlessness of the ocean matches the endless desire for knowledge and power, for a dream of total control, as well as the impossibility of such total power. As such, information must now be visualized as oceanic in the sense that it cannot be fully contained. It seeps out, it leaks, and dissipates. The sheer volume of information today puts paid to any thought of one person or cohort knowing anywhere near everything. As it happens, the Information Age has brought about a new and profoundly anxious form of ignorance. In reference to the seductions of the informational society, Yaeger has noted that the troping of the sea "encourage[s] humans to treat it as an inexhaustible storehouse of goods" (535). She critiques the tendency of poets of the past to insist on the sea's sublimity that, she claims, has rendered it vulnerable to physical sublimation, and she questions the value of such poetics to readers today who are faced with the real threat of a loss of life through pollution and exploitation of the oceans (538). There is a parallel between these unsustainable reading practices alluded to by Yaeger and the common misperception that the sea itself has a near-infinite capacity to self-cleanse and dilute the toxic burden resulting from industrial activities. Similarly, information has been thought of as promiscuously circulating, automatically generating labor-free meaning wherever it shows up without needing to be bound to purpose or intentionality.

Ever since Foucault famously pointed out that "techniques of knowledge and strategies of power" cover the whole field of power and discourse, for between them "there is no exteriority," we have accepted that power is inextricably linked to knowledge (*History of Sexuality*, 93). Pervading every relationship, produced by every encounter, immanent and strategic, power is everywhere "because it comes from everywhere" (93). The question of consent has become sidelined as information has grown exponentially, and subjectivity, or agency as Roach refers to it, is close to extinct. The notion of consent in relation to knowledge is a vexed question today, as discussed in the opening chapter regarding information leaks and espionage. In these days of WikiLeaks we are hardly able to imagine a subjectivity personally able to give or withhold consent to the flow of information. When Hassan asks, "Who rules in the information society?" the answer he comes up with is, "Google" (190). "Google can," Hassan tells us, "provide a measure of what the information society is thinking" (193).[2] Hassan goes on to say that "the social and economic *power* of Google...is reflected in the *value* that capitalism and governments place on such a 'weightless' entity" as what we are thinking (193). If, as Hassan makes clear, following Foucault, power "flows through the structures" (191) both political and corporate, I want to stress that this process can now be located within a global oceanic reimagined with the aid of digital technology for post-Atlantic times. Golding's *Lord of the Flies* and McCarthy's *The Road* circle these matters of exchange, subjectivity, consent, and information the way wrestlers circle their opponents. There is a wariness embedded in the texts in focus here on the matter of where encounters might possibly take place and what knowledge can possibly mean in an apocalyptic world. Increasingly I suspect that a less explored aspect of contemporary terror is constituted by a sense of the end of knowledge, of the terror of bewildering unfamiliarity or lack of competence, of simply not knowing. An aspect of this is that, as discussed in the previous chapter, with knowledge becoming increasingly specialized it often circulates as a form of (far from blissful) ignorance.

The aim of this chapter is to approach knowledge as well as this terror, born of the failure of technology to endow its users with knowledge, as an area with a history of sensible impressions or "muscle memory" not unlike Roach's circum-Atlantic. I believe that if this knowing unease can be recovered into discourse, it will provide guidelines for reading the present as a place fraught with anticipation of a precarious future steeped in diminished subjective agency. The narratives of both *Lord of the Flies* and *The Road* follow human tracks that map a brand new world as well as an old one, in a way that is both forward- and backward-looking. Understanding the coordinates of this area will enable us to speculate on where knowledge and power might congregate. In the same way that meridians are largely arbitrary, functional lines drawn on a map, as aids to navigation, the customary restraints binding, or failing to bind, the actions of the characters in *The Road* and *Lord of the Flies* are a feature of what I call the limits of knowledge. While marooned on a desert island in the Pacific Ocean far from England, the savagery between the boys in *Lord of the Flies* is nevertheless a reaction to a civilization in ruins back home. This way of thinking of area studies insists on the interconnections between social or cultural phenomena that are oceanic in range and constituted by complex tensions stable through time enabling their sustained effects physically to register at great distance.

This stabilized tension, with far-reaching effects, is partly what Marx attributes to capitalism when he writes, "Constant revolutionizing of production, uninterrupted disturbance of all social conditions, *everlasting uncertainty* and agitation distinguish the bourgeois epoch from all earlier ones" (44; emphasis mine). Driven to the end of the world, the quite possibly only remaining atoms of civilization, a father and a son in McCarthy's *The Road*, and a band of schoolboys in *Lord of the Flies*, enact what Marx predicted to be the final reckoning between man and his predicament. Marx famously predicted a loss of moral compass in the death throes of human sociality under Capital with his now famous diagnosis, "All that is solid melts into air, all that is holy is profaned, and man is at last compelled to face with sober senses, his real conditions of life, and his relations with his kind" (44). The "real conditions of life" brought into sharp relief in these novels are what is left finally after the rule of Capital has exhausted its human resources and environmental supplies. It is marked by the lack of any certain knowledge together with the profound absence of an other to offer a fresh perspective (knowledge of the other as well as the other's knowledge) or even a business transaction by which to reflect on one's predicament. The journey of man and boy in *The Road* culminates wretchedly on the Atlantic seaboard of America; the descent of children into brutality in *Lord of the Flies* is set in an island in the Pacific. Both the Atlantic and the Pacific are important ambits of traditional cultural, material, and economic exchange. For now I want to use concepts such as terror and the apocalypse to provide the internal coherence of an alternative set of tensions in helping to locate what threatens encounter and what remains of the possibility of encounter between self and other in the reimagined oceanic of the twentieth and twenty-first centuries.

A year before the attacks on the twin towers, the death of the crew of the Russian submarine K-141 Kursk on August 12, 2000, tragically emphasized the failings and limitations of the Information Age. By associating the word "terror" with the fear of not knowing, I specifically wish to define terror as a result of the failure to provide certainty in the Information Age. To me this is the real root of the word "terror" that since the 9/11 attacks has become the Western *cri de guerre* against ideological opponents and the Muslim world more generally. The death of the crew of the Russian submarine K-141 Kursk highlights some dismal paradoxes that have come to encapsulate the Information Age. How is it that, despite an abundance of scientific knowledge concerning the design and specification of the submarine as well as its precise location, the crew of K-141 Kursk could not be saved? In spite of its being "on the map," so to speak, the Russian submarine with its entire crew could not be saved and so the world was condemned to mute witnessing of its tragic fate.

Golding's *Lord of the Flies* is the story of a group of children stranded on an island when a British plane crashes during an evacuation in the midst of what might be a nuclear war. The novel stages the castaways' slow descent into savagery in which they become lost to the world in both a psychological and geographical sense. Wrenched from the relative security of their boarding school, the children descend into a nightmare world of shadows lacking all sense of how to behave when removed from the structures of civilization and institutional instruction. What remains of the notorious class-based cruelty of the British public school system mutates almost beyond recognition on this island somewhere on the Pacific. There the boys become murderous savages and a regime of survival brutally replaces any structures of civilization and institutional instruction. For all that, though, reassuring traces of past knowledge surface in the novel's protagonist, the fair-haired Ralph, as he remembers something about the order of things as taught by his father: "My father's in the navy. He said there aren't any unknown islands left. He says the queen has a big room full of maps and all the islands in the world are drawn there. So the Queen's got a picture of this island" (41). Ralph derives comfort from this typical colonial view of the world in which a sibylline omniscience is attributed to the Queen now believed to have knowledge of every nook and cranny so long as it is visually represented in her domestic archives. The terror in *The Lord of the Flies* is, of course, that neither Empire nor Queen can map out the darkness that exists within the human heart. My claim in this chapter is that in the apocalyptic wake of world wars and planetary destruction, *The Lord of the Flies* and more recently McCarthy's *The Road* both register the fragility of a civilization whose chief anxiety, despite the prolific circulation of information, is the terror of not knowing.

When faced with great security threats and economic recession, what counts as knowledge and how can it serve us? McCarthy's *The Road* raises such questions again and again throughout its melancholic pages and not just through resonances with so-called Dust Bowl fiction set during the Depression of 1930s. Despite past associations, *The Road* gives those same questions a forward-looking emphasis with its focus on the likely consequences of contemporary forms of scarcity. Indeed, the 2008 failure of the market economy and the unrest associated with the Occupy Movement all occur within a couple of years of the publication of *The Road*. Though the father and son of *The Road* have their eyes mainly fixed on the road and their desperate goal is to reach the coast, they are defined by anxieties related to the atmosphere and the loss of faith in the assurances touted in the Information Age. Father and son in *The Road* are humanist outlaws, staking out a territory of moral difference at odds with the prevailing values of a post-apocalyptic society of cannibals and predatory consumption. Whereas autonomous, self-reliant living frequently epitomizes ecological virtue for many, and is sometimes articulated as a form of ecoterrorism in post-9/11 fiction, in McCarthy's novel, the ecoromantic view of a life "off the grid" (even "off-road" tourism) is reversed.[3] Here, desperate for any guidance, the father clings to the road as the most iconic structure still remaining since the unspecified cataclysm that destroyed most of life on earth. Indeed, the struggle in *The Road* is how *not* to be one with the land, an identification many environmentalists declare to be an ideal. In their arduous and painful crossing of the deathly landscape of a fatally stricken America, father and son need at all costs to distinguish themselves from their setting, for blending in with the territory they must cross would mean death. Rather, their movement must be a kind of reading, or study of their situation, a taking of its measure, even cartographically, so as to assemble a new and fragile knowledge, so as to become a living map of this place (13).[4]

The father is thoroughly immersed in his reading of the landscape and yet the environment has become unreadably resistant to his overtures. To be lost to the world or unable to communicate with it is to experience it almost literally as "autistic" (13), barely responsive. To grasp this landscape at all now, the father must rely on knowledge from the past, "an old chronicle" (13). This old knowledge is different from the information overload of today. It circulates as memory and migrates like stories from generation to generation. The father struggles to survive in order to pass it on to his son so that he may, in turn, pass it on to his son, and so forth. The father's explorations are measured—"marching steps," "counting," "scribing"—all the more precise in order to record "that cauterized terrain" (13). The father and son's existence depends on his knowledge of the scorched environment. Painstakingly slowly, the father's movements in this passage show the beginning of something new, or at the very least the conditions for a new encounter. For this encounter, he "must seek out the upright" (13), as if relearning the stages of human evolution, before the reader's eyes, from homo erectus through homo sapiens and beyond. *The Road* marks the end of what was, but it also, however cautiously, salutes the beginning of other encounters that require a new way of relating to one's surroundings in which both human beings and the stars communicate as "common satellite" (13). To read this with the digitally structured oceanic imaginary in mind is to see it as both a highly fluid locus of encounter and yet, with effort, a place amenable to knowledge. It is to discover hitherto-overlooked interactions between the individual and the world that signal new beginnings for a world in darkness.

The possibility of a new beginning is registered in the destination of the father's movements: the sea. In her seminal *The Sea around Us*, the early founder of the global environmentalist movement Rachel Carson begins by recounting "the beginnings of that great mother of life, the sea" (3). McCarthy's vision of the father's torturous beginnings of a post-apocalyptic life recalls Carson's musings that life begins with the sea and it also ends with mankind's realization that his is, in fact, a watery world "that, in the deepest part of his subconscious mind, he had never wholly forgotten" (15). That said, a trajectory that has as its destination the sea makes a lot of sense in a post-apocalyptic world where the known world on dry land no longer exists and virtually all reference points have been obliterated or fallen into disuse. Based on imperfect knowledge from a time when the sea was a source of food and a means of escape, father and son make their way toward the Atlantic coast, alone. They travel without the boy's mother who chose to end her life rather than survive if survival meant murder and cannibalism, and so the sea has become the only source of life now remaining for the boy and man alike. It is the remembered knowledge, or fantasy, of the sea as the renewed source of all life that motivates their journey throughout the novel. We accompany this bedraggled couple, father and son, for what they might come to learn on the road to extinction. Their survival is essential to the twenty-first-century reader, more likely than not also convinced that this world too is on the brink of destruction. Indeed, for one critic the apocalypticism of *The Road* is very specifically "a response to an immediate and visceral fear of cataclysmic doom in the US after the terrorist attacks on 9/11" (Cooper, 221). Indeed, the novel insists on asking the question that, Morgenstern notes, haunts postindustrial America at large, namely "who or what is a man at the beginning of the twenty-first century?" (37).

The question of what remains of man in the twenty-first century resonates with readers raised on the hopes and anxieties of the Information Age. McCarthy's novel sutures the optimism of a seemingly idyllic past—conveyed in the form of the father's mournful flashbacks to when his wife was still alive—to the fear of an unknown future. The result of this suturing is a thin artery of a "radical present"

(Morgenstern, 48), a balancing act between past and future that is often blocked by cloying nostalgia or panic. It is this edgy sense of being on the brink or threshold of something dire that speaks to the reader powerfully aware of living through the exhaustion of the planet's resources. Being in the present is a luxury that seldom affords the pair in the novel any substantial respite from anxiety, but the father uses these moments as best as he can. Then he aims to remember and impart to his son the values of a pre-apocalyptic past, when moral restrains and table manners mattered. His son's half-hearted attempt to learn the lessons of the past signals the obsoleteness of knowledge from the past in a world in which man eats man. Nevertheless, in his Heideggerian reading of *The Road*, Carlson notes that the "suspension of the world—held up here as story—is not absolute darkness, but the illumination of darkness, the appearance of a disappearance that itself serves to highlight a founding possibility and the condition of all appearance" (59). I am inclined to agree with this reading. In a world flattened by sameness, McCarthy's novel still endorses a belief in the sea as destination and hope in the way the father's burning desire to reach the coast prepares the possibility of an encounter with the transatlantic other.

My emphasis on dystopia as the absence of encounter and loss of any kind of belonging in the world is not meant to deflect from the very physical environmental crises that threaten life on earth. On the contrary, my intention is to interweave, or entangle, the discourses of environmentalism with those of digitally and technologically mediated representation. I want to conceive the oceanic imaginary as an actual and virtual, real and symbolic area in which these discourses encounter each other, where the Atlantic afterlife is lived. McCarthy's coupling of the words "world" and "word" in *The Road* indicates a similar intention to place the symbolic on intimate footing with the actual, the implication being that the destruction of the world might be precipitated by the destruction of literature and lack of faith in language. McCarthy's novel reveals a subjective possibility that Buell refers to (in relation to Ballard) as being marked by "not just awareness of loss" but, more precisely, that entails "awareness *as* the end of everything" (253). Awareness, recognition, and memory all must be present in order to register absence and loss, and they are reliant on, perhaps impossible without, representations.

If encounter and its impossible possibility haunts the pages of McCarthy's novel, it does so as well in Golding's *Lord of the Flies*. The main differences between *Lord of the Flies* published in the 1950s and *The Road* published in early 2000s have to do with the way a calamitous loss of place and belonging is treated by the characters and described by the narrator. The more recent novel expresses a crisis of confidence characteristic of our times, particularly since the recessions of the first decade of the twenty-first century. This is not to say that Golding's novel is not similarly anxious, in particular with regard to control and authority, but the castaway boys in *Lord of the Flies* still exude an attitude of knowing their place in the world, or of having known it once it is lost to them. Even if this knowledge proves to be inadequate when put to the test, all the same, the boys still have a sense of belonging. For Golding the difficult fate of the possibility of encounter hinges on identity. Loss of identity in Golding's novel comes as a result of the loss of the British empire and with it the control of the seas, as well as the crippling of imperialist culture more generally. Loss of identity in *The Road*, on the other hand, is irrespective of America's place in the world and seems to gesture at a loss of order and a profound doubt in civilization. Whereas identity in Golding's novel is inextricably bound to property and ownership, in McCarthy's *The Road*, territory has lost all significance for the father and son as they traverse the road to their destination the sea.

Often McCarthy's novel chronicles the growth of civilization's detritus. The road itself is littered with singular objects from a pre-apocalyptic world that holds no meaning to the son since he was born on the eve of the disaster. These things from the past have meaning only in the father's recollection of them. Alone and aided only by memory, he performs the task of setting the table in a house ruinous with neglect bearing still the faded signs of a past abundance. Such resilient gestures as these in the face of calamity bring the house back to life like a "thing being called out of long hibernation" (177). Likewise, some inherited appurtenances of civilization are evoked, then stowed away, maybe to be preserved in the memory of the son. One of the novel's pervasive tensions is between a legacy of propriety in consumerism, something like table manners, still customary for the father, and a new predatory ethos in which consumerism attains a gruesome, cannibalistic nadir. In this world, where an unspecified event has killed most of its inhabitants, all of its wildlife, and much of the vegetation, including all crops and edible plants, the demands of the stomach are in conflict with the father's now archaic sense of restraint. No money changes hands in the world of *The Road* where currency holds no value and everything is free provided that one can find what one needs before others do. To illustrate the absurdity of the lingering constraints of past consumerism, McCarthy has equipped his characters with the memory of financial transactions (174) as well as the most telltale formality of consumerism: the supermarket shopping trolley. Theirs is a customized, post-apocalyptic example of this ubiquitous signifier of capitalism, now reminding the reader more than ever of the sheer drudgery of mobility.

Objects and especially luxury items help lend human beings their identity both within a community and as individuals. It is often as simple as identifying with the advertising narrative of a product in order to advertise oneself. In *The Road* it is the memory of now obsolete objects that haunts the father. The presence of isolated branded objects in the novel (such as the Coke) recalls the past in which these things mattered. The father chances upon one isolated can of a well-known brand of soft drink and hands it over to his son, asking him to have it all. Here is a gesture haunted by its commercialized simulacrum. The father's offer of *the* Coke instead of *a* Coke as in the slogan "Have a Coke!" underscores the social context of products. The boy's ignorance of the social context of the beverage effaces its significance as a discursive object for him, though because of its past ubiquity (as a product one could literally buy anywhere on earth) this solitary Coke becomes a powerful signifier for worldwide loss.

A far more grotesque passage that presents post-apocalyptic consumerism at its lowest ebb occurs when the pair stumble on a stockpile of people kept alive in a locked cellar to be eaten piecemeal. While the reader recoils in horror at such atrocity, a glance at Marx's *Communist Manifesto* serves to remind him or her of the resonances here with commodification of the labor force. It also recalls the inhuman sweatshop conditions under which many low-cost consumer goods are produced for sale in the West. "Huddled against the back wall were naked people, male and female, all trying to hide, shielding their faces with their hands. On the mattress lay a man with his legs gone to the hip and the stumps of them blackened and burnt. The smell was hideous" (93). In McCarthy's novel the prone human body now must labor on itself as a form of fresh produce. Here society's most abject human remnants are imaged in forms of stains and smells in this gruesome passage. According to Marx, the modern working class was developed only insofar as it served the bourgeoisie: "These labourers, who must sell themselves piecemeal, are a commodity, like every other article of commerce, and are consequently exposed to all the vicissitudes of competition" (49).

The reader is invited to consider terror as the end of knowledge through disturbing scenes with an abject other, but most of all in encounters with the unknowable self. Upon contemplating their chances of survival and his capacity to take his son's life with his own hands, the father asks himself: "Could you crush that beloved skull with a rock? Is there such a being within you of which you know nothing? Can there be?" (96). This question is unanswerable since knowledge is based on predictability. It assumes that what has happened will happen again. To father and son in *The Road*, however, belief is of necessity a frame of mind with operational value, it lets them function. Speculative or existential knowledge regarding, say, one's humanity or bestiality is no longer valid or relevant in the apocalyptic worlds portrayed in both *The Road* as well as *Lord of the Flies*. The extreme circumstances in which the boys find themselves in *Lord of the Flies* cause Simon, himself resistant to the pull toward depravity, to discover that the beast is not on the outside, but inside them (97). The terrifying knowledge the boys come upon in *Lord of the Flies* is that nothing can be known, not even that which is most intimate. In a daze of confusion and existential quandary, Ralph "fell into that strange mood of speculation that was so foreign to him. If faces were different when lit from above or below—what was a face? What was anything?" (85). Losing one's grip on the immediate world, in this case it means having to submit to the ontological insecurity that comes with losing a familiar grasp of reality through representation, this is part of the terror experienced or caused to be experienced by the boys. What makes it acutely traumatic is still remembering what the world used to look like, of being always on the razor-thin threshold of then and now. This much occurs in *The Road* as well, when a lost world is seen through the eyes of the father. There is a difference though, that the loss for the boys on the island is far more limited in scope. While being totally at sea on the island, their residual grip on the world beyond the island constitutes a significant difference between *The Road* and *Lord of the Flies*. The horror of *The Road* is that the destruction is universal; the horror of the latter is that the destruction is isolated and, as far as they are aware, only involves them. To the boys stranded on a desert island in the Pacific, the rest of the world appears unscathed.

Shared fundamental distinctions are essential for civilization to sustain itself, and when the boundaries between acceptable and monstrous behavior have been destroyed, along with everything else, thresholds have to be found elsewhere in the environment. Golding's novel, written in the aftermath of the Second World War, places emphasis on essential social demarcations, as does McCarthy's in its division of the population according to those who eat people and those who refuse to. The struggle to survive in both novels also involves an arduous ascent toward the value of what hard work can achieve, sustaining or rediscovering the social context for actions and customs that were once second nature. If by civilization we mean the production of sustained value, then according to the ethos of these apocalyptic novels, civilization even, or especially, as a remnant, is laborious, a handful of remembered values toward which human beings must strive. When removed from one's accustomed surroundings, the struggle to hold on to civilization is all the more difficult because the burden is shouldered with fewer supports and resources than before. This is especially the case for the father in *The Road*, for whom the task of remembering the time before the apocalypse is both a solitary and anxious one. However, it may just be possible to glimpse an exquisite quality in his situation as well, precisely because he is the last precious atom of civilization at the end of the world. As civilization personified, by keeping himself alive, he is keeping the civilized world alive. Other critics have critiqued the novel's logocentric patriarchal fantasies, and one has pointed out the problematics of a novel contemplating "death that is simultaneously imagined *as*, and as taking place *at*, the end of the world" (Morgenstern, 33). I too note the conflict at hand between survival and personal/cultural extinction. From the point of view of the son's survival, it would no doubt be more practical and far safer for the father to encourage his son to adapt to the new world order of a post-apocalyptic world and learn the ways of the cannibalistic gangs on the road.[5] What I left out of my account of the father as sole flag-bearer of civilization is the simple fact that civilization is meaningless unless it is a concerted activity among others who share a respect for the values that are strived for, which is where I began this part of the discussion. And so it must be added that the final straw of hope the father clings to is the belief that there are others for whom he is keeping the light of civilization burning. His quest then, for himself and his son, is not just to survive as a lone remnant of civilization but far more than that; it is to find others on whose behalf he survives, others for whom his or his son's survival will be precious.

Exceeding the interests of survival alone, the journey portrayed in *The Road* is, as Gretlund notes, a "quest for a meaning" (Gretlund, 46). For this reason, the worst enemy in *The Road* is not the cannibal but "impotence in orienting their journey" (46). Both novels deploy strategies that engage and foreground epistemology, a formalization of what can be known and how, in order to discover the compass points of the post-apocalyptic world, to rediscover in which direction the sun rises so to speak. Specifically, Golding and McCarthy demonstrate that in the liminal or threshold regions associated with endings and the end of a world, new belief systems must be wrung from the available resources in the pursuit of workable knowledge. Taking

Gretlund's idea further, survivors *in extremis* need to know how to orient themselves not just in a mappable physical space but in an ethical space, one that owes a great deal to their imaginary of what is still known, and known to matter, and what is now unknown and may well be a lethal threat to the former. Urgently they must learn how to navigate toward a safe harbor for the values they insist on cherishing, or else stand as a beacon guiding others toward them. This is the significance of the idea of the fire for the father and boy in *The Road*. As a symbol of hoped-for future community, fire gains physical or symbolic significance in both *The Road* and *Lord of the Flies*. At the same time, although fire is highly visible, its ultimate ethical significance is hard to bring to light. Ralph in *Lord of the Flies* attempts to convince the other boys and himself of the significance of fire: "The fire's the most important thing on the island, because, because—" (156). Lost for words, Ralph grasps the significance of the fire without fully understanding its meaning, or without being able to articulate it, which amounts to the same thing, as the boys' survival depends on their ability to communicate leadership and knowhow to the others.

We have seen that Ralph intuitively knows the importance of fire to attract the attention of potential rescuers, but his own conviction cannot shed light on the full significance of this to the others, let alone convince them to keep a fire burning for this reason. The boy in *The Road* also has reason to contemplate a guessed-at, hidden meaning of fire. Although his father has always insisted that they must and do carry the fire, their final dialogue testifies to a similar need to bring this threatened idea into the open:

> I want to be with you.
> You cant.
> Please.
> You cant. You have to carry the fire.
> I dont know how to.
> Yes you do.
> Is it real? The fire?
> Yes it is.
> Where is it? I dont know where it is.
> Yes you do. It's inside you. It was always there. I can see it. (234)

Their attempts to map out the coordinates of the fearful alien landscape that has replaced the past lead them to the one remaining safe place that remains hidden from view: their own interiority. But the values the father tries to inscribe in his son have of necessity to be subject to expression. The invisible idea of fire as a visible sign of shared knowledge (not just of where to go but of who to approach and who to avoid) must itself risk being seen by symbolic externalization. The idea of knowledge has to be lit up in the imaginary in order to continue to be the basis of all other shared values.

The sheer delight with which the boys explore the boundaries of the island at the beginning of the novel is the pleasure of knowledge acquisition. As such they use knowledge in order to conquer the land and their pleasure is palpable (29). At the end of their exploration of the foreign terrain, once they have reached the heights of the island, it remains for Ralph to remark with satisfaction, "This belongs to us" (31). Golding also reminds us here of the importance of a visible record of this attainment, a map, and of how a simple lack of paper makes even this a significant challenge. Despite this hopeful beginning, toward the end of the novel, the boys have exhausted their capacity to discover and share useful knowledge. At that moment the ocean becomes a mindless and ineluctable adversary. Written in the 1950s, Golding's novel is informed by knowledge of genocide, and while it cautions against the destructive force in human beings, it pits the boys against a force of nature as irresistible as it is heedless of them. Nevertheless, when the sea, said to have reached saturation point, turns on the boys by carrying off their bodies (Piggy's being the final one), it does so with an uncanny and impersonal meticulousness:

> The tide swelled in over the rain-pitted sand and smoothed everything with a layer of silver. Now it touched the first of the stains that seeped from the broken body and the creatures made a moving patch of light as they gathered at the edge. The water rose further and dressed Simon's coarse hair with brightness. The line of his cheek silvered and the turn of his shoulder became sculptured marble. The strange, attendant creatures with their fiery eyes and trailing vapours, busied themselves round his head. The body lifted a fraction of an inch from the sand and a bubble of air escaped from the mouth with a wet plop. Then it turned gently in the water. (169–170)

Most striking in this passage is the indifference of the landscape, as well as the ease with which Simon's body becomes absorbed into the natural environment. There is nothing new in the idea that violence and evil lurk deep within the human breast. From an environmental point of view, it is also telling us that when we wage war on nature, it will be we who pay the price.

If we fasttrack forward half a century, our encounter with nature expresses quite a different oceanic imaginary. In McCarthy's novel, life in the sea has been destroyed and with it almost all human existence.

McCarthy is not explicit about what caused the global catastrophe in *The Road*, but its consequence for the ocean is that all life there is extinct and all that remains is the memory of the sea as once a source of life. To the readers of the twenty-first century, this is less a futuristic fiction than an increasingly accepted fact of postindustrial times. The threat our industrial activities pose to life in the sea (and everywhere else) includes the effects of climate change, overfishing, and saturation point pollution to the extent that we now witness "the emergence and spread of dead zones as oxygen is sucked from the water by decaying plankton" (Roberts, *Ocean of Life*, 7). Great garbage patches or refuse eddies circle the oceans gathering in floating human waste, such as plastic and other pollutants, like "ocean black holes" (267). As far as ecodystopian literature goes, *The Road* ticks all the boxes, but it also resists foreclosing on the chance of human intercession, and this makes it a novel that opens up possibilities of faith in effective action and human agency. *The Road* invites the reader to reach deeply within himself or herself for an encounter with the Other, but despite the unreflecting cruelty we witness in the novel, it does not assume that we must find in ourselves a return to a life that is (as Hobbes famously said on the title page of *Leviathan*) "solitary, poor, nasty, brutish and short." With the father we must inevitably ask ourselves the question, "Could you crush that beloved skull with a rock? (96)," and as far as McCarthy's novel is concerned, the answer is not preordained by scripture or coded in our genes but is still ours to give.

If McCarthy offers a cautious hope, it is noteworthy and rather strange that this is sustained in *The Road* by the metaphorical strength of an ocean so lacking in vital force. Diane Luce reads McCarthy's Atlantic shore as unequivocally fatal, at least for the father himself (72). Luce notes further a profound irony that the father should "reverse the westering direction of American exploration, heading instead for the eastern shore and for death" (68). So ubiquitous is the metaphor of going West in American literature (including McCarthy's own *Blood Meridian*) that to most readers the alternate direction taken in *The Road* goes unnoticed. There is no doubt that to the reader who shares with the characters in *The Road* the estrangement, rootlessness, and restlessness of having grown up in "a culture of superhighways precluding rest and a furious penchant for tearing up last year's improvements in a ceaseless search for some gaudy ultimate" (5), as Frederick Turner puts it, a reversal of the traditional American westerly direction of progress certainly must mean something. However, I am not sure I want to follow Luce to the logical conclusion that would equate an easterly direction with the reversal of progress and death, despite the desolation of the ocean the man and boy find at the coast. I do not see McCarthy writing literally or symbolically about an inevitable ecological or cosmological fate already in store for us. Rather, I read *The Road* more allegorically, as a later-day pilgrim's progress in which McCarthy cautiously resists being overly pessimistic and wants above all to foreground the present-day need for a belief in agency founded on encounter with difference.[6] The ecological emergency today is about our "failure to comprehend our citizenship in the biotic community" (Orr, 32). In the oceanic imaginary, the role of the ocean in *The Road* is what remains of father and son's future existence as agents still capable of a belief in a possible encounter with difference and a break with the past. The reality of what awaits them is devastating. Even if the sea is not as blandly malign as it is depicted in Golding's novel, heedless of the significance of the human cargo it bears away, their encounter with the Atlantic translates into a kind of silent terror:

> Out there was the gray beach with the slow combers rolling dull and leaden and the distant sound of it. Like the desolation of some alien sea breaking on the shores of a world unheard of. Out on the tidal flats lay a tanker half careened. Beyond that the ocean vast and cold and shifting heavily like a slowly heaving vat of slag and then the gray squall line of ash. He looked at the boy. He could see the disappointment in his face. I'm sorry it's not blue, he said. (181)

Here McCarthy introduces a nullity all the more chilling because his prose is so measured and controlled.[7] To Luce, the image of the tanker resonates with the prevailing sense of melancholia and devastation of the novel, emblematic of "the global wreckage of the human enterprise" (71) and, as we have seen, for her the destination equals death, a reasonable conclusion. There is no question that the desolation of these final pages, the image of a beach replete with debris and carcasses, "saltbleached ribcages of what may have been cattle" (182), signals a profound halting point. Nevertheless, I think it is needful to frame this scene as a moment of that terror that attends the end of knowledge, which I claim is a feature of our times. If the Atlantic shore in *The Road* marks the utter destitution of all possibility of encounter with difference, then it spells the ends of representation. Here, at the world's end, lit by the stark light of McCarthy's allegory, we can discern the Information Age's worst nightmare, that with all the technology at our disposal we deliver ourselves finally not into knowledge but its opposite. The death of an ocean extinct from pollution, climate change, or other calamity would have been bad enough even if it had not at the same time foreclosed on the chance of some fruitful encounter with genuine otherness. Rather than encountering difference, however, the exhausted pair are met with a deadening sameness. Having entertained the hope that the sea might connect them to something, another shore on the other side of the ocean, the tragedy of their predicament is that father and son are faced with nothing but their own reflection, a mirror image consisting of another father and son who "Slept but a sea apart on another beach among the bitter ashes of the world or stood in their rags lost to the same indifferent sun" (182).

Thus, the end of the world is imagined as a collapse of two discourses, one environmental and the other drawn from an increasingly digital society in which, disappointingly, epistemological certainty is less available than ever at the beginning of the twenty-first century. Here, at what might once have been the frontier of knowledge, the essential distance between self and other, the grounds for any perspective at all, has collapsed. McCarthy's vision of the end of the world has throughout the novel discerned the collapse of representational distance, where father and son constantly encounter "Everything as it once had been save faded and weathered" (7). Having hoped for difference at the end of their journey, it is as if subjectivity and with it the agency elicited by actual encounter is a luxury now extinct. Death, of course, is a great equalizer. For there to be exchange and transaction, there must be difference. Having come thus far only to imagine another father and son "lost to the same indifferent sun" (182) is to come upon death. McCarthy sketches the image of death graphically with a disquieting mathematical precision: "At the tide line a woven mat of weeds and the ribs of fishes in their millions stretching along the shore as far as the eye could see like an isocline of death. One vast salt sepulchre" (187). An isocline is a line on a map extrapolated from a data set of measurements taken from a wide enough area of terrestrial space to warrant being mapped. I read McCarthy's use of this word as meant to evoke any graphical representation of a large set of spatially distant measurements. Here he forces on us the acute awareness of a profound failure in the correlation between knowledge and spatiality. Though this form of data representation predates digital technology, its present potential to graphically represent any and all data sets is now prodigious. McCarthy's use of the word isocline here registers both a past grandeur of information technology as well as its present and final pointlessness for the father and son. Once, he seems to say, we were able to make statistical analysis based on systematic data collection, we could represent such syntheses meaningfully and transmit them efficiently to all corners of the globe. But that was then. For the father and son, the vast set of information this isocline represents is of global proportions—like the World Wide Web—and all it can tell them is that the whole world is everywhere equally dead. The fact that there is nothing for them to set their eyes on other than a replica of themselves interrupts their epic journey with a trajectory of its own, one that calls into question the act of writing and reading in the Information Age.

In "The Scriptural Economy" from *The Practice of Everyday Life*, de Certeau finds a subtle relationship between the space of a blank page and the creation *ex nihilo* on it of a written imaginary space in which words become world: "on the blank page, an itinerant, progressive, and regulated practice—a 'walk'—composes the artefact of another 'world' that is not received but rather made" (134). Here, writing and reading traverse the space of the page, their "itinerant" movement making the world it contains.[8]

McCarthy's compelling intersection of statistics and catastrophe in "an isocline of death" becomes for me finally the territorial claim of the apocalypse itself or allegorically of its ideologues. This line of dead defines the world as no longer needing any borders for all is lost, everywhere the same. It declares that the contest for territory is over, for there is no longer any place worth the struggle, no place better than anywhere else. In the pages of his novel, McCarthy draws the lineaments of a textual world like de Certeau's blank page, awaiting the inscription of some cautious or fearless hope. Though it may be a silent, lead-grey canvas, or a soiled shroud, at the shore of the imagination where ribs of dead fish lie, it is a world that awaits a kind of resurrection. The father and son's harrowing march across an ashen continent resonates deeply with de Certeau's image of a "walk" of words that creates a world. Readers are invited to partake of this creative gesture in the form of reading in step with that march, whereby belief is hammered out of the most desperate circumstance. In the face of devastating sameness, were it not for the possibility of renewal, the world's malady would be terminal and the Atlantic would have an exclusively palliative function.

As knowledge evaporates and takes residence in a sea of sameness in cyberspace, it is often up to each individual reader to create meaning and signification. It is the reader on whom responsibility of interpretation, or simply reception, is bestowed. What remains of the world in *The Road* are its representations, the incarnations, and avatars of real people and things that have survived their destruction in the memory of their correspondents and readers. The "hum" with which the novel ends is the final message from father to son, the father's attempt to enjoin his posterity with his son's: "In the deep glens where they lived all things were older than man and they hummed of mystery" (241). In keeping with the epic proportions of life itself now, the final pages of *The Road* are also a refusal to end the story. The narratological virtue of the novel's ending is that, if it has all along been about a father's struggle to believe in an encounter with renewal, that now depends almost exclusively on the reader's willingness to take up that ethos on behalf of the father. Even if we just turn away from the dead shore to the stream in which remembered trout swim ("On their backs were vermiculate patterns that were maps of the world in its becoming" [241]) without quite knowing why, or if we stare down that Atlantic ocean that, against all odds now, still holds the hope of the father, we are taking up McCarthy's challenge.[9]

Golding's novel is premised on a harsh division between home as civilization at a distance and away as primal brutality up close. While the great ocean separates and differentiates the two, despite the rigor of its rule, it is also a nonpartisan force as well as being what they have between them in common. The strict severity of the division hits the boys hard. When the ocean subsumes the boys into itself with cool efficiency, it reinstates the boundaries between civilization and nature that they have violated. Golding's novel indirectly calls to mind the traditional notion of the commons that has been reinvested with interest in environmental discourses. Put simply, the commons are lands and resources not privately owned but held in common by a community for the benefit of all and as the responsibility of all to care for. The sea can be thought of as just such an area for, as Shewry points out, the sea is "common to all life" and it resists private ownership (303). Lacking this, the entire environment represented in *Lord of the Flies* exists only as an area of contention for the boys, and so the conditions for a creative encounter are nonexistent. "Our nature is to want to grab something that belongs to somebody else," laments Golding in an interview with James Baker, "and we have either to be taught or teach ourselves that you've got to share, you can't grab the lot" (134). What is remarkable in *Lord of the Flies* is the almost complete consensus on the utter unworkability of the idea of sharing, as though such civilized values have somehow been convincingly debunked. In a state of decay, the so-called civilized world back home is "in ruins," perhaps the result of nuclear war, say critics such as Boyd (10). Whether home is in actual ruins or not, what is interesting about this novel is that the way home is now represented as something one finds offshore insofar as the values of the old world are all the more keenly felt on a deserted island in the Pacific, even in their absence. In the face of a deluge of catastrophe, abandonment, and death, the boys attempt to reconstruct a social body on the island with knowledge that has been passed on to them through the public school system. Written not long after the Second World War, *Lord of the Flies* shows the length to which a pack of boys will go to protect their *lebensraum*, a vanishingly small patch of turf surrounded by the Pacific:

> This was the divider, the barrier. On the other side of the island, swathed at midday with mirage, defended by the shield of the quiet lagoon, one might dream of rescue; but here, faced by the brute obtuseness of the ocean, the miles of division, one was clamped down, one was helpless, one was condemned, one was—. (122)

Words routinely fail to reach their mark in this novel—the terror of not being equipped with the referential tools of civilization results in a persistent and chronic muteness. It is as though the famously nonexistent referent of literary theory rears up and, like a linguistic Loch Ness monster, bites off sentences in the midst of their attempt to denote. This inability to make language conform to experience is not only expressed by characters in the novel, here it is the narrator whose verbal powers fall short of expressing the confrontation with the "brute obtuseness of the ocean." The existential angst conveyed through this passage is configured in spatial terms whereby it is the endless expanse of sea that cuts the narrator off from the orderly completion of the sentence. Through the absence of an encounter as the result of a broken text, as in Golding's novel, the reader is confronted with a mute ellipsis, that which cannot be named. Filling such an inchoate void is not in itself difficult but then it remains necessarily within the realm of the private world circumscribed by the body and its immediate needs, failing to become public and part of a commons. Perhaps not unsurprisingly for a novel that so stubbornly insists on drawing out the full consequences of a plunge into the depths of the Hobbesian war of all against all, Golding's text ends with another moment of poignant silence, this time also accompanied by a physical distancing, a turning away from. This occurs, ironically, at the time of rescue, the most anticipated and yearned-for encounter of all. It begins at the point of the formal introductions that whiplash the boys out of savagery, back into civilization although not very reassuringly:

> The officer grinned cheerfully at Ralph.
>
> "We saw your smoke. What have you been doing? Having a war or something?"
>
> Ralph nodded.
>
> The officer inspected the little scarecrow in front of him. The kid needed a bath, a hair-cut, a nose-wipe and a good deal of ointment.
>
> "Nobody killed, I hope? Any dead bodies?"
>
> "Only two. And they've gone."
>
> The officer leaned down and looked closely at Ralph.
>
> "Two? Killed?"
>
> Ralph nodded again. Behind him, the whole island was shuddering with flame. The officer knew, as a rule, when people were telling the truth. He whistled softly.
>
> Other boys were appearing now, tiny tots some of them, brown, with the distended bellies of small savages. One of them came close to the officer and looked up.
>
> "I'm, I'm—"
>
> But there was no more to come. Percival Wemys Madison sought in his head for an incantation that had faded clean away. (222)

Young Percival's failure to introduce himself formally to a British navy fleet officer certainly signals the breakdown of language, an inability to express what has happened. But in the officer's cheerful attempt to make light of the boys' mischief, to infantilize any "war" experience they might have had, I see a more systematic lack, the total absence of any common ground whereby their experiences on the island could be meaningfully brought into the officer's civilized purview. We saw in *The Road* the failure of the oceanic imaginary when the pair reach the Atlantic seaboard and find only a world that has flatlined, a worldwide, lead-grey nullity. Similarly, in Golding's novel, the "obtuseness" of the ocean stands as a barrier between normality (even that of wartime) and the primal ferocity unleashed by the boys on the island. If an oceanic imaginary can offer the locus of widespread, even global, rapport, including space for meeting the radically different other as well as for settling differences, what can we say when that fails? Put simply, the systemic nature of the officer's misrecognition of the situation is oceanic in proportion. The officer's incomprehension refers to an equally widespread—oceanic—repudiation of any sense-making rapport between his world and the island. His refusal or inability to see the actualities of their predicament is a failure to encounter them in their situation. The notion that an officer would know "as a rule" when people tell the truth is far from reassuring here where conventional rules have dissolved. Indeed, no amount of grooming ("a bath, a hair-cut, a nose-wipe and a good deal of ointment") will set things right again. Percival struggles to find what will not come; it is the incantation of his own name as a social morpheme of civilized vernacular that has "faded clean away." The officer's mocking tone when asking whether the boys have been "having a war or something" is dreadfully off the mark, illustrating the violence of language and its limitations when not accompanied by a recognition of agency. The words that do not come in Golding's novel indicate the lack of a common ground wherein might be found shared terms for exploring the predicament of difference. In both cases, however, what is at stake is a symbolically ruled commons wherein agreements can be reached and the shock of difference encountered and given expression.

Let down with the heartbreakingly casual response of an officer unwilling or unable to see and say what he sees, the boys give themselves over to sobbing. Politely, the officer then "turned away to give them time to pull themselves together" while "allowing his eyes to rest on the trim cruiser in the distance" (223). In a deceptively simple shift, the reader's attention is turned to the sea again. Offering merely a palliative function to the father in McCarthy's *The Road*, initially a heedlessly lethal force in *Lord of the Flies*, is it now about to play yet another role in Golding's novel? The outward direction of the officer's glance is a noteworthy narratological moment in a novel that has turned centrifugally and claustrophobically about the axis of the island. From within the barriers of the island, keeping the ocean at bay, the reader is now directed to gaze out toward the horizon, but where the officer sees a "trim cruiser" we see nothingness. In a novel whose narrative hovers on the brink of violence from the first couple of pages and then disintegrates into mayhem, it is perhaps this final scene alone that distils the essence of apocalyptic terror. The officer's embarrassment and shame at the boys' expression of fear and sorrow as they break down into sobs signifies not the promise of civilization but its limits. With no available synthesis of the world of the island and home, offering no insight or perspective, the ocean at this moment acts as a mirror turning our gaze back to the island. Nothing, apparently, can be said or done to respect the boys' experience there. Rescue comes but with it there is no magic incantation that will set things right, for it does not come from a spatial imaginary by which to achieve a perspective that would encompass both where they have been and where they are now returning.

Spanning half a century, Golding's novel, and McCarthy's, tracks the diminishing role of difference as the basis for an encounter. *The Road* presents the reader with an indistinct, yet eerily familiar vision of an unbundling of knowledge, with belief at its lowest ebb at the end of the world as all possibility of fruitful or challenging encounter with otherness dissipates. As we have just seen in the rescue in *Lord of the Flies*, the officer's gaze on that "trim cruiser" brings the blindness of the West into painfully sharp focus. That neat little ship in the immensity of the sea is all that anchors the officer's utter failure to face the island and see in the boys the brutal otherness beneath the surface of his own civilization. Sharing characteristics with the blogosphere, the "maps of the world in its becoming" (241) on the backs of remembered trout in the final paragraph of *The Road* signify the frailty of territorial knowledge, the evaporation of knowledge as territory, with the father's dogged persistence its only faint hope of an afterlife. My claim is that the Atlantic—or the oceanic imaginary—exists now as an afterlife in the complex interactions between individuals and corporate cohorts whose encounters and disputes give the world new and ever mutable shape and form on the World Wide Web. By putting McCarthy's novel in the vicinity of Golding's, my intention has been to show how much of the oceanic lingers as an imaginary in the digital, "atmospheric" age. I will now turn to two novels set in the North Atlantic for thinking through the limits and possibilities of productive exchange of knowledge in an age of global capitalism.

# Part II

# Unsound Waves

# 3

# Through a Border Darkly

## North Atlantic Narratives of Exploitation in Peter Hoeg's *Miss Smilla's Feeling for Snow* and Annie Proulx's *The Shipping News*

In this chapter I want to explore some early warnings of the end times we have just been contemplating writ large, on a global scale, in Cormac McCarthy's *The Road* and confined to a single remote island in Golding's *The Lord of the Flies.* McCarthy's depiction of a post-apocalyptic descent into the most atrocious brutality and Golding's staging of an out-of-the-way reversion to barbarism both present human sociality in radical decline. To understand what might be presently facilitating this decline, as well as what might resist it, I want to turn to two novels of the early 1990s, *Miss Smilla's Feeling for Snow* by Peter Hoeg and *The Shipping News* by Annie Proulx. In these novels, sociality is in dire straits but of a different order. Subject to the dispersing or redistributing effects of global capital, humanity is on the verge of becoming abstracted from the place of its greatest effectiveness: the local. Both novels are set in contemporary society where, according to Hartman, "artificial, bureaucratic, or secondary mechanisms are blocking sources of vitality" (27). We have seen that what struggles to survive against all odds in McCarthy's *The Road* is the most immediate gesture of kindness and care, the nurturing and safeguarding of the young. In Hoeg's novel, this level of care is relegated to the status of an irrelevancy by all except the protagonist, Smilla. Hoeg's novel focuses unswervingly on the plight of the local (families, children, small organizations) overshadowed by global corporations. What the novel strongly suggests is that the sort of rigorous loyalty we see in Miss Smilla, a combination of toughness and tenderness, is always a personal and thus a local phenomenon. In this chapter, I will return to the deterioration of exchange relations, the effacement of difference, signaled by the appalling conclusion of the journey in *The Road* in the transatlantic cul-de-sac encountered by father and son.

Both Hoeg and Proulx give expression to a popular anxiety for the local, seen as being overruled by global capital. Rather than presenting outright antagonism to globalism, they adopt a measured focus on the dialectics of local and global, margin and center. In the context of the abysmal erasure of difference on a global scale in McCarthy's *The Road*—and with it the extinction of any possibility of commerce, the late-twentieth-century globalism of Hoeg and Proulx's novels comes with a degree of optimism. Humanity still has options. Nevertheless, if in these novels there is still plenty of economic and cultural trade across the Atlantic Ocean, it bears the seeds of its own destruction. At the same time, at the core of these North Atlantic narratives is the assumption that the exploitation of natural resources from within a global system of capital accumulation unfairly benefits centralized power structures. In Hoeg and Proulx, what emerges with more clarity is not McCarthy's universal epidemic of loss and destruction, nor the rapidly fading British Empire of *The Lord of the Flies*, but a highly localized prefiguring of the effects of uneven geographical development. Thus we see the consequences of the profit-driven approach of multinational corporations that turn a blind eye to the environmental and cultural damage they visit on the remote northern communities represented in *Smilla* and *The Shipping News*. The ruthless power of the corporate bosses of the 1990s described by Hoeg and Proulx is in the hands of the kind of privileged school boys once stranded on the island in Golding's novel, always poised on the brink of a descent into rampant consumerism. Hoeg and Proulx show the enormous price suffered by the most vulnerable members of the society, including children and the disenfranchised, for the widespread endorsement of progress founded on neoliberal economic principles.

*Miss Smilla's Feeling for Snow* begins with the death of a young Inuit boy in Copenhagen. The boy, Isaiah, is discovered dead on the ground after having fallen from the roof of the building where he lives. With her profound feeling for snow, Smillaraaq Qaavigaaq Jaspersen, of Inuit ancestry herself, is able to read the marks left in the snow on the roof and know that the boy was chased to his death. The only one willing to intervene on his behalf, Smilla sets her mind to uncover the dark forces that are conspiring to keep Isaiah's cause of death hidden. The hard-nosed, yet vulnerable, part Danish, part Greenlander Smilla connects the murder with two covert expeditions to Greenland, one in

1966 and one in 1991. At the center of both of these expeditions is a much coveted meteor in Greenland that, if brought back to Denmark, can be exploited for its powerful, mysteriously life-engendering qualities. The meteor has been found to produce a warmth that enables a deadly tropical worm to thrive in arctic water. The so-called guinea worm is a lethal parasite that has already caused the death of many on these expeditions. The potential for this meteor to cause havoc in the physical and financial world becomes obvious when news of it reaches the Cryolite Corporation and especially the villain, Tork Hviid. In itself the meteor guarantees scientific celebrity to anyone who possesses it, and Hviid will stop at nothing to exploit it for profit, even using the worm itself as a biological weapon. What makes this novel different from other deep-sea thrillers is not just that the plot is centered on the forces of a global market economy and geopolitical conspiracy. In an inspired narrative move, Hoeg shows these forces impacting the body of a child who then becomes emblematic of the oppressed Inuit people living in Copenhagen. Proulx's *The Shipping News* has much in common with Hoeg's *Smilla*. Proulx's novel is largely set at about the same northern latitude as Hoeg's, in the colonial New World isle of Newfoundland, and it too juxtaposes the local and the global, focusing on a traditional, indigenous way of life in a globalized corporate world. In an article published in the *New Yorker* in 2000, Proulx notes:

> For me the strongest influences are the varied landscapes and bare ground of the hinterlands, rough weather and rural people living lives in the pincers of damaging isolation, ingrained loca lisms, and the economic decisions made by distant urban powers. The rush, for me, comes from the effort to put these lives on paper, and through them examine the society that draws the line. (139)

Despite Proulx's own insistence on foregrounding the local as subject to far-reaching economic forces, *The Shipping News* is seldom read as commenting on the fate of small communities in the context of globalization. Instead, it tends to be read as a novel about personal growth, which is how the novel was translated to screen by Lasse Hallström and screenwriter Robert Nelson Jacobs in 2001. In my account I want to focus less on the development and fate of individual characters in both these novels and instead explore the way they can intervene within social settings that are overshadowed by far-reaching economic forces and corporate culture. I will be using Deleuze and Guattari's theory of Capital together with that of the assemblage in formulating a precisely nuanced account of the predicament of human agency in relation to global capitalism. Concepts such as these offer a way of specifying a structure of intervention that takes on the decentering effects now widely recognized in postmodernity.[1] I draw on Ian Buchanan's approach to assemblage theory that affirms that resistance occurs despite it now always being pitted against forces of global Capital that largely efface the durability of traditional movements.

While neither Hoeg nor Proulx identify as members of the communities of Newfoundland and Greenland, their novels offer a devastating critique of the consequences of technological progress in the Arctic Ocean. Theirs is the point of view of Western writers concerned with the cultural, social, and environmental destruction of our planet. Read separately, the two novels seem to tell stories of outsiders whose journeys include revisiting scenes of crimes that mobilize a parallel route of discovery into their own and their family's troubled pasts. Read conjointly however, these narratives from the Arctic Ocean disclose much wider concerns involving the geopolitical exploitation and the desolation of marginalized communities. This conjoint story also bears witness to the local, to the viability of human life, and the connectivity that holds families and communities together in precarious times. Hoeg and Proulx are offering up a number of expansionist metaphors for critical reassessment. In this chapter I will examine these contemporary representations of corporate power in the North Atlantic as depictions of the worldwide pursuit of economic growth at any cost, itself a direct consequence of the greed and corruption of last century's imperialism and still in lockstep with that century. I want to situate globalism within an economy of exploitation, including slavery, so as to further denaturalize these metaphors by reopening their history to critical analysis. What I am calling unsound waves I see as a feature of our contemporary "post-Atlantic" times. These waves are propagated out of a murky past at an accelerated pace under the impetus of an increased proficiency in the ability of technology to obediently further the aims of the world's corporate masters.

There are moments in *Smilla* and *The Shipping News* when I see Hoeg and Proulx proposing forms of resistance to what Gilles Deleuze and Felix Guattari (in *A Thousand Plateaus*) call capitalism's "axiomatic" (143–144). This is the principle in the name of which things and behaviors with traditional or locally situated intrinsic properties (one of the glosses on their term "intensity" [143]) are decoded to be more easily detached from their site of origin and travel as lightly as possible along the paths of exchange and commodification. "The point is," explains Claire Colebrook, "in capitalism it does not matter what we believe or desire so long as the form of our desire can be channelled into the flow of a general value; we must be able to see all desired objects as signs of some underlying general quantity: all goods are reducible to capital" (*Understanding Deleuze*, 48). Importantly, as we shall see, these novels do not simply lament the plight of the decoded local as that which is powerless to resist the tide of Capital's "decoded flows" as they enlist traditional or indigenous life along their trade routes. These authors do not display the outright antagonism to economic neoliberalism of the recent protest movements such as "Occupy Wall Street." Rather, Hoeg and Proulx use narrative to articulate—or "recode"—the past, present, and possible future value of the local without denying the existence and undeniable importance of the global. In their narratives this value intrinsic to the local—always, it must be said, maintained by some labor of productive coding—is necessarily something inseparable from its traditional setting. However, these authors do not shy away from the fact that that very setting now has a global context. Indeed, as we shall see, there is a strong suggestion in Proulx's novel that the local draws from the global strength for its own (local) perseverance.

Proulx's protagonist Quoyle has his name from *The Ashley Book of Knots* that supplies many of the epigraphs of the novel's chapters. He shares his name with a flat, concentric coil of rope "made on deck, so that it may be walked on if necessary" (1). Indeed, Quoyle is a man who can easily be taken advantage of. Quoyle is at first a hesitant, inconsequential character whose wife walks out on him with their two daughters, aged six and four. Quoyle recovers the children after learning that their mother has sold them to a pedophile with whom they are later found naked, skating on "dish detergent on the kitchen floor" with "blank film cartridges all over the place" (26). Thus, at the outset of the novel, a theme whose significance will grow is firmly established: submission. It goes hand in hand with this disturbing instance of the most obscene kind of child labor that is also a theme of significance in the novel. I choose to read this not as an event merely symptomatic of the times we live in but as the present continuation of the Atlantic traffic in slaves. We find another example of this kind of submission in Quoyle's African American friend Partridge's falling for consumerist temptations. Partridge and his wife telephone from California to say they go to parties at black people's places where there are swimming pools and celebrity guests like filmmaker Spike Lee (220). How is Quoyle or indeed the reader to respond to such boasting when in 1992 Los Angeles (LA) was the place of infamous race riots when charges against the LA police for the beating of Rodney

King the year before were for the most part dropped? To me there are strong links between the material that takes flight into the pages of *The Shipping News* via this brief phone call from LA and the place as it exists in an enduring battle for racial emancipation. If I am right, then the high standard of living enjoyed by individuals such as Partridge lacks foundation and, ultimately, only serves as a temporary distraction from the cause of independence and justice, the same struggle Partridge's ancestors endured under slavery. While such a position may risk dehistoricizing this painful past, my point is that it is not just in the past, and it is my intention to repoliticize its endurance into the present as a global practice. Far from being a chilling reminder of the past, it is a practice that continues now to serve instrumental ends in a "post-Atlantic" world. Both Hoeg and Proulx's novels critique the global economy that enslaves us as both producers and consumers locked into a worldwide economy fueled by our own craving for instant gratification. This has widespread—they are global, of course—and long-term consequences.

The familiar notion of postindustrial labor relations involving us as "cogs" in a (now) global economic machine has arguably received its most erudite elaboration and historical accounting from Deleuze and Guattari. For them capitalism has taken us beyond any such "machinic enslavement" (occurring under the archaic "despotic" regimes accessible only to archeology) that they associate with states prior to capitalism (*Thousand*, 427–428). Since the onset of capitalism, Deleuze and Guattari explain, human beings are no longer the "constituent pieces of a machine that they compose among themselves and with other things (animals, tools), under the control and direction of a higher unity." Rather, we are now captured by "*social subjection* [original emphasis]" that is "when the higher unity constitutes the human being as a subject linked to a now exterior object, which can be an animal, a tool, or even a machine" (456–457). Since the first publication of *A Thousand Plateaus* in 1980, the arrival of the Internet more than illustrates the relevance of this concept; it actively mobilizes it more and more exactly. Proulx's depiction of Newfoundland since Confederation with Canada in 1949 is pessimistic. When Quoyle returns with his aunt and his rescued children to his roots in Killick-Claw, the fisheries have been significantly depleted and, like Quoyle, the Newfoundlanders are weakened and trampled on by the global economy of oil production and shipping.

The part of Quoyle's career that is of interest to me is ideally suited to test and interfere with the economic realities evinced above, and this is not just because he finds employment as a columnist covering the "shipping news" at the local newspaper *The Gammy Bird*. More important than this is the fact that sales and circulation are highest on editor and second-in-charge Tert Card's list of priorities. This places him and Quoyle in growing opposition from the start since, apart from his limitations as a journalist, Quoyle eventually becomes something of a writer of conscience. To maintain sales and circulation to the outside world (locally up and down the coast), Tert Card's editorial practice works its own brand of Capital's decoded flows. To promote the paper, he fills it with fake advertising (a matter to which I will return), and for him the violent deaths and sexual depravities of his community must be made sensational, always with pictures if at all possible and always with the aim of simply increasing sales.

It soon emerges that the newsroom is a hotbed of debate over the socially corrosive consequences of neoliberal economic policies. Soon after Quoyle joins the team of motley locals who give the community the stories that matter to them, the paper's owner, Jack Buggit, gives him a rundown of Newfoundland since Confederation, explaining how the community was lured by the promise of "electricity and roads, telephone, radio...health care, mail service, good education for me kids" (65). Instead, complains Buggit, they were cheated out of the only source of real income available to them: "goddamn Canada government giving fishing rights to every country on the face of the earth, but regulating us out of business" (65). Proulx's choice of location in *The Shipping News* is deliberate as her intention was to depict a traditional society on the verge of collapse in the face of economic change (Rood, 61). Proulx presents both sides of the story: *The Gammy Bird* provides the nexus for a debate that gets to the heart of that transition. There are those like garrulous editor Tert Card who believe Newfoundland to have been a backward colony in the middle of nowhere with no marketable resources other than fish and whose people died from poverty-related diseases. To him the disenchantment of having joined the Confederation seems hypocritical. He argues that "they give you antibiotics and oxygen and all and you live to bite the hand that saved you. Nobody, nobody in their right mind would go back to them hard, hard times. People was only kind because life was so dirty you couldn't afford to have any enemies. It was all swim or sink" (200). In keeping with this, Hunt and Doty see Proulx strongly suggesting that Newfoundlanders are partly complicit in their own economic exploitation by not having protected their natural resources against short-term gain (4).

Under the benign dictatorship of Jack Buggit, *The Gammy Bird* listens in to the heartbeat of the coastline and reports not what journalists in Toronto deem appropriate, but what locals want to read.[2] The epigraph of the chapter in which Quoyle first encounters the writers and editors of *The Gammy Bird* informs us that "gamming" refers to the practice of sailing ships falling in with each other at sea, maneuvered to keep close enough to shout news to each other (56). In *Moby-Dick*, Melville explains in the chapter entitled "The Gam" that letters could be delivered as well (265). I want to read this from a present-day perspective as a significant response to those decoded flows Deleuze and Guattari describe, that feed commodities into Capital's axiomatic circulatory system of trade routes and delivery schedules, its calibrated supply of mass-produced demand. To imagine a successful "gam" happening today, it would not be as if the ships simply "back their yards" so as separately to resist the pressure of wind and current. As Hoeg points out in *Smilla*, the sheer tonnage of today's container ships means that they proceed inexorably on course as though external local forces and pressures, such as weather conditions and other ships, are nonexistent (315). Originally gamming meant that, largely by chance and in mid-ocean, ships unexpectedly discovered a new destination for an alternative cargo of stories, news, and letters. My feeling is that, for Proulx, encounters like these are precious and probably becoming rarer as the Information Age gathers momentum. Certainly, *The Gammy Bird* is the place of just such an encounter. Thus, Quoyle's arrival at the paper is a form of contemporary "gam" in which an unplanned yet fruitful exchange of views becomes newsworthy.

In his career at the newspaper, Quoyle discovers that shipping is news and, it seems, news is a kind of shipping. Sometimes it can circulate "contraband" ideas, even if they are simply a matter of insisting on the value and significance of the local. With Buggit at its helm, *The Gammy Bird* succeeds largely in sticking to local ways and resisting the fashions and business imperatives the editor-in-chief refused to learn in Toronto, the siren songs of modernization. And Quoyle also succeeds for, under the wings of *The Gammy Bird*, he gains an alternative, rather commanding voice in place of his lifelong hesitant mumbling. Indeed, some critics read the novel in part as the development of Quoyle's voice from mute to articulate (Seiffert, 515). *The Gammy Bird* acts then as a new beginning for Quoyle who slowly learns to confront his past by articulating it rather than suppressing it. Smilla in Hoeg's novel is similarly forced to overcome lifelong fears. Surprisingly, she is afraid of the ocean. We see her at the beginning of her journey to Greenland looking out over the sea, feeling disoriented and frightened at the sight of "an amorphous, chaotic shifting of directionless masses of water that loom up and break and roll" (231). The threat of drowning is not the reason she fears water, however. "I'm not afraid of the sea merely because it wants to strangle me," she insists, "I'm afraid of it because it will take away from me my orientation, the inner gyroscope of my life" (232). Hoeg contrasts Smilla's acute sense of direction on land and her fear of losing it. Here the oceanic imaginary as radical fluidity (not unlike the World Wide Web) challenges any attempt to establish fixed coordinates, while at the same time it provides the possibility of the most surprising, testing, and sometimes fruitful encounters. DeLanda's now famous account of exteriority, developing Deleuze and Guattari's notion of the assemblage, helps to think about Quoyle's agency as leveraging within the stormy straits between "the properties defining a given entity [and] its capacities to interact with other entities" (10).[3] In the same way that *The Gammy Bird* provides Quoyle with his rite of passage, what DeLanda calls "relations of exteriority" (10) ensure that he brings a surprising shake up to the paper itself, its staff and management, its prevailing ethos. Assemblage then partakes of the oceanic imaginary through access to as well as resistance to its radical fluid exteriority. In keeping with these reflections, Smilla's sea journey on the ship *Kronos* in Hoeg's novel takes her across an abyss both spatial and temporal, bringing fear and isolation on the way to her homeland, Greenland.

*Kronos* is the father of Zeus. Sometimes associated with "Cronus" or possibly "Chronos," the ship in which Smilla sails can be read as representative of the destructive ravages of time. In *Smilla*, there are competing notions of time. The local, experiential notion of time upheld within the Inuit traditions of Smilla's childhood proves devastatingly incompatible with a unified, global sense of time as regulated by the clocks on Wall Street or Greenwich. Most poignant in the novel is, of course, the child as an emblem of potential time rendered vacant, absent. That Isaiah's lifetime is cut short right at the start of the novel leaves the reader with an appalling sense of time emptied, of human potential annulled. Hoeg's novel encourages us to think of Isaiah's (or anyone's) absence, not as something that no longer is but as a mark in the present carved repeatedly into the text of Hoeg's novel and into the presence of those who remain. Hoeg insists via Smilla's point of view that Isaiah remain present to us as one who is lost and he partly achieves this by using present tense in the flashbacks to Smilla's time with Isaiah.

In this way the story is sometimes told via careful focalization on Smilla and what, in these present-tense flashbacks, seems to be her still growing recent attachment to the absent child. His absence is also a presence as well as a mute yet powerfully felt witness to events in the present. There is also the suggestion that even had he not died, his lack of real agency means he would still have had a minimal chance to intervene in matters that proved fatal to him. (We also know that that would not have stopped him trying since he was a feisty lad who reached for his knife once when Smilla slapped him, and we know he took to the icy waters to save his father.) It is worth noting that child-like status is given to adults and whole cultures as they are framed by Western colonial interests. Ashis Nandy points out that colonies are generally viewed and treated as children (54). Indeed, Poddar argues that Denmark has persistently been portrayed by its publicists as the "benevolent and nurturing parent, and Greenland as the grateful child" (164). This notion of colonized populations not having grown up, of their being behind the times, is a prevalent feature of imperial sentiment.

Rather than portraying Greenland as primitive, a parenthetical episode in the history of Denmark, Hoeg's novel creates a far more complex portrait of this island and its history. *Smilla* depicts lives deeply affected by the greed of colonial business practices and Western consumer culture. Hoeg uses flashbacks of Smilla's past, often of times spent hunting with her mother, now lost to her and as a way of life forever lost to all Inuits. In a way similar to her memories of Isaiah, all these losses for what no longer is take on an almost palpable presence, something which still can be felt to this day. Hoeg carefully represents international criminality as inseparable from the colonial enterprise in Greenland. The three illegal, and fatal, secret expeditions to Greenland, undertaken to assess and to exploit the meteor, take place over five decades. That the expeditions continued through five decades despite proving fatal to the Inuit workers testifies to a criminal commitment to exploit them and their land, a commitment comparable in historical scale to colonization itself. It keeps in perfect step with the operations of the Cryolite Corporation whose activities and records were used in the cover up of the deaths and the expeditions. Most acutely affected is Isaiah's family, decimated by greed of such criminal proportions. During the second secret expedition, Isaiah's father and other Inuit men who dived into the parasite-infested waters became infected while exploring the meteor and never returned from the expedition.

Although he swam in the same waters to rescue his father, Isaiah was unharmed. For this reason, Isaiah has been monitored by Tork Hviid and his team in order to assess this unusual metabolism of the parasite in his body. The significance of the word "parasite" resounds here. In Isaiah's body Hoeg sees the combined stories of colonized Greenland, "child" of the Danish authorities, as well as that of the suffering of Inuit families and their children. Living and dead Isaiah's body, beloved by Smilla, has been merely a useful site of research for this parasitic enterprise for even after being chased off the roof to his death by Tork, and before paramedics arrive, a muscle biopsy is taken from Isaiah in order to assess the postmortem effect of the parasite. Patchay reads this in terms of residual colonialism and suggests that the biopsy represents the ultimate form of control, one that even assumes authority over children's corpses (26). It is useful to recall Foucault here whose economy of power is premised on the inquiring gaze that "insidiously objectifies those on whom it is applied" (*Discipline and Punish*, 216). Foucault in *The History of Sexuality (Volume 1)* has demonstrated how "bio-power was without question an indispensable element in the development of capitalism" (140–141) and how scientific attention to the performances of the body "characterized a power whose highest function was perhaps no longer to kill, but to invest life through and through" (139). The ability to absent oneself from the inquiring gaze is, conversely, a form of heroic resistance. After Smilla's mother disappeared in her kayak, her body was never recovered, and for Poddar this makes her "a figure of anti-colonial resistance" (173–174). This entails a symbolic power passed on to Smilla who for much of her career manages to escape the probing and the surveillance of the colonial gaze. Ultimately, Patchay argues, the parasite of *Smilla* is "the desire for power by Danish authorities" (21). The implication is that Danish progress is at the cost of those living on its fringes, such as Isaiah's mother whose life has been ruined largely through alcohol-related diseases.

Smilla's own family has suffered too, either through failing to adapt their traditional Inuit way of making a living to a capitalist society or by conforming too successfully. Her brother, it is said, committed suicide when he could no longer hunt for a living. Smilla's father, on the other hand, is an unscrupulous, outstandingly successful Danish professor of medicine, a coroner, as well as a former employee of The Cryolite Company, now headed by the thoroughly corrupt Tork Hviid. Smilla's life so far has managed to avoid these corrosive forces impacting the Inuit people, though she does suffer alienation. She is a hybrid character, motherless and uprooted from Greenland, far more educated and knowledgeable in her discipline of glaciology than most, yet socially still an outsider in Denmark. In his reflections on exile, Said warns that one of the effects of decolonization and modernization is the creation of territories where "immense aggregates of humanity loiter as refugees and displaced persons" (286). Hoeg's novels spotlight those shadowy demographic crevices of our civilization where displaced persons must dwell. This is a challenge to the Danish welfare system as noted by Moller (31) and often a critique of contemporary Western culture more generally. As with Proulx's novel, Hoeg's critique of global capitalism focuses on the North Atlantic ocean both as a natural environment as well as a stage on which economic and industrial activities are played out. More precisely, with globalization in Hoeg and Proulx's novels exacting such a calculated tribute from the most vulnerable human resources at its disposal, I am put in mind of how the Atlantic Ocean was the original site of a business practice that entailed the buying and selling of human beings.

Paul Gilroy and Charles Long have convincingly argued that the Atlantic slave trade was the beginning of the attempt to globalize the world. Referring to plantation slavery as "capitalism with its clothes off," Gilroy has called for a renewed focus on the Atlantic to achieve "one single, complex unit of analysis... to produce an explicitly transnational and intercultural perspective" (15). Gilroy's term the "black Atlantic" has come to stand for how a particular historical conjunction has a bearing on British black citizens. Similarly, Roach draws attention to the invention of the New World and the horrendous violence of this creation. He argues that while these brutalities "may have been officially forgotten, circum-Atlantic memory retains its consequences, one of which is that the unspeakable cannot be rendered forever inexpressible: the most persistent mode of forgetting is memory imperfectly deferred" (4). My idea of an oceanic afterlife owes much to this notion of memory held in abeyance in which the gesture is itself a dynamic record alive in the present and still further affected by the passage of time. It is not based on the assumption that once remembered the past can somehow be recovered. In this I incline toward Hall's argument in which cultural identity "belongs to the future as much as to the past" and that its temporality involves it as much in processes of becoming as in brief or long periods of stability (131). Proulx and Hoeg's novels show how slavery endures both in the internal logic of global Capital and in the kind of suffering it visits on exploited populations.

When Quoyle and his aunt arrive in Newfoundland, the aunt pauses to consider the long line of predecessors, those who had arrived there from remote ports: "Vikings, the Basques, the French, English, Spanish, Portuguese. Drawn by the cod, from the days when massed fish slowed ships on the drift for the passage to the Spice Isles, expecting cities of gold" (32–33). Whereas his aunt can imaginatively position herself in the company of these seekers of fortune, Quoyle is unable to see the role he himself plays in an economy of exploitation. This is not to say that either of them is "drawn by the cod," but that they are hoping to fulfil a desire for something different, a new start, a new enterprise. For Quoyle to do this, however, he must face down his own past and his lineage with a criminal ancestry. This begins quite gently on a trip to the rugged and uninhabited Gaze Island with fellow journalist Billy Pretty who tells Quoyle about Canada's history of white slavery. Billy tells Quoyle of the Irish and Scottish orphans shipped off to Canada, "just swept them up by the thousand" (167) to be "worked to the bone, treated like dirt, half starved and crazed with lonesomeness" (168). While Quoyle is not personally guilty of the fact that the Canadian economy flourished through child labor, and therefore not terribly unsettled by this, Billy's disclosures soon bring him to a crisis point. Billy next tells him that Quoyle's own ancestors were pirates, pointing out that Gaze Island is perfectly situated to command a view of all the shipping coming from Europe, an advantage that was regularly exploited by Quoyle's forebears. Billy softens it somewhat:

> "Truth be told," said Billy, "there was many, many people here depended on shipwrecks to improve their lots. Save what lives they could and then strip the vessel bare. Seize the luxuries, butter, cheese, china plates, silver coffeepots and fine chests of drawers. There's many houses here still has treasures that come off wracked ships. And the pirates always come up from the Caribbean water to Newfoundland for their crews. A place of natural pirates and wrackers." (172)

It is at this point that we are invited to see how the novel situates human agency within time and pitted against the decentering effects of Capital. To some extent it is true that to end the abovementioned cycle of past exploitation Quoyle must somehow revisit the scenes of earlier crimes and, as Flavin notes in relation to Quoyle, "exorcise the ghosts and demons of his family's past" (241). However, as I said at the outset of this chapter, Quoyle's personal development is not in itself the main concern in this chapter. If he does detach himself from his personal lineage with pirate ancestors, and from any trace of complicity in Canada's involvement in slavery, as we shall see, this is necessary for him to act most effectively on matters beyond his private and personal existence. Nevertheless, for him to become an agent of change at the newspaper, giving his local community access to and even influence in global affairs, Quoyle must undergo a baptism not unlike Ishmael's at the close of *Moby-Dick*.

Quoyle has been afraid of water since he was terrorized by his father whose idea of teaching his young son to swim was to throw him in the deep end. It is not until Quoyle nearly drowns that he overcomes this lifelong incapacity in the water. When his barely seaworthy boat capsizes, he rapidly learns to swim and, by implication, to fight for a life of his own, under the same conditions his father imposed. In that moment, the novel's temporal and spatial structure is gathered into one place in a single knot of significance. In those same waters that his ancestors committed acts of piracy, Quoyle severs both the bond of fear originating in his childhood as well as the one linking him to those criminal associations. Quoyle survives by holding on to a floating ice-chest that surfaces from his capsized boat, clinging to it until he is rescued by Jack Buggit with his uncanny sense of knowing when people are at risk of drowning at sea. This scene echoes the ending of Melville's *Moby-Dick* in which Ishmael is saved by clinging to a floating coffin. Like Melville, Proulx draws a powerful narrator from this moment of near-drowning. Like Ishmael saved by a passing ship and liberated to begin his tale of Captain Ahab and the whale, Quoyle also soon finds a voice capable of addressing matters beyond any personal limitation when he takes up the position of editor of *The Gammy Bird*.

As editor of the local paper, Quoyle becomes a local who is keenly aware of what threatens the sustainability of local ways. This does not make him more insular to the outside world. On the contrary, Quoyle uses the paper to raise environmental and political awareness through his editorials that feature the widespread consequences of policies governing the oil and fishing industries. I suggested earlier that *The Gammy Bird*'s name, by translating the metaphor for the early meaning of "gamming" to apply it to present-day shipping, can be read as suggesting an intentional resistance to what Deleuze and Guattari refer to as Capital's axiomatic of coded flows. Gamming, or the communication en route between ships, invites the human element into the mechanical or axiomatic flow of capital. Further to this then, under his editorship, Quoyle asks Buggit that the space taken up with fake advertising be released to be used for news instead. Indeed, the advertising Quoyle rejects is a perfect example of Capital's axiomatic since, rather than advertising actual local products and services the bulk of the ads were fictional, they referred to nonexistent companies. In these ads, Buggit falsely advertises the power of the paper's advertising. The content of the fake ads was so thoroughly "decoded" that the "commodity" actually being touted by them was nothing but advertising's fundamental mendacity. The masses of ads served only as a falsified measure of the paper's prestige to the few legitimate advertisers.

Deleuze commentator Ian Buchanan has a particular take on the notion of assemblage that is relevant here. For Buchanan, an assemblage is not just any social or natural aggregate at all. Rather, it must bring together a number of agencies, some of which can in fact be in conflict with each other, and at the same time the assemblage must be understood as enduring *for* something or someone. In addition, an assemblage does not grow merely in size by the addition of features or members; rather, anything or anyone added to an assemblage changes its function. I think it is worth letting Deleuze and Guattari's oft-repeated formulation "assemblage of enunciation" (*Thousand*, 23) resonate here since it is especially relevant when discussing the properties and capacities of the press. The concept of assemblage then helps us to identify more precisely the initial significance of the newspaper to Quoyle and now his significance to the paper. Even at first, the job on the paper was not just another job for Quoyle, it was a turning point for him. More importantly though, Quoyle becoming an editor now is not just the (decoded) replacement of one man for another. In Quoyle the paper acquires a more outspoken conscience that until then was only expressed in arguments between the staffers. As well as dropping the pretence of fake advertising, its editorials take on global issues that affect locals, and opposed voices are also allowed to speak via the paper. If we ask "for whom" or "for what" the paper now exists, it is for something altogether different from before. Its purpose is truly multiple in seeking for all locals the benefit of their having a say in matters global without being one and the same as the global. Indeed, the concept of the assemblage permits us to understand that any number of interventionist agencies can arise to stand as the "other" of global capital.

Proulx's novel goes hand in hand with a widening discourse surrounding ecological decline generally, and more specifically her novel intersects with a heightened awareness of sustainability in the fishing industry in the Arctic Ocean. The Canadian government imposed a cod moratorium in 1992 (Cooke, 194) severely restraining the locals the right of access to traditional fisheries. Thus, as Cooke explains, at the time of writing the novel, the harvestable stock of cod had almost disappeared due to technological advances, lack of government regulation, and large-scale international profiteering (200).[4] This industrialized, profit-driven approach to fishing is criticized by the locals in the novel. Billy Pretty bemoans the trawlers and the draggers that catch the fish long before the inshore fishermen even get a fair chance

(292). Group solidarity and a strong belief in regional identity and a traditional way of life can provide consolation at a time of economic precariousness when over thirty thousand fishers have lost their livelihood (Whalen, 65–66). Both Hoeg and Proulx evoke the idea of a fragile home, a specific and localized place of shelter and belonging under threat by the decoded flows of a homogenizing global consumer culture. Though the Arctic environment is particularly harsh, both novels make the point that the dangers pre-globalism were preferable to the threats imposed by global capitalism today. Billy Pretty says to Quoyle: "the sea was dangerous and men were lost, but it was a satisfying life in a way people today do not understand" (169). Billy's vision of a globalized Newfoundland sees a morally corrupt landscape emerging, one in which large businesses bring with them drugs, crime, prostitution, vandalism, divorce, and abandoned children (199).

A similar economy is visualized in Hoeg's novel via its representation of the sea and the ship *Kronos* especially. Afloat in the North Atlantic, *Kronos* illustrates the contradiction at the heart of globalization. Globalization has been idealized by its supporters as offering, in Massey's words, "unfettered mobility" as well as "free unbounded space" (81), and yet the ship enables Hoeg to critique the limited shelter for human congregation in the contemporary world. The *Kronos*, a "piazza in the middle of the ocean" (328), presents a claustrophobic, isolated habitat for a motley group of crew members from all corners of the world. Essentially the entire crew are slaves of capitalism and exploited for their drug addictions and other dependencies. Hoeg's representation of the ship *Kronos* is an indictment of capitalist recruiting methods and a spoof of globalization. Smilla observes the paradoxical immobility of a ship under way, "a fixed platform of steel, framed by a permanent cyclorama with a cold grey winter wind blowing across it, placed on top of a moving yet always uniform abyss of water. Convulsed by the monotonous exertion of its engines, the ship pounds in vain on one spot" (259). Instead of offering a smooth passage, the sea is folded and punctured by occasional makeshift harbors offering in mid-ocean the barest of platforms on which to trade and conduct associated commercial activity. Here in this unlikeliest of places people still come together to feed into the wheel of capital. These places include the casino and the floating oil platforms outside of Nuuk "like a universe floating on posts" (321), where in the Arctic Ocean an entire floating dock able to service container ships can be dismantled in 12 hours (322).

The coastal landscape portrayed in *The Shipping News* has similarly been interrupted with ugly constructions of oil rigs since oil was discovered in the 1970s. Predictably, the neoliberal Tert Card of *The Gammy Bird* swears by the oil projects of the Arctic Sea: "Newfoundland is going to be the richest place in the world. It's a new era. We'll be rolling in money" (199). While Proulx's novel recognizes that oil provides significant economic growth in the region, she does not shy away from cautioning against the dangers associated with the oil industry, including unsafe working conditions, precarious employment, and pollution. In her reading of the novel, Cooke points to the connections between the fictional oil rig *Sevenseas Hector* and the real-life *Ocean Ranger* disaster in which 84 crew members perished because of a laissez-faire approach by government that colluded with multinational companies and turned a blind eye to worker safety (200). In Hoeg's novel, the ship *Kronos* represents a capitalist enterprise flipped upside down to expose the underbelly of globalism. As one part of a corrupt and illegal trading system, the ship itself stands metonymically for the global network of business deals and the trade routes they inscribe. It is no longer the case that the transatlantic relationship anchors the imaginary to either side of the Atlantic Ocean. As globalism has shrunk the world, this imaginary is no longer tethered to any particular part of the ocean. It shows up here, there, and everywhere.

Slavery, once confined to the middle passage between the west coast of Africa and the United States, now reappears in narratives set in the North Atlantic. Indeed, as I am suggesting, slavery is still a feature of the lives of consumers as well as exploited cultures. Édouard Glissant, in *Poetics of Relation*, describes a circum-Atlantic history of slavery linked to today's relational cultures, including multiculturalism and hybrid cultures. What I have been saying about the fertile space of hazardous and fruitful encounter with the past via the oceanic imaginary corresponds with Glissant's recommendation that we use our literary imagination to realize the present-tense afterlife of Atlantic slavery. In Glissant's account, the particulars of Caribbean reality are recovered and patterns of relation made concrete through the act of listening and imagining. "Imagine," Glissant implores the reader, "two hundred human beings crammed into a space barely capable of containing a third of them" (1). To imaginatively board that ship in the company of those African slaves, Glissant implies, is a prerequisite to our fullest understanding of the injustice they suffered, the perils they risked, and the possibilities they encountered. Glissant's account of what I am calling the Atlantic afterlife challenges us to face present-day social problems such as those attendant on globalism with a keen awareness of how even now we might just intervene in their past causes to produce hitherto unimagined alternatives.

Glissant's heartfelt appeal to our understanding of the complexity of a relational society in terms of risk, discomfort, and even danger is a far cry from the jubilant celebration of ease and comfort with which globalism has attempted to win our hearts and minds in recent decades. Far from a triumphal story about the collapse of distance and the celebration of connectivity over difference, *Smilla* is a foreboding tale that leaves the reader with a renewed conceptual and emotional appreciation of distance between people, one that can take into account the complex and varied Atlantic frames of reference. Smilla herself can stand as an emblem of these complexities. At first we are guided by her feelings. Smilla channels the brutality of the past as told by the mysterious depths of the Atlantic Ocean. Through her we see the surroundings for what they really are, not for what they are made out to be by those who profit from our easy acceptance of globalism. What we are permitted to see via Smilla's perspective is an ocean that presents another set of coordinates for understanding its place in global capitalism. Seen in this light, the Atlantic is far from cleansing, neutral, smooth, and enabling of passage. Instead we see an ocean still festering with unbearable pain and human suffering, an ocean that stifles movement. Smilla hears on our behalf the relentlessness of its unsettling song of sorrow. Her body bears witness to this brutality when, toward the end of the novel, Smilla catches a glimpse of herself in the mirror. Then we are shown, like stigmata, the many injuries she has sustained. The description that follows is visceral and shocking, aimed at pulling the reader back into the physical world where the fragility of the body is made disturbingly real:

> There's no skin on my kneecaps. Between my hips is a wide yellowish-blue path of blood that has coagulated under the skin where Jakkelsen's marline-spike struck me. The palms of both hands have suppurating lesions that refuse to close. At the base of my skull I have a bruise like a gull's egg, and a spot where the skin is broken and contracted. (358)

The detached forensic detail used to describe the many wounds inflicted on her body is also confrontingly visceral. It underscores the pain endured by a woman who is alone and vulnerable. It also seems to serve another purpose. I think it is no exaggeration to say that this image of injured woman draws attention to the fragility of the entire terraqueous globe more generally. If we can see that the wounds she has been subjected to testify to those still not healed in victims of past capitalist ventures such as the covert expeditions to Greenland in the novel, as well as Danish colonial policy, why not also see in them the suffering of the Atlantic slave trade? Lives have been absorbed into the history of the Atlantic, largely silenced by progress and continuity. When Smilla closes her eyes desperately seeking guidance from all the sounds of the mid-ocean dock, she feels "all noise is being sucked out into the emptiness above the vast Atlantic Ocean" (327). At the same time, all that is valuable to us, including the planet and our children, remain unshielded from irreparable damage and destruction. While there are personal reasons why Smilla dreads the ocean since she lost her mother to it, the state of being motherless should nevertheless be read in the wider context of losing one's bearing of not belonging but of traditional roots and of life's prolific and multiple stories all coming to a sudden end. When on board the *Kronos*, Smilla is overwhelmed by disorientation. Perhaps she is experiencing an unadulterated dose of what we all feel in a globalized world of mass communication.

Despite Smilla's disorientation, there are grounds for hope in Hoeg's novel and in particular in Smilla's "feeling for snow." Globalization, accelerated by the World Wide Web of information technology, features multiple encounters, interactions and articulations of relations, processes, practices, and experiences. As I see it, present-day virtual flows of capital and information convene an oceanic imaginary that represents the actual afterlife of the Atlantic Ocean since both draw on metaphors of network, flows, and connectivity. In William Boelhower's introduction to *Atlantic World*, for instance, the Atlantic is described as "a tensive, exuberant, and often incommensurable space bunched, folded, striated or simply mapped according to the strategic interplay between circulation and sites" (1). The capacious possibilities afforded by this space are well matched by the global reach of the Internet's web of intersecting trajectories and influences. Nethersole notes that the "Web, like any mesh configuration, knows no centre or periphery but only nodes of (electronic) intensity and sites—not places—of accumulation and exchange. Sites that can be substituted for one another simultaneously create an ever-proliferating metonymic chain of information flows, defined by speed, not distance" (640). For these reasons, Smilla stands to fail against what appears to be an impossible adversary, despite her ability to read the deep significance of snow and ice and her other heightened sensitivities both interpretive and perceptual. Despite these obstacles, however, Smilla gains insight, intelligence, and power by listening in to her world. For Smilla, the loss of orientation through loss of her senses ("deaf, blind, and helpless" [232]) signifies the final stage of her sequestering herself from civilization. Rather than forging connections via conventional means of communication, Smilla reaches inward for an expressivity whose syntactical roots have been internalized over time.

The unsound waves that Smilla forgoes in favor of the ancestral syntax she shares with her mother are comparable to those global capitalist traces that lock individuals into a vocabulary of exploitation. What the reader is not aware of until Hoeg draws our attention to it, by lending her such terrific powers of observation, is how well-equipped she is to survive, even though she (like the rest of us) is "at sea." Far from deploring her chance of survival, it is as if Hoeg suggests that the loss of one's orientation in a world of mass communication and digital literacy opens up other possibilities for understanding the world, opportunities that habit or familiarity would render indiscernible to us. Also, related to this, Hoeg seems to be pointing toward paths of survival that do not lead to the oppression of others. Obviously, it is possible to argue that Smilla's virtuosity signifies little more than Hoeg's adherence to the conventions of his genre, after all the traditional hero or heroine of suspense narratives draws on highly idiosyncratic personal resources to overcome insurmountable obstacles. However, I have suggested at the outset of this chapter that Hoeg is offering a very nuanced account of the plight of contemporary subjects and communities in the face of global capital. In many respects it may be that Smilla's feeling for snow is a dying art, a traditional cognitive acuity that is soon to be lost to the world. Indeed, it very much resembles an endangered reading practice that may soon be extinct.

However, in my reading, Smilla's ability to "read" snow is analogous to the ability of many of us to navigate the web. Seen this way, she is not a lone survivor of a dying culture but rather someone that contemporary readers not only relate to but a hero with cognitive abilities many of us share. Nethersole notes that "Empty, undulated, and unlimited cyberspace surrounds our corporal existence with an ever-present digital membrane that separates the actual...from the virtual" (640). Another way of referring to this loss of orientation as felt by Smilla is to point toward the lack of borders and structure in our digitalized, globalized world. In her reading of the novel, Patchay reminds us of the Greenlander's advanced understanding of multiplicity and difference in the manifestations of snow that "can only be read with regard to its variation" (23). The Greenlander's perception of snow assumes no uniformity. Another example of Smilla's advantageous mindset is her remembered Inuit understanding of space as she recalls measuring journeys she took with her mother in *siniks*, the number of sleeps that a journey requires (278). This materiality of lived experience aside, what makes Smilla most equipped to tackle the rootlessness of the globalized world is the fact that as an indigenous woman she has already been severed from her roots and adapted herself to this predicament. The profound disorientation of globalism makes manifest the skills that have been latent in Smilla, such as, primarily, her ability to *feel* what rootlessness means. A question I will return to is how similar to Smilla we are as we contend with a world where any digitally mediated stability has come to resemble the fragility and fluidity of ice and snow. Through a border darkly, Smilla and her readers navigate a post-Atlantic world.

Similarly, the forces of globalism in Proulx's *The Shipping News*, however devastating and powerful, at times also point unexpectedly toward a sense of deep connectivity that paradoxically places Newfoundland with all its uniquely local qualities within the wider world. This occurs when the ferocious storm toward the end of *The Shipping News* is global in scope and scale, yet this very globalism reveals an intimate set of connections between the near and the far. Proulx imbues this wind with familial qualities, calling it an "uncle wind"

> to the Alaskan Williwaw and Ireland's wild Doinionn. Stepsister to the Koshava that assaults the Yugoslavian plains with Russian snow, the Steppenwind, and the violent Buran from the great open steppes of central Asia, the Crivetz, the frigid Viugas and Purgas of Siberia, and from the north of Russia the ferocious Myatel. A blood brother of the prairie Blizzard, the Canadian arctic screamer known simply as Northwind, and the Pittarak smoking down off Greenland's ice fields. (317–318)

The winds that reach the settlement of Killick-Claw are to be understood as related with Europe and Asia, by a mythical association as or more powerful than blood. Proulx seems to underscore that one of the peculiar effects of globalization is an increasing awareness of the world itself as a singular place, especially, as Featherstone notes, "in the sense of its fragility, its finitude and openness to irreparable damage and destruction" (175). Thus, the local in *The Shipping News* is kin to the global and meets with global concerns at the level of their own extreme vulnerability. Symbolically and literally the novel's regional focus is overruled by the forces of these global winds when the house at Quoyle's Point is simply blown away.

The novel's shift away from regional-specific concerns notwithstanding, it still remains faithful to the idea of home and a sense of belonging being fundamental to human well-being, though, as we have just seen, the idea of home in the novel undergoes considerable evolution to the point of opening on to the world. The imagistic possibilities of water and the oceanic imaginary make it possible still to imagine a sense of belonging for Quoyle and the other characters in Killick-Claw despite the defacement of place and the threats it is continually subjected to. In her reading of *The Shipping News*, Polack discusses the novel as a quest for home via the unique medium of water as that which both dissolves as well as purifies bodies. She argues that the "compensation for being pulverized by water is an openness to a range of stories for reconstituting the self, stories which facilitate homecoming" (101). Proulx's novel invites a reading of redemption as sheer survival, reminiscent of Ishmael's deliverance from drowning after the sinking of the Pequod. Water destroys, but it also purifies. Billy Pretty's nostalgic complaint against globalism for eradicating the neighborly ways of the past is worth recalling now. Newfoundland was once knit together by a "joinery of lives," he said, "smooth in places, or lumpy, but joined" (169). I think these words are also appropriate for describing what remains at the end of the novel.

In Hoeg's novel, the ship *Kronos* constitutes a smuggling operation wherein, due to Smilla's unstoppable efforts, the past crimes of the smugglers come back to haunt the present. For much of the novel the ship's cargo remains a mystery to Smilla and the crew. Apart from the three felonious individuals whose names Smilla is able to discover, the true nature of the corrupt economic forces that direct the ship's course is similarly unidentifiable. "Behind the three of them," she remarks, "is something else, something bigger, something more ruthless" (171). What this "something else" is remains unsaid, but, as I have shown, it expresses itself in practices that let us read the Atlantic slave trade within capitalism today. Smilla asks, "Hasn't Europe always tried to empty out its sewers into the colonies? Isn't the *Kronos* once more the convicts on their way to Australia, the Foreign Legion on its way to Korea?" (279) A close look at *Kronos* confirms Nandy's argument that all Western ideas of progress are "tinged by the worldview of imperialism" (54). Indeed, and as with the third force in Graham Greene's *The Quiet American* discussed in the opening chapter of this book, there is an unnamable, infinitely more powerful force that in turn fuels globalism and capitalism.

This force is symbolically visualized in Hoeg's novel as a force so powerful even First Officer Sonne, that "little piece of what's good about Denmark" (297), cannot escape its gravitational pull. Despite his "blue eyes, pink cheeks, and honourable intentions," Smilla reflects, "all around him are powerful forces: money, development, abuse, the collision of the new world with the old. And he doesn't understand what's going on. That he will only be tolerated as long as he cooperates" (298). In their reading of the novel, Poddar and Mealor point out that this "quintessential" Dane Sonne is as far away—culturally and geographically—from the metropolitan center as he possibly could be and that this, therefore, suggests that the text identifies a true and honest Denmark to be located in areas "less ravaged (or un-touched) by the forces of modernisation" (185). If, as Poddar and Mealor suggest, Sonne represents the virtues of an original and untarnished folk culture, a similar case can be made for the Captain of *Kronos*. Prior to being subjected to the forceful incentives of the most venal aspects of capitalism, the Captain used to decide the speed and the route of the journey. But now "it's the shipping companies that decide," he laments, "now it's the offices in the big cities that are sailing the ships. And *this* is what you measure time by" (310). Seamen have ceased to exist (317) and the Captain is "just a gear-box that transfers impulses to a complex machine" (315). The Captain's role on this ship is increasingly titular, perhaps even decorative.

Again, those "powerful forces" are allusively present when Smilla's survey of the ship reaches its climactic point in the engine room. Described in hyperbolical terms, the engine room is customized to fit an oversized engine that is said to be "a distillation of civilization" (283). Its force is all-powerful, yet mundane, "Something that is both taken for granted and incomprehensible" (283), of which Smilla says, "Even if I had to, I wouldn't know how to stop it. In a certain sense, maybe it can't be stopped" (283). The ship's engine is here conceived as the actual driver of trade and smuggled commerce, as well as symbolic of the immeasurably larger and ruthlessly efficient forces of Capital. Economically, they are of course linked. Since Hoeg has turned the ship upside down, corporations are represented in a different light to what they are usually, but this is not to say that Hoeg's representation is misleading. Corporations exist solely for the purpose of creating wealth. Nothing must get in their way. Hoeg's spoof on globalism includes populating *Kronos* with a whole array of petty criminals, heroin addicts, prostitutes, and other such marginalized characters living on the edge of society. I have already said that these people are slaves to capitalism. It would perhaps be more accurate to say that they are the underbelly of corporations. Hoeg's burlesque of corporate practices shows how addiction (even more than money) makes the world (of consumerism) go round, representing that which is usually hidden from view, yet without which the market could not function. The lingua franca on board *Kronos* is a hotch-potch of European languages, including a lot of slang used primarily to register threat, rumor, and innuendo, the result of desperate people of various nationalities from difficult circumstances temporarily sharing a confined space. *Kronos* might in this regard be thought of as a "contact zone," a term coined by Mary Louise Pratt (313).[5] This ship of fools comments darkly on the truism that global capital is shrinking the world. In this case, however, the result is not a global village but rather a sort of capitalist black-hole with, as we have seen, a similarly astronomical gravitational field. At times, the *Kronos* is a ludicrously condensed global corporation in its own right; at others, it is like an adventure cruise ship visiting the most extreme destinations of the world of global capital.

The market forces alluded to in Hoeg's novel are not always portrayed as sheer strength. Even as the army has evacuated the Arctic and the military colonization of Greenland has come to an end, Denmark still retains an administrative grip on its former colony, not least to secure its mineral rights (72). The novel makes it clear that if the engine represents the distillation of civilization, so does a raspberry tart, the "union of exquisitely sophisticated crowning achievements and a nervous, senselessly extravagant consumption" (142). Clearly global capitalism addresses itself effectively to all sensibilities and, according to some, including the members of the Inuit Circumpolar Council (ICC), is to all intents and purposes inescapable. The Danish version of colonialism, according to ICC, took the form of a mental dependency on the elite and a paternalistic information flow directed toward Greenland (Shadian, 118–119). The ICC was formed to assure Alaskan, Canadian, and Greenlandic Inuit participation, planning, and benefit from the drilling of oil in Arctic territory (Shadian, 203). The wish of those enslaved to consumerism ("that particularly Western mixture of greed and naiveté" [316]) is not to coerce locals, wherever they are, for greed is enough to secure their cooperation. No, what must be coerced now is "the Other, the vastness, that which surrounds human beings" (316). Enter the floating oil platforms once again. An oil rig outside of Nuuk is described in the novel as consisting of "25,000 linked metal pontoons anchored to the sea floor 700 metres below us, half a square kilometre of desolate, windblown, green-painted metal, ugly as sin, twenty sea miles from the coast" (316).

Hoeg and, especially, Proulx's novels reveal that the oceanic imaginary surfaces in today's metaphorical conjuring of flow and connectivity as an expression of digital communication networks. But if they show glimpses of possibility once afforded by the Atlantic Ocean, they also now reveal the colossal damage that is the flip side of those connections. Winchester notes that people tend to overlook the polluting traffic exerted on the Atlantic, as if, somehow, its sheer bulk and immeasurability has also disguised the "immense amount of systemic misuse" it sustains (333). The shipping industry as well as, of course, the airline industry contribute to carbon emissions that threaten the sustainability of the Atlantic Ocean as a living organism, host to a rich marine life. The ships, such as those we see in Hoeg and Proulx's novels, create low-level clouds that linger in the atmosphere for weeks and months. These are known as "ship tracks," replenished by a continuous traffic of mostly cargo ships that generally stick to preestablished routes, so-called "shipping lanes" (Winchester, 349). Both Hoeg and Proulx bear testimony to the unsound waves that linger in a post-Atlantic world attending the shift from an oceanic to an "atmospheric" (digital) transfer of goods and information. The following chapter will return to the scene of an oceanic imaginary as it haunts the present both in prescriptive and cautionary terms. I want to show how the aspects of the compression of space and time recognized by David Harvey as emblematic of postmodernity derive from early- to mid-twentieth-century developments especially affecting personal life. I then want to suggest that these more traditional "oceanic" patterns of expressivity from a time when the ocean was the main medium for imagining the transatlantic other constitute a reprise for thinking about the role of digital technology today. By looking at the contentious aftermath of Sylvia Plath and Ted Hughes's marriage, I discover practices of reading and writing that we today associate with the limits and possibilities of online communication.

# 4

# A Post-Atlantic Divorce

## Reading and Writing Ted Hughes and Sylvia Plath in the Digital Age

Amplified by their supporters and detractors, the voices of Ted Hughes and Sylvia Plath are still reverberating long after their deaths. The readings and writings that they inspire form part of an Atlantic afterlife that surfaces in the Digital Age. Plath's death left a void that has been filled with a large body of critical responses much of which overlaps with the emotional investments of devoted readers who continue to discover her prodigious talent as a poet and also identify with the pain she suffered. Fueled by cultural rivalry across the Atlantic, devotion to Plath has also generated equal measures of hostility toward Ted Hughes who is still held accountable by some for Plath's suicide in 1963. As her widower, he also became the chief editor of her estate and, therefore, responsible for the posthumous publications of her poems, letters, and journals. The story of Hughes and Plath was already a highly charged text further refracted and readable through a lens of great social upheaval and the development of personal autonomy in the 1960s and 1970s. The aftermath of Plath's suicide until the publication of *Birthday Letters* by Hughes shortly before his death in 1998 also provides an opportunity to trace the development of the Information Age in the latter half of last century.

Though their marriage and overlapping literary careers began prior to the full onset of worldwide digital communication, my contention is that Plath and Hughes's story provides suggestive guidelines for negotiating the rapidly changing relationship between private and public in the twenty-first century. We need to reflect back on the visions our culture once entertained in relation to public knowledge and writing the self. In this light, I see Hughes's vigorous written resistance to being swept up against his will in Plath's transatlantic literary afterlife showing how we might think through the intellectual and ethical responsibilities that come with the increasing public availability of private information. Digital culture in its present form is arguably historically contingent; not just a sign of greater technical power, it is also a response to the exigencies of capitalism, warfare, the Cold War, as well as the elements of abstraction, codification, self-regulation, virtualization, and, of course, programming (Gere, 18). In this chapter I want to work through the strategies for reading the themes of secrecy and visibility via the text that Plath and Hughes have become.

Reference in the title of this chapter to a "post-Atlantic divorce" is meant to draw together both the well-known straining of relations between Hughes and Plath (at the time of Plath's suicide, Hughes was having an affair with Assia Wevill, whom he later married and had a child with), as well as the unsettled relationship between writers and readers on either side of the Atlantic, most of whom were unable to remain impartial in the matter. I also want to think about the virtual existence assiduously sought by many today that echoes Sylvia Plath's desire for an existence not circumscribed by the body. Plath's desire as well as its recent digital realization is also a "divorce" from the physically and socially situated self. This resonates with what I see as a force in Hughes's poetry that seeks austere kinship with a post- or prehistoric humanity that subsists agonistically in the present, responsive to though quite apart from the familiar social world as well as from nature. Not secure or welcome in either place, this usually solitary figure is seen in the pages of *Crow Poems*, *Cave Birds*, as well as many other of Hughes's poems. Since Plath's death, it would seem that only a mutually exclusive appreciation of their work is possible. To be an admirer of Plath often means to be staunchly anti-Hughes, and vice versa (Churchwell, "Corpus," 100). Gender plays a role in this division among readers, fans, and critics. It is common to refer to the "war between the sexes," except in this case, the marriage between Plath and Hughes attracts enormous interest because, as Middlebrook asserts, the war seems more real (82). There certainly have been more casualties, as only a passing knowledge of Hughes's marriages reveals. Transatlantic cultural rivalry is also at stake. When Ted Hughes's letters were published in 2007, Elaine Showalter wondered why in the United States there was so little interest in the Poet Laureate other than as the lesser of the two poets. She asks, "Does our economy of fame condemn Hughes to live forever as merely her unfaithful, less gifted English husband, played by Daniel Craig in a dull movie?" (5). The nature of the critical division prompts the answer, yes and no. This chapter will argue that the Hughes and Plath saga certainly reprises the transatlantic divide, but in doing so, it also recalls the significance the ocean once played as that which unites and separates the old from the new. Afloat in a sea of discourse and dispute, the Plath and Hughes controversy has resurrected the ocean and situated it within what I call the "atmospheric" age of technology-mediated communication.

That the publication of Hughes's letters received a terse silence on one side of the Atlantic and an enthusiastic reception on the other testifies to the enduring afterlife of Plath as poet and cultural icon, as well as the similar endurance of the stand-off between the Hughes and Plath camps. This afterlife, begun after Plath's death, was first sustained by predigital communication chiefly in the press, including letters, as well as in journals. To my mind, even at the outset, this afterlife of the Plath–Hughes phenomenon illuminates the urgent human desire of readers and observers to express and share considered responses as well as strong or even virulent opinions about others. Soon digital technology would enable these disputes to surpass the bounds of the Atlantic, riding on a wave of powerful new forms of communication. Castells stresses that "conscious communication is the distinctive feature of human beings" the acceleration of the speed and reach of personal communication means that here is "where society has been most profoundly modified" by technological advances (Castells, Preface, xxv). Of particular interest in this regard is the most recent rise in the sharing of user-generated content that Castells refers to as "mass self-communication" (xxvii). This is growing rapidly on the back of the Internet's vast processing power "distributed in all realms of social life" (xxvii). Sylvia Plath's literary and personal fate in the hands of a highly mobile and divided transatlantic community of readers reveals something about the entanglements of life and the written word in the modern world that were just beginning to increase shortly after her death.

Needless to say, there were international scandals before this, but the Hughes–Plath story is of particular interest because it involves a rupture within an international group of professional readers and writers that can be read as a prototype for later, digitally mediated clashes. The postmodern world, as famously noted by David Harvey, can first and foremost be understood in terms of speed; specifically it is marked by an acceleration of the speed at which capital moves about the world (*Postmodernity*, 230). Harvey notes how the production, exchange, and circulation of capital now occurs at an increasing rate, which results in what he refers to as time–space compression (229).

The idea suggests a novel way of conceptualizing the impact of economic aspects of communication technology on spatiality and geography, which in turn lends precision and timeliness to our understanding of the more familiar notion of a shrinking world. A similar, obvious connection exists between, on one hand, the mobility of readers and, on the other, the production, exchange, and circulation of text. What is perhaps less obvious is that it is this narrative connection between the production and reception of text that paved the way for strategies of reading that are conducive to the way we write ourselves or imagine writing ourselves via social media today. This chapter takes the Plath and Hughes story as a myth of origin for the overlapping voices and competing territories now seen in the Information Age. The shouting for textual authority that emerged in the aftermath of Plath's death is an early indicator of the kind of writing and reading that leaves multiple and fragmented traces on the Internet via social media today. Today's virtual rooms comprise information that is "fluid, virtual, simultaneously gathered and dispersed" (Lévy, xv). The reason for this dispersion of information is that the boundary between writers and readers has largely collapsed.

De Certeau distinguishes between writers and readers in terms of their spatial conditions. Writers, he argues, are "founders of their own place . . . diggers of wells and builders of houses," whereas readers are travelers, moving "across lands belonging to someone else, like nomads poaching their way across fields they did not write" (174). Some of Hughes's poems stage a similar blurring between the writer and the reader as a reversal between nature and culture. In "The Thought Fox" (*Hawk*, 15), the observer of the fox finds a blank page filled with print toward the end of the poem, as if the subject of his observation has left readable paw prints on the page. De Certeau also imagines worlds in the making, created by writers, made available for readers to cross as nomads or, perhaps slightly less eloquently, as tourists on a temporary visa. Far from being passive denizens of this textual land, however, de Certeau describes the reader's role as being one of invention and juxtaposition: the reader "invents in texts something different from what [the authors] 'intended' [and] combines their fragments" (169). We see thus in the literary reception of Plath and Hughes that readers recreate the poets' posthumous existence in textual sites similar to the way groups of settlers inhabit and contest a new territory. Today the word "site" has a virtual, web-based sense beyond de Certeau's meaning. As such, the afterlife of Hughes and Plath even at the outset as a contested space of readers and observers' responses constituted an early analogue of the Information Age in which the distinction between writing and reading is far more smeared.

The list of visitors to this Plath and Hughes site is enormous, far too long to attempt to list here. What many have in common is that often they begin their chapters and their books with the caveat that they will not write about the personal lives of Sylvia Plath and Ted Hughes. Despite these intentions, many end up doing precisely the opposite, speculating on the inner lives of their subjects with the authority of someone on intimate terms with both poets. In her now infamous book *The Haunting of Sylvia Plath*, Jacqueline Rose adopts this approach. "I am never talking of real people," she assures her readers early on, "but of textual entities" (Rose, 5).[1] Yet, her interpretation of Plath's poetry does venture to speak of Plath herself and her relationship with Hughes and skates very close at times to being a psychoanalytical reading of their psychic lives. How could her subject then not be the people themselves as real? Others, such as Dianne Middlebrook, Terry Gifford, Neil Roberts, and Elaine Feinstein, attempt to recreate the Plath and Hughes literary and biographical topography in the interest of delivering an actual and historical account of the poets' lives. There cannot, of course, be a singular narrative or truth of Plath and Hughes's marriage and literary partnership, especially not in an age when fact and fiction are increasingly blurred. What emerges instead are multiple terrains that subsequent readers may selectively draw on in order to confabulate, via a reading that has the properties de Certeau associated with writing, a settlement of their own on the site of Plath–Hughes. While the Plath and Hughes dispute for many might originally have been about the attribution of culpability to a morally fallible husband, it has since grown exponentially more complex. Amplified by digital technology, the ambit navigated by writers and readers now offers multiple platforms for supporters and critics of Hughes to voice their views on Hughes's professional and personal conduct after Plath's death.

Such spreading of the territory in question challenges de Certeau's notion of writers as sedentary builders and readers as itinerant nomads since the sheer magnitude and mode of construction of the territory crossed is far more complex than what de Certeau could have imagined. Since the proliferation of technology-mediated discourse, every form of consumption on the Internet becomes a form of survey in the form of a provisional territory or encampment of true believers and dissenters even if believers are merely counted as having clicked on the thumbs-up icon. Clusters of views and counterviews have been mushrooming since Plath's death, and no one, least of all Ted Hughes himself, could control the proliferation of gossip, interpretations, hearsay, and so on. One gets a sense of Hughes's powerlessness from the numerous letters written by him, such as this excerpt from a letter to Gerald and Joan Hughes written in 1963: "All I've ever been interested in is simplifying my existence so that I could write, & all I've ever done is so involve myself with other people that now I can't move without horrible consequences of all kind, on all sides" (Reid, 221). The overlapping, largely hostile discourses proved too much even for someone with Hughes's command of language to withstand. Whoever shouts the loudest ended up ruling this disputed textual territory, even if only for a time, and what had become of the aftermath of Plath and Hughes's encounter that Hughes called the "Plath Fantasia" (554).

Lyotard sheds light on this antagonistic relationship between authors and readers across vast, temporal, and spatial distances. He intensifies and makes more complex de Certeau's account of a written topography through the notion of telegraphic culture. By this he means, literally, "writing at a distance" referring specifically to the way in which technology expands the territory created by writers and, in the same gesture, "removes the close contexts of which rooted cultures are woven" (*The Inhuman*, 50). Fueled by the desires and the reach of the Information Age, territorial disputes are erupting (still) between readers and writers who are continuing to invest in the Plath and Hughes saga. Making more complex the distinction between authors and readers, Ted Hughes was opposed to being made the textual subject of writings about Sylvia Plath. In a sense he insisted on being her author, as Churchwell argues ("Corpus," 100).[2] Hughes's insistence on editorial authority over Plath has been severely criticized, as has his resistance to joining the dispute or to defending the role he played in her life. In a letter to the editor of the *Guardian*, Hughes angrily wrote, "my refusal to have anything to do with the Plath Fantasia has been regarded as an attempt to suppress Free Speech" (Reid, 554). In letters to friends and family, he has candidly expressed his growing paranoia about his own response to this "Plath Fantasia." In a letter to Lucas Myers written in 1987, Hughes summarizes decades of scrutiny to which he has been subject, saying his responses and comments have been "magnified, amplified, spectrally analysed & crazily polemicised in the auditoriums & laboratories & court-houses of the U.S. National Plath Investigations Committee & Patriotic Publications Inc" (Reid, 535). Here, Hughes captures well the sense of being ambushed and beleaguered by a many-voiced adversary that claims the kind of authority that Senator McCarthy assumed during the House Un-American Activities witch hunts of the 1950s.

Indeed, the Plath and Hughes story begins at a point in history when a conservative and repressive 1950s' America is in the grip of the Cold War. This is also the context of a literary and cultural shift in the poetics of expressions of self that inaugurates the concept of "personal life." At the same time, an equally powerful force for the institutionalization of psychoanalysis sought a formal and medically recognized means to both promote and control this new private life. There are thus two forces at play here, one facilitating the autonomy of self and one that seeks to constrain it. A look into the women's magazines of the time sheds light on these contradictory forces at play in 1950s' America. They exalted domesticity all the while exhorting readers to pursue careers and independence (Walker, 208). Plath, and many women like her, was caught in a dilemma that found expression in her early writing. Plath's first and only novel, *The Bell Jar*, portrays a woman enjoying the outgoing life of someone who is living out her public existence while still submitting to a hidden life of someone paralyzed by the controlling forces of convention and tradition. Plath wrote *The Bell Jar* under a pseudonym in 1963 at a time in her life when she was, like her protagonist in the novel, leading the glamorous life of an intern at a prominent Ladies' Magazine (*Mademoiselle*). Plath uses the voice of Esther Greenwood to express feelings of depression, but she also summarizes something of the contemporary zeitgeist. America at this time was reeling from what Matthews calls "a massive dislocation" following the Depression, the rise of fascism, and the aftermath of the War (344). Through the theorization of the unconscious and sexuality, Freud had authorized the celebration of a "unique, idiosyncratic interiority that could never be fully aligned with the shared public culture" (Zaretsky, 379–380). Psychoanalysis, and Freud's work especially, paved the way for thinking about personal identity as something unique and mysterious, utterly distinct from social roles such as the place assigned in the family or the work place.

This development of a strong distinction between a publicly constrained exterior and a liberated private interior prepared the way for the programmatic freedom of expression found in technologically mediated communication today. Hand in hand with this development of interior richness, as already mentioned, there was also a growing expectation to conform to societal standards. It was expected that women especially had to conform to certain publicly held norms. Failure to conform, Macpherson argues, was considered a form of sickness, and there was a rush to seek diagnosis or diagnose oneself as a form of self-policing in line with the standards of 1950s' America (3). Plath's

*The Bell Jar* is informed by both the fear of diagnosis as well as the urge to self-monitor. Her protagonist Esther suffers from disillusionment and a spirit of rebellion, but is unable to articulate these feelings other than as symptoms of her nervous breakdown (Macpherson, 38). Interdicted by powerful internal and external forces, the body itself becomes readable. Its symptoms in the novel are articulated already on the first page as Esther identifies with the fate of the Rosenbergs, convicted of treason and awaiting their execution on death row. Her morbid identification with the victims of McCarthyism in its crusade against communism masks a more personal anxiety about her own containment within a patriarchal society that insists on objectifying her as a woman, a realization that grows on her during her time as an intern at the fashion magazine. Ester's inability to speak out about these concerns with her peers reflects the way many women, including Plath herself, kept their interiority hidden from the public gaze. Effectively treated as a second-class citizen because of her gender, Esther discovers what this lack of a dialogue or rapport between her innermost existence and others means in terms of being and becoming herself. Her condition overlaps with the Althussarian problematic of interpellation. This occurs when powerful interests (institutional, political, economic, corporate, etc.) discursively address subjects in ways that forcefully exploit their desires, desires which are themselves also created and installed in subjects by the same discursive means. In this way subjects are understood as called by social symbolic forces into positions of conformity to agendas originating from outside. Seyla Benhabib discusses the operation of this discursive push and pull within "webs of interlocution and narrative," and in her terms, at its most pragmatic level, Ester's difficulty plays out at the level of knowing, or in her case not knowing, "how to answer when one is addressed and to know how to address others" (Benhabib, *Culture*, 15). This succinct account rather pointedly indicates that, as well as imposing the conditions of an address, the symbolic network also provides avenues of response to that address which, I suggest, are also potential sites for agency.

*The Bell Jar* contains images of self-presentation that are vividly conceived, many evoking cinematic effects. For example, in a social situation Esther feels herself "getting smaller and smaller" (Plath, *Bell Jar*, 17), the description calls up the sense of a movie camera being dollied away from a scene, or else zooming out.[3] Elsewhere the cinematic technique of the fade dominates the imagery as when Esther, enjoying a favorite moment in the bathtub, feels the rest of the world dissolving and fading out of view (21). At an extreme stage of her alienation, Esther becomes the "skin shed by a terrible animal," and though relieved to have escaped the animal, she is distraught that it has taken her spirit with it (107). Finally, Esther loses the will to live and this too is expressed in a terrifying image of zooming out, seeing "day after day glaring ahead of me like a white, broad, infinitely desolate avenue" (135). The novel's ending, however, stages a sudden turnaround from this alienation. Instead of expressing defeat through distance and a departure from the company of others, Esther identifies a sign of recovery in herself in the way she turns toward others in order to address them. The final sentence of the novel sees her stepping into the world, not away from it. Ultimately, this will enable her departure from the mental institution where she has been confined under the care of the maternal Dr Nolan: "The eyes and the faces all turned themselves toward me, and guiding myself by them, as by a magical thread, I stepped into the room" (258). A similar stepping into relation with the outside can be seen in bouts of extreme productivity in the life of the author herself. However, until the immensely prolific period of writing toward the end of her life, a creative outlet that saw the birth of poems such as "Daddy" and "Lady Lazarus," Plath's private thoughts were often confined to the pages of her diary, letters, and unpublished poems and stories.

In her foreword to the collection of Sylvia's *Letters Home*, Aurelia Plath closes with a few excerpts from her daughter's diary of 1949, when Sylvia was 17 years old. These pages convey an ambiguity regarding the relationship between the self and the public. On one hand, Plath expresses the desire to stand apart from the crowd and "to be an observer . . . to be omniscient" (*Letters*, 40). This observer figure questing after knowledge beyond the confines of the life defined for a postwar American teenager never really fit in with the social situation on either side of the Atlantic. This figure recalls Hannah Arendt's notion of the pariah. When Arendt writes about such individuals, she is primarily referring to the Jew, for example in texts such as *Rahel Varnhagen: The Life of a Jewish Woman* and elsewhere. The critical distance from circumstances and social setting available to the pariah has much in common with the storyteller, the poet, and the refugee. Michael Jackson understands Arendt's outsiders as transgressive figures able to breach conventional social boundaries and therefore possessing a greater capacity to observe the society from which they are ostracized (256). There is no doubt that the story Plath tells via her alter ego Esther in *The Bell Jar* is one of being an outsider and not fitting in. For all that, though, she identifies all too easily with specific oppressed others, such as the Rosenbergs destined for the electric chair. She lacks what Jackson refers to, citing Lisa Jane Disch, as the "visiting imagination" of the pariah, having "neither an objective standpoint (the pariah does not seek disinterestedness or distance from the other), nor an empathic one (the pariah is not interested in losing himself in the other)" (257). The pariah thus puts himself or herself in the place of a series of others and the "result is neither a detached knowledge of another's world nor an empathic blending with another's worldview" (257). Rather it is an "*impartial* understanding attained through storytelling" (257) conditioned by the impossibility of endorsing any one perspective, which is to say, by the condition of being an outsider.

I mentioned at the outset that Plath wished to get beyond the limits of her cultural setting; it was another reason for using the word "divorce" in the title of this chapter. Plath's wish "to be omniscient" is doubtlessly rooted in the equally strong fear of never being able to exist outside of a socially and physically circumscribed self. Seen in the light of Jackson's notion of the untethered, nonaligned storytelling imagination, this is ultimately a collapse of representational distance or a failure to escape the constraints of her own body and selfhood: "Yet if I were not in this body, where *would* I be—perhaps I am *destined* to be classified and qualified. But, oh, I cry out against it" (Plath, *Letters*, 40). Plath's burning question "where *would* I be" (if I were not in the body of an American teenage girl) haunts us still. It would seem that the Digital Age has come to our rescue if not Plath's. As though in answer to questions such as hers from two generations back, Castells notes that twenty-first-century "technologies, devices, and applications...support the proliferation of social spaces on the Internet," which, if they do not soothe away all sense of isolation (*Network Society*, 387), do permit users to engage in "avatar interaction in three-dimensional virtual spaces" (Preface, xxvii). Castells is cautious about the benefits of social interaction online. He points out that while allowing "an egalitarian pattern of interaction where social characteristics are less influential in framing...communication" we must not overlook the fact that it is "particularly suited to the development of multiple weak ties" (Castells, *Network Society*, 388).

To have dared ask where else one could be in Plath's times, on the other hand, would have seemed unrealistic and for someone of an earlier generation, such as Plath's mother, unheard of. "I was totally imbued with the desire to be a good wife and mother," declares Aurelia Plath of how she saw her options as a woman and mother around the time Sylvia was born in 1932 (*Letters*, 11). The difference in the tone of writing between a daughter's detachment from and her mother's attachment to the conditions of her existence could not be more striking! Plath's ideal for herself can largely be attributed to the neo-Freudianism of the early 1950s and the growth of a domestic ideology that included a greater emphasis on romance, excitement, leisure, consumerism, and sexuality (May, 573). It is in this context that readers must understand the mutinous nature of Plath's vision of herself in an alternative place to the one expected of her as a future wife and mother. The notion that womanhood could ever boil down to a matter of choice would have appeared baffling to a woman of Aurelia Plath's generation whose future was already defined on the basis of her gender.

At the same time, what Aurelia Plath's generation had that Sylvia Plath's lacked was a strong, albeit socially restricted, sense of purpose. Women of Aurelia Plath's generation dared not share their daughters' dreams of an autonomous self as separate from the domestic sphere. As well as that the Cold War, during which Plath came of age, contributed to a general feeling of deep insecurity. The fear of being unprepared, and of not being able to handle the outside as described by Plath in *The Bell Jar*, afflicted many, and it was a fear exacerbated by the spiraling nuclear arms race. Zaretsky argues that the rise of twentieth-century capitalism also contributed to an inner life that increasingly "reverberates with the voices of others, the imperatives of social production" (76). Aurelia Plath's generation had secured a sense of self-worth based on the family unit as inextricably linked to private property. Halfway into the twentieth century, Zaretsky argues, our "lives and social capabilities" took the place of property, which was further supplanted by "our dreams, our desires, our fears, our sense of ourselves" (76). Instead of property, what emerges "on a mass scale" is the notion "of human relations, and human beings, as an end in themselves" (76). Zaretsky warns that such a view cannot in itself be the foundation for a transformation of society since a new society would have to be organized around new modes of production and labor (77). If so we can perhaps understand the contribution of Sylvia Plath and other women to this social change via their productive labor on new literary forms reflective of this turning away from property and toward self.

Whereas Plath found no real answer to the question of where she could be if she "were not in this body," women today are far more likely to escape the sociocultural conditioning of their private selves and find themselves a speaking position that is not circumscribed by the body. Today online avatars can be devised and made to inhabit virtual spaces purpose-built for all manner of interactions with similarly configured others, attendant as they are on the discovery of the multiple ways of being ourselves. What I want to stress is that this reaching far beyond ourselves is unexpectedly consistent with Jackson's account of the pariah who seeks "neither a detached knowledge of another's world nor an empathic blending with another's worldview" (257), though now it can be located within a global oceanic reimagined within the context of digital technology for post-Atlantic times. I need to adapt and modify the notion of the pariah to accommodate the notion of the literary outsider, with the overlapping themes of secrecy and visibility that jostle with one another in my reading of Sylvia Plath and Ted Hughes's afterlife. These themes are explored by the poets themselves, especially in Sylvia Plath's early work and in the writing as well as the reception of Ted Hughes's *Birthday Letters*. Before I move on to a closer reading of the afterlife of their work, let me add to Plath's diary excerpt and *The Bell Jar* a further fictional example of the difficulty of addressing another or the world. Doris Lessing's story "To Room Nineteen," popular in feminist discourse, also lends itself to a slightly different critical inquiry. My focus is slightly less on the gender problematics presented in the story and more on the aspect of encountering and addressing that which lies beyond the self. The story reveals the now familiar blurring of traditional boundaries, painfully overcome by Esther at the end of *The Bell Jar*, between public and private, visibility and invisibility. Lessing's story brings further nuance to a theoretical discussion of the private that chimes with the concerns of digital visibility prevalent in today's society. Specifically, I find in this story the basis for a discussion regarding narrative as something which is encrypted and secret and information as open and effortlessly assimilable in the Plath and Hughes text.

In Lessing's story, a woman comes to the realization that once her children are going to school they are off her hands and at that point there is nothing else for her to do, no inner life to preoccupy her thoughts and dreams. At first Susan Rawlings believes now she has all the time to use as she pleases, but left in her home she discovers nothing remains that pleases her once relieved of her household duties. The solution that she hits on is a total annihilation of her new self and the freedom that comes with anonymity. To this end she rents a dingy hotel room for three days a week between 10 am and 5 pm where she finds relief from the role that comes from being a mother and a wife. Room number 19 allows Susan a place where she can walk out on her own life. As she abandons the role of mother and wife, even temporarily, she exits the symbolic order, that notorious network of interlocution through which she feels called to conform. However, recall that

Benhabib's nuanced summation of the force of interlocution includes the option to speak back to its address. In seeking fully to absent herself from where she is called to conform to societal expectations, Susan is also sacrificing her own chance to publicly announce herself as reshaping the new form of her life. Susan's removal of herself from the domestic and the familiar, to occupy a rented hotel room under a false name, comes to signify the end of any further possibility of encountering others or discovering herself via others. Susan turns to room number 19 as a place where she can conceal herself and encounter from a distance the men and women who pass her window (376). Susan is almost a pariah, but lacking the power to speak back to the other from across the distance she sets up. Once her secret is discovered by a detective hired by her husband, Susanne is cornered. While her suicide places her literally beyond the reach of any social demand to conform, it also forecloses on her chance to declare herself as refusing that call and perhaps herself making a forceful call of her own to other women in the same position.

The capacity to sever or in any way overcome one's connection with subjective confinement, even if only by virtual means, is commonly available in the Digital Age to an extent Plath and her contemporaries could only have imagined, if at all. Since the development of the Information Age, digital technology has given us the ability to walk out on ourselves and, in effect, divorce what we feel to be limiting conditions of subjectivity. While Castells notes in 2001 the weakness of online ties, he also admits that in times of "rapid individualization and civic disengagement" these do still constitute a real expansion of communication options (*Network Society*, 388). When we engage with others online, we separate ourselves from our place-based identity and with it the social constraints addressed to us there. Online spaces free users to inhabit multiple roles. Advances in communication technology have also seen greater fragmentation, dislocation, and anxieties about identity and belonging. Lima notes that because of its ability to decentralize and democratize, online communication has contributed to a radical shift in the stratification of society (61). Lash cautions that for community to survive there must also be recognition that "presupposes not just blind alterity but understanding, a certain kind of intersubjectivity, and some sort of shared tradition" (252). It is too easy to posit the pariah figure as an ideal, and in her discussion of Arendt's notion of the pariah, Benhabib takes a moderate stand on the freedoms available to us in opposing culturally imposed norms. While she notes that "socialization and acculturation do not determine an individual's life story," she also warns against "the risk of becoming an outcast or a convert, a marginal figure or a deserter of the tribe" ("The Pariah," 15). Certainly *The Bell Jar* shows the tragic and futile consequences of being an outsider, divorced from a sense of place and belonging. When Plath moved to England on a Fulbright Scholarship to study literature at Cambridge University, she took on the role of an American abroad. Shortly after her arrival at Cambridge in 1956, she met Ted Hughes. Scholars such as Janet Malcolm, Anne Sexton, Linda Wagner-Martin, and others have noted the profound cultural shock that Plath would have suffered among the English literati (Malcolm, 73–75). Malcolm argues that Plath "did not write—and could not have written—*The Bell Jar* or *Ariel* in her native Massachusetts" (53). A transatlantic move, especially at a time when such a relocation was rare, signifies a new beginning, one that allowed Plath to shed parts of her identity that she no longer felt to be true, and the move offered her the chance to experiment with new creative options for herself and her writing.

Hughes also experienced his own break with the familiar when he crossed the Atlantic with his American wife for the first time in 1957, a year after they had met. At the time Hughes's attitudes toward the United States were decidedly conflicted. His introduction to the United States came through his relationship with Plath, and through her he became acquainted with a wide tradition of American literature and poetry that helped fuel his own creativity (Gill, 62). Hughes especially admired American postwar writing, and his admiration was to be reciprocated when American periodicals and poetry competition organizers awarded him prizes for poems that were later to become part of his 1957 debut collection of poetry, *The Hawk in the Rain.*[4] Nevertheless, although invited to read at respected American venues, Hughes very rarely accepted (Feinstein, 76, 187) and he often spoke disparagingly of American culture. This did not mean, however, that he identified strongly with British culture. Despite being honored with the title of Poet Laureate, Ted Hughes was not a typical British gentleman. His strong affiliation with the working class and, later in his career, a strong interest in environmental issues set him apart. Hughes's outsider status intensified as a result of the controversy that surrounded him since Plath's suicide and until the end of his life, especially culminating in the publication of *Birthday Letters.* In many respects, this collection of poems steadfastly refuses to satisfy the curiosity of readers wanting more information on the marriage and Plath's suicide. Indeed, poems in the collection often follow a tradition Hughes began with his Crow poems in which human concerns are situated within a defamiliarized, mythic, or prehistoric landscape.

Hughes's public life was one compromised by a series of scandals, and, I argue below, the poems in *Birthday Letters*, as well as in *Crow*, testify to Hughes's resistance to being dragged into debates regarding his private life.

We have seen how Plath in her novel *The Bell Jar* examines personal identity under erasure from societal pressures. While the novel ends on an optimistic note for the protagonist who regains the means to be heard, Plath herself died alone and alienated on the other side of the Atlantic. Writing about the "enigma" that is Sylvia Plath, Malcolm clearly states that it is her transformation from a "housewify little woman of America" to a poet "thin and white in Europe, who wrote poems like 'Lady Lazarus' and 'Daddy'" that is "at the heart of the nervous urgency that drives the Plath biographical enterprise, and of the hold that the Plath legend continues to exert on our imaginations" (66). For English poet and critic Al Alvarez, suicide is "central to contemporary writing" and it is this that continues to fascinate Plath's readers (xiii). Insofar as he refers to the notion of a disembodied poetry, Alvarez is surely correct since Plath's continuing ability to haunt her readers is doubtless because something of herself is felt to move in her writing more freely as a result of her physical absence. Similarly, Banita finds in Plath a tension between, on one hand, "the blistering friction of the voice" and, on the other, "the false self that houses it" that lends the poetry its immediate effect (42–43). Wishing to divorce from her self, "the torment caused by the inability of the speaker to define her identity raises the intensity and necessity of these impersonations," as Banita argues (42). Multiple avatars of Plath's own invention now circulate among her readers via her poetry for Plath's text is now more than ever an exercise in role-playing and the virtuality of identity that seems uncannily to have anticipated the expressive opportunities the Digital Age would bring to writers and their readers.

In her investigation of what she calls the Plath "shrines" on the Internet, Banita describes the phenomenon of fan-based Plathian poetry to be a journey reprising Plath's own "elusive foray into a pacifying emptiness" (46, 48). I take her comments to be diagnostic of a certain mood prevalent in today's Digital Age more generally. The transatlantic contrasts that once helped define the relationship between self vis-à-vis other seem literally to have no place any more. Nevertheless, web-based encounters that now blur the boundaries between self and other, reader and writer, take place in an oceanic imaginary, though now it is facilitated via digital technology. Room number 19 to which Susan fatally retreats in Lessing's story now threatens to become everyone's virtual spare room. The virtual Plath shrines are an example of such rooms that nourish readers' desires and appetites for an elusive subject without allowing for the need for challenging encounters with the other. To seek omniscience, divorced from one's body, is now widely available to many; all it takes is a broadband connection. Put in another way, the Atlantic is everywhere in the form of its virtual afterlives. Indeed, the Internet has been likened to large oceans (Eriksen, 105). The Plath site invites participants to become like messages floating in bottles adrift in the ocean. When Bayleye and Brain remark that Plath has become simultaneously visible and hidden and therefore an "insoluble mystery" to her readers (7), I take this to be a consequence of the virtualization of her text and the subsequent blurring of readers and writers. Instead of affirming the singularity of her existence, the many voices that make up the Plath site have contributed to the erasure of her identity. Banita's realization that the Plath Internet shrines are forays into "pacifying emptiness" also comes with the argument that "Sylvia Plath as such does not exist" and that "it is through invention and fabrication that she comes alive" (46, 40).

This is the prototype for the peculiar mixture of effusive online creativity coupled with personal anonymity that has become common in expressions of subjectivity in digital media today. Sylvia Plath has become a mirror image for whoever is blinded by her open and confessional style of expressivity only to, as Banita notes, "prove the imprecision of reflection and the ethical responsibility of confronting otherness in its painful specularity" (43). Also Egeland notes that Plath's popularity is a corollary of today's insatiable demand "for authenticity and personality, for what is 'real' and 'true'—qualities made so important in a mediatized world characterized by the reification of individuals" (43). The paradox of the secretive yet visible Plath noted in these examples points to the particular predicament of Plath and Hughes's celebrity status and it is as such that their story serves as an early analogue of today's virtual room. The controversy attached to their story comes from the enormous variation in their public ratings in terms of their gender, their poetry, and, perhaps above all, their cultures. The notion that Plath's transformation from a "housewify" American woman to a poet "thin and white" in Europe is at the heart of her hold on readers' imaginations (Malcolm, 66) becomes more credible when we consider how the transatlantic differences between Hughes and Plath continue to shape their textual afterlife. To what extent can fan-based virtual communities such as the ones dedicated to the life and poetry of Sylvia Plath resist the bland "echo chamber" effect of self-selected online content that communication theorist Hassan sees as an increasing feature of the Information Age (205, 211–212)? What Banita identifies as "pacifying emptiness" (46), Hassan sees as an acceleration "towards destinations unknown, to an existential emptiness, where the past and its lessons rapidly disappear and the future is a permanently dark horizon" (223).

Plath's desire to be omniscient and divorced from her body led to an erasure of identity where she, her life, and her poetry have now become the destinations of the multiple desires and appetites that frequent the virtual rooms set up in her honor. Ultimately, what Hannah Arendt so admires in Rahel Varnhagen is her ability to transform her outsider status "from being a source of weakness and marginality into one of strength and defiance" (Benhabib, "Pariah," 11). A fictional attempt to do precisely this can be found in Plath's *The Bell Jar*. In addition, though her poetry often falls under the banner of confessional women's poetry, there are good grounds for reading her work as in fact "radically engaged in historicity" (Wolosky, 126).[5] In this vein, Jonnes reads Plath's poem "The Colossus" advocating a "primal lawlessness" giving expression to an oppositional youth culture whose poetry rebels against patriarchy (144). Readings such as these that look in Plath's poetry for the ways in which it intersects with public culture, reflecting the discontents of a 1950s' America, for instance, are valid, provided they do not overlook the reality of Plath's predicament. In real life, Plath's attempt to escape 1950s' programming of American womanhood ultimately failed. As an outcast, she was victimized, alone, and caught under the bell jar. In his reading of Plath's "The Rival," Ellis argues that Plath's poems contain images of letter writing as a conversation that she had with herself rather than with other people (23). Similarly, Van Dyne returns to the destabilizing effect of words on the self in Plath's poetry. In her reading of "Words," Van Dyne sees the flow of language imaged as "sap" that "Wells like tears" in the process of rupturing the poet's autonomy and authority (178). In this poem, words are the audible result of the axe blows made to trees, the sounds of wood ringing that seem to flee the scene of sap-spilling violence like the echoes of spooked horses. Later, the speaker in this poem encounters these fugitive sounds, with an image that could just be turned to remark what becomes of utterance detached from place and person, as it often is in the Information Age: "Words dry and riderless" are what these "indefatigable hoof-taps" have become (*Ariel*, 86).

Plath's wish to be other than the sum total of her experience as an embodied human being epitomizes a crisis now felt by many, caught in the Net, as Castells refers to it. Indeed, Castells claims that in the present day "*societies are increasingly structured around a bipolar opposition between the Net and the self*" (*Network Society*, 3; emphasis original). By the Net, he is referring to the interwoven net of information for which individuals often figure as mere data. Despite the attractions to high-speed information and access to an ever-widening circle of social bonds, however "weak" they may be, no one wants to be programmed and caught like an insect in the spider web of the Information Age, a veritable contemporary "bell jar." Perhaps, as Arendt maintains, our pariah status is our only real means of resistance. In what remains I want to explore the ways in which Hughes's own poetics can be read as expressing the voice of the pariah. Navigating the borderline between private and public, mundane death and the improbable triumph of life, Hughes's poetry is populated with quasimythical creatures (such as Crow) to reveal humanity as exiled from, even spat out or excreted from nature, surviving on its wits. Hughes's poetry frequently stages a blackly comic struggle between socialized ideals, of men or his gods, and the pull toward an animal destiny often couched in explicitly mythic terms. I wonder to what extent the story of the conflicting claims of the individual and the powerful sway of the Net can be read as a reprise of this visceral struggle? I suspect that the dizzying, mathematically sublime prospects offered to users of the World Wide Web have parallels with the vast temporal scope of the prehistoric settings or mythic timelessness of many of the poems. Hughes manages to couple his particular sublime with an earthy eroticism in "Low Water" from *River* in which the "river is a beautiful idle woman" who "eyes you steadily from the beginning of the world" (88). The individual is cast aside, insignificant, were it not for the fact that his own (presumably masculine) sexuality is engaged in mute dialogue with the ancient and gravid meanderings of the River.

The sublime is there also in the violent encounters found in Hughes's work, when an overwhelming inhospitality to individual life, which may simply be sublime indifference, meets with a surprising and granular resistance. Like a blackly comic pariah, the figure of Crow in *Crow: From the Life and Songs of the Crow* haunts a landscape as bare of hope as anything Beckett imagined. There Crow repeatedly demonstrates a grim defiance of the odds against him (13) without ever attaining the sanctuary of a secure moral advantage over his conditions. Similar moments occur in *Cave Birds: An Alchemical Cave Drama* when insight is extracted from poetic virtuosity in the teeth of the appalling inexorability of death and judgment. Bentley remarks of the poems in *Crow* that they are told in a voice that belongs to an individual "on an escape route from a social and cultural system that is felt to be unable to contain the self" (38). This accords to some extent with my contention that the poems voice a pariah's perspective, but I cannot concur with Bentley's suggestion that Crow stands for backing down from the challenge. Bentley reads "Crow's Account of the Battle" as a window into alienation of the most traumatic kind, one that registers the "*intractable* nature of the site of pain" (38; emphasis original). In "Crow Tries the Media," we see the futile battle against a discursive mass media that transforms every song into a commodified item (46). Bentley sees symptoms of severe depression here, with justification, for by 1970 when *Crow* appeared the poet had lost two wives by suicide. At the same time, possibly as a result of Hughes's own suffering, the poetic expression of Crow amounts to a forceful and eloquent denouncement of the public misuse of language. Despite the hopelessness of the situation (after all, how do we communicate without words?), the poem expresses defiance.

Almost the entirety of the short poem "Examination at the Womb-door" is in the form of an incantatory call and response designed to establish the triumph of death over all that is humanly worthwhile. The poem establishes a liturgical rhythm in which death is the name of a dark god to whom the examinee must submit before he is allowed to be born. Death in this poem constitutes an impasse of sublime proportion, the poem itself being just a sample of an endless litany of death's strengths and achievements. As well, the poem is a blackly comic joke at death's expense, and when the punch line comes it never fails to surprise. I suspect this is simply because everything said in the poem of death is true, and so with death being no joke, to joke is sublime. "But who is stronger than death?" comes the final question like the last hammer blows on the last nail in a coffin. "Me, evidently" counters Crow, who is then allowed to be born (15). The Crow is a riposte to any existing structural principle that would refuse to allow for his very existence as an exception to its rule; Crow thereby becomes another, rebellious structuring principle. At times, Crow is allied with the speaker of the poem, but more often than not, Crow is bent on following mutinous ends of his own, a trickster aiding and abetting the folly of mankind.

With the publication of *Crow*, Hughes was accused of nihilism and of being antihuman (Bentley, 27), and it is not hard to see why. However, I want to read Hughes's poems as invoking creation myths wherein life and human life emerge with a triumph that draws status from the vast scale of the cosmological and prehistoric cycles in which they emerge. Steeped in this deep time, there are poems in *Crow*,

*Cave Birds*, and also in *River* that invite the reader to situate human existence as a remarkable intervention within a larger, perennial context. There is also in this a sublimity in Hughes's work, since the stake of life increases in scale when seen juxtaposed with the temporal immensity from which it emerges with vanishingly small likelihood of ever having happened at all. As such, the interjection of any life, however brief it may be, attains pariah status as a mutinous refusal of the terms laid down by death. Rather than portraying lives nihilistically crushed by the tragedies of his time, Hughes's poetry allows readers to consider humanity as an achievement prehistoricized as it were and rebelling against annihilation. Immunity to time is what interests Hughes in "The Knight" from *Cave Birds.* As insects pick over the carcass of a dead cockerel in this poem, slowly uncovering all of the bird's skeleton, the poem becomes a eulogy to life's tenacity as well as of the capacity actively to die. Hughes adopts the conceit of nobility to praise the ceremonious formality of the bird's remains as though they are themselves a literature worthy of the name of scripture: "His spine survives its religion, / The texts moulder— / The quaint courtly language / Of wingbones and talons" (28). This poem celebrates the pure power of metaphor and narrative.

*Cave Birds* is strikingly illustrated with ink drawings by Leonard Baskin, the American sculptor and printmaker who was a lifelong friend of Plath and Hughes since he and Plath were colleagues at Smith College from 1957 to 1958 (Loizeaux, 21). Recalling Bentley's reading of "Crow's Account of the Battle" as "the site of pain," Baskin's illustration of "The Knight" in *Cave Birds* gives graphic form to the injurious conditions endured by Crow, and, remarkably, its style seems to indicate the scene of drawing echoing the writing. The skeletal remains of the bird are depicted from above on a ground of scrupulously tight and even horizontal crosshatchings hinting at the sheet of paper on which the poem and drawing appear. The disintegration of the body, notes Loizeaux, "does not produce complete decomposition, either in the narrative or the book" (37). This is a vision of any death as that of a fallen knight submitting with the utmost dignity to the ethical code of his kind that, though he dies, is a code that endures, like literature. Far from having abandoned a human perspective, Hughes's primordial poetry is able to situate mortality within a myth striking not least of all for its reverence for the immortalizing power of poetry itself.

The collaboration between Baskin and Hughes produces, especially in moments such as this in *Cave Birds*, a meaningful liaison between word and image that becomes itself part context part content for more complex conceptual and literary sense than text alone could convey. What interests them, notes Loizeaux, is "relation across difference: words and images orbit each other, held in active tension, exchanging across the gap" (38). The combined effect in "The Knight" of text and image presents us with what Loizeaux refers to as an image of the "afterlife" (38). The graphic image and poetic imagery together suggest that the knight's remains are a form of writing that embodies a living tradition of courtly values involving an unswerving and heroic gaze on life and its often appalling settings. The knight's body contains, Loizeaux argues, "the material for a new body/book" (37). What can this afterlife offer us, presented as it is on these facing pages comprising Baskin's almost calligraphic rendition of a bird's skeleton painstakingly drawn, like an excavated fossil, yet animated forever by Hughes's ennobling, imagistic couplets? Initially, it gives the reader a context that is not fixed to the here and now. Recalling Plath's wish to be omniscient and physically absent from herself, it suggests a reading practice that can access a timeless setting for human temporality that does not deny human time. Another way of looking at this is to refer to finite memory as private and the nonpresent context as public. Memory that is finite is that which ends when a human life ends. Public memory, on the other hand, exists beyond the singular individual. Culture is its custodian whenever exemplary lives are celebrated and memorialized. These poems of Hughes ruminate on culture as distinct from the vicissitudes of individual lives, and, insofar as that independence is maintained, culture is then immune to the depredations of time from which all living things suffer. The poems also bear upon the possibility of the loss of culture's everlasting capacity to endure from generation to generation.

In a bid to keep his distance from the ongoing controversy of his life after Plath, even in what on the face of it promised to be his most private correspondences, such as *Birthday Letters* published in 1998, Hughes stages his most acutely felt awareness of Sylvia Plath via the sort of mythic or prehistoric settings that we saw in *Crow* and *Cave Birds*. To many, the publication of *Birthday Letters* after 30 years of controversy and silence around the topic of Sylvia Plath symbolizes a breakthrough, a release of "pent-up emotion," as Wagner has it (3), or a "sampling" from a 30-year dispute, as Churchwell says ("Secrets," 105), from a man who finally breaks his vow of silence (120). Critics may have exaggerated this expressivity slightly, or at least failed to see it in the context of a self-mythologizing that Plath and Hughes always engaged in. Indeed, as Egeland argues, one reason for the mythologizing of the Plath and Hughes text is that they themselves "consistently interpreted their own lives and each other in mythic terms" (283). From the very beginning of their relationship, then, there was a complex overlap of secrecy and visibility, the private and the public. To my way of thinking, the poems in *Birthday Letters* continue to speak in the voice of a pariah adapted from the style Hughes established in *Crow*. This outsider refuses to gratify the appetite for scandal, nor does it add to the transatlantic bickering that attends the Plath–Hughes aftermath. Here, Hughes is speaking with authority and an artistic insouciance that seems to say, "I may stink to high heaven, but here is what I have to say in the way only I can say it." The result is a divided narrative, one open in the way "The Knight" lies revealed for all to see, and the other in which local biographical data is withheld in favor of the deeper revelations of myth.

In her analysis of the literary phenomenon that is *Birthday Letters* (for there is no denying that the publication of these poems, addressed to the poet's deceased first wife, caused a minor sensation in the literary scene), Churchwell argues that the collection is "best understood as an 'open secret,' a volume hesitating uneasily between disclosure and encryption, unsettled by its inability to fix the boundaries between public and private" ("Secrets," 104). Hughes's biographer Neil Roberts touches on a similar tension when he suggests that in *Birthday Letters*, Plath is an "addressee who exists not only in the private world of the poet, but in a public world of ideological discourse" (202). I agree with Churchwell's reading of the collection as an "open secret," perhaps recalling Poe's famous story of an extremely sensitive letter hidden in plain view. However, where Churchwell describes this volume as something "hesitating uneasily" and "unsettled" by it being neither public nor private, I see Hughes situating the private within a public recast in terms that are all his own, drawing on the mythic or prehistoric, in which individual lives become a feature of what constitutes and disrupts the wider world. This shifts the focus from seeing the collection as a public display of private guilt to seeing it as a vehicle for Hughes's literary values as these help form his response to public scrutiny. *Birthday Letters* offers a portrait of human matters, here the relationship between a woman and a man, untouched by the wrangling in the media and critical press of the past three decades. So, do these letters hidden in plain view offer a revelation of some kind? Churchwell correctly notes that while it was marketed as that which would break a vow of secrecy, most of what was disclosed in the poems was already known by all ("Secrets," 121). Even so, a revelation in the form of a psychoanalytical truth emerges from reading the collection. It is this truth that is coded and concealed. This mixture of revelation and concealment animates the reading of *Birthday Letters*. It also provides strategies for reading the Information Age as partially open (information) and coded (narrative).

As I argued in the opening chapter regarding the espionage fiction of Graham Greene and WikiLeaks, information by itself is data, decentered and unnarrated, lacking the durability of narrative. We have seen in this chapter that there is an increasingly virtual aspect to the discourses that follow in the wake of the encounters between Plath and Hughes that, I argue, take on an enduring form only insofar as they are convoked by narrative. Moulin claims that one of the greatest paradoxes of Hughes's career is that "his whole work is an exploration of the inner life, in an age which was, at best, sceptical of this concept" (14). I agree in part with this claim though it would be more precise to think that Hughes's fascination is with an encounter between an inner private life and an outer dimension of immense power and duration. This vast prehistoric and sublimely indifferent setting is what people must struggle to contend with, to interrupt its perennial cycles with a vital and shockingly beautiful mortality worthy of lasting inscriptions in literature. As such, Hughes's poetics is profoundly concerned with countering whatever undermines the human stake in immensity. His poetics prepare the way for a reading and writing practice that can resist the prodigious power of the Internet without ignoring it as the terrain that contemporary subjects must inhabit. We can deduce that this accords with his intentions from his refusal to weigh in to transatlantic squabble that was the media event he called the "Plath Fantasia." Whether in his collaborative work with Baskin in *Cave Birds* and *Crow*, or in "letters" to his late first wife, Hughes's interest is in what lies intimately between people in ordinary life while also connecting this life with an extraordinarily deeper context that his poetry enjoins us to encounter together, in community.

To explore the world that our inner life must inhabit, that inner core of humanity often beset with prehuman forces, Hughes enters a primordial or mythic moment. In "Badlands" from *Birthday Letters*, Hughes reflects on death, but in a curious reversal of the emphasis in "Examination at the Womb-Door" (wherein all-powerful death is overruled by "Me, evidently"), the lovers contemplate the awful presence of life, at which she concludes,

> Here where there's only death, maybe our life
> Is terrifying. Maybe it's the life
> In us
> Frightening the earth, and frightening us. (*Birthday Letters*, 86)

"In us" Hughes has Plath find all that is needed to contemplate the vast reaches outside any conventional sense of time and beyond familiar and comforting dichotomies such as life and death. "In us" we find our own lives contain a prodigious vitality fit to scare off even death. Hughes's enchantment with a metaphysical poetry that sees him stepping outside of self is akin to Plath's desire to divorce her own self and be omniscient or God-like.[6] Conformity is a kind of death as well, and so a degree of pariah-like rejection of that role is also required in order to form a community with others if one is to be truly and vitally an other among others. Does this suggest more of the ways in which Hughes's poetics and his public life exemplify a stance that contemporary subjects may assume in relation to communication technology? Hughes locates *in us* the utmost hope for a sublime encounter with otherness, shocking enough well and truly to take on the numbing death of sameness and bland, fruitless conformity.

The Information Age enables powerful connectivity through technologically mediated encounters between self and the other. However, as Willson points out, that same technology "also disconnects the individual from the embodied interactions surrounding her/him" (646). Put simply, the Net is no more nor less than the setting for any kind of interactivity one cares to name, and it is indifferent to that specifically human potential for heroic encounter with the vital force of an, at times, terrifying otherness that leaps out at us from the lines of Hughes's poems. "Interactivity" such as this does not just happen; it must be fomented like revolution, it needs the pariah, and narrative is its incitement. Facing the annihilating, programmatic pull of technology, the pariah constitutes an interruption to the endless recycling of information that threatens to impose a deadening conformity on the life of language and textuality. It is for this reason that Lyotard in *The Postmodern Condition* recognizes that transparent, empirical or scientific knowledge "has always existed in addition to, *and in competition and conflict with*, another kind of knowledge, which I will call narrative" (7; emphasis mine).

The Plath and Hughes text offers strategies for navigating the private and the public in the Digital Age. In his *The Inoperative Community*, Jean-Luc Nancy offers a philosophical foundation that supports the kind of community that together endures and celebrates its capacity to shock itself with its own vitality, the life *in us* and also coming from beyond us. For Nancy the very fabric of community lies in a shared exposure to the world where a "singular being *appears*, as finitude itself: at the end (or at the beginning) with the contact of the skin (or the heart) of another singular being, at the confines of the *same* singularity that is, as such, always *other*, always shared, always exposed" (28). Individuals, on the other hand, according to Nancy, are constituted by "communication, contagion, or communion" (27). Nancy's understanding of community to be a space of appearance between beings suggests that the shape of the community cannot be prescribed in advance. As well, it confirms Gere's notion that the global communications network society is capable of both joining and separating members of society (222). A community does not preexist its members. Willson clarifies Nancy's position: "being is not common because it differs with each experience of existence, but being is *in* common: it is the *in* where community resides" (651). A community, as I understand Nancy, is not where one furthers oneself, but rather, it is the site of a shared exposure to the shock of otherness of which the community is capable. Translated into terms such as the public and the private, we see how the self must in fact be divorced from the community in order to offer traces of enduring memory, to be capable of standing as its other, but not only as its pariah. Nancy refers to this split between self and community as an intrusion into the equanimity of a self-consciousness that might otherwise take the community simply for its own backyard (19).

Hughes's *Birthday Letters* does not present an inventory of disclosures to gratify the reader by tipping her or him in favor of one or another interpretation of what happened between himself and Sylvia Plath. Instead of this information, we are treated to a narrative that is located in deep time where the poet addresses an absent Sylvia Plath as if she were present (what his biographer Neil Roberts refers to as "apostrophic elegies" [202]) while also recalling how she was shockingly other even when present to him. At the moment of willed, shared exposure to this otherness, readers and writers not only of the Plath and Hughes text but all who are engaged in communication and textuality contribute to what Nancy calls "ecstasy of the night of immanence" (19). And though it comes in the form of letters that are in this way revelatory, Hughes's final volume obscures rather than discloses the events of the poets' matrimonial life. A writing practice is challenging only to the extent that there are readers who promote bare text to the status of textuality or narrative. For that to continue to happen, there must be an exchange and a communication divorced from the confines of the self. Scott Lash asks, however, "how can this be possible in an age, not of symbolic exchange, but of dead, digitized symbols; not of forms of life, but a virtualized habitus?" (110). Where Lash echoes Benjamin's own sense of loss of storytelling, my discussion of what Hughes offers readers reveals in his work a marked alliance with storytelling and grounds for a hope in its future. In the following chapter on Anne Michaels's narratives of mourning, I shall further explore the role of storytelling as supporting a political narrative of loss.

The problem faced by the pariah, the voluntary outcast in our midst, brings Benjamin's concern for the demise of storytelling into sharp focus. For Benjamin, I noted in chapter 1, the storyteller, whose future he feared for, offers "the communicability of experience," which, at the same time, is also "the epic side of truth" (86). Now it is possible fully to appreciate that for Benjamin "experience" was precisely the bracing encounter with otherness that is the epic truth of the storyteller's outsider role within his or her community. Storytelling, or narrative, looks encouragingly forward to the vital interruption to conformity of the subjectivities that will arouse it and back in respectful memory of their achievements. I wish to end this chapter by noting that Sylvia Plath's desire for omniscience beyond the enclosure of the private self for the sake of a unique and difficult poetic perspective is a noble one. Plath and women like her growing up in 1950s' America struggled to be the shocking other that their community needed, without enjoying the benefit of acceptance, as the bracing voice of the other, for the difficult challenge to stand outside the shelter of the self that wants to conform must be faced by writers as well as readers. Unlike Sylvia Plath, Hughes was able to maintain a persistent outsider status throughout his poetic career, but although his poetry flourished, there can be little doubt that for him also his stance came at great personal cost. Even now, after his death, Hughes continues to maintain some authorial control over his literary output, balancing privacy and visibility. Not until at least 2023 will his final papers be disclosed at the archives of Emory University where Hughes himself transferred all his written work. Rather than expect further as yet undisclosed information on the marriage of Plath and Hughes to emerge then, scholars and readers of these two poets would be wise to engage with their textual remains not as detectives on the lookout for clues but as fellow mortals. In so doing, we will leave behind traces of our humanity as unsound waves in an oceanic imaginary that interrupts the information flows of the Digital Age.

# Part III

# The Coastless Sea

5

# Bridging Bereavement

## Narratives of Loss and Loss of Narrative in Anne Michaels

In the final pages of *Moby-Dick*, Ishmael is clinging to a coffin that bobs to the surface just after the *Pequod* goes down. The sole survivor of a shipwreck, Ishmael finds himself almost overwhelmed by nature, by the sharks, the sea-hawks, the fowls, and above all by the waves that keep coming toward him. Despite this, Ishmael refuses to surrender to "the great shroud of the sea," which, he tells us, "rolled on as it rolled five thousand years ago" (634). Instead, Ishmael performs the heroic feat of interrupting the endless passage of time, by staying alive long enough to tell, to have told, his tale. The novel closes under the banner of an address to the reader from the book of Job: "And I only am escaped alone to tell thee" (634). The singularity of Ishmael's achievement, the "only" and "alone" (matched by the singular "thee" at the receiving end), makes of his telling a highly personal, even unique, form of address. As such it is very different from the modes of address made popular via the Internet. The exchange is powerful because it is intimate and personal. That such a voice has the power to enlist his reader's sympathies from the middle of the ocean and after having exhausted his readers with an endless number of whale stories is nothing short of remarkable! Melville's novel is the exultation of the narrative voice that survives the sinking and therefore constitutes an afterlife for narrative itself.

Ishmael's life has been spared solely, it seems, "to tell," so that he may narrate the story of Captain Ahab's pursuit of vengeance on the white whale. The final scene in *Moby-Dick* is simultaneously a moment of reckoning and beckoning. Here Ishmael takes stock of what has brought him close to death while begging his listener to come closer, and closer still. Here, narrative voice itself has somehow, impossibly it seems, managed to keep its lone head above the waters of oblivion to tell thee, me, us, in defiance of mortality, how the story narrowly escaped being lost. Buoyed up by a coffin, Ishmael comes close to dying. The proximity of death may be what accounts for the stillness of the passage. The tumult of the whale's attack is over now, the shouted orders and cries of exaltation and despair that filled the closing pages have all fallen silent. Even the screeching of the small fowls has come to a stop. The story too is, of course, at its end, but this quietude feels more like an intermission that silences all extraneous sound except this one voice that has said and is yet to say, "Call me Ishmael." The sharks glide silently past Ishmael "as if with padlocks on their mouths" and the beaks of the sea-hawks are "sheathed" (634). If a funereal atmosphere is evoked in the final pages of Melville's novel, it also pays tribute to a voice that refuses to die. The novel begins with a simple mode of address to the reader "Call me Ishmael." In its final pages, it recalls that scene of introduction by showing the reader the imperative to narrate at a moment of great loss and the threat of a loss greater still. There are two distinct thematizations of loss in this passage: the loss of the Pequod as well as the potential loss of the narrative voice. This passage foregrounds the immunity of the storyteller and the vitality of a narrative power that is baptized in the icy waters of the Atlantic.

What if the immunity of that voice were to come under threat? What if the mythological river of Lethe that flows through the Underworld has burst its banks and the waters of oblivion now swirl around us, dulling the possibility of an alert readiness to encounter the new? This is the first of two chapters that fall under the heading "The Coastless Sea." I have suggested throughout *Atlantic Afterlives* that, our digital connectivity notwithstanding, we seem tragically disconnected from the plight of others today. Another way of visualizing this is to say that worldwide we are all *at sea* often without Ishmael's mode of address to direct our attention. By "coastless" I am referring to a technologically mediated, homogenizing tendency at work in culture today, something that tends to produce a sea of sameness uninterrupted by borders or markers of strong differentiation. The Information Age, I argue in this chapter, puts pressure on our coasts, erasing or effacing geographical and cultural borders. Paradoxically, there are at the same time more countries than ever that are now working to define themselves by their physical coasts and the policing of these coastal boundaries. Australia is one such country. I write this from Melbourne, one of several cities situated at this vast island's edges threatening to spill over into the oceans like the crayon marks of a child's erring attempt at coloring in. There are no signs that the current government is going to weaken its border control. Indeed in 2014, in the High Court of Australia, the conservative Prime Minister Tony Abbott announced his government's commitment to secrecy in the pursuit of its military-led Operation Sovereign Borders.[1] *Atlantic Afterlives* in general, and this chapter in particular, is written in the wake of recent refusals by Australia to offer passage to refugees who attempt the dangerous crossing from Afghanistan, Iran, Iraq, Sri Lanka, and other places. "The Pacific Solution" is the name given to the Australian government's policy of transporting asylum seekers to detention centers on island nations in the Pacific Ocean rather than accommodating them in Australia. The success of the implementation of this so-called solution points to one of the most painful ironies of the Information Age regarding the relationship to the Other. The oceans continue to enable passage and refuge, but they offer no belonging, no place, as it were. As the presenter of "The National Interest" on ABC Radio National in Australia and the author of *Borderline: Australia's Response to Refugees and Asylum Seekers in the Wake of the Tampa*, Peter Mares, says, the Tampa affair marks an erosion of the principle of rescue at sea (Mares).[2]

This chapter urgently asks, via Canadian author Anne Michaels's *The Winter Vault*, what reading and writing positions are available to us whereby narrative can shelter the exiled and the dispossessed even after death. Throughout this book I maintain that an afterlife comes into existence and is mediated through narrative, specific types of narrative. It is through such narrative that the lives of those we have lost are prolonged even beyond death; it is only through narrative that their significance to us can grow into its fullest stature. By afterlife, I am not referring to a spiritual existence beyond death, but rather an actual, physical afterlife sustained when the living ensure that the precious contributions made by the dead outlive them. This is mediated through technology or through processes of curation, restoration, conservation, and especially narrative. Michaels's novel speaks of tremendous loss and the kind of suffering that comes from an absence that words cannot yet fill in. The dead have been preserved prior to burial, but they have not yet acquired an afterlife through a narrative. Michaels's point in my account is that such an afterlife may never be achieved because narrative itself is increasingly an outmoded form of representation. The form of Michaels's novel registers the absence of a coherent narrative and the consequences of this loss without feeling obliged to satisfy a certain set of traditionalist criteria for the novel as form, but nor has she committed herself to a postmodern aesthetic.

I see Michaels as a storyteller clinging to the coffins in the coastless sea of our post-Atlantic world. In her work, the symbolism of water and passage across the ocean establishes tentative coordinates for thinking about the contingencies of communicating individual and communal experiences of the most desperate loss amid the wreckage of a transatlantic dialogue. This oceanic imaginary still constitutes a real geography, an area which once could be imagined as constituted by the intersecting ships that meet and pass in the world's oceans. It is still legible in the same way that the wake left behind the paths of ships is. I would like to use the work of human geographer Doreen Massey to give this notion of area some theoretical grounding. Massey reminds us of the danger of a view of space that constitutes an extreme of instantaneity. She proposed instead that we imagine the spatial as a site of interconnecting multiple trajectories or movements (76). I interpret the Information Age as a threat to area along the lines of Massey's account of "claustrophobic holism in which everything everywhere is already connected to everywhere else" (77). Instead of an imaginary completeness, Anne Michaels gives us a space for multiple trajectories of loss to exist simultaneously. Grief and abandonment are ever present. As such, this space of loss registers the demise of an Atlantic community. Her first novel *Fugitive Pieces* from 1996, a novel about a boy who narrowly escapes being killed during the Holocaust and whose life is haunted by his traumatic past, shares the themes of loss and remembrance with the author's more recent *The Winter Vault* from 2009. Neither *Fugitive Pieces* nor *The Winter Vault* offers a recuperation of any kind of wholeness, even a porously bounded expanse such as the transatlantic relationship.

Michaels has published collections of poetry that also reject any notion of a final consolation for the losses of the twentieth century. Collections include *The Weight of Oranges*, *Skin Divers*, and her recent *Correspondences* from 2013, an elegy for her father in which she weaves his absence into the narrative of a more generalized loss. *Correspondences* is a book that unfolds literally to a single long sheet of paper. It contains tantalizingly brief selections of the poetry written by many known and lesser known poets and authors, some of them victims of the Holocaust. At times, it is as if she has had to create a cemetery to bury her father. There are other voices, such as W. G. Sebald for instance, who postdate the Holocaust but whose work has been in part an emotional response to it. It is as if Michaels has chosen this form of printed object in order to critique the tendency to homogenize all victims of the Holocaust. She allows the narratives of loss to be discrete and thus each able to encounter otherness wherein a "layered kinship is formed, a touch across the pages" (*afterword*). The book physically resists being comfortably held all at once. Once folded out, it becomes a most fragile artefact whose spine can easily tear if stretched too far. Conceptually, the work also resists becoming an archive or an inventory of loss since Michaels's long poem occupies the entirety of the reverse side. Her living voice produces a stark contrast with the voices of the dead. Her book speaks to Roland Barthes's famous musings regarding the death of the author whereby her reading of their absence becomes a departure point for her own narrative of mourning for her father. It would seem that hers is a product of how Barthes envisages the development of text when he wrote that "the text is a tissue of quotations drawn from the innumerable centres of culture" (146).

The "correspondence" in question is that between the living and the dead, as well as between the dead themselves posthumously. In this way, Michaels creates an afterlife for these authors and poets through the vitality of her response to them. Michaels's lengthy one-page poem produces another kind of kinship of voices that occupy an unusual literary space reminiscent of Massey's spatiality in which a "dynamic simultaneity" supports multiple processes and practices that encounter each other as a series of what she calls "Loose ends and ongoing stories" as opposed to a unified space of "completed simultaneity" (107). Thus, for Michaels, there are multiple Holocausts and multiple encounters between survivors and their readers as well as victims. The loss is multiple and it cannot be mourned in any simple gesture. Similarly, this chapter argues that there are multiple Atlantics as well as a growing number of afterlives. It agrees with William Boelhower's definition of the Atlantic as "a tensive, exuberant, and often incommensurable space bunched, folded, striated or simply mapped according to the strategic interplay between circulation and sites, nomos (an oceanic order) and peoples, shifting scales and multiple narratives" (1). Importantly, in her recent novel *The Winter Vault*, Michaels emphatically registers loss as well as the call for narrative to continue to record moments of loss. There is an incompleteness to her novel, a refusal to entertain the idea of closure. This resistance is at the level of structure and also registered as the thematization of representation. In short, the novel conveys the limitations of representation as it reaches an impasse that is simultaneously a passage as well as the foreclosure of an itinerary beyond the narratological.

It has been my argument throughout *Atlantic Afterlives* that since the beginning of the Information Age the transatlantic relationship has an afterlife that continues to reverberate elsewhere, beyond the traditional routes of discovery and trade, up to the present. In this chapter, I want to examine how Michaels in *The Winter Vault* contributes to the literary existence of this afterlife through her treatment of mourning as well as that which hinders mourning. The situation depicted in her story presents itself as an unbridgeable gulf, but in her narrating these aporia, Michaels's writing offers "the experience of the impossible" (Spivak, *A Critique of Postcolonial Reason*, 427) and by so doing contributes to the narratological construction of an afterlife. There is an ideological aspect to the impasse one comes across in her novel. Michaels is more interested in bearing witness to the disjointedness of the twentieth century than pretending that hers or anyone else's account of it can reproduce the past as a seamless whole. As with her assemblage of poems in *Correspondences*, her prose can be viewed as a staging of encounters that takes us beyond the quotidian and toward an aesthetic practice that is attuned to both the past and the present as well as the future. She allows the fragmentation of her fiction and poetry to remain on the page as a mark of untranslatability. Rather than retelling history through her characters, Michaels keeps something safe from endless reproduction and reiteration. By so doing, Michaels salvages something precious and unique that remains safe from the passage of time precisely because it is not easily reconstructed.

Aspects of Derrida's foreword to *The Wolf Man's Magic Word* by Nicolas Abraham and Maria Torok are relevant here for exploring the difficulty of mourning in relation to the Atlantic afterlife generally and Michaels's novel specifically. There are parallels between what Derrida calls a "crypt" and Michaels calls a "vault." The internal logic of Michaels's novel develops the notion of a vault where the dead are kept during winter. A "winter vault" then is the place where the dead wait to be buried when the earth is frozen too hard for grave-digging. It acknowledges that when the time is not right, one must wait to bury the dead. Michaels's novel reminds us that in our relations with the dead there are times when we are faced with the impossibility of forgetting the rawness of their loss, which is at the same time the inability properly to remember their lives, via narrative. What remains is an all-pervasive sense of loss, of grieving, and of sobbing. In Derrida's reading of the Wolf Man case, he differentiates between introjection and incorporation as two different aspects of the way trauma such as loss is handled. *Introjection* is the means by which a subject conventionally internalizes trauma as something nameable via narrative that "expands the self" (Derrida is following Ferenczi), by which "it advances, propagates itself" (xvi). *Incorporation*, on the other hand, sets up a foreign enclave within the self; it encrypts the loss—effectively via a refusal narratively to remember and mourn—and it thereby renders part of the self unavailable, taken up by the structure of this internal crypt. A perhaps surprising aspect of Michaels's novel is in the way it presents loss rather than represents it, and in so doing Michaels in fact goes some way toward a fictional demonstration, even an expose, of the mechanism of incorporation or encryption at work.

The crypt then is a psychoanalytical concept referring to a response to death or trauma that actually kills or at least silences part of the self. Rather than symbolically sequestering knowledge of the trauma in the self where it can be sensed and even narratively "lived" via symptoms accessible to analysis, the crypt is "a disguise hiding the traces of the act of disguising, a place of silence." The "incorporation" of a Word-Thing, as Derrida calls it, makes it unreadable because it is meant to encrypt by hiding (including hiding from) the reality of a painful loss. It is not available to artistic or poetic rendition since poetry uses metaphor and metonymy that are the analogues of the conventional means for naming unconscious or absent things. Nor is it legible in an analysis via the conventional means of substitution and displacement whereby a symptom speaks to the analyst. *Incorporation* is a highly covert operation in which the trauma of a loss is itself rendered somehow dead and buried in the place of living memory. Michaels's novel *The Winter Vault* is less concerned with individual expressions of suffering, a point taken up by her reviewers, some of whom, on moral grounds, criticize her almost off-hand attitude to characters in the novel.[3] But to deplore Michaels's omission of singular personal cases of suffering is to overlook the real insight her vision is offering us. To follow a linear path taken by a singular character would be to attempt to reconstruct, and in some way to reproduce, a chain of events comprising both loss and recovery. To emphasize the loss of many is instead to acknowledge the impossibility of such a recovery because of the sheer magnitude and scale of the loss in question.

For these reasons, Michaels's novel insists on following the material traces of a history of loss sustained by the community at large. *The Winter Vault* begins in Egypt in 1964 in the upper part of the Nile, just after the confluence of the Blue and White Niles. During the decade of the 1960s, the Aswan Dam was constructed and as a result Lake Nasser was formed inundating the region of lower Nubia, forcing close to 120,000 people to be resettled in Sudan and Egypt. As well, a number of historical monuments and temples that were threatened by the flooding were dismantled and reassembled on higher ground. The Unesco Nubia project invested forty million dollars to save this area and its people and their livestock from total destruction or drowning from flooding due to the filling of Lake Nasser. In Michaels's novel, the fictional engineer Avery oversees the dismantling and subsequent reassembly of the great temple at Abu Simbel at a place above the water level. Avery and Jean's marriage comes to a tragic turn when Jean suffers a stillbirth. With Avery's blessing, Jean returns to Canada where she encounters the artist Lucjan, a migrant from Poland who himself mourns both the death of his family after the Nazi invasion of Warsaw as well as the loss of the city itself.

This second half of the novel serves as a contrast to the Egypt part in that it counters the exclusive intimacy of a young married couple with a different kind of shared intimacy of a more communal kind found among the Polish exiles in Toronto. It must be said though that neither the pairing of two lovers in Egypt nor the more open constellation of lovers in Toronto offers a solution to pain and loss. However, in my account, the apparent failure of Michaels's narrative to resolve the different kinds of loss felt by its many grieving characters, as well as its refusal to satisfactorily suture the two halves of the story, is also its success. Included in this achievement is Michaels's unswerving study of profound disappointment experienced by those whose work it is to safeguard the past when they realize that their contribution is but another aspect of the destruction that attends all human labors. By not falling into line with readers' expectations of closure and resolution, *The Winter Vault* resists the urge to reproduce the historical content of the Holocaust.[4] Instead, Michaels's novel renders legible the bodies of the dead through the experience of radical alienation in which the reader gains a momentary awareness of the loss and grief of the other in the form of a crypt or a vault, necessarily hidden away from the Self, logically inaccessible, though not unconscious. The winter dead wait, Lucjan explains to Jean, "for the earth to relent and receive them. They wait in histories of thousands of pages, where the word love is never mentioned" (242).

Lucjan's comment aims at the heart of what narrative as opposed to historical accounts can achieve. Whereas thousands of pages may provide merely an inventory of loss, it takes a narrative and the desire for narrative to create an afterlife. Michaels's novel is a calling to the artist to apply the powers of narrative in order to prolong, even immortalize, the significance of the lives of the dead. To say that the dead wait in histories of thousands of pages for the earth to receive them is to suggest that the dead are concealed by denial rather than via the revelatory power of poetics and narrative. They are curtained off and not mentioned, love or no love. Michaels's novel reminds the reader of the many deaths that remain unnarrated to this day and forever more, even though the remains of the dead have been preserved in vaults. The mention of "thousands of pages" suggests that a narrative that contains the word love, in other words a viable afterlife, exists at a different scale, less heartless and imposing.

The reference to "thousands of pages" also signifies exhaustion regarding a perception of what constitutes knowledge. Michaels's novel offers an antidote to the belief that all there is to know about the world has already been or could be communicated. In this regard, her novel recalls Walter Benjamin's famous essay on the vanishing role of storytelling coinciding with the increasing value placed on the dissemination of verifiable information (84). For Benjamin, we are growing "poorer in communicable experience" having lost something "that seemed inalienable to us, the securest among our possessions . . . the ability to exchange experiences" (84). Instead, what is now exchanged is "anything but experiences that goes from mouth to mouth." He tells us "never has experience been contradicted more thoroughly" than since the First World War, when "the tiny, fragile human body" was suddenly subject to "a field of force of destructive torrents and explosions" hitherto never experienced, in the form of strategically arrayed military and economic pressures (84). *The Winter Vault* attempts to bring back storytelling by suggesting that, contrary to the thousand pages, not everything is verifiable and can be brought into visibility. Narrative is incomplete. Much remains hidden, and even to the most careful reader, the page is full of ellipses and aporia that gesture toward something that cannot be captured. For this reason, it is impossible to impute meaning to events without retaining a perspective on what is simultaneously lost in the process. What of that which cannot be translated? her novel seems to ask.

Readers seeking a greater investment in individual loss might be tempted to see Jean avoiding the loss of her stillborn child by identifying instead with loss as sustained by Lucjan and his companions. Here, in my account, I see the novel performing a kind of "bridging" work. What is given to readers is an afterlife in which loss is suffered, recognized, respected, as well as shared as loss. The novel offers two painfully unresolved halves that demand a methodology or a reading practice that secures the role of writing in an age deluded into thinking that the battle against loss has been or could be won, through simulation or online archives. This point is all the more significant in the aftermath of our lost oceanic connectivity. Why, in an age of "global witnessing," as Michaels puts it in an article for *The Atlantic* about reading Canadian literature on a world scale, do we remain distanced from the suffering of others? Relentlessly, Michaels's novel does not attempt to exorcise suffering through denial. Ultimately, both character and reader remain inconsolable. Throughout her work, and particularly in *The Winter Vault*, Michaels resists suturing the gaping wound of destruction, refusing to offer any false sense of security or therapeutic balm to her readers. After all, what purpose would it serve to believe we are inured against loss? Since one can never *have* the loss of others save in the imagination, Michaels insists on exercising that faculty. Her novel lends a compelling counterperspective to the overwhelming power of information technology that has persuaded us that nothing from now on should ever be lost. Our digital culture gives us false promises of mastery over our representations, our "story," our publicity, our afterlife.

Despite the fantasy that all can be preserved or reproduced, Michaels's novel suggests that loss is an integral part of our humanity. It is for these reasons that narratives such as *The Winter Vault*, in refusing to offer consolation or any sense of mastery over our fate, is an important expression of loss. Michaels's interest in *The Winter Vault* is to remind the reader of an all-pervasive sense of cultural loss touching every individual. In overseeing the demolition of Abu Simbel, Avery is struck by the futility of his work, and his feeling of defeat combines with the novel's many expressions of failure to suggest something about the experience of loss in the Digital Age. It is as though all that this monumental labor has achieved is a simulation. When Avery has saved the parts that make up the Abu Simbel temple and presents the work-in-progress that is the reconstruction of Abu Simbel to the Ministers of Culture and the diplomatic corps, his heart is filled with shame, not pride. He might have preserved something of history, as a relic, but in the process, he suspects, he has failed to imbue his work with narrative (5). His reconstruction of the temple is a physical relic lacking any content. The temple was uprooted from its natural place and in the process something of its mystery, Avery surmises, has gone missing. He asks himself how much, if anything, can be rescued and what remains in the wake of such demolition?

The temple's imposing facade, its interior spaces, its physical mass and proportion have all been recreated just as they were, but what of its spirit and its art? What of its purpose? And what of the trauma of those who lost a way of life and a culture in the region of Nubia? By being encrypted, both the living culture and the antiquity are memorialized out of memory. Taking the form of a successful transplant that then needs no further discussion, the underlying sense of loss is largely forgotten. Avery intuits this and he laments his contribution to history and what it encrypts in its thousands of pages of documentation. Perhaps this is what leads him to support and encourage his wife Jean to seek out ways of expressing her sorrow over their stillborn child, even if it means leaving him behind. What seems to be missing for Avery is, I believe, evinced, albeit rather obliquely, in Raymond Carver's well-known short story "Cathedral." In Carver's story, a man tries and fails to describe a cathedral to a blind man through conventional means of representation. When the blind man suggests that they try drawing a cathedral together, literally hand in hand, neither one seeing the result, something of a cathedral's religious purpose of bringing people together in mystery is conveyed to the suspicious protagonist as well as to the reader. As a result of their joint efforts to recreate an unseen cathedral on paper, a bond is formed between the two men. The act of drawing together performs bridging work. Where at the beginning of the short story the narrator was uneasy at the blind man's disability, there is now empathy, and something approaching reverence.

Avery longs for this sense of connectivity on the Egyptian construction site in *The Winter Vault*. As the two men in "Cathedral," one blind and the other eventually working with his eyes shut, join forces to represent a cathedral, they enact the meaning of congregation. I see their efforts to bring a cathedral into shared understanding as a sacred ritual that the documentary on cathedrals playing on the TV in the background cannot offer. What the documentary offers is information about the architectural history of cathedrals, the visual equivalent of Lucjan's thousands of pages. What the men's attempt at jointly drawing a cathedral achieves, on the other hand, is much more than this, because it is less. Surely, while they must have failed to draw a cathedral, they have made a concerted effort to represent what they both lack. Interestingly, the story reinforces the loss of difference between a copy and its original as theorized by Baudrillard. Both the reconstructed Abu Simbel temple in *The Winter Vault* and the cathedral represented on the television screen in Carver's story approach the status of *simulacra* (as Baudrillard would have it) insofar as they deny or make no mention of the loss of the original. This is another way to understand what I mean by a coastless sea: it is a pervasive locus of unmourned loss, oblivion, an endless supply of copies that are reproduced without recourse to or memory of an original source or a creator. This homogenization is the ultimate crypt supplied seamlessly and efficiently by the Digital Age. It leaves people hankering for authenticity in a world that no longer recognizes the original except perhaps in those who find themselves grieving over a loss hidden by its substitutes, a loss they can therefore hardly name.

Narrative interrupts this seamless homogeneity when it creates the conditions for an abrupt encounter with otherness, the strange and the unprecedented. Think about Ishmael's narrative voice on the final page of *Moby-Dick*: "And I only am escaped alone to tell thee." Such an address shortens the distance between reader and narrator, even if not in a physical sense such as when death has rendered such an encounter impossible. Would it be out of place to suggest that narrative performs the work of religion in the Information Age? The word religion comes from the Latin *ligare*, meaning to tie together, to bind. What distinguishes *The Winter Vault* from other contemporary novels is the way its structure resists a linear reading. Like the temple at Abu Simbel that must first be taken apart piece by piece in order to be transported, the novel itself is also constructed out of fragments that may or may not be joined up at the end. *The Winter Vault* does not offer closure. What is incomprehensible remains so, loss is pervasive, and as for memories and recollections of the past, these augment and complement one another without there being a final easeful word. "To make peace," Sontag warns, "is to forget. To reconcile, it is necessary that memory be faulty and limited" (115). The winter vault is a place where dead bodies lie in wait for the ground to thaw so that graves can be dug (241). In the meantime, and not in lieu of burial, but contingent with it, Michaels's work offers "non passages" what Spivak refers to in the spirit of Derrida as the experience of the impossible (*A Critique of Postcolonial Reason*, 427). The bridging work, says Spivak quite strongly, also after Derrida, has to be supplied by the reader "who provides connections in order to make the text work" (427).

By privileging the act of memory and especially the obligation to remember the loss of many, Michaels's novel recognizes along with Susan Sontag that remembering "is, achingly, the only relation we can have with the dead" and that for this reason it has "an ethical value in and of itself" (115). Both in this novel as well as in her recent *Correspondences*, Michaels is deeply invested in a writing of encryption and decipherment that frustrates easy progress through the narrative, always demanding the joining together of separate parts. This partly invites the reader to abandon his or her assumptions of commensurability and partly frees her work from the constraints of any straightforward interpretational framework. As a thinker, Michaels's values are in synch with Emily Apter's who in her work as a theorist in translation studies and comparative literature has recently warned against the shallow congeniality of a "reflexive endorsement of cultural equivalence and substitutability" (2). Michaels's work begins with the assumption that her narrative fulfills its destiny only when it finds a reader who can encounter its brokenness without attempting to reconstruct a satisfying whole thereby. Another way of referring to this reading strategy is a process of bridging bereavement in which not closure or comfort but bereavement itself is the bridge. To recall Benjamin again, now in the spirit of Derrida and the process of encryption, when the surviving soldiers returned from the battle fields of the First World War, they were mute. He writes of the delayed response to the expression of their suffering: "What ten years later was poured out in the flood of war books was anything but experience that goes from mouth to mouth" (362). A similar stumbling block is seen in the construction of *The Winter Vault* as a novel. Its two halves resemble the walls of a structural vault that attempts to join the inconsolable Jean with a displaced Polish community in Toronto.

The second half of *The Winter Vault* devotes itself to the loss experienced by Lucjan and the exiled Polish community he is part of. Lucjan and his migrant friends from Warsaw make up the *Stray Dogs*, a group of elderly Polish musicians haunted by the almost complete destruction of their city by the Luftwaffe, as well as by the attempts to rebuild the city in the aftermath of the war. In a moving passage, Lucjan explains how the rebuilding of the city deranged people's memories of that same city, leaving survivors bereft of their own private recollections of their city. He attempts to convey to Jean the feeling of being in a city both the same and different from the one he grew up in. He speaks of streets and doorways as both familiar and "yet not quite," a city that is at once less and more real than the way they remembered it from before the destruction (232). Despite the reconstruction of their city, now a near perfect *simulacrum* of what it once was, the survivors are by no means inured from their loss. On the contrary, the rebuilt city houses a grief all the more inconsolable because it alienates its citizens from the past. Recalling Derrida's account of the crypt, the rebuilt city blatantly denies the reality of loss so that in effect that loss has been lost. Lucjan's Warsaw is Avery's Abu Simbel temple writ large. What Kandiyoti argues in relation to Michaels's debut novel *Fugitive Pieces* is perhaps also appropriate to say about *The Winter Vault*, namely that "every place is two places (or more) for the survivor for whom predisaster and exilic places are superimposed upon another" (315). If this is true, then what Jean's husband Amery says of his labors on the Great Temple can equally apply to the rebuilding of

Warsaw: "the reconstruction was a further desecration, as false as redemption without repentance" (140).

There is, however, an important difference between the relocation of the temple and the rebuilding of Warsaw since for Warsaw there is an afterlife, though it is not founded on the rebuilt city itself. In her novel, Michaels evokes the spirit of migrant communities in some of the most memorable passages of the novel. Through them the values of the old Warsaw have been relocated and survive in places far from their original location. And so Michaels tells us of an overt smuggling operation in which something of the spirit of Warsaw has been trafficked out of Europe and into migrant communities in Toronto and other places. A remembered Warsaw bravely survives both its destruction and the reconstruction, enduring in diasporas around the world. Michel de Certeau places much power in memory precisely on account of this footloose vagrancy: "memory derives its interventionary force from its capacity to be altered—unmoored, mobile, lacking any fixed position" (86). Michaels's novel sets the Holocaust beside and on equal terms with personal as well as with other non-Eurocentric cultural losses (such as the displacements due to the building of waterways in Egypt and Canada) in ways that may provoke some readers to whom nothing measures up to the evil perpetrated on the Jewish communities of Europe by the Nazis. Michaels preempts this feeling by having Jean convey doubt in her right to feel pain: "What was personal loss in the face of universal devastation—the loss of Nubia, the destruction of cities. Her misery shamed her" (248).

The lived and remembered Warsaw resembles a wound that cannot heal. As an encrypted city, it resurfaces on the other side of the Atlantic in fragments and it leaves its former citizens hankering for a pattern, a narrative, a way in. The same could be said for readers of the novel. This longing for completion is also mirrored in the feelings of the audience who the Stray Dogs leave "sick with longing" (254) for a recognizable tune. The arrangements of standards played by the Stray Dogs are desecrated, falling apart at the seams. Longing becomes a kind of unsettled homesickness throughout the novel through a perpetual shifting of the site of loss. This is the subject of Lucjan's personal art work as well as Jean's scent trails. Lucjan's project consists entirely of maps of a city, including maps of invisible things, maps indicating where people had experienced moments of fear or of hope (250). Jean's work complements Lucjan's when, in unexpected places, she physically sows the seeds of remarkable experiences for others, providing them with surprising moments of remembrance. She leaves signals that she hopes will be received in years to come when people walk by and catch the scent of a flower they might not have smelled for some decades (202). Both Lucjan and Jean perform what de Certeau would call "practiced space." Jean especially manipulates space memory by secretly installing such dislocated reminders as to constitute for someone a rupture in time. De Certeau refers to this as a "foreignness" that "makes possible a transgression of the law of the place" (85).

In what remains of this chapter, I wish to consider the possibility of a similar transgression via the reconstitution of a singular central speaking and reading position addressed to many through Roland Barthes's thoughts on mourning. In Barthes's *Mourning Diary*, a public place of encounter with loss itself after the death of his mother on October 25, 1977, becomes newly possible through his resolution to make of his private loss a contribution to public knowledge. Barthes recognizes that even the announcement of death has qualities of an event that "mobilizes, interests, activates, tetanizes" (50). The absence of narration, Barthes fears, would allow death to slip into something fixed, sedentary, and *grim*: "And then one day it is no longer an event, it is another *duration*, compressed, insignificant, not narrated, grim, without recourse" (50). It is not a coincidence that in the translation of Derrida's essay on the significance of the crypt in the "Wolf-Man," the verb "vault" is used throughout to indicate the relation between movement and the maintenance of focused feeling. The implied distance in the verb "vault" suggests mobility as well as the necessity for a bridging operation as already made possible through narrative. The act of vaulting, of hurdling, of throwing oneself across or over obstacles, or of leaping into the unknown, across an abyss, are all features of the risky business of narrating loss. In Barthes's case, perhaps even a convulsive ("tetanized") gesture serves to allow death to develop into a narrative for the living, thereby creating its afterlife. By means such as this, death remains in the present. Michaels draws attention to the way the dead are sometimes doubly lost to us, in the winter vault, where they numbly await the power of narrative to bring their death acutely to life.

Where Michaels's evocation of the winter vault stages a frozen impasse that immobilizes the progress of mourning that would move loss into narrative, Roland Barthes's *Mourning Diary* reminds the reader of the necessity to keep the dead as if alive. There is, however, a winter vault that holds Barthes captive at the beginning of his mourning after his mother's death. Before Barthes can attend to his hankering after the roving chaos of a life touched by death, he must overcome a winter vault of his own. Put another way, Barthes finds himself as the sedentary occupant of a cryptic incorporation that Derrida tells us, "always marks an effect of impossible or refused mourning" (xxi). Barthes finds himself in transit, bereft of place, a man *sans papiers* awaiting deportation. Made homeless by the loss of his mother, he sees himself alienated from the time and place before her death: "Sometimes, roused by desires (say, the trip to Tunisia); but they are desires of *before*—somehow anachronistic; they come from another shore, *another country*, the country of before.—Today it is a flat, dreary country—virtually without water—and paltry" (53). Here Barthes strikes a chord with Derrida in his lecture "Mnemosyne" dedicated to the memory of Paul de Man, in which Derrida rejects the capacity to live with loss if it means translating the existence of the departed one into a memory or a monument: "Is the most distressing, or even the most deadly infidelity that of a *possible mourning* which would interiorise within us the image, idol, or ideal of the other who is dead and lives only in us?" (6).

What makes Barthes's position even more complex, worthy of public note, is that his refusal to bury his mother in "the country of before" has to do with his difficulty in refounding afresh a self-image distinct from who he was for her when she was still alive. Having lost the woman to whom he was everything, he now feels he "must gain recognition all over again" (133). The diary is the work of someone who is attempting to make himself matter once again and in a most unexpected way:

> For me, at this point in my life (when *maman* is dead) I was *recognized* (by my books). But strangely—perhaps falsely?—I have the obscure feeling, now she's no longer here, that I must gain recognition all over again. This cannot be by writing another book: the idea of *continuing* as in the past to proceed from book to book, course to course, immediately struck me as mortiferous (looking ahead *to my dying day*). (Whence my present efforts at resignation). Before resuming *sagely* and *stoically* the course (quite unpredictably moreover) of work, it is necessary for me (I feel this strongly) to write this book around *maman*. In a sense, therefore, it is as if I had *to make* maman *recognized*. (133; emphasis original)

The hesitation expressed in the many sub-clauses in this diary entry tells us something about the striking and radical novelty of just what Barthes is attempting to achieve. He wants nothing less than that his mother's passing should mark the end, and the beginning, of an epoch. Rather than making himself matter by looking backwards at an already immortalized past marked by a series of significant publications, Barthes suggests that his mattering depends on something new performed in the present moment on behalf of one for whom he no longer matters at all. His suggestion is of a significant action, a performative convergence of word and deed, wherein action is itself readable and interpretable and memorable. I see Barthes striving for something very like the status of Benjamin's storyteller, but with added power, since the action he envisages as memorializing his mother is meant to refound his own memory as well.

Barthes's *Mourning Diary* speaks of the role of poesis in making action into something worthy of attention. Hannah Arendt in *The Human Condition* declares that only the human is capable of originating something new and unprecedented. Arendt refers to action as the human ability "to start new unprecedented processes whose outcome remains uncertain and unpredictable whether they are let loose in the human or the natural realm" (*The Human Condition*, 231–232). Indeed, for Arendt, humanity's defining attribute is the capacity for risky action that is an unprecedented addition to the public realm. For Barthes to make his mother "*recognized*" for who she was is an example of such an act. As a celebrity author and critic, Barthes needs to recast himself as another public figure with the event of his mother's death. In the three years that followed his mother's death and leading up to his own, Barthes published *Camera Lucida*. This book on photography and the image is simultaneously his mother's afterlife as narrated by her son. Early on in the *Camera Lucida*, Barthes clarifies how the private and the public converge in the act of photography. He writes, "Alas, I am doomed by (well-meaning) Photography always to have an expression: my body never finds its zero degree, no one can give it to me (perhaps only my mother?" (12). Barthes registers how in the process of becoming photographed he becomes an object and how this is a "micro-version of death" (13). What is only implied in Barthes's *Mourning Diary* is explicitly told in *Camera Lucida*:

> If, as so many philosophers have said, Death is the harsh victory of the race, if the particular dies for the satisfaction of the universal, if after having been reproduced as other than himself, the individual dies, having thereby denied and transcended himself, I who had not procreated, I had, in her very illness, engendered my mother. Once she was dead I no longer had any reason to attune myself to the progress of the superior life Force (the race, the species). My particularity could never again universalize itself (unless, utopically, by writing, whose project henceforth would become the unique goal of my life). (72)

Arendt's critique of the private sphere, as opposed to the public, is on account of its reducing subjects to mere private consumers of their lives. For Arendt, the individual human subject demands a public arena in which to be seen as unique. Lacking this we become objects of exchange, valued for what we do and what we make, never for who we are. The caution that is registered in Barthes's diary as well as given expression in *Camera Lucida* is a mark of the frailty that by necessity accompanies these acts precisely because they are unprecedented. To Barthes, the written work that he henceforth engages in is inseparable from the struggle to bring about remembrance of his mother, a secular immortality. Action in a public sphere as Arendt defines it, accompanied by a separate storytelling gesture, is the only chance humanity has for actions that outlive the time of their doing and so partake of immortality.

Barthes's diary calls into question the status of writing and literature in the face of extreme anguish. Put simply, and literally, words have not yet proven to be adequate to the task of describing this particular loss. In addition, Barthes's "fear of making literature" out of his mother's death (23) signals a more general ambivalence regarding the use of discourse as a means of addressing private pain. Barthes's diary is also the expression of intensely private anxieties regarding the role of literature and the author, in particular. Scattered throughout its entries is the persistent worry that Barthes might after all not have dedicated himself enough to her, a realization that comes to him toward the end of her life: "Since I've been taking care of her, the last six months in fact, she *was* 'everything' for me, and I've completely forgotten that I had ever written" (16). Mourning to Barthes becomes a complex assemblage of new challenges: a project of excruciating introspection, the desire to fight against the oblivion of his mother's memory, as well as a burgeoning fear of his own mortality. Barthes fathoms in *Camera Lucida* that mourning for him cannot remain a private affair. His memorialization of his mother aims to memorialize himself as well by memorializing his private loss as a matter of public relevance.

Seyla Benhabib glosses Arendt's public realm as "a competitive space, in which one competes for recognition, precedence, and acclaim; ultimately it is the space in which one seeks a guarantee against the futility and the passage of all things human" (193). Arendt notes that "one discloses one's self without ever either knowing himself or being able to calculate beforehand whom he reveals" (*The Human Condition*, 192), and it is in part this unpredictability that brings uncertainty to the endeavor. Arendt argues that the agent, the one who acts, cannot at the same time be his own storyteller. Barthes's mourning diary recognizes this in that, aside from the painful loss felt by its author, these pages also speak of a timidity regarding the written word as a form of disclosure as well as the limits of writing and narrative. "Less and less to write, to say," Barthes notes in one entry, "except this (which I can tell no one)" (40). And so Barthes takes us to the heart of mourning, namely the nonexistence of things, the profound emptiness and silence that death leaves behind in the world of the living. The loneliness felt by Ishmael when the world of Moby-Dick and Captain Ahab disappears along with the sinking of the Pequod comes close to describing the feelings that Barthes struggles with in his diary. But as with Ishmael, whose story can only really begin once he is utterly vulnerable, facing his own mortality and unknown destiny, Barthes also must create meaning out of desolation. In this sense, Barthes attempts to bring something into existence the way his mother did for him: "Confusion, defection, apathy: only, in snatches, the image of writing as 'something desirable,' haven, 'salvation,' hope, in short 'love,' joy" (59). What makes his endeavor all the more heart-rending is that Barthes is resigned to the fact that what he brings into existence will be second-rate to what his mother enabled.

Barthes, in other words, is resigned to the fact that he will not ever appear to himself (or others) as whole. Without *maman*, Barthes cautions himself, he will forever be incomplete, "henceforth you will always keep something broken about you" (171). Despite this realization, however, a bridging process can take place and Barthes is not destined to remain inside his winter vault for times on end. However imprecise and lacking, language nevertheless keeps him buoyed in a sea of utter despair: "My suffering is *inexpressible* but all the same *utterable*, speakable. The very fact that language affords me that word 'intolerable' immediately achieves a certain tolerance" (*Mourning Diary*, 175). Language renders tolerable by approximation. Language cannot bring the dead back to life. What it can do, as Michaels, Barthes, and Arendt recognize, is to fill the void and provide some sheltering against pain. This shelter is not exclusively of an existential nature. Perhaps more importantly, it is our guarantee for civilization. In "The decline of the Nation-State and the End of the Rights of Man," Arendt reminds the reader that the sole possibility for humanity's survival is to exist within a community: "We are not born equal; we become equal as members of a group on the strength of our decision to guarantee ourselves mutually equal rights" (*Origins of Totalitarianism*, 301). In her work on the public sphere and its intersections with trauma, Noëlle McAfee similarly cautions, after Arendt, against the complete withering of the public sphere as created by the expressivity of the individual voice: "Without people engaged in talking, writing, expressing, demonstrating, signifying, performing in a world with and for others, there would be no public sphere. It is not that a space would be waiting and empty, it would no longer exist" (17).

I would like now to return to the question of the storyteller's role post-Information Age in bringing home the tragedies of the sea. Two representations of mourning have emerged from my readings of Michaels's novel and Barthes's mourning work. First, we have encrypted memory waiting to come into circulation via narrative. This is an account of something in the past that is not yet available for public access. Encrypted memory is allegorized as the winter vault in the novel of the same title. Second, we have memory that is released from its crypt in the form of "narration, as the inchoate intent to tell" (Brooks, 53). Barthes is an example of this release of loss into the public realm as expression and text. Where the winter vault is armor against the passage of time, narrative as shared in the public sphere is "subject to the processes of desiring and dying," as Brooks writes (53).

It is ironic to witness this afterlife in the author of "Death of the Author" via a reconstitution of a central speaking and reading position. A place of encounter with loss itself becomes newly possible through his resolution to render his own private loss a contribution to public as well as self-knowledge. Barthes exposes himself to the gaze of the world as he attempts to think, create, imagine the significance of his loss, and, as is clear from *Camera Lucida*, it is not just for himself. Barthes needs to be remembered as the one who strove to make his *maman* memorable. He was after all the only one who could do it, or who needed to do it. In the manner of Ishmael, crying out the story of those whose hopes were sunk beneath the waves, Barthes's *Mourning Diary* offers counsel to grieving others. In the Information Age, that communication between narrator and reader seems rare. Tossed out like an anchor to the reader, Ishmael's "And I only am escaped alone to tell thee" is particularly moving in today's world of increasing displacement and fragmentation. From these preliminary observations, I want to suggest that the communication between narrator and reader is what effectively constitutes area. While the Internet has put us in contact with more strangers than ever conceivable in the pre-Digital Age, it has unfortunately not diminished the fear of face-to-face encounters with the stranger. All too often, we confuse a virtual nearness with an encounter. But software-mediated access to place and people at our fingertips is rarely these days an encounter with the strange. What happens "out there" at sea is as remote as that which happens in the virtual world, in some cases more so.

Whether this legacy from the Information Age is one that we can change—or even want to change—remains to be seen. Until then, we will continue to dive into the drifting wreckage of the Pequod on the Atlantic Ocean for help in surviving whatever separates us from others, whether it be grief, isolation, or exile.

Next I discuss ideas relating to the "coastless sea" as framed by a post-apocalyptic narrative. My particular interest in the following chapter is in the millennium crisis as brought about in the months leading up to the year 2000. At this point in time, it was widely believed that the so-called "Y2K bug" would wreak mayhem on information systems around the world. The global economy was then (as it is today) thoroughly dependent on the smooth functioning of high-speed, multimodal connectivity, but what was so revealing about the scare was how tenuously situated this networked society felt itself to be, despite the sophistication of its technology. Although the Y2K bug turned out to be a nonevent, in a few years the global economic crisis was to hit, ably assisted by improvements in the automation of economic decision making and the growing efficiency of the global communication network. As the machinery of connectivity triumphed, consumer confidence plummeted. The crisis brought with it a sense of disempowerment dramatized by novels and films from the turn of the century. In her *Essays on Extinction*, Claire Colebrook sees in the post-apocalyptic motif the opportunity to approach the question of the very real possibility of the actual extinction of the human species, while addressing the "barely perceived and half-articulated problem of how and whether humans ought to survive" (190). My focus on the apocalyptic is in the way it frames narratives of these anxieties in fiction on either side of the Atlantic. While the Y2K bug itself was harmless, rarely even needing a software intervention, a lingering sense of human impotence impacted masculine virility especially. These tensions between a sense of growing technical prowess at the peak of the Information Age, on one hand, and a sense of being under the thumb of our own creation, on the other, were played out across the Atlantic. The dialectic of the known and unknown, old and new, prowess and impotence reaches a peak of intensity in Michel Houellebecq's *Atomised* and Philip Roth's *The Human Stain*, two novels published on the brink of the new century, and the subject of my final chapter.

# 6

# Future Perfect

## The Problem of the Human in Michel Houellebecq's *Atomised* and Philip Roth's *The Human Stain*

Examples of masculinity in decline emerge in Michel Houellebecq's *Atomised* and Philip Roth's *The Human Stain* in the way they register, on the cusp of the twenty-first century, the growing autonomy of technology together with the dependence of humans on it, just as they problematize individual resistance to this dependence. Deflated by masculine infirmity, Roth's detumescent narrator, Nathan Zuckerman, seeks another form of connection while reporting the amorous exploits of his Viagra-charged hero, Coleman Silk. Here, medical technology provides a prosthetic aid to the ageing Silk's "connectivity," which then (connection begetting connection) gives Zuckerman an "in" to a story he can only know vicariously. Houellebecq's characters, Michel Djerzinski and Bruno Clément, face different challenges in holding themselves together individually or as half-brothers of an inattentive hippy mother, and their narrative ends up atomized, but not before bearing witness to an irreversible technology-driven desiccation of the human. Specifically, in these novels we see the terror of impotence or loss of resourcefulness as male characters search for any kind of immortality in the face of emergent technologies of reproduction and representation—"connectivity"—that place the function of master signifier (what is sometimes called the phallic or linguistic copula [Bristow, 86]) beyond the reach of mortals. Roth's novel turns to the campus as a predictable site where knowledge might still achieve immortality, while Houellebecq resorts to science, though in neither case does the human emerge with a satisfactory personal stake in the impending future.

In the previous chapter, we have seen that Roland Barthes and Anne Michaels endow narrative with memory in the form of story that provides a form of bulwark against the passage of time. No such hope is to be found in either Roth or Houellebecq's novels. Rather, *Atomised* and *The Human Stain* close with terrifying visions of an oceanic imaginary that seem to confirm the apocalyptic anticipations of McCarthy's *The Road* and Golding's *Lord of the Flies* (chapter 2). When the blanketing fog rolls in from the Atlantic toward the close of *Atomised*, the reader discovers that the novel that has so far held his or her attention has been narrated retrospectively by a clone from a bleak future no longer populated by human beings. A similar contest between authorial control and a rogue denouement resulting from Coleman Silk's scientifically aided adventures is played out at the end of Roth's novel. There we leave the narrator on a frozen lake in New England desperately contending with the jealous husband who has likely murdered his own ex-wife and Silk, two of Zuckerman's main characters. The worry that science was getting out of control was voiced in the 1960s by critics who warned that humans would not be masters over technology. Postman called it "the Frankenstein Syndrome" (23), and Ellul referred to the human as "a slug inserted into a slot machine" (135). In an age of accelerating technological autonomy, both Houellebecq and Roth present narrators who incarnate terrifying visions of crippling powerlessness to control or predict the consequences of a technologically purified humanity.

I want to start with a more recent novel of Houellebecq, *The Map and the Territory* from 2010. This novel, published a decade into the twenty-first century, takes an unflinching and acutely perceptive look at Europe's art industry, its technological methods and motifs, within a dystopic Europe, living out its last days in moral and cultural decay. Europe is the rotten tooth Houellebecq cannot leave alone: most recently in 2015 his focus is on its vexed relationship with Islam in *Submission*, and its pornography and sex tourism are examined in his 1999 novel *Platform*. *The Map and the Territory* chronicles the career of visual artist Jed Martin whose work is hilariously described at times in an autistic attention to detail. The novel ends zooming in on Martin's final installation in which the decrepit artist uses time lapse photography to film the decomposition of a toy diorama signifying the slow festering of France, and Europe more generally. The narrator indulges in a curatorial tone of voice to describe the installation with the critical distance of someone who still has a finger on the pulse of the contemporary art scene, however faint that pulse may now be:

> one tries to make sense of the unease that grips us on seeing those pathetic Playmobil-type little figurines, lost in the middle of an abstract and immense futurist city, a city which itself crumbles and falls apart then seems gradually to be scattered across the immense vegetation extending to infinity. (291)

At first it seems rather odd, the assured tone of the expert adopted by the narrator to whom surely the irony cannot be lost that what he is describing is no longer a representation, a map, but the territory, Europe, itself. However, Houellebecq's novels, like those of his contemporary Cormac McCarthy and to a lesser extent William Golding, curate culture for posterity. The voice of the Houellebecqian narrator, across all his novels, is insistently and clinically diagnostic, a compulsive cataloguer of the symptoms of social decline. With chilling precision and in a black comedic voice, it remains for him to observe and eulogize the life that was, reminiscent of the level of detail McCarthy's narrator uses, though not the tone, in chronicling the remains of culture and civilization that against all odds still turn up at the end of the world in *The Road*. Also comparable is the way that the narrators of both *Lord of the Flies* and *The Road* note in encyclopedic detail the decay in the bodies of animals and humans, for Houellebecq's narrator focuses on progress of decomposition in the human body with the connoisseurship of a pathologist. In *Atomised*, this aspiration for scientific accuracy makes a mockery of the fiction in which it appears, overtaking it, overshadowing it. Following mention of the death of Bruno Clément's grandfather in 1967, we learn:

> In temperate climates, the body of a bird or mammal first attracts specific species of flies (*Musca*, *Curtoneura*), but once decomposition has begun to set in, these are joined by others, particularly *Calliphora* and *Lucilia*. Under the combined action of bacteria and the digestive juices disgorged by the larvae, the corpse begins to liquefy and becomes a ferment of butyric and ammoniac reactions. (42)

And so on. *Atomised* is narrated from a chillingly inhuman remove. Houellebecq's prose is disposable, reminiscent of reportage, a text that delivers information but avoiding sentiment or human interest, it does not amount to knowledge. Instead, the reader is expected to consume the information given and then move on rather than being weighed down by sentiment or further significance. The author made this blend of infotainment a stylistic feature of *The Map and the Territory* and was consequently accused of plagiarizing Wikipedia shortly after its French publication. The question of copyright and fair use of citation aside, my interest is in what this steadfast refusal of the sensibility of pathos has to tell us about knowledge and its transmission. This chapter will raise questions regarding the technological promise of post-Atlantic times. An unrestrained "ultra-connected" oceanic imaginary aided by technology and prosthetics suggests a proliferation of deadening sameness to Houellebecq, while Roth sees an occasion for the elegiac exultation of the dying author. Through close reading of Houellebecq's *Atomised* and Roth's *The Human Stain*, this chapter will stage the Atlantic as a topos of the end of knowledge as encounter with otherness, and the end of human, specifically male, resourcefulness. Those "pathetic Playmobil-type little figurines" at the end of the *The Map and the Territory* constitute an artistic means of expressing a pessimistic view of human progress that comes into effable relief in both Houellebecq and Roth's novels. Death or the narrow escape from death haunts the pages of Roth's novel from start to finish in the form of anxiety related to sex and reproduction. *The Human Stain* is the final novel in a trilogy that begins with *American Pastoral* and is followed by *I Married a Communist*. The trilogy clings to the vestiges of a romantic myth of the outcast receding toward the horizon of the superhighways of information in a highly networked world.

The narrator of *The Human Stain*, Nathan Zuckerman, has willfully sequestered himself in a Thoreauvian style in a cabin surrounded by woods in the Berkshires, New England, partly because of his decision to withdraw from the sexual arena:

> My point is that by moving here I had altered deliberately my relationship to the sexual caterwaul, and not because the exhortations or, for that matter, my erections had been effectively weakened by time, but because I couldn't meet the costs of its clamoring anymore, could no longer marshal the wit, the strength, the patience, the illusion, the irony, the ardor, the egoism, the resilience—or the toughness, or the shrewdness, or the falseness, the dissembling, the dual being, the erotic *professionalism*—to deal with its array of misleading and contradictory meanings. (36–37)

Here too, as with Houellebecq's decomposition scenes, the prose veers into reportage. There is also an overproduction of prose as if to compensate for the emptiness Zuckerman fears, whether death or the lack of libido. The litany of reasons justifying his decision to retire from the sexual arena is unconvincing; he is protesting too much. Indeed, a sentence like this, coming in at just under one hundred words, suggests that for Zuckerman writing is to be his way of demonstrating prowess in connectivity, and there is validity in that. The point, though, is that by the time Zuckerman finds out about the cancer in his prostate, and becomes both impotent and incontinent as a result of the prostatectomy, on his own account he has already decided on a monastic lifestyle. In lieu of sex, Zuckerman seeks out spiritual guidance ("sustenance" [44]) in Hawthorne, his literary New England ancestor. As with Hawthorne, who famously claimed not to write novels as such, but romances removed from "the possible or probable course of ordinary experience" (Porte, 95), Zuckerman also seeks romance as a buffer against the real of his infirmity. Indeed, romance in lieu of procreation becomes a measure of humanity in Roth's novel.

At stake in both *Atomised* and *The Human Stain* is the ability to know and extend knowledge beyond the physical, surpassing as well as the symbolic, or expressive, limits of self. Procreation is called into question in both novels, and human beings are either condemned to the eternal half-life of clones in Houellebecq, or in Roth we settle on the more familiar desire simply to prolong sexual potency for as long as possible via pharmaceutical intervention or, failing that, to live a long but necessarily celibate life. Indeed, as we have seen in chapter 2, the apocalyptic novel is routinely devoid of male and female interactions. Both *The Road* and *Lord of the Flies* remain chaste around the question of physical love and the creation of life. The boys marooned on the island in *Lord of the Flies* have not entered puberty and, apart from the father's vague reminiscences of his dead wife in McCarthy's novel, nothing in *The Road* is overtly sexual. Similarly, Houellebecq's *Atomised* centers around boys unrestrained by maternal caution and care. It takes as normal the cruel behavior of boys in Golding's dystopic vision:

> From his first week at primary school in Charny, Michel had been struck by the cruelty of the boys. It's true that the little beasts were farmers' sons, and therefore closer to animals than most. Nevertheless, it was startling to witness the instinctive, unaffected way they stabbed frogs with a compass point or a dip-pen; violet ink blossoming beneath the skin of the unfortunate animal as it slowly died. They would gather in a circle, their eyes bright, to watch its final agony. Another of their games was to cut the antennae off snails with their round-ended children's scissors. All of the snail's sensory awareness comes from its antennae, crowned by the eyes. Without them, the snail is reduced to a pulpous mass, suffering and bewildered. (195)

This repulsive description of animal suffering stands out if only because the novel seems unconcerned with human suffering, though paradoxically the aim of Michel Djerzinski's ground-breaking biological research is to end the vicissitudes of sexual reproduction. The novel charts the life of Michel as a notable scientist whose work in fusing molecular biology with quantum physics paves the way for the first cloning of a human being in the novel on March 27, 2029. *Atomised* is in fact narrated by one such unnamed human clone (readers discover this in the novel's epilogue) who salutes the end of the human race along with its disastrous sexual reproduction, replete as it is with aggression and despair. The tour de force of Michel and the other scientists is their ability to manipulate subatomic material to the point of eliminating human error and suffering. The cost of doing away with this intrinsically human "stain" is not just in the way individual lives are damaged along the way. There is an even more devastating price to be paid by a society that places so much importance on the pursuit of certainty. I read Houellebecq's novel as a warning against this pursuit of perfection that rules out the unforeseeable, the serendipitous, and the surprise encounter as legitimate in the path to discovery. Strictly, in Houellebecq's dystopic vision even the possibility of any further discovery of what it means to be human becomes extinct. Cloning in *Atomised* is represented as a form of embodied knowledge muted by its very assurance. Houellebecq exults experience as the last bastion of humanity and asks the reader what will happen if experience itself is cloned. We have already seen in chapter 2 that a transatlantic exchange is reliant on difference. Facing that homogeneous sameness, as on the shores of the Atlantic in McCarthy's *The Road*, individuals are no longer able to imagine encounters based on exchange. Instead, as Roth and Houellebecq suggest, the old borders of encounters are revisited in the pursuit of improbable romance.

The romance celebrated in *The Human Stain* by its romantically challenged narrator, secluded in the woods of New England, is the cult of eternal life. Having narrowly escaped his own death at the cost of sexual impotence, Zuckerman proceeds to narrate the tumultuous and fatal affair of Coleman Silk. The septuagenarian Silk, former dean of faculty at Athena College, is involved with Faunia Farley, a 34-year-old illiterate janitor at the same college. Silk's progress is propped up by Viagra, as well as the thrill of being able to share his conquest with Zuckerman, his personal narrator. Zuckerman's narrative aims to immortalize the intimacy shared by Silk and Farley, at least he works at elevating their affair to something that will survive its violent end even if by doing so Zuckerman contributes to the fetishization of the penis. This prolongation of the efficacy of the male generative organ in both *The Human Stain* as well as its supersession in *Atomised* is an attempt at immortality. By a prolongation of the organ, I am not simply referring to its extended functional life through Viagra but also the immortalization of the act of copulation as well as the love and life story of Silk himself via Zuckerman's prose. Zuckerman's vicarious enjoyment of the older man's sexual adventures is somehow compensated for by the fact that Silk, a scholar no longer allowed to produce knowledge, is now the subject of Zuckerman's next novel. This new novel, the novel within the novel, is also entitled *The Human Stain*. It tells Silk's story of how, due to his perceived racism on campus and his involvement with a woman almost 40 years his junior, he is pilloried by the academy and the wider community.

Firmly anchored in New England, *The Human Stain* and its author Philip Roth exult in the cultural capital of this outpost of the Old World. Cast down from his role as an academic, Silk is then vilified again for refusing to bow to Puritan notions of civility and decency. It is the work of Zuckerman the storyteller to transform tawdry bits and pieces of biographical information about Silk into a narrative of wider human relevance, a larger narrative about desire, suffering, and ageing. Houellebecq does not exult the romance and power of storytelling in quite the same way. In his much bleaker vision of Europe, human reproduction is managed by medical technology in order to eradicate all risk of error, to wipe the proverbial board clean, rather than romanticize and exult its imperfections through literary embellishment. Despite the pleasing fantasy of Californian hippie communes in *Atomised*, Houellebecq's vision of the new millennium is grim, imparting none of the wisdom and counsel Walter Benjamin so prized, that we found in Graham Greene's work (chapter 1) and in the poetry of Ted Hughes (chapter 4). Knowledge as a specifically human achievement in the world of cloning has become disembodied, lifeless, removed from place and country. Hardly deserving of the name, knowledge as discovery is incapable of being communicated via Benjaminian storytelling as the experience of a chance-driven encounter with the unexpected. In the atomized world, place is nonexistent; the absence of home and the absence of knowledge go together. Information as Houellebecq describes it is atomized knowledge, not anchored to any recognizable source.

Although Roth's novel centers on the campus, the academy has ceased to be a place of productive intellectual exchange. Instead, in Silk's own faculty, cloying fantasy, anxious rivalries, and baseless rumors congeal into a self-serving mass of distractions having scant bearing on the real world. Stubbornly surviving as a place of privilege, and threatened with extinction as an institution built on principles of exclusion, the academy is both a public collective space as well as a deeply intimate one. The more vulnerable a place is to attack from the outside, the more private it becomes. Such intimate confines, argues Berlant, are constituted by threats to the image they seek to sustain (7). Roth displays two visions of the academy in *The Human Stain*. The first is of the academy as a place of superiority, sequestered from the outside world. It is worth remembering that the historical background of the university is as a safeguard and defense against heterodox outside influences. Scholars in Medieval Europe typically went to the Near or Middle East to broaden their minds. By the same route Islam returned with these scholars to the West as part of their intellectual attainment. As a result, universities (Bologna, Paris, Montpellier, among others) were established to stand as an intellectual front of resistance. In short, the university was there to protect Christian values. A similar fear of contamination from the outside world circulates in Roth's depiction of the academy. The second vision of the academy Roth offers is very different. Here he sees it as supporting public knowledge as a service to the broader community. Roth's novel is nothing if not a stern reminder that the "human stain" of error and discovery is an important link in the chain of knowledge acquisition and that nothing can be gained by sanitizing it. *The Human Stain* depicts the affair between a woman of lower socioeconomic status, intellectually and financially barred from campus, and a former dean of faculty. Although revealing how porous the barriers are between the "real" world and the campus, their intimacy ultimately confirms the fantasy of a transgression both possible and foreclosed in a place where existing paths of knowledge transferral are rarely violated, except at considerable personal cost. As the part-time janitor of the college, Faunia Farley is at the very bottom of the social order, presumed ignorant and unworldly. Moreover, her direct contact with America's underbelly in the form of her pathologically jealous ex-husband Les Farley threatens the status quo of the university and the perceived superiority (as well as the lives) of its academics.

Roth questions the notion of the university as an ivory tower through the character of Coleman Silk who, despite being twice her age and utterly removed from her world of domestic abuse and personal hardship, falls passionately in love with Farley. Their affair becomes a vehicle for querying some familiar academic methods and practices. Outlandish textual interpretation, for example, is taken to task in Roth's novel where the subject of so much analysis and theory, Faunia Farley herself, proves the most impenetrably resistant of "texts." Farley embodies the New World heritage of struggle to overcome adversity that was not accomplished without bloodshed and trauma. Roth connects her story with the twentieth-century personal and cultural trauma of American violence through her ex-husband, a Vietnam War veteran whose rage and jealousy has become psychopathic. She is also a woman who struggles to keep a dairy farm, who is thus also deeply connected to the American settler tradition of working with the soil for the nourishment of the community. A strangely pastoral scene early in *The Human Stain* effectively counters the claim of the campus to be the primary scene of learning with an alternative of its own. Silk invites his friend, the author Nathan Zuckerman, to "Organic Livestock," the dairy farm where Farley lives and works. Although the dairy farm is organic and so free from "the 'stain' of pasteurization and homogenization," as Royal perceptively notes (129), the farm signals a refusal to submit to the obsession with cleanliness manifested in attempts to produce a blemish- and germ-free product. Arguably, the purity renounced has its corollary in the ideal of the academy as ivory tower. It is significant that inside the university Farley works as a cleaner, whereas in her own place, as it were, she is in contact with all the dirt and muck associated with a dairy. Coleman enjoys watching his mistress milk the cows, partly because it is erotic to him, but also because the very act of extracting milk from cows seems more productive and less sanitized than extracting new meaning from old texts in his line of work.

Exactly how incompatible the jargon that circulates at university is with human experience becomes obvious in *The Human Stain*. Among the first to discover this, rather surprisingly, is Silk himself for, despite preferring to see his lover among cows rather than books, he intuits that she has formidable thinking powers. Early on in the novel, Silk informs Zuckerman of Farley's "savage" wisdom, her lack of formal education notwithstanding. That suffering and grief enable people to learn is not a novel idea. In Roth's novel, however, Faunia Farley's treatment by the "school of hard knocks" alienates her from her upper-class origins as well as the university community with which her job as college janitor puts her, however peripherally, in contact. *The Human Stain* raises important questions regarding the university's ability to impart real and useful knowledge that is not derivative. Critical of scholars like Delphine Roux who teaches Greek plays within a feminist framework, Silk is of the opinion that the university apes rather than critically examines current trends, thereby failing to uphold strict academic distance from the fashions and opinions of the day. Of a female student who complains that Silk's reading of Euripides is misogynistic, he protests that to conclude reading *Hippolytus* and

*Alcestis* with "nothing to say about either of them other than that they are 'degrading to women' isn't a 'perspective,' for Christ's sake—it's mouthwash. It's just the latest mouthwash" (192).

Silk does not simply blame the university for its lack of intellectual standards; he also holds little regard for students. In conversations with Delphine Roux, Silk displays a dismal view of the students (191). A similar pessimism for self-improvement is professed by Houellebecq's characters in *Atomised*; most of whom are victims of the late capitalist *zeitgeist* of liberalism. The half-brothers Michel and Bruno of *Atomised* are the neglected children of parents who found parenting incompatible with their pursuit of personal freedom. Both these lifestyle junkies and their children are products of an aggressively competitive capitalist individualism as well as the sexual revolution of the 1960s and 1970s. Houellebecq sees to it that a good measure of New Age religion is thrown in, especially the sort that slowly came to infect business culture. In every way critical of the cult of the individual, Houellebecq and his characters often hold America to blame for our atomized world of emaciated social involvement and smeared personal responsibility. The characters in *Atomised* attempt to replicate the liberated hippie culture of places like California, but their attempts fall short of the real thing and the result is lifeless and bland. Bruno, a sexually frustrated man whose frantic search for personal satisfaction leaves him depleted, vents his frustrations to whoever cares to listen. This raises a separate problem, Houellebecq seems to suggest, because nobody listens anymore except for those who get paid.[1] In an earlier novel, *Whatever*, Houellebecq makes cruel fun of psychoanalysis, for woman especially, though he targets the dangers of the talking cure more generally.[2] The fact that there is both a personal narrator who is also a devoted listener to the slandered Coleman Silk's tale of woe in *The Human Stain* suggests that romance still has currency in America for those who can afford the time to pay attention.

*Atomised* depicts a very different world where individuals are cut off from their environment and detached from relations of human reciprocity. Who pays attention to Bruno and Michel's failings as men, fathers, and lovers? While some critics agree that *Atomised* is concerned with larger questions pertaining to the historical possibilities and limits of humanism (Wallace, 142), others challenge the success of Houellebecq's critique of late capitalist society on the grounds that its overtly sexual content merely titillates many readers. Varsava holds that the novel says "very much more about insecure, sexually obsessed European men in early middle age than it does about European society at large" (162). However, for all its free love posturing and its graphic descriptions of casual sex, it has to be said that *Atomised* is in fact rather asexual. Instead of the pleasure of discovery of self and other, *Atomised* proposes a world in which the desire for scientific progress has superseded the natural sexual urge in human beings, as the scientist Michel notes:

> Truth is, I'm just not interested in sex any more. Knowledge, on the other hand... There's still a desire for knowledge. It's a curious thing, this thirst for knowledge... very few scientists have it, you know... There is no power in the world—economic, political, religious or social—that can compete with rational certainty. (322)

On the eve of the millennium, alongside the pervasive fear of a software bug that might wreak havoc on our information systems, human progress here is still measured by the degree of control we have over our certainties. The stain of humanity that will not budge, despite its hopeless prospects in Roth's novel, has been obliterated in Houellebecq's *Atomised*. Technological intervention has ensured that nothing, not even sexual reproduction, has been left for human imperfection to bungle. While Philip Roth depicts an America whose Puritan strictures serve as the perfect setting for the fantasy of transgression, Michel Houellebecq imagines a Europe too naive (unless it is really stupid or worse, lazy) for original thinking and self-invention. When the hippie movement begins to ebb in California in the 1970s, Francesco di Meola, one of the founder members of Esalen near Big Sur in California and lover of Bruno and Michel's mother Janine, transfers his business for "liberating the individual's innate potential" (82) to rural France. There, near Avignon, di Meola successfully attracts hordes of "particularly repressed" (94) as well as "thick" (96) young people.

A feature of the contemporary transatlantic knowledge industry that registers clearly in *Atomised* is the way the United States, offspring of the Old World, is often the parent of ideas that are then taken up in Europe. This is observed by the characters in *Atomised*; so it is not surprising that Bruno derides his father's decision not to expand his cosmetic surgery business by picking up the fad of silicone breast enlargements. "Nothing has ever caught on in America," Bruno declares, "that didn't engulf Western Europe a couple of years later, nothing" (84). If Bruno is right then he should expect to see in Europe a resurgence in the kind of amorous passion practiced by Coleman Silk in *The Human Stain*. Maybe, but if so, this particular import from the New World (which clearly is not the same as that Californian free love) is rather slow in coming. In an article about Houellebecq, Morrey points out that the "ruthless competition and demand for excellence that drive the labor market and economic relations have gradually encroached upon the private sphere in such a way that personal relationships and sexual practices are now subject to the same pressure" (143). In Houellebecq's eyes, love "has become an outmoded sentiment, structurally incompatible with a free sexual marketplace based around narcissistic competition" (146). Certainly, neither Michel nor Bruno is able to love and be loved, even though they are both given the chance to step up to the challenge by the women in their lives. Michel, we are told, "had contributed to the sum of human knowledge; that was his vocation, it was the way he had found to express his talents; but love was something he had never known" (345). As for Bruno, he is unable to rise above his simple needs for sexual stimulation. It is true, as Morrey observes, that the world of Houellebecq is a world in which sex is simultaneously highly visible and inaccessible (142), while quite the opposite is true of *The Human Stain*. But if Bruno and his sort are correct to surmise that the United States is always ten steps ahead, what does Roth's novel have to say about the possibilities for authenticity and integrity in human relations, especially of the amorous sort?

Well, in the United States, despite Roth's efforts on its behalf, *amour* is also a threatened form of human interactivity. Nevertheless, thanks to the miracle of Viagra, Professor Coleman Silk is able to step into the role of a veritable Priapus, even if it means he must cease teaching the Greek classics. This medical enhancement to his sexual connectivity also confers on the sensitive man one last chance at the real thing, love. Faunia's generous offer of herself to Silk ("I am whatever you want" [Roth, 234]) stands in marked contrast to the finicky, narrow-minded criteria people apply to their romantic lives—think of the selection process for partners in online dating. Through her, Roth also discredits the preprogrammed, closed attitude of the academy. Only carnal knowledge and Faunia Farley herself retain some of the mystery of humanity in Roth's novel. Most of all, academics are portrayed as foolish, Silk for his solipsism and the others for their lack of empathy and their sanctimony. Silk receives an anonymous note that reads, "everyone knows you're sexually exploiting an abused, illiterate woman half your age" (38). In a move that surely mocks the very idea of research and literary analysis, Silk has the note examined to verify its author, based on "slant, spacing, letter formation, line quality, pressure pattern, proportion, letter height relationship, connections and initials and terminal stroke formation" (55). The academy is made a fool of in Roth's novel, but only because there is the strong sense of it having let the public down at a time when it most needed guidance. Concurrent with the impeachment of President Clinton for lying about his affair with Monica Levinsky, the fictional Coleman Silk is barred from teaching due to a total misreading of his referring to two recalcitrantly absent students as "spooks" when it turns out that they are African American. For this he is accused of racism and that, together with his affair with Faunia Farley, is enough to suspend him from teaching (32).

Even after withdrawing from his public position as dean and lecturer, Silk's lawyer Primus warns him of "the malevolent puritanism" (76) that will be his downfall unless he completely disassociates himself from Farley also in his private life. Unable to change the opinion of others, Silk resolves, if he can, "to live beyond the jurisdiction of their enraging, loathsome, stupid blame" (64). The narrator of *The Human Stain*, Nathan Zuckerman, dreams of draping a banner across the White House bearing the words "A HUMAN BEING LIVES HERE" (3). While this kind of shared humanity could, in a less complex age (or novel), be the basis of a stand against the social control of individuals in the West, Zuckerman here is complicit in peddling a sentimentality in the service of a disguised puritanical repression. He calls to mind the spread of what cultural commentator Alan Liu refers to as a systemic and fatal "friendliness":

> Alienation is everywhere, but it is no longer the Marxist drama of antagonism; it is instead a drama ("deep act") of friendship. One may be feeling glum or doomed, but there is no escape. Friendliness, like fate, is everywhere. (123)

In Liu's terms, when Zuckerman reveals that he too is at the service of this endemic push toward conformity that suppresses the human stain, he is only fulfilling his role as part of "the convergence of information and service work" (123). While laboring at a narrative that seems to want to rescue flawed human beings from public shame and vilification, Zuckerman is also complicit in a process that smooths the way for "the external control of emotional labor" (122), which Liu notes is essential for corporate culture to function. Loose ends in Zuckerman's narrative are most clearly revealed when it comes to his narrating the part played by the illiterate janitor and dairy farmer

Faunia Farley. Here is how Zuckerman imagines Farley reflecting on the stain of humanity in the company of a caged crow:

> It's in everyone. Indwelling. Inherent. Defining. The stain that is there before its mark. Without the sign it is there. The stain so intrinsic it doesn't require a mark. The stain that precedes disobedience, that encompasses disobedience and perplexes all explanation and understanding. (*Human Stain*, 242)

Recall that Zuckerman is master of the hundred-word sentence. Clearly, here he thinks his friend's lover would feel the strain of putting two or more words together. Brought to us filtered by Zuckerman's prejudices, her meditation on the stain reveals more about his intrusiveness in this narrative than it does about her. Most apparent is the vocabulary he uses, this and the voice are quite unlike Farley's own. At this moment we can begin to appreciate Roth's achievement in explicitly refracting a narrative honoring our flawed humanity through the eyes of a particularly flawed narrator such as Zuckerman. Both part of and removed from the story, his role is similar to that of the chorus in one of the Greek plays formerly taught by Silk at the University. The prose Zuckerman imagines for Faunia is contrived, obviously constructed out of a montage of potted psychology and New Age wisdom. The reader is invited to watch the narrator in the process of manufacturing reality by ventriloquizing a range of different characters in the novel. Why, when he is capable of honestly disclosing his sexual infirmity, does Zuckerman give Faunia Farley a phony intellectual speech register? Zuckerman's power as a narrator is compromised here and, we could be forgiven for adding, it is compromised in the same way Silk's Viagra-induced copulative prowess testifies to a weakness at the level of truth.

This disjunction or dissonance between Zuckerman's and Silk's narrative suggests a problem that Viagra or any other technologically enhanced connectivity among human beings cannot heal. Indeed, I suspect that Roth's aim is to celebrate and flaunt the human stain of a narrator's impotence as a genuine improvement on any sanitized, politically correct alternative. Incontinent and impotent after a prostatectomy, Zuckerman's reclusive lifestyle has kept sexual urges under control, until his new friendship with Coleman Silk awakens a new vicarious pleasure in sexuality together with a desire to narrate it. Sex and psychoanalysis theorist Joseph Bristow sees verbal prowess of Silk and Zuckerman as allied with a phallic power that is possibly more than metaphorically traceable to the sexual copulative function.

Outside of the Lacanian theory of language and the psyche on which Bristow bases his remarks, the word "copulative" has, distinct from its sexual sense, a grammatical meaning that rejoins Bristow's account: the phallic function, as "the linguistic copula," is "the verbal unit (enshrined in the verb 'to be') that yokes disparate elements together, securing the chain of shifting meanings" (86). Nevertheless, engaging this verbal power does not always result in a strong sense of security. Regardless of being master of the prolonged sentence, what Zuckerman hears of Silk's sexual exploits threatens to expose his fragile masculinity at a time of diminishing relevance for his profession as storyteller in the Information Age. Though Faunia Farley is depicted as the wise sage, the one who possesses what her paramour refers to as "negative wisdom" from "thirty-four years of savage surprises" (27), it is the portrait of the male body and especially the phallus (in both senses of the word) in *The Human Stain* that reveals most clearly the tensions regarding productivity and reproductivity at the end of the Information Age.

A few pages into the novel, it becomes clear to Zuckerman that he is subservient to Silk for what is revealed about himself while telling the story of Silk's life. It dawns on Zuckerman after a particularly poignant scene between the two men dancing together that in telling Silk's story he is also telling his own: "And my having danced around like a harmless eunuch with this still vital, potent participant in the frenzy struck me now as anything but charming self-satire" (37). As ecstasy awakens after decades of slumber in the newly Dionysian Silk; it also becomes possible to observe the ritual origins of tragedy. In the private theater of Coleman Silk, a self-made man who has concealed his African American origins to everyone in his life, the viewer begins to see that the narrative will be adapted by the tragic vision of Zuckerman in whom something else also begins to stir after years of forgetfulness. Envy? Resentment? Desire? Whatever it is, it is true that a novelist seeks conflict, something to write about, a point not missed by Silk himself who begins to see the power Zuckerman possesses over him: "Catastrophe is cannon fodder for him. But what can *I* transform this into? I am stuck with it. As is. Sans language, shape, structure, meaning—sans the unities, the catharsis, sans everything" (170). Although here Silk feels exposed so too is Zuckerman, for a veil is lifted and the storyteller is no longer protected by whatever fourth wall his skill might erect for him to hide behind. Even so, in sharing his story with Nathan Zuckerman, Silk discovers the power that the storyteller has over him. For his own as well as his narrator's benefit, all that remains for him to do is to follow his desire with Faunia

Farley, "because to be able to abandon oneself to this freely, someone has to know it" (33). That was once a simple idea, that we exist as far as we are witnessed and reported, but at the turn of the twentieth century, Roth's novel testifies to the personal disempowerment that comes when sexual connectivity relies increasingly on technology. Beyond Viagra for the aged, think of social networking, as well as the prevalence of Internet dating for the young. While representational technologies usurp the control we have over our self-representations, Silk's story is outsourced to Zuckerman, leaving Silk bereft of language. That Silk is unable himself properly to translate his experience of Faunia Farley into narrative is a loss more deeply felt for his having cultivated and enjoyed oratorical skills of his own. Silk's simple yet profound question, "what can *I* transform this into?," registers the limits of anyone's power to use language to control experience or its reportage.

This is a commentary on the complexity of the relationship between subjectivity and automation at the height of the Information Age. What autonomy remains with the singular individual after she or he has relinquished control to machines that prosthetically work to extend the reproductive and representational abilities of the human? Silk's role is relegated to that of action hero in his own life. No longer able to narrate his experiences himself, they come into effable relief only through Zuckerman's grasp of the adventures Silk lives through. According to technology author Shoshana Zuboff, a machine "can be controlled according to a set of rational principles in a way that human bodies cannot" and, she adds, this is because a machine is "mute" (8), it does not talk back. Zuckerman's narrative, however limited it may be in its pretention to omniscient knowledge of the private thoughts of characters, is nevertheless allied with a force that seeks to publish what without it would be merely a cul-de-sac of private and unreportable experience. The fulfillment of a desire that would otherwise die with the body is given a life after death in Roth's novel through Zuckerman's compelling narrative. A body that is essentially mute can be controlled, as Zuboff says, because it is "precise and repetitive" (8). To the extent that human beings act resistlessly in obedience to the compulsion of external forces, they too are like machines, and they are mute in the sense that they do not protest their conditions or narrate them. The compulsion of the pleasure principle, Freud tells us, seeks only a decrease in tension for the human animal who thereby follows the path of least resistance to pleasure, and ultimately to death. When Silk and Farley die in a car accident, presumably orchestrated by Farley's jealous and war-damaged ex-husband, we have an uncanny reminder that the pleasure principle is no less powerful a compulsion than the death drive with which Freud equated it. Silk's pursuit is fated to end in death, unmodified as it is by the "reality-principle" that, according to Freud, would have ensured his *not* getting what he wanted when he wanted it, "dancing their way stark naked right into a violent death" (204).

There may well be something to Zuckerman's quest for a substitute phallic verbal command, for without his reporting, Viagra in and of itself provides only for the possibility of a prolonged sex life. One of the stakes in Roth's novel is the phallic force that must be supplied by the impotent narrator, cut off from the physical act of sex, but not necessarily from the power to tell its story. However, the final scene of the novel that sees Zuckerman in conversation with Les Farley sheds doubt on the power wielded by him as the narrator of Silk's libidinally inspired outpourings. Whereas Faunia fails to provide much interest for Zuckerman, her ex-husband Les Farley exerts a magnetic appeal to him. The passages in which Zuckerman renders Les Farley's trauma as a Vietnam veteran belong to the more moving passages of the novel because the narrative voice breaks, unable to remain aloof from the masculine frailty it depicts. Zuckerman speaks via Les Farley's damaged psyche about the tragic consequences of war on the individual in this group therapy session with other war veterans:

> The group consisted of Vietnam vets like Farley except for two from the Gulf War, crybabies who got a little sand in their eyes in a four-day ground war. A hundred-hour war. A bunch of waiting in the desert. The Vietnam vets were men who, in their postwar lives, had themselves been through the worst—divorce, booze, drugs, crime, the police, jail, the devastating lowness of depression, uncontrollable crying, wanting to scream, wanting to smash something, the hands trembling and the body twitching and the tightness in the face and the sweats from head to toe from reliving the metal flying and the brilliant explosions and the severed limbs, from reliving the killing of the prisoners and the families and the old ladies and the kids. (73–74)

Readers who have grown accustomed to Zuckerman's style of narrative so far are surely entitled to ask, whose point of view this is? Whose macho opinion is he actually ventriloquizing in this scene? Who exactly believes that Gulf War vets suffering posttraumatic stress are "crybabies"? At the same time, the performance is rather convincing in its disarray in the face of this suffering. Perhaps this is a changed Zuckerman, for he invests a lot of narratological blood, sweat, and tears in describing Les Farley, an outlaw and wife-beater, and the novel ends when the two men meet, face to face. The reader expects a showdown as is customary when desperadoes compete for the same treasure though in Roth's novel the competition still ends up being centered around narrative control in an age of symbolic disempowerment. This prose, touching on acute masculine uncertainties, reveals the flawed nature of literature in contrast to the predictability of scientifically enhanced protocols of encounter, a feature of the Information Age. Unlike information, literature demands a reading that observes the inconsistencies of its real-world human subject matter as well as those of the text itself, "making claims not subject to any verification," declares Michael Wood, "except the kind that comes from within the work itself" (100). The act of writing is revealed in Roth's novel as a rather desperate attempt to reach out and connect with readers, and for the reader to accept the author's offering on these terms, she or he must read, as Wood suggests,

> with a mixture of scepticism and belief; of trust in fiction and awareness of fakery; of submission to syntax and imagery and alertness to technique, of dependence on internal cross-reference and constant checking with our often rather casually held notions about lived historical life. (100)

While expressing an intense skepticism regarding the comforts offered by narrative, Roth nevertheless seeks to offer these treasures.

In the novel's final scene, a somewhat chastened Zuckerman still inhabits his first-person narrative but now his reach is limited, as if housebound, while he narrates only his own memories with no taste, it seems, for any further attempt at the flights of omniscience that disappointed him in his waning powers. Leaving his car by the side of a New England road, Zuckerman finds himself crossing fields on foot, conscious of himself trespassing, uneasily observing his reaction to the "pristine" landscape before him (345). In a final reprise of the themes inaugurated by the novel's title, he reflects that this beauty is conventionally assigned to such places insofar as their Edenic purity is unmarked by the hand of man. However, when Zuckerman comes across Les Farley fishing through the ice of a frozen lake, it turns out that the place is in fact marked by the human, by a kind of writing in fact, although there is nothing about what follows to reassure us about the future of the life of letters. Zuckerman approaches Farley with dread, armed only with the extreme caution usually reserved for a dangerous animal, or a psychopath. As if for a parlay, they face each other on the ice with an auger between them, the one Farley has used for drilling his fishing hole: "The auger out on the ice. The candor of the auger. There could be no more solid embodiment of our hatred than the merciless steel look of that auger out in the middle of nowhere" (352). This meeting on ice between author and this renegade narrative loose end recalls the final encounter between Victor Frankenstein and his creature on a glacier in Shelley's *Frankenstein*. Farley does not plead for his creator's mercy as Frankenstein's creation does, rather he adopts a threatening attitude to the author for having the temerity to include him in his novel. In an unsettling closing image, Farley ends up representing a barely human force that would undermine any respect for literature's attempt to represent us to ourselves: "the icy white of the lake encircling a tiny spot that was a man, the only human marker in all of nature, like the X of an illiterate's signature on a sheet of paper. There it was, if not the whole story, the whole picture" (361). In a world seduced by the promises of information, and increasingly suspicious of that "mixture of scepticism and belief" (Wood, 100) demanded by narrative, this could be the picture we are left with.

Claire Colebrook makes a compelling if disturbing case for a thoroughgoing questioning of the role and value of the human. Imagining the possible rights of an other-than-human life that might emerge in some not-so-distant future brought about by human or natural influences, Colebrook says of that encounter on the glacier between Frankenstein and his monster, "The creature's plea to his maker is also an allegorical questioning of humanity's relation to production: how can we leave a populace of the future so miserably orphaned?" (195). This sheds light on a difference between the desperate pathos of Shelley's creature and the far less sublime sense of loss Roth inscribes in his own surrogate author, Zuckerman. The imagery in the scene Zuckerman paints underlines loss of agency for both the storyteller and the told locked in static immobility, as frozen as the ice beneath their feet: "Here we are alone up where we are, and I know, and he knows I know. And the auger knows. All ye know and all ye need to know, all inscribed in the spiral of its curving steel blade" (354). Knowledge now is so diminished in value that the toolmaker knows little more than his tools. The narrative Zuckerman tells in his own *The Human Stain* has far-reaching implications for himself and for representational distance as well. It becomes clear after facing Les Farley on the ice that, once the book is published, Zuckerman can no longer stay in the cottage where he has lived as a recluse for the last five years of his life, for Farley would, Zuckerman is certain, avenge the slanderous way the author has revealed his secrets. No longer the biographer of Coleman Silk's libidinous progress, Nathan Zuckerman now finds himself caught in a much more perilous game. He walks away from the threat posed by Les Farley and the auger, reassuring Farley that his secret is "safe with me" (360). The scene suggests that Roth himself is fearful for the future of literature and learning and the sort of knowledge offered by novelists, however incomplete in contrast to the totality expected of information. There is a worrying sense as the novel closes, of fiction under threat from reality. It calls to mind the danger of the university ceasing to offer a distinct perspective on whatever is happening in the economy, the corporation, politically, and so on, because it has become identical to these processes. The fearful self-censorship of the narrator's power by something outside invading his text signals the frailty of agency in an age of endless production, whether of text or other consumer objects.

The story ends in more than one sense of the word, with its attention not on Coleman Silk or Nathan Zuckerman (although it is, of course, through his eyes the reader is looking) but on Les Farley and the repudiation of the role of the storyteller that he stands for, that "X of an illiterate's signature on a sheet of paper" (361). We are not simply leaving this novel but, considering its urgent concern with threats to authorial agency and intellectual critical distance, we may well be entering, with the coming century, a new dark age for literary freedom. The storyteller leaves his story for the world to do with it as it wishes, which may ultimately be nothing at all. The actors have all exited the stage either through death (Silk and Faunia) or the careful preservation of a foreshortened life seen in how cautiously Zuckerman retreats from Les Farley "shuffling backward a half-step at a time" (359), more impotent now than ever. *The Human Stain* ends with a chilling image of Zuckerman seeming for all the world to be capitulating to the pressure to misrepresent Les Farley, to whitewash both his crimes as well as the political decision making that led to them: "Only rarely, at the end of our century, does life offer up a vision as pure and peaceful as this one: a solitary man on a bucket, fishing through eighteen inches of ice in a lake that's constantly turning over its water atop an arcadian mountain in America" (361). Surely he is being ironic, for otherwise the only truth here is the merely veridical fact of the threat that Zuckerman is succumbing to in offering readers this sentimental, sanitized mouthwash. It denies what Farley has just told him so insistently, that far from being "a solitary man on a bucket" in an idyllic setting there are "thousands and thousands of other guys," battle-scarred guys like him who are "doomed" to endure the nightmare of their postwar trauma (355). Nothing remains but for the storyteller to abandon his post as the observer of life. Instead of dissent and rebellion, the storyteller retreats into loneliness, an existential exile from the world of storytelling. In a word, where the production of text is no longer reliant on the mediating role of human perception and receptivity, storytelling has turned flaccid. In Colebrook's words, this vision of a solitary man fishing reveals the possible reification not just of mankind but also of the text that follows him. In speculating on what literary theory would be in the hands of a species after humans, Colebrook urges her readers to think of remaining texts not as holders of intent and meaning but "more likely encountered as marks or traces without animating hand" (39).

We leave Roth's novel poised beside a frozen lake in New England, where narrative and its narrator are left to fend for themselves, endangered and alone, all but effaced except for an illiterate's mark. Turning to Houellebecq's Europe, where the storyteller has already been subdued and defeated by technologies of representation, the narrator is extinct and narrative looks unsentimentally and with an archivist's twenty-twenty hindsight at a past that is consistent, unsurprising, and, from now on, uncannily like the future. Stateside traces of an American dream ensure that hope in values that are recognizably human still remains, whereas in *Atomised*, a chronicle of the malaise of the 1990s, agency has already died out to be replaced by a posthuman conformity. Bereft of a narrator such as Zuckerman, and therefore cut off from the narratological production of belief and literary knowledge (however errant), Houellebecq's novel is also bereft of the pathos that still exists in Roth's. That neither Michel nor Bruno is able to love their women is a feature of their "atomized" society. It is true that Bruno comes to life as a fuller character toward the end of the novel, but this is largely because of his having an interlocutor in Christiane, someone to whom he can direct his phallic drive, even as "linguistic copula" that, recall, aligns it with the verb "to be" (Bristow, 86), to produce a coherent and satisfying record of his own personal history. During these confessional moments, the reader is given relief from the otherwise desiccated surface of *Atomised*. Bruno's narrative constitutes a few momentary islands of delightful continuity in an otherwise rigorously fragmentary novel, although it would be a mistake to think of these episodes expressing more than his own need for pleasurable release. His tendency toward premature ejaculation corresponds with his half-brother Michel's weak erections and preference for cuddles rather than penetration of his rediscovered lover Annabelle. Both men give expression to a specifically masculine susceptibility to castration by technology, though in Michel's case there may still be a feminism that would elevate him as an ideal: the lover as friend, as sensitive guy, even as honorary woman (Mills and Mullany, 37). Whereas Roth's novel attempts to fuse the notion of the self-made man with the dangling promise of a potentially strong and powerful coalition of male identity, Houellebecq's protagonist Michel despises males, his research being fueled by the desire to do away with the need for males altogether. Michel's posthumously successful attempt to clone the first human being is acknowledged by a descendant of that first success in a dry-eyed tribute to the humanity, now extinct, that created him, her, or it:

> History exists, it is elemental, it dominates, its rule is inexorable. But outside the strict confines of history, the ultimate ambition of this book is to salute the brave and unfortunate species which created us. This vile, unhappy race, barely different from the apes, had such noble aspiration. Tortured, contradictory, individualistic, quarrelsome, it was capable of extraordinary violence, but nonetheless never quite abandoned a belief in love. This species which, for the first time in history, was able to envisage the possibility of its passing and which, some years later, proved capable of bringing it about. As the last members of its species are extinguished, we think it just to render this last tribute to humanity, a homage which itself will one day disappear, buried beneath the sands of time. It is necessary that this tribute be made, if only once. This book is dedicated to mankind. (379)

The tone is urbane and expert, as incapable of irony as it is of pathos, or even of selecting the wrong word. With clerical precision this voice effortlessly applies a perfectly calculated measure of acknowledgment to the passing of humanity. In Houellebecq's novel, all the real heroes have left the scene decades before, along with the villains, and whoever or whatever remains to imbue their memory with some immortality is a life-form that, strictly speaking, knows nothing of death. In the final analysis, what most grates in the tone of voice of the clone is its pusillanimous propriety, because its utter imperviousness to any chance mistake means it does not even need the courage of a conviction. Now that humans are extinct, it is possible and "just" to speak about their flaws and their achievements, the greatest of which has been to put an end to themselves in submitting to be supplanted by clones, or so the clone narrator implies above.

This reportage about the passing of the human species points to the victory of reproductive as well as information technology over the all too human sex and storytelling romanticized by the figure of the storyteller in Roth's novel. As Zuboff argues, information technology (as opposed to the machine) is far from mute since whatever it provides comes with a "dimension of reflexivity" by which it notifies us of its presence, very like the clone that narrates *Atomised*:

> The action of a machine is entirely invested in its object, the product. Information technology, on the other hand, introduces an additional dimension of reflexivity. It makes its contribution to the product, but it also reflects back on its activities and on the system of activities to which it is related. Information technology not only produces action but also produces a voice that symbolically renders events, objects, and processes so that they become visible, knowable, and shareable in a new way. (9)

The clone's *memento mori* for its human antecedents is all-encompassing, touched by a historian's generalizing tendency to speak on behalf of the subjectivities whose history it narrates: "All across the surface of the globe, a weary, exhausted humanity, filled with self-doubt and uncertain of its history, prepared itself as best it could to enter a new millennium" (354). If the millennium culminates in such a widespread sense of insecurity, it is well to remember that these very conditions cry out for a narrative that will shelter that vulnerability. The brave new world of the clones by contrast claims total certainty, and insofar as the technology functions or aims to function perfectly correctly, it recalls Hannah Arendt's famous summation of tyranny in *The Human Condition*: "The trouble with these forms of government is not that they are cruel, which often they are not, but rather that they work too well" (221). Writing over 50 years ago in 1958, she might be voicing Houellebecq's concerns even as he situates the consequences of Michel's research 50 years further on, as she goes on to say:

> It is the obvious short-range advantages of tyranny, the advantages of stability, security, and productivity, that one should beware, if only because they pave the way to an inevitable loss of power, even though the actual disaster may occur in a relatively distant future. (222)

In Houellebecq's vision of the future, human beings have been excised from life by a quest for scientific control all the more dispiriting because it so clearly leads to individual oppression; a more profound castration en masse is unimaginable. For Houellebecq, the increased "automatism in human affairs" that Arendt foresaw as "by no means a harmless scientific ideal" has finally come to bear fruit in a life-form now fully "at peace with the scientific outlook inherent in its very existence" (*The Human Condition*, 43). As a result, the quest for narrative and knowledge has no meaning anymore and, in Arendt's words, "events will more and more lose their significance, that is, their capacity to illuminate historical time" (43). Michel, himself a scientist, ponders whether "the need to find meaning [is] simply a childish defect of the human mind?" (360). Through this gloomy outlook, Houellebecq analyzes the way in which the individual is used and defined by corporate materialist Europe, pinpointing the exact area where the precision and reliability of information claims victory over the tentative, exploratory quality of narrative. "A culture," Roszak reminds us, "survives by the power, plasticity, and fertility of its ideas" (88). Critics who point out that Houellebecq's prose excels in its elevation of the mainstream tend to overlook the significance of suggestions like those toward the end of *Atomised*, that what happens to the mainstream there is something profoundly tragic and rather exceptional in the history of humanity.[3] Houellebecq's narrative treatment of twentieth-century alienation is all the more disquieting because the voice he uses to tell this tale has no stake in individual struggle, the clone knows nothing of the tragic. Interestingly, the clone's style bears many of the hallmarks of what Liu identifies in "cool" culture: a numbing, "detached cynicism," and "inability to feel agon" (87). The clone delivers its account of the passing of the human species with the smugness of a company report acknowledging the staff cuts that were necessary to achieve this quarter's profits.

At the end of *Atomised*, Michel arrives on the Clifden peninsula in Ireland where a laboratory has been set up to begin developing the process that will lead to the cloning of the first nonsexually reproduced human being. It seems fitting that the approaching end of the human takes place at the extreme "edge" of Europe: "This was the westernmost point of Europe, the very edge of the Western world. Before him, the Atlantic Ocean stretched out four thousand kilometres to America" (352). Houellebecq discloses a bafflingly human side of his protagonist as Michel contemplates the cows whose genetic code he has created and gives way to feelings of an unaccountable sort of inadequacy. How, he wonders absurdly, can those cows continue the business of being cows without acknowledging the presence of their maker: "To them, he should be like God, but they seemed completely indifferent to his presence" (349). Michel, being human and so able to be confused and irrational, feels the lack of appropriate awe or even idolatry from his bovine creations, but these are merely symptoms of other feelings of misgiving that attend his particular research. It is not the cows' fault but through them Michel seems here dimly to perceive that with the new millennium his work is introducing a problem worse than all the sexually derived waywardness that it might have cured: life from now on has a proclivity toward indifference.

In Ireland, Houellebecq introduces another character, Walcott, an Englishman and head of the scientific unit there, whose impressions of the Irish countryside resonate with Michel's. While the novel has chronicled a generalized despair from the beginning, especially Bruno and Michel's, it now makes the following attempt to show the possibility of a reconnection with the landscape, and with it a potentially fruitful encounter with otherness:

> As they came into Galway, Walcott spoke: "I'm an atheist myself, always have been, but I can understand why they're Catholic here. There's something very special about this country. Everything seems constantly trembling: the grass in the fields or the water on the lake, everything signals its presence. The light is soft, mutable. You'll see. The sky itself is alive." (350)

Perhaps Houellebecq is having a dig at the English, for Walcott's futile remarks are, given the future he is bringing to pass, anachronistically sentimental, even dishonest. They strike a false tone not unlike Zuckerman's "Hallmark" rendition of Les Farley fishing. Why does this Walcott recall the shimmering beauty of life and use it to justify the misguidedness of religious belief, while at the same time he is actively engaged in a project that sees life as needing the corrective of science? The answer to this question is not hard to find if we consider that the diction selected for Walcott by the clone narrator, as well as in the narrative above, reveals a historicism whose language has been co-opted by corporate culture. I wonder what sort of bells that might ring for us in our own epoch? If we can see it for what it seems to be, part of a sanitized creation myth for the clones, as contemporary human readers we may see ourselves slighted at the notion that the world of the clone is in fact an allegory for our own, unless we simply feel vindicated, by Houellebecq's perspicacity, as the endangered life-form that we are. The clone replays a time when language was used to express not just information but also profound emotion as a touchstone of knowledge or truth, and the posthuman context of this narrative is what falsifies. However, it falsifies in not quite the same way that Roth's novel reveals the dissonance between narrator and narrated, as in his attempt to ventriloquize Faunia Farley, for example—Zuckerman is simply not an omniscient narrator. The tendency of a doctored humanity to spin-doctor its past in *Atomised* shows that in the brave new world of the clone (whenever it happens to take place), language capitulates to be ruled by the style-sheet of the corporate prospectus with its smug, self-congratulatory rhetoric.

When his job in Ireland is at an end, Michel Djerzinski, we are told, makes his way to the coast and gazes out over the Atlantic from that westernmost headland of Europe. Significantly, the scene he observes is "completely covered by a thick blanket of fog rolling in from the Atlantic" (352). In the clone's official record of events, Michel commits suicide by drowning in the sea, his body melding with the vapors of the Atlantic fog. Houellebecq's grim vision of a Europe smothered under an Atlantic fog emphatically signals that the end of the human is the end of difference and variation, end of an errant history, and the inauguration of an era ruled by the scientifically mediated eternal return of the clone. This moment in Houellebecq's novel also calls to mind that numbing sameness, discussed in Chapter 2, faced by the man and boy at the end of *The Road*, summed up in the words "isocline of death" (187). There the language of precise measurement and wide-ranging data collection meets the worldwide ruin of the biosphere that science may well have been instrumental in bringing about or was at least powerless to avert. Writing of *Atomised* in an analysis of place in contemporary fiction, O'Beirne also pauses to reflect on the significance of that fog, seeing there Houellebecq's moment of an "unexpected Atlantic apotheosis" (O'Beirne, 400).

Having removed his character from the claustrophobic streets of the Continent, Houellebecq further releases Michel into the vastness of space, including the opacity of the sea and the translucence of the sky. These expanses, argues O'Beirne, are non-places, "keeping no trace of our passages" (400). Such places do not know us and we no longer recognize them because there we can leave no enduring mark of our passing or record of what we have encountered. Certainly, the fog as well as the disappearance of the inventor of human cloning into the featureless ocean suggests an undistinguished and featureless future. Here is the triumph of reproductive technology even as it fails to record the passing of the human, without mark or adequate basis for remark. I read the closing imagery of *Atomised* as symptomatic of a prevalent anxiety at the turn of the millennium as we turn away from paths of knowledge and discovery that cross in the oceanic imaginary toward an algorithmically enhanced control of information distribution in the virtual dimension of the atmospheric. It seems, for Houellebecq, to be a final species-wide exodus for the human from place-based knowledge to information detached from any place of further departure or arrival. Far from signifying what

Catherine Malabou courageously anticipates as a viable Nietzschean eternal return, an "ontological cloning" whose triumph she envisages as action "without being different but without returning to the same either" (28),[4] the clone as offered up for our consideration by Houellebecq is a pure avatar of fearful ressentiment of life's astonishing variety. This weak-willed spectral double of mankind, phantom of reactivity, is evidence of a profound refusal to say yes to the whole of life's challenges whether they arrive on foot, by sea, or via communication technology.

If the clone is the embodiment of an ineluctable sameness, born of the fear of encountering strangeness in ourselves and each other, what might be the consequences of this or indeed any other technology for the safe duplication and sanitized dissemination of human achievement, for literature, and the archives of knowledge? Without the insistence on difference through interpretation, something that might satisfy Malabou's quest for a way to comprehend the eternal return "that would substitute synthesis for difference" (28), knowledge risks being reduced to or replaced by mere information, promiscuously available everywhere and nowhere. Michel's body is never found and his tale ends up being narrated with none of the pathos, however flawed and self-indulgent, that a storyteller such as Zuckerman could bring to it. Houellebecq's novel peters out into abstraction with the erasure of Michel; he vanishes, literally, into thin air. *Atomised* imagines the potential of the virtual world through an abstraction of mankind that is made possible by Michel's romanticized ideal to cure the human of all trace of malady but ends up with a resulting life-form that is indistinguishable from its founding conditions.

Indeed, Michel's brilliantly informed scientific discoveries that lead to the birth of the posthuman are even deprived of the personal recognition of his achievement without which this vision struggles and fails to maintain an ethical commitment to life on earth. Not long after the widespread introduction of the personal computer in businesses, the computer was voted "Man of the Year" by *Business Week* in 1982 (Liu, 142). Ten years later, the World Wide Web appeared and the computer became more powerful and mobile (143). The cults of masculinity used to characterize the brothers Bruno and Michel in the novel, and which are so central also to Roth's attempts to secede from mainstream Americanism, have in Houellebecq been reduced to rhetorical devices of the free market (he-man, go-getter, pornstar, honorary woman—the list goes on). While Wallace argues that "the desperate reduction to these postures is also human" (141), the intention of this chapter is to remind the reader not of the bare minimum aspects of the human but of the most we dare hope for, that very capacity to hope and dare now, more than ever, a necessary measure of our humanity.

A central question of the future of humanity, of whether or not the Atlantic afterlife can be anything other than a mere confirmation of the elapse of the individual contra the Network, provokes my reading of both *The Human Stain* and *Atomised*. Neither Houellebecq's nor Roth's response to our times is optimistic regarding that future. The struggling attempt at self-exaltation by the male narrator in Roth's novel is marked by incapacity. Zuckerman's encounter with his nemesis Farley peters out into a waning of the intent to confront and is far from the celebration of autonomy, of authorial hutzpah, that he wishes it to be. Likewise, Michel's seclusion on the Irish peninsula is far from the enclave of the human technological sublime Walcott's speech (courtesy of his clone historian) suggests it might be, far even from the diminished ideal the clone narrator merely enunciates, though it can hardly be expected to believe it (unless belief too has been reliably cloned). Instead, both Zuckerman's protracted meeting with the homicidal Les Farley and Michel's sojourn in Ireland are portraits of idiosyncratic characters made hollow by the early phases of a shift from the human to whatever comes next. They are defeated by the superior phallic control of technology as it delivers exactitude in reproduction and accuracy in representation, by which even now subjectivities are being reproduced in the same way commodities are.

Posthumanism and the atomization of our times are foreshadowed in both Roth and Houellebecq's novels. While there are those such as Colebrook who say agency is not a proper goal for human beings, this is not to say that it is not showing up, relentlessly in fact, in contemporary fiction. The Atlantic haunts these novels and reminds the reader of coastal boundaries, both real and virtual, that are now in the process of erosion in the Information Age. These boundaries include the distinctions, however frail and frayed, between subject and object, the strange and the familiar, man and machine, and even between information and knowledge. What these boundaries reveal is not the exceptional in humanity, but its ordinariness. It is in the gestures of ordinary life that the literary asserts itself, in the way we stubbornly "call something by a name that is not its own," as Wood reminds us (7). It is to the folly of humanity, not its efficiency, that Roth's novel mournfully bids its farewell. The posthuman narrator in Houellebecq's novel, by contrast, has mastered a literacy of the future of which we know little at this stage except that it is as incapable of memorable folly as it is of spectacular failure, no longer able to offer readers a category for the nameless and the not yet known. With a literacy shaped by the reproductive technologies imagined by Roth and Houellebecq, the pleasures of being at sea will be neither the author's nor the reader's.

# Conclusion

## Beyond the Information Age and Sustainable Reading Practices

I noted toward the end of my final chapter the gradual erasure of what Philip Roth refers to as "the human stain" in his novel of the same name. By bringing Roth into dialogue with Houellebecq, I showed two very different narratives of how technology attempts to smooth out the flaws in humanity, producing predictable or even calculable results, but with destructive consequences for narrative and the tentative, exploratory sensibility that it stands for. Clearly, science can try to erase narrative's mark in the quest for a blemish-free expression, improving on the unreliability of the merely human, as is evident in Houellebecq's novel in which human cloning eradicates all chance fluctuations in favor of radical uniformity. We saw too in Roth's novel how human connectivity was enhanced via the aid of medical science, with Coleman Silk's love life flourishing on regular doses of Viagra. The novels show how narrative power takes a considerable beating from technology, and it has been my contention throughout these pages that knowledge requires narrative and both are distinct from information, there being no automatic or guaranteed support for them in the Information Age. Our age is also a post-Atlantic age, a time of the Atlantic's afterlives, which I have been referring to in terms of a shift from an oceanic to an atmospheric locus of communication and exploration.

The Atlantic has been a specific terrestrial locus through which movement, growth, and influence could be measured between Europe and America. It lay between them while offering passage to and from these continents, and as such, it was also a place of encounter. Importantly, the errant and chance-driven nature of these interactions is a defining feature of what I mean by narrative, sign of the human stain, which is often a casualty of the ethos of calculability that presides over information. However, I am suggesting that while technology might erase that stain, it can also help situate a reimagining of its significance and value. Musicologist Joel Dinerstein sees a hopeful alliance between art and technology in his account of the role of automation in the cultural production of African American storytellers, dancers, singers, and especially musicians. In his history of swing at the time of the Information Age, Dinerstein asserts that "Americans needed both technology and survival technology to imagineer themselves into the unpredictable future" (311). The distinction between technology and "survival technology" is compelling for here Dinerstein emphasizes the need for an imaginary coupled with technology in order to confront and explore alternative futures. I welcome this account of a symbiotic relationship between information and knowledge, technology and narrative, machine and body, which, like the oceanic imaginary, can be incorporated into contemporary reading practices.

The oceanic imaginary forms a resistance to the pull toward automated uniformity. This is where I stake a claim for narrative as an itinerary for subjectivity; it is where storytelling resurfaces to dialogue with the Information Age and so constitutes a "survival technology" of its own. *Atlantic Afterlives* proposes a new and tenuously located setting for literature. My focus began with transatlantic novels, then moved further afield, and it remains for the reader to take up the challenge to anchor narrative, storytelling, and poetics in something deeper and more solid than information alone can supply. This is not to deny that digital technology has irreversibly changed the way we imagine literature's place in the world. Indeed, throughout this book I have affirmed that the breadth of virtual space is actually oceanic for contemporary readers. The American scholar and educator on ecological literacy, David Orr, argues that water is a large part of the beauty of language (54). As well, he notes that it has given rise to our most elegant technologies such as the water clock, the ship, and the waterwheel, for water is the "truest indicator of human intelligence, measurable by what we are smart enough to keep out of it" (55). My hope is that among the most elegant of technologies traceable to water is the survival technology that is the oceanic imaginary.

Houellebecq's clone narrator manifests what happens when people become like the information they consume, endlessly and faultlessly reproduced, applicable to everyone and everything. The sanitized, politically correct purity of the discourse of the clone seems to offer a corrective to the sort of flawed and inconsistent, subjectively biased narrative in Roth's novel. The clone's utter self-sufficiency is very different to what knowledge or narrative offers, for they are incomplete, relying on the chance encounter with, and subsequent engagement of, readers and interpreters, for their meaning. Contemporary literature will continue to respond to the increasing atomization of life, by emphasizing survival technology in the encounter with radical otherness. *Atlantic Afterlives* addresses the question of how to read texts that have been informed one way or another by technologies introduced in the Information Age. My approach throughout this book has been to treat narrative and the ability to respond to it as rare and precious, like finite resources, water, fuel, or clean air. Rather than attempting to live the Information Age dream of infinite growth and endlessly proliferating, promiscuous relevance, I argue that the texts in focus demand a methodology for reading contemporary literature as constrained by materially finite intellectual resources of time and energy.

The most far-reaching responses to the expansionism of information take place in post-Atlantic literature itself as it negotiates, distils, and translates technologically mediated modes of communication into new topographies of knowledge. It is imperative that we consider these not only for what they say about the last century but, more urgently, for what we presently face. To do so, we need to rethink our reading practices though not, I feel, by following a conventional comparativist approach. Although Paul Giles is among those who have an eye on the future of our discipline, in *Virtual Americas* his thoughts on where we might take American studies diverge markedly from mine. Giles sees transatlantic dialogues now operating as enablers of the "radical aestheticization" of ideas (274). He takes the notion of American freedom as an example of a paradigm communicated and readable across the Atlantic and argues that, rather than finding "a pure or transcendent freedom," we look instead for "a virtual image of liberty, its simulacrum" (274). Thus, he argues, "America is valuable not for what it might be in itself, but for the interference it creates in others" (275). Finally, it remains then for American studies as a whole to "work as a virtual discipline, a means of disrupting the self-enclosing boundaries of other areas, whether academic disciplines or geographic territories, by its projections of dislocation and difference" (275). From this we gather that, as far as Giles is concerned, America is none other than his current reading methodology; it is found wherever a boundary is blurred in any area of aesthetic and intellectual life. Giles suggests that America is located, writ small or large, wherever it or one of its avatars interferes with other locales.

I resist Giles's notion that discovery is purely disruption, that it occurs in every boundary dispute. By placing so much value on the notion of the potential ubiquity of disruption or "interference," its function as an intervention becomes meaningless. Further, I strongly reject the corollary to Giles's argument, that virtual readers and scholars have nothing to do with the actual world. Giles's insistence on the virtual and aesthetic in ideology ignores it as the mechanism through which powerful material interests strive for ends that are far from virtual and certainly not aesthetic. In chapter 5 on the afterlife of the Ted Hughes and Sylvia Plath text, I suggest, in lieu of a virtual, placeless proliferation of disruptions, the oceanic imaginary is an enduring site of resistance to uniformity embodied in the voice of the pariah. To see America as showing up wherever a boundary is crossed or a disruption caused is to reproduce the diffuse formations of the Information Age without situating any enduring resistance to or perspective on it. When Deleuze and Guattari, writing about Kafka, value resistance in the form of a "minor literature" operating within the dominant language, they see Kafka's as a "minor practice of major language from within" (*Kafka*, 26). They welcome this practice, in which Kafka is "a sort of stranger within his own language" (26) who yet challenges the language while calling for restraint, by "making it follow a sober revolutionary path" (19). Deleuze and Guattari remind us that the resistance offered by "minor literature" must not seek to erase the major literature, for the perspective the minor supplies is valuable only as a unique perspective on that mainstream culture. My approach to the authors I treat in this book sees them embarked on discrete trajectories or itineraries, forming within the major field of the Information Age the minority of the oceanic imaginary's pathways and perspectives. Where Giles wishes to void the concept of the major altogether, as if there is no longer an America in itself, Deleuze and Guattari express no such need to invalidate what is. Rather, a minor literature co-exists with the major and offers "the possibility to express another kind of community" (19).

Thus, it is possible to speak of characters such as Greene's Fowler from *The Quiet American* and Hoeg's Smilla as being in touch with or even enmeshed in the Information Age, even or especially when they themselves are articulating their own "minor" path within the field of this major force. Wai Chee Dimock similarly sees the potential for community and what she refers to as kinship in *Through Other Continents: American Literature across Deep Time* (2006). For Dimock, literary genres are as "widely dispersed" and "unpredictable as human beings themselves" (78), and literature cannot be circumscribed by periodization nor for that matter by any other form of categorization. I am certainly sympathetic to what she sees as the "unfinished business" (78) of reorganizing texts endlessly according to new criteria and evolving motivations. I am less convinced, however, that this kind of reading practice is sustainable when any kinship network can propose an endlessly expanding proliferation of new texts. This, in my view, is a reading practice that emulates the boundless reach of information itself. I wonder if to honor our textual imprint on earth, we need now to rely more on our capacity to think in terms of degrees of restraint rather than a reach that goes off the scale. As well, the endless proliferation of reworked contexts, as deliriously seductive as it is, ceases to be a distinct minor literature when it is, like the web, universal and pervasive. To recover the meaning of exploration and discovery, we need to reclaim the actual existence of some boundaries or limits, and with them the right to synthesize rather than surf, to navigate rather than drift. The study of literature in the Information Age needs at all costs to avoid becoming identical with the never-ending network that delivers so much of its textual material. The risk is seen in the image from Borges's fable (it fascinated Baudrillard in *Simulacra and Simulation* [3]) in which the cartographers of the Empire draw up a vast and futile map at the same scale as the Empire itself. Without the restrains of selection and compression, the twin coordinates that structure representation and other meaning-making processes such as the art of storytelling, this pointless duplication of the world is what literary cartographers would end up reproducing.

By way of an alternative to the extreme reach and expansion imaged by Giles and Dimock as well as promised by the web itself, I would like to close with two contemporary authors whose impressions of our age reveal the world's frailty and the overall ineffectiveness of endless growth. David Markson's *Wittgenstein's Mistress* from 1988 follows the progress of an unhinged protagonist set loose in what might best be described as a virtual environment of global scale, although there is no explicit mention of any technology behind it or, indeed, how everything got this way. Despite playing a bit fast and loose with our sense of a foundation, ultimately this novel convinces of its stake in a real world by the level of care and caution it recommends to its readers regarding space and expansion. Michel Faber's recent novel, *The Book of Strange New Things* (2014), offers a comparable blend of critical (indeed, interstellar) distance together with profound concern for what the world might well be coming to. *Wittgenstein's Mistress* is narrated by an amateur painter Kate who believes herself to be the only person still alive on earth. Part of Markson's remarkable achievement in this novel is that Kate's predicament does not seem implausible. As the single citizen of the world, her itinerary is strangely private and public at the same time. She can wander at will, make the Louvre her home, and use its walls on which to hang her own paintings beside those of the masters. There are no doors closed to her, no obstacles to hinder her usually ambulant movements. She makes use of whatever vehicles are left stranded on the roads, abandoned by their owners for reasons never disclosed. If she feels like a shot of tequila, she need only walk into a deserted Mexican restaurant in order to satisfy the urge.

Markson's prose and syntax is often serially structured, conveying an entire world in the form of an arbitrary inventory of what shows up for Kate when she takes one step at a time, follows one whim at a time. In this way a spirit of careless happenstance pervades *Wittgenstein's Mistress*, with an almost somnolent or trance-like obsession with minor details. One might say that the novel is simply a screen where things happen, usually without human intervention. What remains then is a depiction of an environment, a world of objects, as if seen from the perspective of one among its objects. Nothing in the novel explains how Kate's routinely pedestrian progress transports her across the Atlantic Ocean as easily as it does on a regular basis, nor for that matter, why such obsessive attention is dedicated to the road motif in Europe and the car in particular. As quickly as it can be said or read, she is in Paris or London, or any other European or American city, literally transported by words. The effect of this on the reader is neither alienating nor particularly disturbing, but it does impart a sense of the frailty, the uncertainty, and the smallness of life. Markson's novel also restores the notion that the world is at the mercy of the reader. With an acute tenderness for place comes an extreme compression of distance and a Eurocentric selection of transatlantic items that constitute this world. This produces an explicitly skewed vision that must offer a surprising challenge to area studies, since only a fraction of civilization is captured, incompletely, even naively. In Kate's hands, the reader is treated to a history of the arts, not just painting, but also music, philosophy, and literature. Everything is of relevance it would seem, simply because it comes by Kate who filters a plethora of impressions. This sensory overload is bewildering in its transgression of conceptual boundaries, but the resulting selection imposes an order to life and perception that marches in time with the click-and-drag rhythms of the Information Age. Thus, the menstrual cycle, the washing of underwear (inexplicable as all consumer goods are free for the taking in this virtual world of Kate), and other such rituals jolt the reader into a meaning-making process that imposes subjectivity through narrative in a virtual world.

In a review of Max Nicholson's seminal *The Environmental Revolution* (1970), Ted Hughes describes how the author's detailed descriptions of the world paradoxically shrink it. After reading Nicholson, Hughes explains that it is now clear that this "miniature earth has our stomach, our blood, our precarious vital chemistry, and our future" (134). In the oceanic imaginary of Markson's novel, the world wandered by Kate is also condensed as though it is a virtual simulacrum, though if so it is an emphatically embodied idea of the virtual, one that coexists with the real without excluding the organic. Though it is a world devoid of human life, in which case it is a post-apocalyptic world as in McCarthy's *The Road*, the artistic and intellectual traces left by humans and rendered legible through Kate's musings move the reader to consider the fragility of all representation rather than the plight of the terrestrial orb. Dinerstein's term "survival technology" stands out here. For me it reveals that at the heart of life is the never motionless machine that is the human body and with it the technology of narratives that further mobilizes its experiences. Ultimately then, we reach a "survival technology" when private experience goes abroad, when it is publicly represented and narrated and thereby takes on enduring value. Storytelling is thus an index of Kate's survival, both in the technical and the spiritual sense. Stefik in *Internet Dreams* argues that we should be drawing on our collective experience of cultural archetypes and metaphors "when we make choices about the information infrastructure" (xxiii). Liu is pessimistic, warning that, "Strip away all the colorful metaphors of information seas, webs, highways, portals, windows, and the rest (like picture calendars tacked to the wall), and what comes to view is only the stark cubicle of the knowledge worker" (76). The view of the Information Age offered by *Wittgenstein's Mistress* is less grim, even bemused at the power of words to marshal feeling. In Markson's novel, those metaphors are moving, for they are the only transports available to stir life into the human condition.

This ethos of storytelling in resistant dialogue with the Information Age is remarkably different from what we find in Kurt Vonnegut's fiction, for example. Well known for his skepticism of the benefits of automation on our lives, in stories such as "EPICAC," Vonnegut also displays susceptibility to the Orwellian horrors he often conjured. In this love story, a machine and a human are rivals for the love of the same woman. Eventually the woman succumbs to the human's bid for marriage, but only because he seduces her with the eloquent and heartfelt poetry that the machine has produced on his command. In the process of writing the love poems, however, the machine decides that life is not worth living unless it can participate in life fully as a human being. The machine self-destructs, deleting itself from their lives forever, but not before printing out a veritable archive of love poetry to maintain the connubial feelings between wife and husband come rain or shine for all eternity. Vonnegut seems to suggest that exploitation, subjugation, and rivalry are at stake in any interaction between machine and human. There is no sense of partnership in the exchange between robot and human, and even the love that flourishes as a result of the robot's creative output is a cruel reminder of its extinction rather than a "survival technology" that might give meaning to life beyond sheer survival.

Encounters between human and alien life forms are central in Michel Faber's most recent novel *The Book of Strange New Things*, dedicated to the author's wife who passed away during the writing of the book. It is a story of a British minister Peter Leigh, employed by the mysterious global conglomerate USIC as an intergalactic pastor to the alien populace of a distant planet. At the start of the novel, he boards a one-way flight to America and thence to a destination beyond our galaxy. Where Markson's oceanic imaginary sidesteps the ocean, Faber's spans interstellar space. Peter's beloved wife Beatrice remains on earth and their only form of communication is via a laborious and expensive interstellar email system, "Shoot." Though the novel's detailing of the alien planet and its inhabitants is intriguing and at times wondrous, Faber's novel is equally concerned with a very down-to-earth disquiet regarding the fate of the earth. Planet Earth, Beatrice reports back to Peter, is under duress. Mass flooding, tidal waves, war, whole chunks of continents washed away, inexplicable eruptions of violence, and a drastic temperature increase mean home, as remembered by Peter, is becoming more alien than the strange planet, "Oasis," where he now resides. Peter's first meeting with the indigenous population of Oasis puts in question his purpose as a Christian missionary since, needing no convincing of the benefits of his religion, the aliens are already able to quote the Bible back to him chapter and verse. Despite extreme bodily differences between humans and aliens, what is most dispiriting for Peter is that in them he encounters not a satisfying challenge to his spiritual or rhetorical skills, no disbelieving otherness to gather into his fold, but a textually bestowed sameness. What is intended to be the "good news" of the Christian teaching turns into something bland, all too familiar, like yesterday's news. The extraterrestrial world of Oasis has much in common with the sameness met with in the Information Age. The planet's moist, vaporous environment represents the sea of sameness, the atomization of the Atlantic detached from place and gravity.

Faber's novel is essentially about the difference between communication and information, witnessed in the otherness that enriches the liaison between lovers, and the sameness that falls like a pall between strangers. It is also about the faith that knows nothing of distance, binding correspondents such as Peter and his impossibly far-off wife in a rigorous protocol of address. The immense sadness of the novel is felt when communication breaks down. Strung out between an alien world that is all too familiar and the familiar world on the brink of destruction, the words between husband and wife fail to reach their destination. Thus, Peter's one-way ticket to America and beyond becomes allegorical of information's itinerary in our age when messages are projected outward homelessly, with no singular sense of where they came from or if they are ever received. Like Faber and Markson, the authors I have examined in this book offer representations of social and subjective experience that ride on the ebbs and flows of exchange in the Information Age while keeping their distance.

# Notes

## 1 Narrative without Borders: Reading Graham Greene in the Information Age

1. Professor Buchanan elucidated his latest position on assemblage theory at his Melbourne workshop, "Assemblage Theory and its Discontents," October 14, 2014. See https://news.federation.edu.au/files/29-09-14_Workshop_Assemblage_Theory_3_.pdf.
2. See Marc Pitzke in *Spiegel Online International*, July 15, 2013, on the National Security Agency revelations initiated by Edward Snowden and also involving *Guardian* reporter Glenn Greenwald: "A growing number of mainstream media outlets have been focusing their criticism on the leakers—Snowden in Moscow, Greenwald in Rio—instead of the content of their leaks. American headlines aren't being dominated by the latest details of the seemingly endless scandal, but by the men who brought them to light." http://www.spiegel.de/international/world/nsa-spying-scandal-focus-on-edward-snowden-by-us-media-a-911185.html, accessed April 10, 2015.
3. Incidentally, this notion of detection as exponential growth of knowledge, threatening to consume the individual, is what the public witnessed in relation to Assange of WikiLeaks when subject to investigation in Sweden for sexual misconduct.

## 2 Apocalypse Then and Now: *The Road, Lord of the Flies*, and the Ends of Knowledge

1. For a wonderful description of the multiple beginnings and ends of the Atlantic Ocean as well as its vast geographical, economical, cultural, and political influence, see Simon Winchester's *Atlantic: A Vast Ocean of a Million Stories* (London: Harper Press, 2011).
2. This is a later-day version of the power wielded through the intimacy of the confessional (of particular interest to Foucault).
3. Ahlberg, Sofia, "Within Oceanic Reach: The Effects of September 11 on a Drought-Stricken Nation." In this chapter I argue against the over-

mobilization of identity that attacks difference whether in the defense of nature or retaliation against terror.

4. "He rose and stood tottering in that cold autistic dark with his arms outheld for balance while the vestibular calculations in his skull cranked out their reckonings. An old chronicle. To seek out the upright. No fall but preceded by a declination. He took great marching steps into the nothingness, counting them against his return. Eyes closed, arms oaring. Upright to what? Something nameless in the night, lode or matrix. To which he and the stars were common satellite. Like the great pendulum in its rotunda scribing through the long day movement of the universe of which you may say it knows nothing and yet know it must." Cormac McCarthy, *The Road* (New York: Alfred A. Knopf, 2006), p. 13.
5. Interesting to consider in this context is Freud's *Civilisation and Its Discontents* in which he argues that the price individuals pay in order to be part of a community is high, often involving the necessary repression of atavistic behavior deemed antisocial by the group.
6. In a broadcast panel discussion on the relation between art and science, McCarthy denied that a scientific worldview made him pessimistic: "Well, some of my friends would probably tell you that making me pessimistic would be a difficult chore indeed," he said, "I'm pessimistic about a lot of things, but... there's no reason to be miserable about it." See http://www.npr.org/2011/04/08/135241869/connecting-science-and-art, accessed March 21, 2015. It is perhaps not surprising then that McCarthy is a resident author at the Santa Fe Institute with a particular interest in complexity theory and the science of climate change among many other things.
7. The scene recalls Beckett's *Endgame*: when Hamm demands to know what the ocean is like outside the window, he is similarly told that the waves are "lead," that everything is grey, and the ocean is inaudible (26).
8. De Certeau helps articulate the battle over knowledge and belief as anxiously sought and as fearfully defended territories in symbolic and actual space (134). Foucault may have emphasized power's pervasive and decentered mobility, but he also affirmed its concentrations based, for example, on tactics. While affirming that power operates from everywhere, Foucault argues that tactics end up "becoming connected to one another, attracting and propagating one another, but finding their base of support and their condition elsewhere, end by forming comprehensive systems" (*History of Sexuality*, 95). De Certeau makes of this aspect of power a more traditional conception of the problematic in which power "stocks up" and "sifts out" and "gives itself the means to expand" (de Certeau, 135) so as to control not just an area or a site or a situation among many competing others but rather to make the universe conform to a particular worldview outlined in black on white.
9. Incidentally, the sound toward the end of *The Road* is similar to the "Boum," the echo encountered in the Marabar Caves in E. M. Forster's *A Passage to India*.

## 3 THROUGH A BORDER DARKLY: NORTH ATLANTIC NARRATIVES OF EXPLOITATION IN PETER HOEG'S *MISS SMILLA'S FEELING FOR SNOW* AND ANNIE PROULX'S *THE SHIPPING NEWS*

1. See Claire Colebrook, *Understanding Deleuze* (London: Allen and Unwin, 2002), p. xlii. "We need to do away with the idea that…man decides his being," Colebrook explains, "for it is less the case that we decide who 'we' are than that forces 'decide' us." See also Jonathan Roffe, "Exteriority/Interiority," in *The Deleuze Dictionary Revised Edition* (Edinburgh: Edinburgh University Press, 2010), p. 97. Roffe explains that Deleuze's critique of interiority means "there is no natural interiority (conscious willing, for example) involved in human subjectivity."
2. Jack Buggit explains to Quoyle that "They sent me off to Toronto to learn about the newspaper business. They give me money. What the hell, I hung around Toronto what, four or five weeks, listening to them rave at me about editorial balance, integrity, the new journalism, reporter ethics, service to the community. Give me the fits. I couldn't understand the half of what they said. Learned what I had to know finally by doing it right here in my old shop. I been running *Gammy Bird* for seven years now, and the circulation is up to thirteen thousand, gaining every year. All along this coast. Because I know what people want to read about. And no arguments about it" (67)
3. Like Roffe's reading of Deleuze, DeLanda rejects interiority though he favours a useful distinction between the properties of "a given entity" and its capacities. The distinction may be a little arbitrary but it does allow us to give a name to and think about agency as a result of the potentially immeasurable difference between "the properties defining a given entity [and] its capacities to interact with other entities" (10). Manuel DeLanda, *A New Philosophy of Society: Assemblage Theory and Social Complexity* (London: Continuum, 2006).
4. "This crisis arose partly due to technological advancements: echo-sounding to find the fish, drag nets to trawl the ocean (resulting in vast amounts of overkill, with immature fish being thrown back, dead, into the ocean), efficient boats that could travel farther and faster, and the development of the factory-freezer ship. Compounding the problem, the Ottawa government tended to overestimate the number of fish and how quickly stocks could be replenished, while also allocating quotas based on economic rather than ecological criteria. Lack of regulation until 1977—the year in which Canada restricted foreign fishing around most of the island—meant that large overseas fleets were free to exploit. 'Extractice' practices, the Frankenstein effect of technology run riot; distant, sometimes ill-informed, administrators; and large-scale international profiteering were, thus, all key to the crisis." Dervila Cooke, "Tradition, Modernity, and the Enmeshing of Home and Away: *The Shipping News* and Proulx's 1990s Newfoundland," *Studies in Canadian Literature* 38.1 (2013): 190–209, at p. 200.

5. By "contact zone" Mary Pratt is referring to "the space in which peoples geographically and historically separated come into contact with each other and establish ongoing relations, usually involving conditions of coercion, radical inequality, and intractable conflict." Mary Louise Pratt, *Imperial Eyes: Travel Writing and Transculturation* (New York: Routledge, 1992), p. 313.

## 4 A Post-Atlantic Divorce: Reading and Writing Ted Hughes and Sylvia Plath in the Digital Age

1. "In this book, in the analysis of those writings, I am never talking of real people, but of textual entities. (Y and X) whose more than real reality, I will be arguing, goes beyond them to encircle us all." Jacqueline Rose, *The Haunting of Sylvia Plath* (London: Virago Press, 1991), p. 5.
2. See Perloff's "The Two Ariels: The (Re)making of the Sylvia Plath Canon" for a detailed reading of Hughes's editorial changes to Plath's *Ariel* collection, changing the trajectory of the work from an internal story that emphasizes growth and hope to one that leaves a prevailing sense of hopelessness and doom.
3. "It's like watching Paris from an express caboose heading in the opposite direction—every second the city gets smaller and smaller, only you feel it's really you getting smaller and smaller and lonelier and lonelier, rushing away from all those lights and that excitement at about a million miles an hour" (17). Sylvia Plath, *The Bell Jar* (London: Faber and Faber, 1963).
4. Plath typed and sent off poems from *The Hawk in the Rain* for the Harper Brothers and New York Young Men's Hebrew Association Poetry Center's competition judged by W. H. Auden, Stephen Spender, and Marianne Moore, a contest that Hughes won. Neil Roberts, *Ted Hughes: A Literary Life* (London: Palgrave Macmillan, 2009), p. 41.
5. In her reading of "Getting There" and "The Thin People," Wolosky reads Plath as someone who is "describing, registering, and exposing the culture and history around her" (26).
6. It is, therefore, all the more sad and ironic that Plath now features on all her book covers and often as if the photographs are windows into a very private world that "promotes nostalgia, and, by virtue of their subject no longer being alive, they acquire a certain degree of pathos," as noted by Banita (44–46).

## 5 Bridging Bereavement: Narratives of Loss and Loss of Narrative in Anne Michaels

1. See Amy Maguire's article in "The Conversation," July 9, 2014. http://theconversation.com/australias-global-reputation-at-stake-in-high-

court-asylum-case-28951. For some background, see Mungo MacCallum's piece in "The Drum," January 14, 2014. http://www.abc.net.au/news/2014-01-13/maccallum-operation-sovereign-borders/5196708

2. It was the so-called Tampa affair, a much publicised tragedy in August 2001, that put maritime law generally and Australian border control policies specifically in the spotlight. The Tampa, a Norwegian vessel, responded to the mayday call from an Indonesian fishing boat (the official term is Suspected Illegal Entry Vessel) containing 438 men, women, and children just north of Christmas Island. Captain Arne Rinnan changed course in order to intercept the stricken vessel and begin the rescue operation of the passengers of the sinking boat. Rinnan deemed his vessel unseaworthy given its load and lack of safety equipment, but his request for permission to dock on Christmas Island was denied. Although faced with Australian threats of prosecution, Rinnan felt he had no choice but to enter Australian territorial waters given the danger he and his passengers were in. In a preposterous move toward manipulating public opinion, the seafaring asylum seekers were accused of throwing their children overboard in an attempt to secure passage to Australia. Although these claims were proven false, the liberal government at the time under Prime Minister John Howard was still able to adopt stricter border protection measures by demonizing asylum seekers and exploiting voters' fears of a wave of illegal immigrants entering the country. Peter Mares, "Comment: Ten Years after Tampa," *The Monthly*, August 2011.
3. "Michaels' willingness, along with Jean's, to abandon Avery (we have just glimpses of him throughout the second half) cheats us of experiencing the grief of a character we have come to care about. It also makes us rather suspicious of Jean, who seems to give little though to whether her relationship with Lucjan constitutes any sort of betrayal." Sylvia Brownrigg, "Movement of the People," *The Guardian*, May 9, 2009. http://www.theguardian.com/books/2009/may/09/anne-michaels-winter-vault
4. In an attempt to rid herself of the shame she feels in the face of her own sorrow, Jean writes to one of the men working on the reconstruction of the temple with Avery. Daub allays her fears: "Perhaps there is a collective dead. But there is no such thing as a collective death. Each death, each birth, a single death, a single birth. One man's death cannot be set against millions, nor one man's death against another. I beg you not to torment yourself on this point" (249).

## 6 Future Perfect: The Problem of the Human in Michel Houellebecq's *Atomised* and Philip Roth's *The Human Stain*

1. One need only compare his predicament with that of an early Roth antihero, Portnoy, also a frustrated man on the hunt for transformative experience with the opposite sex. In 1969, Philip Roth's *Portnoy's Complaint*

reads like one monologue from the New World to the Old. Portnoy airs his grievances to his psychoanalyst trained in the Freudian school and it is as if all of Europe listens.

2. "Handsomely remunerated, pretentious and stupid, psychoanalysts reduce to absolute zero any aptitude in their so-called patients for love, be it mental or physical; in fact they behave as true enemies of mankind. A ruthless school of egoism, psychoanalysis cynically lays into decent, slightly fucked-up young women and transforms them into vile scumbags of such delirious egocentrism as to warrant nothing but well-earned contempt. On no account must any confidence be placed in a woman who's passed through the hands of the psychoanalysts. Pettiness, egoism, arrogant stupidity, complete lack of moral sense, a chronic inability to love: there you have an exhaustive portrait of the 'analysed' woman." Michel Houellebecq, *Whatever*. Trans. Paul Hammond (London: Serpent's Tail, 1998), p. 102.
3. Katherine Ganz sees the value of Houellebecq's respect for a "middle-of-the-road" readership: "Reflecting on the mainstream as both a member and an observer, the Houellebecqian narrator offers introspection without the unpleasantness of self-reproach. In championing their sensibilities—a bland mix of racism, egotism, and ill-informed apathy—works like *Les particules élémentaires* and *Plateforme* allow middle-of-the-road readers to feel that they are not only normal, but worthy of recognition by one of the West's most influential literary figures." Katherine Gantz, "Strolling with Houellebecq: The Textual Terrain of Postmodern 'Flânerie,'" *Journal of Modern Literature* 28.3 (2005): 149–161, at p. 158.
4. "What would a reading of Nietzsche give that would refuse to turn difference into its guiding thread? It is with this question that I will end this text, leaving open the possibility of a new understanding of the eternal return, that is to say also of life, that would substitute synthesis for difference, and the equally unsettling figure of the clone for that of the phantom. I thus state very simply, in the form of an announcement, the possibility of reading the doctrine of the eternal return as a thought of ontological cloning. And what if, in the end, everything were to redouble, if all the ontological knots were to reduplicate, without being different but without returning to the same either? What if the philosophical challenge of our epoch, prefigured by Nietzsche, was precisely to come to think without identity and without difference?" Catherine Malabou, "The Eternal Return and the Phantom of Difference," *Parrhesia* 10 (2010): 21–29, at p. 28.

# References


Ahlberg, Sofia. "Within Oceanic Reach: The Effects of September 11 on a Drought-Stricken Nation." *From Solidarity to Schisms: 9/11 and After in Fiction and Film from Outside the US*. Ed. Cara Cilano. Amsterdam and New York: Rodopi, 2009.

Apter, Emily. *Against World Literature: On the Politics of Untranslatability*. London: Verso, 2013.

Arendt, Hannah. "The Decline of the Nation-State and the End of the Rights of Man." *The Origins of Totalitarianism*. London: George Allen & Unwin, 1951. 267–302.

———. *Rahel Varnhagen: The Life of a Jewish Woman*. New York: Harcourt Brace Jovanovich, 1974.

———. *The Human Condition*. Chicago and London: University of Chicago Press, 1998.

Arthur, Charles. "The Dangers of Big Data." *The Guardian Weekly*, August 30–September 5, 2013: 1.

Ash, Timothy Garton. "Foreign Reporting Needs New Strategies." *The Guardian Weekly*, December 17–30, 2010: 22.

Banita, Georgiana. "'The Same, Identical Woman': Sylvia Plath in the Media." *The Journal of the Midwest Modern Language Association* 40.2 (2007): 38–60.

Barthes, Roland. "The Death of the Author." *Image—Music—Text*. New York: Hill and Wang, 1978.

———. *Camera Lucida: Reflections on Photography*. Trans. Richard Howard. London: Vintage: 2000.

———. *Mourning Diary*. Trans. Richard Howard. London: Notting Hill Editions, 2011.

Baudrillard, Jean. *Simulacra and Simulation*. Trans. Sheila Faria Glaser. Ann Arbor: Michigan University Press, 1994.

Bayley, Sally and Tracy Brain. "'Purdah' and the Enigma of Representation." *Representing Sylvia Plath*. Eds. Sally Bayley and Tracy Brain. New York: Cambridge University Press, 2011: 1–9.

Beckett, Samuel. *Endgame*. London: Faber & Faber, 1958.

Benhabib, Seyla. "Hannah Arendt and the Redemptive Power of Narrative." *Social Research* 57.1 (1990): 167–196.

———. "The Pariah and Her Shadow: Hannah Arendt's Biography of Rahel Varnhagen." *Political Theory* 23.1 (1995): 5–24.

Benhabib, Seyla. *The Claims of Culture: Equality and Diversity in the Global Era*. Oxford: Princeton University Press, 2002.

Benjamin, Walter. "The Storyteller: Reflections on the Works of Nikolai Leskov." *Illuminations*. Trans. Harry Zohn. Ed. Hannah Arendt. New York: Schocken Books, 1969: 83–109.

Bentley, Paul. "Depression and Ted Hughes' *Crow*, or through the Looking Glass and What *Crow* Found There." *Twentieth Century Literature* 43.1 (1997): 27–40.

Berlant, Lauren. "Intimacy: A Special Issue." *Intimacy*. Ed. Lauren Berlant. Chicago: Chicago University Press, 2000: 1–8.

Boelhower, William. Intro. *New Orleans in the Atlantic World: Between Land and Sea*. Ed. William Boelhower. New York: Routledge, 2010: 1–9.

Borges, Jorge Luis. "On Exactitude in Science." *Collected Fictions*, trans. Andrew Hurley. London: Allen Lane, The Penguin Press, 1999.

Boyd, S.J. *The Novels of William Golding*. New York: Harvester Wheatsheaf, 1990.

Boym, Svetlana. *Another Freedom: The Alternative History of an Idea*. Chicago and London: The University of Chicago Press, 2010.

Bristow, Joseph. *Sexuality* (2nd ed.). Milton Park: Routledge, 2011.

Brooks, Peter. "Narrative Desire." *Reading for the Plot: Design and Intention in Narrative*. New York: Vintage Books, 1985: 37–61.

Brown, Wendy. *Walled States, Waning Sovereigny*. New York: Zone Books, 2010.

Brownrigg, Sylvia. "Movement of the People." *The Guardian*, May 9, 2009.

Buchanan, Ian. Melbourne workshop, "'Assemblage Theory and its Discontents," October 14, 2014. https://news.federation.edu.au/files/29-09-14_Workshop_Assemblage_Theory_3_.pdf

Buell, Frederick. *From Apocalypse to Way of Life: Environmental Crisis in the American Century*. New York and London: Routledge, 2004.

Carlson, Thomas A. "With the World at Heart: Reading Cormac McCarthy's *The Road* with Augustine and Heidegger." *Religion and Literature* 39.5 (2007): 47–66.

Carson, Rachel. *The Sea around Us*. New York: Oxford University Press, 1961.

Carver, Raymond. *Cathedral*. London: Vintage, 2009.

Castells, Manuel. *The Informational City: Information Technology, Economic Restructuring, and the Urban-Regional Process*. Oxford: Blackwell, 1989.

———. *The Information Age: Economy, Society and Culture*. Vol.1. *The Rise of the Network Society* (2nd edition). London: Wiley-Blackwell, 2001.

———. Preface to the 2010 edition of *The Rise of the Network Society*. http://www.abstract.xlibx.com/a-economy/60264-4-manuel-castells-john-wiley-sons-ltd-publication-the-informatio.php, accessed April 27, 2015.

Churchwell, Sarah. "Ted Hughes and the Corpus of Sylvia Plath." *Criticism* 40.1 (1998): 99–132.

———. "Secrets and Lies: Plath, Privacy, Publication and Ted Hughes' 'Birthday Letters.'" *Contemporary Literature* 42.1 (2001): 102–148.

Colebrook, Claire. *Understanding Deleuze*. Crows Nest, Australia: Allen & Unwin, 2002.

———. *Death of the PostHuman. Essays on Extinction*, Vol. 1. Ann Arbor: Open Humanities Press with Michigan Publishing, 2014.

Cooke, Dervila. "Tradition, Modernity, and the Enmeshing of Home and Away: *The Shipping News* and Proulx's 1990s Newfoundland." *Studies in Canadian Literature* 38.1 (2013): 190–209.

Cooper, Lydia. "Cormac McCarthy's *The Road* as Apocalyptic Grail Narrative." *Studies in the Novel* 45.2 (Summer 2010): 218–256.

Damrosch, David. *Reading across Time*. Oxford: Wiley-Blackwell, 2009.

De Certeau, Michel. *The Practice of Everyday Life*. Trans. Steven Rendall. Berkeley, Los Angeles, and London: University of California Press, 1984.

DeLanda, Manuel. *A New Philosophy of Society: Assemblage Theory and Social Complexity*. London: Continuum, 2006.

Deleuze, Gilles and Felix Guattari. *Kafka: Toward a Minor Literature*. Trans. Dana Polan. Minnesota: University of Minnesota Press, 1986.

———. *A Thousand Plateaus: Capitalism and Schizophrenia*. Trans. Brian Massumi. Minneapolis: University of Minnesota Press, 1987.

———. "Desert Islands." *Desert Islands and Other Texts 1953–1974*. Ed. David Lapoujade. Trans. Michael Taormina. Los Angeles: Semiotext(e), 2004: 9–14.

Derrida, Jacques. "*Fors:* The Anglish Words of Nicolas Abraham and Maria Torok." Foreword to *The Wolf Man's Magic Word* by Nicolas Abraham and Maria Torok. Trans. Barbara Johnson. University of Minnesota Press: Minneapolis, 1986.

———. "Mnemosyne." Trans. Cecile Lindsay. *Memoires for Paul de Man*. New York: Columbia University Press, 1986: 1–43.

———. *Specters of Marx: The State of the Debt, the Work of Mourning and the New International*. Trans. Peggy Kamuf. New York and London: Routledge, 1993.

Dickinson, Emily. *The Complete Poems*. Ed. Thomas H. Johnson. London and Boston: Faber and Faber, 1989.

Dimock, Wai Chee. *Through Other Continents: American Literature across Deep Time*. Princeton and Oxford: Princeton University Press, 2006.

Dinerstein, Joel. *Swinging the Machine: Modernity, Technology, and African American Culture between the Two World Wars*. Amherst and Boston: University of Massachusetts Press, 2003.

Domscheit-Berg, Daniel and Tina Klopp. *Inside WikiLeaks: My Time with Julian Assange at the World's Most Dangerous Website*. London: Jonathan Cape, 2011.

Egeland, Marianne. *Claiming Sylvia Plath: The Poet as Exemplary Figure*. Cambridge: Cambridge Scholars Publishing, 2013.

Ellis, Jonathan. "'Mailed into Space': On Sylvia Plath's Letters." *Representing Sylvia Plath*. Eds. Sally Bayley and Tracy Brain. Cambridge University Press, 2011: 10–31.

Ellul, Jacques. *The Technological Society*. London: Cape, 1965.

Eriksen, Thomas Hylland. *Tyranny of the Movement: Fast and Slow Time in the Information Age*. London: Pluto Press, 2001.
Faber, Michel. *The Book of Strange New Things*. Edinburgh and London: Canongate, 2014.
Featherstone, Mike. "Global and local cultures." *Mapping the Futures*. Eds. John Bird, Barry Curtis, Tim Putnam, and Lisa Tickner. 169–187. Taylor and Francis (e-book).
Feinstein, Elaine. *Ted Hughes: The Life of a Poet*. London: Weidenfeld and Nicolson, 2001.
Fielding, Nick, Ian Cobain, and Dominic Rushe. "US Military Taps 'Sock Puppets.'" *The Guardian Weekly* 25.3 (2011): 9.
Flavin, Louise. "Quoyle's Quest: Knots and Fragments as Tools of Narration in The Shipping News." *Critique: Studies in Contemporary Fiction* 40.3 (1999): 239–247.
Forster, E. M. *A Passage to India*. London: Penguin, 2005.
Foucault, Michel. *Discipline and Punish*. Harmondsworth: Penguin, 1979.
———. *The History of Sexuality (Volume 1)*. Trans. Robert Hurley. London: Penguin Books, 1990.
Freud, Sigmund. *Civilisation and Its Discontents*. New York: Norton, 2005.
Gantz, Katherine. "Strolling with Houellebecq: The Textual Terrain of Postmodern 'Flânerie.'" *Journal of Modern Literature* 28.3 (2005): 149–161.
Gere, Charlie. *Digital Culture*. London: Reaktion Books, 2008.
Giles, Paul. *Virtual Americas: Transnational Fictions and the Transatlantic Imaginary*. Durham and London: Duke University Press, 2002.
———. *Antipodean America: Australasia and the Constitution of U.S. Literature*. New York: Oxford University Press, 2013.
Gill, Jo. "Ted Hughes and Sylvia Plath." *The Cambridge Companion to Ted Hughes*. Ed. Terry Gifford. Cambridge: Cambridge University Press, 2011: 53–66.
Gilroy, Paul. *The Black Atlantic: Modernity and Double Consciousness*. Cambridge: Harvard University Press, 1993.
Glissant, Édouard. *Poetics of Relation*. Trans. Betsy Wing. Michigan: University of Michigan Press, 1997.
Golding, William. *Lord of the Flies*. London: Faber & Faber, 1971.
———. "Interview with James R. Baker." *Twentieth Century Literature* 28.2 (1982): 130–170.
Gordon, John Steele. *A Thread across the Ocean: The Heroic Story of the Transatlantic Cable*. New York: Walker & Company, 2002.
Greene, Graham. *The End of the Affair*. New York: Viking Press, 1951.
———. *Our Man in Havana: An Entertainment*. Middlesex: Penguin, 1962.
———. *The Quiet American*. London: Penguin Books, 1973.
———. *The Heart of the Matter*. Middlesex: Penguin Books, 1974.
———. *A Burnt-Out Case*. Harmondsworth: Penguin, 1975.

———. "Under the Garden." *A Sense of Reality.* Middlesex: Penguin Books, 1981: 9–64.

———. *A Life in Letters.* Ed. Richard Greene. London: Little, Brown, 2007.

Gretlund, Jan Nordby. "Cormac McCarthy and the American Literary Tradition: Wording the End." *Intertextual and Interdisciplinary Approaches to Cormac McCarthy: Borders and Crossings.* Ed. Nicholas Monk. New York and London: Routledge: 41–51.

Hall, Stuart. "Cultural Identity and Diaspora." *Identity: Community, Culture, Difference.* Ed. Jonathan Rutherford. London: Lawrence & Wishart, 1990: 222–237.

Hamsun, Knut. *Night Roamers and Other Stories.* Trans. Tiina Nunnally. Seattle: Fjord Press, 1992.

Hartman, Geoffrey. *Scars of the Spirit: The Struggle Against Inauthenticity.* New York: Palgrave Macmillan, 2002.

Harvey, David. *The Condition of Postmodernity.* Oxford: Blackwell, 1989.

———. *The New Imperialism.* Oxford: Oxford University Press, 2003.

Hassan, Robert. *The Information Society.* Cambridge and Malden: Polity, 2008.

Herman, Michael. *Intelligence Services in the Information Age: Theory and Practice.* Hoboken: Taylor and Francis, 2013.

Herriman, George. *A Katnip Kantata in the Key of K.* Forestville: Eclipse Books/Turle Island Foundation, 1991.

Hobbes, Thomas. *Leviathan.* London: Penguin Books, 1985.

Hoeg, Peter. *Miss Smilla's Feeling of Snow.* Trans. F. David. London: Flamingo, 1994.

Houellebecq, Michel. *Whatever.* Trans. Paul Hammond. London: Serpent's Tail, 1998.

———. *Atomised.* Trans. Frank Wynne. London: Vintage, 2001.

———. *Platform.* Trans. Frank Wynne. London: William Heinemann, 2002.

———. *The Map and the Territory.* Trans. Gavin Bawd. London: William Heinemann, 2011.

Hughes, Ted. *Crow: From the Life and Songs of the Crow.* London: Faber and Faber, 1973.

———. *Cave Birds: An Alchemical Cave Drama. Poems by Ted Hughes and Drawings by Leonard Baskin.* London: Faber and Faber, 1978.

———. *Selected Poems 1957–1981.* London: Faber and Faber, 1982.

———. *River: Poems by Ted Hughes, Photographs by Peter Keen.* London: Faber and Faber, 1983.

———. *The Hawk in the Rain.* London: Faber and Faber, 1986.

———. "The Environmental Revolution." *Winter Pollen: Occasional Prose.* Ed. William Scammell. London and Boston: Faber and Faber, 1994: 128–135.

———. *Birthday Letters.* London: Faber and Faber, 1998.

Hunt, Alex and Alexander Doty. "Proulx's Allusions to Shakespeare's *Richard II* in *The Shipping News.*" *The Explicator* 70.1 (2012): 1–4.

Isin, Engin F. *Citizens Without Frontiers*. New York, London, New Delhi, and Sydney: Bloomsbury Academic, 2012.

Jackson, Michael. *The Politics of Storytelling: Variations on a Theme by Hannah Arendt*. Copenhagen: Museum Musculanum Press, 2013.

Jonnes, Denis. "Death's Child: Lost Fathers, Bereaved Daughters and the Rise of Postwar Feminism—Rereading Sylvia Plath." *Cold War American Literature and the Rise of Youth Culture: Children of Empire*. New York and London: Routledge, 2015: 133–145.

Kandiyoti, Dalia. "'Our Foothold in Buried Worlds': Place in Holocaust Consciousness and Anne Michaels's *Fugitive Pieces*." *Contemporary Literature* 45. 2 (Summer 2004): 300–330.

Lash, Scott. *Critique of Information*. London, Thousand Oaks, and New Delhi: Sage Publications, 2002.

Lessing, Doris. "To Room Nineteen." *To Room Nineteen: Collected Stories Volume One*. London: Harper Collins Publishers, 2002.

Lévy, Pierre. *Collective Intelligence: Mankind's Emerging World in Cyberspace*. Trans. Robert Bonnono. New York: Plenum Trade, 1997.

Lima, Manuel. *Visual Complexity: Mapping Patterns of Information*. New York: Princeton Architectural Press, 2011.

Lincoln, Kenneth. *Cormac McCarthy: American Canticles*. New York: Palgrave MacMillan, 2009.

Liu, Alan. *The Laws of Cool: Knowledge Work and the Culture of Information*. Chicago and London: The University of Chicago Press, 2004.

Logan, Robert K. *Understanding New Media: Extending Marshall McLuhan*. New York: Peter Lang, 2010.

Loizeaux, Elizabeth Bermann. "Reading Word, Image, and the Body of the Book: Ted Hughes and Leonard Baskin's 'Cave Birds.'" *Twentieth Century Literature* 50.1 (2004): 18–58.

Luce, Dianne C. "The Painterly Eye: Waterscapes in Cormac McCarthy's *The Road*." *Intertextual and Interdisciplinary Approaches to Cormac McCarthy: Borders and Crossings*. Ed. Nicholas Monk. New York and London: Routledge, 2012: 68–89.

Lyotard, Jean-Francois. *The Postmodern Condition: A Report on Knowledge*. Trans. Geoff Bennington and Brian Massoumi. Minneapolis: University of Minnesota Press, 1979.

———. *The Inhuman: Reflections on Time*. Trans. Geoffrey Bennington and Rachel Bowlby. Stanford: Stanford University Press, 1991.

MacCallum, Mungo. "Asylum Seekers and the Language of War." *The Drum*, January 14, 2014. http://www.abc.net.au/news/2014-01-13/maccallum-operation-sovereign-borders/5196708

Macpherson, Pat. *Reflecting on the Bell Jar*. London and New York: Routledge, 1991.

Maguire, Amy. "Australia's Global Reputation at Stake in High Court Asylum Case." *The Conversation*, July 9, 2014. https://theconversation.com/australias-global-reputation-at-stake-in-high-court-asylum-case-28951.

Malabou, Catherine. "The Eternal Return and the Phantom of Difference." *Parrhesia* 10 (2010): 21–29.

Malcolm, Janet. *The Silent Woman: Ted Hughes and Sylvia Plath*. London and Basingstoke: Picador, 1994.

Manne, Robert. "Robert Manne on Julian Assange." *The Monthly*, March 2011: 16–35.

Manning, Susan and Andrew Taylor. Eds. *Transatlantic Literary Studies: A Reader*. Baltimore: The John Hopkins University Press, 2007.

Mares, Peter. "Comment: Ten Years After Tampa." *The Monthly*, August 2011. http://www.themonthly.com.au/issue/2011/august/1316394350/peter-mares/comment-ten-years-after-tampa

Markson, David. *Wittgenstein's Mistress*. Champaign, Dublin, and London: Dalkey Archive Press, 1990.

Marx, Karl and Frederick Engels. *The Communist Manifesto: A Road Map to History's Most Important Political Document*. Ed. Phil Gasper. Chicago: Haymarket Books, 2005.

Massey, Doreeen. *For Space*. London, Thousand Oaks, and New Delhi: Sage Publications, 2005.

Matthews, Fred. "The Utopia of Human Relations: The Conflict-Free Family in American Social Thought, 1930–1960." *Journal of the History of the Behavioral Sciences* 24 (1988): 343–362.

Maupassant, Guy de. *Afloat*. Trans. Laura Ensor. London: George Routledge and Sons, 1889.

May, Elaine Tyler. "Myths and Realities of the American Family." *A History of Private Life: Riddles of Identity in Modern Times*. Eds. Antoine Prost and Gérard Vincent. Trans. Arthur Goldhammer. Cambridge and London: The Belknap Press of Harvard University, 1991: 539–592.

McAfee, Noëlle. *Democracy and the Political Unconscious*. New York: Columbia Univeristy Press, 2008.

McCarthy, Cormac. *The Road*. New York: Alfred A. Knopf, 2006.

McLuhan, Marshall. *The Mechanical Bride: Folklore of Industrial Man*. London: Routledge & K. Paul, 1967.

Melville, Herman. *Moby-Dick; or the Whale*. London: Vintage Books, 2007.

Michaels, Anne. *The Weight of Oranges*. Toronto: Coach House, 1985.

———. *Fugitive Pieces*. Toronto: McClelland, 1996.

———. "Reading Faust in Korean." *The Atlantic*, August 1, 2009. http://www.theatlantic.com/magazine/archive/2009/08/reading-faust-in-korean/307532/

———. *The Winter Vault*. London, Berlin, and New York: Bloomsbury, 2009.

———. *Correspondences*. London: Bloomsbury, 2013.

Middlebrook, Diane. *Her Husband: Hughes and Plath—A Marriage*. New York: Viking, 2003.

Mills, Sara and Louise Mullany. *Language, Gender and Feminism: Theory, Methodology and Practice*. Milton Park: Routledge, 2011.

Moller, Hans Henrik. "Peter Hoeg and the Sense of Writing." *Scandinavian Studies* 69.1 (1997): 29–51.

Moretti, Franco. *Graphs, Maps, Trees: Abstract Models for a Literary History.* London and New York: Verso, 2005.

Morgenstern, Naomi. "Postapocalyptic Responsibility: Patriarchy at the End of the World in Cormac McCarthy's *The Road.*" *Differences: A Journal of Feminist Cultural Studies* 25.2 (2014): 33–61.

Morrey, Douglas. "Sex and the Single Male: Houellebecq, Feminism, and Hegemonic Masculinity." *Yale French Studies* 116/117 (2009): 141–152.

Moulin, Jenny. "The Problem of Biography." *The Cambridge Companion to Ted Hughes.* Ed. Terry Gifford. Cambridge: Cambridge University Press, 2011. 14–26.

Murray, Jack. *The Landscapes of Alienation: Ideological Subversion in Kafka, Céline, and Onetti.* Stanford : S University Press, 1991.

Nancy, Jean-Luc. *The Inoperative Community.* Ed. Peter Connor. Trans. Peter Connor, Lisa Garbus, Michael Holland, and Simona Sawhney. Foreword by Christopher Fynsk. Minneapolis and Oxford: University of Minnesota Press, 1991.

Nandy, Ashis. "Imperialism as Theory of the Future." *Cultural Imperialism: Essays on the Political Economy of Cultural Domination.* Eds. Bernd Hamm and Russel Smandych. Toronto: Broadview Press, 2005: 52–59.

Nethersole, Reingard. "Models of Globalization." *PMLA* 116.3 (2001): 638–649.

*New York Times.* http://atwar.blogs.nytimes.com/2010/07/25/the-war-logs/, accessed April 12, 2015.

Nietzsche, Friedrich. "On Truth and Lying in a Non-Moral Sense." *The Birth of Tragedy and Other Writings.* Trans. Ronald Speirs, eds. Raymond Geuss and Ronald Speirs. Cambridge: Cambridge University Press, 1999. 141–153.

Norseng, Mary Kay. "House of Mourning: Fröken Smillas fornemmelse for sne." *Scandinavian Studies* 69.1 (1997): 52–84.

O'Beirne, Emer. "Navigating 'Non-Lieux' in Contemporary Fiction: Houellebecq, Darrieussecq, Echenoz, and Augé." *The Modern Language Review* 101.2 (2006): 388–401.

Orr, David. *Earth in Mind: On Education, Environment, and the Human Prospect.* Washington, Covelo, and London: Island Press, 2004.

Patchay, Sheena. "Not Just a Detective Novel: Trauma, Memory and Narrative Form in Miss Smilla's Feeling for Snow." *Journal of Literary Studies* 26.4 (2010): 17–35.

Paulson, William R. *The Noise of Culture: Literary Texts in a World of Information.* Ithaca and London: Cornell University Press, 1988.

Perloff, Marjorie. "The Two Ariels: The (Re)making of the Sylvia Plath Canon." *The American Poetry Review* 13.6 (1984): 10–18.

Persson, Magnus. "High Crime in Contemporary Scandinavian Literature—The Case of Peter Hoeg's Miss Smilla's Feeling for Snow." *Scandinavian*

*Crime Fiction*. Eds. Paula Arvas and Andrew Nestingen. Cardiff: University of Wales Press, 2011: 148–158.

Phelan, James. "Narrative Judgments and the Rhetorical Theory of Narrative: Ian McEwan's *Atonement*." *A Companion to Narrative Theory*. Eds. James Phelan and Peter J. Rabinowitz. Malden and Oxford: Blackwell Publishing, 2005: 322–336.

Pilkington, E. "Wikileaks' Alleged Source Bradley Manning Held in 'Punitive' Conditions." *The Guardian*, February 5, 2011.

Pitzke Marc. *Spiegel Online International*, July 15, 2013. http://www.spiegel.de/international/world/nsa-spying-scandal-focus-on-edward-snowden-by-us-media-a-911185.html, accessed April 10, 2015.

Plath, Aurelia Schober, Ed. *Sylvia Plath Letters Home: Correspondence 1950–1963*. London and Boston: Faber and Faber, 1976.

Plath, Sylvia. *The Bell Jar*. London: Faber and Faber, 1963.

———. *Ariel*. London: Faber and Faber, 1965.

Poddar, Prem and Cheralyn Mealor. "Danish Imperial Fantasies: Peter Hoeg's *Miss Smilla's Feeling for Snow*." *Translating Nations*. Ed. Prem Poddar. Aarhus: Aarhus University Press, 2000: 161–202.

Polack, Fiona. "Taking the Waters: Abjection and Homecoming in *The Shipping News* and *Death of a River Guide*." *The Journal of Commonwealth Literature* 41.1 (2006): 93–109.

Porte, Joel. *The Romance in America: Studies in Cooper, Poe, Hawthorne, Melville, and James*. Middletown: Wesleyan University Press, 1969.

Postman, Neil. *The Disappearance of Childhood*. London: W.H. Allen, 1983.

Pratt, Mary Louise. *Imperial Eyes: Travel Writing and Transculturation*. New York: Routledge, 1992.

Proulx, Annie. *The Shipping News*. New York: Charles Scribner's Sons; Toronto: Maxwell Macmillan Canada, 1993.

———. "Big Skies, Empty Places." *New Yorker*, December 25, 2000: 139.

Reid, Christopher. Ed. *Letters of Ted Hughes*. London: Faber and Faber, 2007.

Roach, Joseph. *Cities of the Dead: Circum-Atlantic Performance*. New York: Columbia University Press, 1996.

Roberts, Callum. *The Ocean of Life: The Fate of Man and the Sea*. New York: Viking, 2012.

Roberts, Neil. *Ted Hughes: A Literary Life*. London: Palgrave Macmillan, 2009.

Roffe, Jonathan. "Exteriority/Interiority." *The Deleuze Dictionary Revised Edition*. Ed. Adrian Parr. Edinburgh: Edinburgh University Press, 2010.

Rood, Karen Lane. "The Shipping News." *Understanding Annie Proulx*. South Carolina: University of South Carolina Press, 2001: 60–88.

Rose, Jacqueline. *The Haunting of Sylvia Plath*. London: Virago Press, 1991.

Roszak, Theodore. *The Cult of Information: A Neo-Luddite Treatise on High-Tech, Artificial Intelligence, and the True Art of Thinking*. Berkeley, Los Angeles, and London: University of California Press, 1994.

Roth, Philip. *Portnoy's Complaint*. London: Transworth Publishers, 1971.
———. *The Human Stain*. London: Vintage, 2005.
Royal, Derek Parker. "Plotting the Frames of Subjectivity: Identity, Death and Narrative in Philip Roth's *The Human Stain*." *Contemporary Literature* 47.1 (2006): 114–140.
Said, Edward. "Reflections on Exile." *Transatlantic Literary Studies: A Reader*. Eds. Susan Manning and Andrew Taylor. Baltimore: The Johns Hopkins University Press, 2007: 285–290.
Sanders, Barry. *The Private Death of Public Discourse*. Boston: Beacon Press, 1998.
Saussy, Haun. "Exquisite Cadavers Stitched from Fresh Nightmares: Of Memes, Hives, and Selfish Genes." *Comparative Literature in an Age of Globalization*. Ed. Haun Saussy. Baltimore: The John Hopkins University Press, 2006: 3–42.
Seiffert, Rachel. "Inarticulacy, Identity and Silence: Annie Proulx's *The Shipping News*." *Textual Practice* 16.3 (2002): 511–525.
Shadian, Jessica M. *The Politics of Arctic Sovereignty: Oil, Ice, and Inuit Governance*. London and New York: Routledge, 2014.
Shelley, Mary. *Frankestein; or, the Modern Promotheus*. New York: Tom Doherty Associates, 1988.
Shewry, Teresa. "Pathways to the Sea." *Environmental Criticism for the Twenty-First Century*. Eds. Stephanie LeMenager, Teresa Shewry, and Ken Hiltner. New York and London: Routledge, 2011: 247–260.
Showalter, Elaine. "Who Remembers Ted Hughes?" *The Chronicle of Higher Education*, March 14, 2008: 5.
Sontag, Susan. *The Pain of Others*. New York: Farrar, Straus and Giroux, 2003.
Spivak, Gayatri Chakravorty. "Explanation and Culture: Marginalia." *Out There: Marginalization and Contemporary Cultures*. Eds. Russell Ferguson, Martha Gever, Trinh T. Minh-ha, and Cornel West. New York: The New Museum of Contemporary Art and Massachusetts Institure of Technology, 1990: 377–393.
———. *A Critique of Postcolonial Reason: Toward a History of the Vanishing Present*. Cambridge: Harvard University Press, 1999.
Stefik, Mark. *Internet Dreams: Archetypes, Myths, and Metaphors*. Cambridge and London: The MIT Press, 1996.
Thompson, Robert Luther. *Wiring a Continent: The History of the Telegraph Industry in the United States 1832–1866*. Princeton: Princeton University Press, 1947.
Toth, Josh. *The Passing of Postmodernism: A Spectroanalysis of the Contemporary*. Albany: State University of New York Press, 2010.
Turner, Frederick. *Beyond Geography: The Western Spirit against the Wilderness*. New York: Viking, 1980.
Van Dyne R., Susan. *Revising Life: Sylvia Plath's Ariel Poems*. Chapel Hill and London: The University of North Carolina Press, 1993.

Varsava, Jerry Andrew. "Utopian Yearnings, Dystopian Thoughts: Houellebecq's *The Elementary Particles* and the Problem of Scientific Communitarianism." *College Literature* 32.4 (2005): 145–167.

Virilio, Paul. *The Lost Dimension.* New York: Semiotext(e), 1991.

Vonnegut, Kurt. "EPICAC." *Novels and Stories 1950–1962.* New York: Library Classics of the United States, 2012: 727–733.

Wagner, Erica. *Ariel's Gift: A Commentary on Birthday Letters by Ted Hughes.* London: Faber and Faber, 2000.

Walker, Nancy A. *Shaping Our Mothers' World: American Women's Magazines.* Jackson: University Press of Mississippi, 2000.

Wallace, Jeff. "Atomised: Mary Midgley and Michel Houellebecq." *Towards a New Literary Humanism.* Ed. Andy Mousley. New York: Palgrave Macmillan, 2011: 127–142.

Walsh, Dorothy. *Literature and Knowledge.* Connecticut: Wesleyan University Press, 1969.

Wark, McKenzie. *The Virtual Republic: Australia's Culture Wars of the 1990s.* Sydney: Allen & Unwin, 1997.

Wasko, Janet. *Hollywood in the Information Age: Beyond the Silver Screen.* Cambridge: Polity Press, 1994.

Whalen, Tracy. "'Camping' with Annie Proulx: *The Shipping News* and Tourist Desire." *Essays on Canadian Writing* 82 (2004): 51–70.

Whitman, Walt. *Leaves of Grass.* London, New York, Toronto, and Melbourne: Cassell and Company, 1909.

Willson, Michele. "Community in the Abstract: A Political and Ethical Dilemma?" *The Cybercultures Reader.* Eds. David Bell and Barbara M. Kennedy. London and New York: Routledge, 2006: 644–657.

Wikileaks. https://wikileaks.org/About.html, accessed April 12, 2015.

Winchester, Simon. *Atlantic: A Vast Ocean of a Million Stories.* London: Harper Press, 2011.

Wolosky, Shira. *Feminist Theory across Disciplines: Feminist Community and American Women's Poetry.* New York and London: Routledge, 2013.

Wood, Michael. *Literature and the Taste of Knowledge.* Cambridge: Cambridge University Press, 2005.

Yaeger, Patricia. "Editor's Column: Sea Trash, Dark Pools, and the Tragedy of the Commons." *PMLA* 125.3 (2010): 523–545.

Zaretsky, Eli. *Capitalism, the Family, and Personal Life.* London: Pluto Press, 1976.

Zuboff, Shoshana. *In the Age of the Smart Machine: The Future of Work and Power.* New York: Basic Books, 1988.

Zuckerman, Ethan. *Rewire: Digital Cosmopolitans in the Age of Connection.* New York and London: W.W. Norton & Company, 2013.

Zweig, Stefan. *The Royal Game and Other Stories.* Trans. Jill Sutcliffe. London: Jonathan Cape, 1981.

# Index

CPSIA information can be obtained
at www.ICGtesting.com
Printed in the USA
LVOW04*1627030516
486513LV00009B/187/P